Mexico Versus Texas

Anthony Ganilh

LITERATURE HOUSE / GREGG PRESS
Upper Saddle River, N. J.

Republished in 1970 by
LITERATURE HOUSE
an imprint of The Gregg Press
121 Pleasant Avenue
Upper Saddle River, N. J. 07458

Standard Book Number—8398-0652-3
Library of Congress Card—79-104459

Printed in United States of America

MEXICO

VERSUS

TEXAS,

A DESCRIPTIVE NOVEL,

MOST OF THE CHARACTERS OF WHICH CONSIST OF

LIVING PERSONS.

BY A TEXIAN.

" C'est le quaternieme siecle aux prises avec le dixneuvieme."
Abbé Drolichon.

Philadelphia:
N. SIEGFRIED, PRINTER, No. 26 NORTH SECOND STREET.
1838.

TO HIS EXCELLENCY SAMUEL HOUSTON,

PRESIDENT OF THE REPUBLIC OF TEXAS.

———

To whom with more propriety than to your Excellency can I inscribe a work whose principal theme consists of the glorious and successful struggles by which your fellow citizens attained their independence? It is, under God, to your valor, prudence and humanity they are indebted for their success, and now you stand before the world as one of those master-spirits by whom mighty changes are wrought in the economy of human affairs.

Texas may be considered as leading a crusade in behalf of modern civilization, against the antiquated prejudices and narrow policy of the middle ages, which still govern the Mexican republic.

The vast plains of Cohahuila, the rich mountains of Chihuahua expect their deliverance at the hands of the Texians, and if our adoptive country is faithful to the call of Providence, power, glory and immense wealth await her among the nations of the earth, while millions of human beings, now degraded through ignorance, will learn to bless her name, as that of a benefactress, and rejoice in her success, as that of an adoptive mother.

That you may live to see the meridian of her splendor is the ardent wish of

> Your very humble and
> Obedient servant,
> THE AUTHOR.

PREFACE.

A republic extending through more than twenty degrees of latitude, possessing a fertile soil, the greatest comparative mineral wealth on the face of the globe, and a population distinguished by docility, has, after shaking off the yoke of her European metropolis, opened her gates to modern lights and refinements. The preceding lethargy had, nevertheless, been so deep, that the dazzling glare thus suddenly flashing on the country has produced rather a painful sensation. Like a man who, from the obscurity of a dungeon, suddenly finds himself exposed to the meridian sun, and is, by that instantaneous transition, deprived of the faculty of vision, till the pupil of his eye adapts itself to his new situation; Mexico, emerging from the darkness into which the policy of Spain had plunged her, as yet supports with difficulty the brilliancy of modern civilization. She is wincing and making *wry faces!* There is an illiberal and fierce opposition against the introduction and spreading of knowledge, as well as puerile attempts at reaction; still the pupil of the national eye is dilating and the light is making a rapid progress.

It is this contest and moral strife between the imperfect civilization of the fifteenth century, which still sways the land of *Anahuac*, and that of modern times, which has already effected an entrance into the country

1 *

that we have, in the present work, undertaken to depict. As the collision between the two opposite systems became more strongly developed during the last campaign against Texas, we have thought that, by connecting the information we could communicate on the subject, with the adventures of an officer who highly distinguished himself during that sanguinary struggle, we should render our work more entertaining.

No one will deny that the subject is interesting as well as original. We are aware that it required greater talents than have fallen to our lot to do it justice, yet we hope we can claim some merit for having pointed it out, as well as for the labours which the compiling of this work has rendered indispensable. Our observations are the result of two years travels through Mexico. Nearly all the localities mentioned herein have been personally visited by us, and, as most of them lie in the Northern provinces, never, till now, described by travellers, we may presume some of our remarks possess at least the merit of novelty.

A few words now on the defects of the work. The story is loosely put together, and, in its plot, presents none of the complicated *imbroglios* accounted so essential in modern novel writing for stirring the imagination of the reader. To the first count, we plead guilty; but answer, with Sir Walter Scott, "who the devil minds the frame of a picture, provided the painting itself be well executed?" To the second accusation, we answer that we would rather think it a motive of praise, should we be found to have interested our reader by faithful descriptions of the workings of the human heart.

A friend who has obliged us with numberless correc-
tions suggests the idea that the ceremonials and clergy
of the Romish Church are too frequently introduced on
the scene. The charge, if it be a defect, is well founded;
yet we must plead, in self defence, that we cause those
clergymen to act in so diversified a manner, as, we
hope, will afford amusement to the reader; and, moreover, the church has so much sway in Mexico, and the
practices of bigotry are so closely interwoven with
every kind of business, civil, criminal, military and
commercial, that, in justice to the proportion things
bear to each other, we could not allot a lesser space to
those reverend personages.

The work, we are conscious, has a thousand other
defects; yet it gives a more faithful and detailed portraiture of Mexican manners, than any other book
published on that country, since its emancipation from
the Spanish power. May we hope that this merit,
which we boldly assert it possesses, will atone for its
wanting those beauties which proceed from the vagaries
of the imagination!

The political events with which we have connected
our moral and statistical details, in order to impart to
them the literary interest resulting from a dramatic
form, are of too recent a date, and have made too much
noise in the world to have left us at liberty to introduce
the alterations that our fancy might otherwise have
suggested. It is what will happen to any novelist
attempting to interweave his fiction with a point of
history not yet mellowed by time. It was, however,
impossible to shun such an inconvenience in fulfilling
the project we had in view, of giving a sketch of modern
Mexican manners, and the thousand curious incidents

resulting from the moral contest in that country, between modern civilization and antiquated prejudices.
More than once we have applied to ourselves the
famous line of Horace "incedis per ignes suppositos
cineri doloso." Now, it is for the public to pronounce
how far we have succeeded in picking our steps along
this dangerous path, without damage to our socks.

MEXICO *versus* TEXAS.

—

CHAPTER I.

In that singular region of Mexico, where the high table land begins to sink, by gradual descent, towards the valley of the Rio Bravo; there extends, through a space of more than four hundred miles in length and three hundred in breadth, a desert, known, in the maps, under the name of " Bolson of Mapimi," so utterly devoid of water and vegetation as to be intransitable. Its interior is, of course, entirely unknown; and although it is supposed to contain metallic riches to an immense amount, no one, except, every now and then, some wild Indian, ventures on crossing its skirts. Nature, however, which often delights in contrasts, has blessed with fertility and enriched with perpetual verdure a small district, which occupies the south-east verge of the dreary wilderness. That enchanting *oasis* is fertilized by the waters of the river Nassas, which, rising in the rich mountains of the state of Zacatecas, flows in a north-east direction, until it loses itself in the lakes of Parras and Mapimi, between which it divides its waters. The various channels into which it branches off, and by means of which its beneficial influence pervades every part of this beautiful plain, form a thousand meanders. Groves of tall and elegant saplings, interspersed with trees of gigantic size, adorn their banks, offering to the traveller's eye a spectacle which may be said to be *unique*, in a journey from the mouth of the Rio Bravo, to the foot of the western chain of the *Sierra madre*. (1)

In the spots which the scanty population of the country has begun to cultivate, the productions of the

temperate zone are intermingled with those of tropical climates, and the equable temperature, together
with the perpetual absence of frost, insure to the labourer the varied reward of his toils. Here, luxuriant fields of wheat are inclosed by quick hedges of orange trees, and vineyards are defended from the in-
roads of wild animals, by thick set rows of cactus,
upon which the brilliant cochineal insect multiplies in
myriads of millions, or the varied species of Indian figs
grow in abundance. In the orchards, the avigato pear,
the citron and banana alternate with the apple, the
plum and peach tree of Europe. On the banks of the
streams, the arundo gigantea is extirpated, in order
to make room for the sugar cane, while the driest spots
produce abundant crops of the finest cotton. In a word,
the agriculture of that fertile plain, although yet in its
infancy, may be considered as the richest and most
varied it is possible to imagine; but nature, as if desirous to impart to her gifts a greater value, by contrast-
ing them with scenes of the most awful aridity, has
raised on every side of this rich district of country,
except on the south eastern edge, a circumvallation of
mountains, whose jagged summits tower in chalky nakedness above the neighbouring level. Not one single
spring, not the least rill of water issues from their
base. Not one single tree, not the least bush adorns
their sides. Hardly can one find, here and there, a
sturdy agave, or a half withered opuntia sadly vegeta-
ting in the rocky crevices. Belonging, generally, to the
trap formation, these rocks affect regular shapes, and
rise mostly in perpendicular ledges, so that their summits are often inaccessible. Even the climbing goat is
inadequate to the task. There are, however, at intervals, deep cuts, called puertos, in the language of the
country, through which nature has opened a communication from one valley to another, and it is at the entrance of one of those narrow passages, by which the
inhabitants of the della of the river Nassas communicate with their neighbours, that is situated the little
town of Phelipa, where the scene of our story opens.

    That place could, at the period to which we refer,

boast of some illustration rather uncommon in the
North of Mexico. Its first Alcalde, who had been gov-
ernor of the province of Cohahuila, was a man of education, who, having, in his youth, studied divinity, with
an eye to a rich benefice in the gift of one of his
uncles, had, when the war of independence broke out;
abandoned it for the study of law, but who, still, plu-
med himself upon his double knowledge, and used
sometimes to boast that he was "*in utroque jure lau-
reatus.*" Amongst the members of the *Ayuntamiento*,
(anglice, the board of aldermen,) there were four or
five persons who were acquainted with Latin, and
possessed a little knowledge of Spanish literature.
Two foreign physicians, the one a Frenchman, the
other an American, exercised the healing art *in Co.*,
and gave a zest to the social tone of the place; and,
lastly, the parish priest, who was accounted a prodigy
of learning, by his influence and polite behaviour, har-
monised the whole, and never failed to repair what
little breaches of good manners jealousy or illiberality
might produce among those worthies.

This dignitary was a great and good man in every
sense of the word, and, as he plays a distinguished part
in our history, it is proper we should make our readers
minutely acquainted with his character.

Don Fernando de Larribal (such was his name) was
the youngest son of a Biscayan gentleman, who, having
little else to leave to his children than the example of
his virtues, had despatched our Fernando, yet almost
an infant, to Mexico, in order that he might make his
fortune under the patronage of his eldest brother, who
had been an inhabitant of that country for several years
previous. The elder brother, being subtle and insinu-
ating, after entering into holy orders, attached himself
to the Bishop of Durango, and became his secretary, a
post of great authority and profit. He was already in
possession of that comfortable situation, when his
younger brother came from Spain to join him, and was
by him placed in the college of San Juan de Leteran,
the best seminary of learning then extant in Mexico.
Here, young Fernando made great progress, and, by

his good conduct, so highly recommended himself to
the rector of the institution, that, upon his brother's
benevolence growing too scanty for his support, he was
assisted out of the director's private purse. Thus protected, the young man went through what was, then
and there, supposed to constitute a complete course of
education ; that is to say, he learned thoroughly Latin
and Arithmetic—went through Algebra as far as the
equations of the third degree—dabbled a little into
Spanish literature—became a proficient in theology and
metaphysics, and was solemnly admitted to the degree
of bachelor of arts, in the university of San Ildefonso,
by receiving, with great pomp and formality, the power of *interpreting Aristotle all over the earth!*

Being thus invested with academic honours, he was,
by his brother's interest, presented to the living of
Phelipa, which, in point of income and respectability,
was the third of the large diocese of Durango.—
There, he had, by his zeal, learning and charity, recommended himself to the universal love and respect of
the inhabitants. Out of an income of five thousand
dollars a year, he spent upon himself barely what was
sufficient for the actual necessaries of life, and employed the remainder in supporting a public school and
relieving private distress. Not content with these ben-
efactions, he kept a little pharmacy, in order to administer, gratuitously, remedies to the poor, and even, when
requested, practised medicine, with which he was well
acquainted. It is true that, as he had not the Pope's
permission to that effect, he was shy and scrupulous of
prescribing for the sick ; yet he could never withstand
the calls or tears of the poor, and this was, as his
vicar observed, a greater stumbling block to him, than
all the other canons of discipline put together. Fur-
thermore, at his leisure hours, he taught Spanish and
Latin grammar to the children of several of his rich
parishioners, who were desirous of having them prepared for college, free of expense—a thing which is as
frequent in Mexico as in any other part of the earth.

That man, thus endowed with the spirit of philanthropy, was entirely free from the moral defects which

are too frequently found to disgrace the Mexican clergy. He had a great zeal for the good of souls, without intolerance—great learning without pride—and, to say all in a few words, he was a *holy priest*, in the Catholic sense of the expression, and yet an honest man. It was no wonder, then, that he was respected and beloved by his parishioners. They were the more attached to him by comparing him with his fellow clergymen of other parishes; and they had, in order to express their attachment, generally adopted an Indian epithet which they applied to him by way of eminence. They called him *Tata padre*, an endearing expression, by which Mexican Indians designate a degree of moral excellence almost superhuman, and which, in the halcyon days of religious fanaticism, they thought it was a great honor to grant to the illustrious Don Vasco de Quiroga, first bishop of Mechoacan, after he had, by arduous labours, civilized the Tarascos, and introduced among them agriculture and the mechanical arts. (2)

To our clergyman, so virtuous and benevolent, providence had afforded numerous occasions of exercising his charity, by placing him at the head of a large parish, chiefly composed of Indians, who, although civilized and acquainted with the arts necessary to social life, were still ignorant, improvident and apathetic in the extreme. The numberless calls made upon him at all hours, by night and by day, seldom tired his patience, and, though he sometimes grumbled, he always ran to the assistance of his parishioners, whenever they insisted on being attended by him rather than by his vicar, which was generally the case, and rendered the latter's office almost a sinecure.

On the day on which the hero of our story was ushered into the world, our worthy clergyman had been called to the sick four times already, and feeling much fatigued by his repeated rides, he was resting himself, and enjoying the cool of the evening breeze, under a spreading orange tree, in his *huerta*, when his servant, a silly old Indian, called Tio Pedro, precipitately rushed towards him with a countenance in which astonishment mingled with terror was depicted, and

said, in a hurried tone, "Now, Tata padre, may the
most holy virgin of Guadelupe defend us, (3) but there
is another sick call! And in the most strange manner
ever seen in Phelipa. A four wheeled coach, senor,
has just stopped at the main gate of the court yard,
and, to my notion, it was never made in this republic.
The wheels are so slender! And with bright iron
bands, all of a single piece! And the body of the
coach, senor,—oh, it is a sight! Varnished, olive green,
picked out with yellow. The grand carriage of the
bishop of Durango, when he came down to give confirmation, last summer, was nothing to it! And he that
rides in it is a strange gentleman, senor—very strange.
He is dressed like the Alcalde's son, when he returned
from Mexico, and has a narrow brimmed hat, for all
the world like the one your worship brought from Durango, at your last trip. And his face, senor. Oh, it
is so white and so smooth! The man must be a Jew!
He certainly is an American. He cannot be a Christian: he looks so much like those pictures Tirilla
brought from France and wished to palm upon the people for images of saints. Now you won't go, Tata
padre. I hope you won't go. The man is certainly a
Jew!"

This address was delivered by Tio Pedro with so
much volubility, that his master had no chance to utter
a single word; but, rising up from his seat, he was
walking towards the parsonage, when he was met, at
the gate of the huerta, by the gentleman whom Tio
Pedro had described. He was a man of twenty-three
or twenty-four years of age, of a handsome appearance;
but evidently a prey to violent grief. He accosted the
priest with politeness, and informed him, with tears in
his eyes, that a lady, who was travelling towards Bejar,
had been seized with the pains of premature labour,
and compelled to remain at a village of the name of
Larza, three leagues distant, and that he had come with
haste to seek for temporal and spiritual assistance.—
She was in great danger, and he wished to know whether
there was any medical man in the place.

To this, the priest answered that they had two phy-

sicians in Phelipe, but that unfortunately both were
absent and at a considerable distance. At this piece
of information, the stranger seemed to be thrown into
a paroxysm of grief. He wrung his hands, looked up
towards heaven, and then upon the priest, with such an
air of supplication, that the latter was unable to withstand its eloquence. He had resolved within himself
to send his vicar to administer spiritual consolation to
the sick lady, for he felt so much tired from his preceding rides, that he did not think himself adequate to
the task; but he could not resist that dumb appeal, and
immediately changed his resolution; for, though spiritual ordinances conferred by his vicar would be, as he
knew, as efficacious as his own; yet, in the absence of
the physicians, none but he was able to administer
medicine. He, therefore, consoled the stranger in the
best manner he could, and added he would go himself
to the lady's assistance, and that, as he understood a
little medicine, he hoped to be of some service. There
was also, he said, an old midwife, who lived in the
place, and had often, in difficult cases, acted under the
direction of the physicians. They would take her
along with them, and, in the mean time, despatch messengers to the two physicians, in order to hasten their
return.

They had, by this time, reached the dwelling house
of the priest, who immediately despatched his servant
to bring, with all possible haste, Tia Rachela, the above
named priestess of Lucina, who was to accompany
them; but the servant, who did not like the errand,
manifested some repugnance and even undertook to
reason the case with his master.

"Tia Rachela," said he, "will hardly be prevailed
upon to come, when she finds out in whose company
she is to ride."

"How?" said the priest, " you forget yourself, Tio
Pedro;—my kindness has spoiled you. Am I not good
company enough for Tia Rachela?"

"Ah, senor," resumed the servant, "sure, your worship is good company enough. It is not of you that I
speak; but I know what I know," added he in a whisper;

"and if a poor servant might advise, I think you would do well to send the vicar and not go yourself. Consider, senor, as I told you—"

"And consider, Tio Pedro," resumed his master, waxing wroth, "that, as your parish priest, I do command you to go immediately and fetch Tia Rachela hither, and answer not a word."

Tio Pedro went away, grumbling, and soon got to Tia Rachela's house, to whom he imparted his errand in such a manner as inclined her rather to conceal herself, in order to eschew the contamination of riding in the same coach with a man suspected of being a Jew, than to perform what she would in other circumstances have considered as an office of charity. She was arguing and debating the matter with Tio Pedro, when the clergyman, tired waiting, came to decide her by his authority. His commands, delivered by himself in person, she could not resist, and, donning on her best shawl, she reluctantly went with him and entered the coach. The Tata padre and the strange gentleman mounted afterwards, and drove away with great speed towards the *rancho*, or village of Larza.

They were no sooner gone, than Tio Pedro flew to the house of Dona Salas, an old *beata*, who, having become a widow at the age of sixty-three, and enjoying the satisfaction of seeing her twelve children married and comfortably settled, had, through a desire of participating in the merits of the order of St. Francis, renounced the world, made a *simple* vow of celibacy, and taken the habit of the *terciarias*. By merely wearing the gown of the institute, and reciting a few additional prayers every week, she became possessed of an individual share in the large stock of spiritual graces and indulgences which are the exclusive property of the Franciscans, and even had as much merit as the Capuchin nuns themselves, who live in complete seclusion and rigorous poverty. That beata, though sufficiently faithful to her religious vows, by which she had got a cheap bargain of salvation, had, nevertheless, a great antipathy against what is generally accounted the monastic observance most painful to a female; I mean, silence and recollection. Her house was the news room of Phelipa and the place of rendezvous for all the comadres of the vicinity. This, being very well known to Tio Pedro, was the secret though unavowed motive which prompted him to resort thither, in order to give a quicker and wider spread to his suspicions and surmises.

He found, at Dona Salas', a little club of female gossips, who had seen the coach drive up to the priest's house, and had immediately met, in order to deliberate on the purport of that strange incident. Tio Pedro's countenance indicated that his tongue was pregnant with some extraordinary piece of news, of which it longed to be delivered; for he kept his mouth shut up with great rigidity and wagged his head to and fro with no less solemnity. There is a kind of free-mason-ry among news-mongers, to what degree soever they may belong, which enables them, at one single glance, to guess when a brother or sister of the craft has some-thing worth knowing in his budget, and their natural eagerness to get at it is not a little heightened by their secret pride, whose flame is fanned by a consciousness of their penetration.

Upon Pedro's entering, they did not fail to assail him with a confused multiplicity of queries, to which, however, he, out of a sense of his own importance, de-clined answering, until he had been invited to sit down by the lady of the mansion, and was *categorically* in-terrogated by her.

"Now, Tio Pedro," said Dona Salas, who knew well how to manage him; "you have been running up and down the town, in a great hurry, for I saw you pass by three or four times, and you will not, I think, be the worse for a little glass of *vino mescal.* (4)

"Indeed, senora," answered Pedro; "I hardly ever taste it, for the Tata padre can smell it, should I swal-low but a thimble full; but, as he will not return till to-morrow, I think I can venture it without any danger."

"He will not return till to-morrow!" resumed Dona Salas. "Is he then gone so far?"

"He is not gone farther than the *rancho* of Larza,"
2*

replied Tio Pedro; "but for all that, he will not return till to-morrow; that is to say, if he return at all."

"If he return at all!" exclaimed all the women, alarmed. "Mercy on us, Pedro, what is the matter?"

"The matter, senora," returned Pedro, "is that my master is gone off with an outlandish gentleman, who is no Christian, I am sure, because he speaks rather broken Spanish, and when he came to the door of the house, he knocked and knocked, without ever calling out *Ave Maria.*—His wife is unexpectedly brought to bed, yonder at Larza, and if he be a Jew, she, of course, is a Jewess. So, master is gone to give her extreme unction, and Tia Rachela to assist her in her own way. But I am afraid it will turn out worse than we think. They may kill my poor master, and, as for Tia Rachela, they may throw a spell upon her, and even should she escape unhurt, by whom can she expect to be employed, after assisting a Jewess."

Upon hearing Tio Pedro's surmises, the female senate became horrified, and thinking, as well as he, that their beloved Tata padre was in danger, they began to deliberate upon the means of rescuing him. Dona Salas proposed to send the sacristan with the grave digger and the singing boys, armed with swords and daggers; but, Tio Pedro remarking that the boys were too young and the sacristan too old to fight, it was, after mature deliberation, agreed to go to the Alcalde's and lay the matter before him, expecting that he would, in his wisdom, send a party of the civic guard to insure the priest's safety.

The first Alcalde of Phelipa, although he had, in his youth, studied divinity, was, by the knowing ones, supposed a little inclined to *modern philosophy*, and of all the women in town, the one he hated most was Dona Salas, on account of her blue gown and white cord of St. Francis. He was, therefore, most disagreeably surprised when he saw that female entering his office, accompanied by four or five of the most meddlesome comadres in the whole parish; but when they laid before him the subject of their visit, he became more displeased still, for he had no mind to make himself

ridiculous by acceding to their wishes, and yet he knew
that a refusal would give them occasion of prattling
against him, and representing him as inimical to religion.

Unwilling, therefore, to incur the odium of a flat de-
nial, he represented to them that there was not the
least probability of their beloved pastor's life being in
danger, since the person who had called upon him appeared to be a gentleman of great respectability; that
the village of Larza was populous and the road to it
quite safe; and that he could not concur in a measure,
which, without any adequate motive, would not fail to
create an unusual excitement, and perhaps alarm the
person to whose assistance the priest had been so
ready to fly.

All these plausible reasons, did not, however, satisfy
the women, and, least of all, Dona Salas, who entered
into an elaborate argumentation with the Alcalde, in
order to prove the reasonableness of what she had proposed; but that magistrate's mind being made up, and
seeing that all her eloquence availed nothing, she, at
last, lost patience, and left the office in a pet. The
female squadron who accompanied her participated in
her displeasure, and they were no sooner in the street
than they held a council among themselves, and it was
agreed to go to the captain of the civic guard to beseech him to do what they, under the present circumstances, judged necessary.

They found that functionary more tractable than the
Alcalde, yet, not thinking that a great display of military force was wanted upon this occasion, and also, for
fear of committing himself with the Alcalde, he contented himself with summoning, as secretly as possible,
eight privates, whom he rather begged than commanded, to go without noise towards Larza, and watch over
the priest's safety.

CHAPTER II.

Whilst the members of the guard are trotting off, on their errand, we will overtake the priest and the strange gentleman, who are riding ahead of them, in order to listen to their conversation. After a long silence, during which the stranger's grief seemed at every step to increase in intensity, the priest, desirous of alleviating it by consolation, observed:—"My calling, sir, which makes it binding upon me to keep secrecy in every thing relating to the spiritual welfare of my fellow men, and my desire of being useful to you as much as lies in my power, persuade me that I cannot be thought indiscreet in manifesting a wish to be informed more in detail of your present circumstances, which may enable me to be more serviceable than I could otherwise expect to be; yet I would not be thought to court a confidence which you may have powerful reasons to withhold, nor would I violate the sacredness of misfortune, by an importunate curiosity. I make the suggestion merely because you seem to be struggling within yourself."

"It is true, father, you have guessed right," answered the stranger; "I have a painful communication to make; for I shall want your counsel and your aid. From your reputation, your character is known to me, and I am aware of the inviolable sacredness of the seal of confession, under which alone I will communicate to you the cause of my grief and of my fears. It is indeed urgent that you should be informed of all, before you reach the bed side of her whom you are going to visit;—but how shall I communicate it within this woman's hearing? Is there any language unknown to her, which we could use?"

"Are you acquainted with Latin?" interrupted the priest.

"Too imperfectly for the purposes of conversation," returned the stranger. "But do you understand English?"

"If you will articulate slowly," replied the clergyman, "I think I shall be enabled to understand your meaning, for I read and have some practical knowledge of the language."

"Well, then, father," resumed the stranger, in his vernacular tongue; "I am an American.—i am the youngest son of a planter of the State of Maryland, of the name of Faring; but, having embraced the mercantile profession, I was sent to Mexico, in order to transact business for one of the principal commercial houses of New York. I had been living four months in that city, when certain affairs of importance obliged me to undertake a journey to the State of Mechoacan. The persons with whom I had business lived in the city of Pasquaro, on the banks of the lake of the same name, and the scenery of its shores, which is the most picturesque I ever beheld, afforded me so much delight that I made them the theatre of frequent rambles, during which I was wont to study the beauties of Nature, in silent admiration.

"I was, I believe, the first American ever seen in that part of the country, and although this circumstance naturally made me the object of curiosity, yet on account of my supposed difference of religion, it was mingled with a certain degree of hatred, which not unfrequently broke out into open insults. I have sometimes seen Roman Catholics, in the United States, exposed to a similar species of persecution, in a land where, certainly, there are, on account of the superior information it possesses, fewer excuses. My heart had always bled within me, whenever I witnessed an instance of so gross a spirit of intolerance. But now, I was, though perfectly innocent, exposed to suffer a species of retaliation. I was looked upon, by that ignorant people, as a person by whose contact they would be defiled, and with whom it would be a sin to be upon habits of intimacy, or to exhibit the common civilities of life. My neglect in paying to the ceremonies of religion the external marks of reverence which are exacted from all, though it proceeded merely from ignorance, was construed into open disrespect, and being accidentally present, one day, when the *host* passed by, without taking off my hat, I was stabbed by an ignorant shoemaker, near whose booth I was standing.

"I was left in the street, weltering in my blood, till, happily for me, the coach of the count of Letinez passed by; and his daughter, who was riding in it with her governess, seeing me. thus abandoned without succour, out of compassion, caused me to be carried to her father's house, which was only a few steps distant.

"The old count was absent, and the servants, in the idea that the wound I had received was but a just punishment for what they considered a sacrilegious act, would not have waited upon me without disgust; but I was indebted, for a more humane and generous treatment, to a clergyman, a brother of the count, who, during his absence, superintended his household and governed his family. My eternal gratitude is due to that worthy priest. He had a mind enlarged by reading, perfectly free from bigotry and prejudice, and he sincerely lamented the fatal effects of the intolerant ideas planted in Mexico by the Spanish government. He had been conversant with Humbolt, was fond of the company of foreigners, and acted towards me with genuine philanthropy, since, notwithstanding my being a Protestant, he procured me the best medical attendance, visited me frequently, and did not disdain to administer to me medicines with his own hands. His conversation was interesting, and he was passionately fond of literature. A similarity of taste on my side formed between us a bond which soon ripened into intimacy, and as soon as I was able to rise from my bed, he introduced me to the distinguished visiters of the house and instaled me, as it were, a member of the family.

"I had not been long in that house, before the count's only daughter, Maria del Carmen, made an irresistible impression on my heart. Her beauty was of a superior order, and though she had not enjoyed the advantage of an education corresponding to her rank, the goodness of her heart and delicacy of her feelings in a great measure supplied the deficiency. She reciprocated my attachment, and her uncle perceived our growing intimacy without checking it; still, there was a great, and, as I thought, an insuperable obstacle to the accomplishment of our wishes:—the difference of religion. No marriage between a *Protestant* and a female of the country had ever taken place, and though that objection could be obviated by the Pope's dispensation; still the Pope was so far off, and the communications with the holy See so difficult and precarious, that it might be considered as insuperable. Our mutual love kept increasing, notwithstanding all the difficulties we foresaw, and, at last, the lady's uncle, becoming alarmed for the consequences, in a firm but polite manner, signified to me, that propriety would no longer permit me to remain an inmate of the family, adding, that, as a union with his niece was not to be thought of, our further intimacy must cease.

"Before leaving the house, I had a private interview with Maria. Her uncle had already intimated to her his resolution, but I found her less grieved than I had reason to expect; because, knowing his love for her, she hoped to induce him to change his determination, and had already sketched a plan for that purpose. In order to give her scheme, (of the success of which she was very sanguine,) time to take effect, she requested me to absent myself during the space of a month, and not to show myself in the neighbourhood until I should hear from her. I expostulated with her, but to no purpose, for she insisted on my immediate disappearance, prescribing, at the same time, that I should remove to the island of Tzintzunzan, situated in the middle of the lake of Pasquaro, where the ruins of the capital of the ancient kingdom of Mechoacan are still to be seen, inhabited by three or four thousand Indians.

"Blindly following her directions, I took a boat, that same evening, and caused myself to be ferried over to the place of my temporary exile. I had no idea of the artifices to which she, in the mean time, had recourse, in order to work upon her uncle's fears, and induce him to accede to our mutual wishes. But on the twenty-second day after my leaving Pasquaro, I received a letter from her, in which she gave me to understand that matters being made up, her family were going to remove to Valladolid, the capital of the province, where they had a house, and that I might make my appearance in that city, as though I were returning from a long journey. She had availed herself of my absence, to feign the most violent grief, and even seemed to fall into a rapid decline, which her old nurse, (who still lived with her, in quality of governess, but entirely devoted to her wishes,) asserted would infallibly cause her death. She was careful, indeed not to attribute her young lady's sickness to the repulse I had met with; but the skilful hints she continually insinuated persuaded every body that it could proceed from nothing else. Many people began to blame the old uncle for his cruelty, and he became himself alarmed for his niece. He tried to console her, and to dissipate her sorrow by the recreations most adapted to her age, but she remained inconsolable, and, often in the midst of the most enticing diversions, tears would fall, which she affected to conceal, until, at last, the old gentleman, relenting, *pretended to guess at her secret* and promised to render her happy.

"There was yet the old count's scruples to our union to be overcome; but, as he was, in all things, directed by his brother, the task was not supposed to be very difficult, yet another obstacle stared us in the face we needed a dispensation from the ecclesiastical court and without it the marriage could not be celebrated For the purpose of soliciting that necessary permission it was thought proper the family should remove to Valladolid, and Maria del Carmen having owned to her uncle that I had not left the country, as had been supposed, but would be found in that city, the old man hastened the preparations for the journey.

"For my part, in six days time from the date of the letter I had received from Maria, I arrived in the capital of Mechoacan and the family of Letinez got there soon after me.

"When Maria informed me of the artifice to which she had had recourse to overcome her uncle's scruples I was not a little surprised, for I believed her too plain

and unaffected to be capable of what could not be considered in any other light than duplicity; but, as she
had been actuated by an ardent affection, of which I
was the object, I could not possibly resent her conduct.
We now abandoned ourselves to the most delightful
anticipations of future happiness, and her father, who
soon returned—though he made, at first, some show of
resistance—was, at last, persuaded by his brother's
entreaties and his daughter's tears to ratify our mutual promises.

"The next obstacle we had to encounter was to obtain
from the ecclesiastical authority, permission for the
celebration of our nuptials. The Bishop was absent,
but he had delegated his jurisdiction to the Dean of the
Cathedral, who was a particular friend of the family of
Letinez, and under great obligations to them. This
dignitary was sufficiently disposed to grant us the
favour we sued for, but it was thought above the power
even of episcopal authority, such dispensations being,
by the canons, reserved to the Pope himself. The
count, however, found various divines of great reputation who decided in our favour. In order to oblige us,
a particular point of the canon law was strained. It
was said that, when recourse to the sovereign pontiff is
either physically or morally impossible, the bishops
are, in their dioceses, authorised to give all the dispensations commonly reserved to the Apostolic See. In
our case, such a recourse was *morally* impossible,
because it was exceedingly difficult, in the present
disturbed state of affairs, in Mexico and Spain, to
communicate with his *Holiness*. These reasons prevailed on the Dean's mind, and he granted us the
dispensation. There were many other formalities
which we should have had to comply with, had not the
indulgence already granted us rendered it ridiculous
to exact things of minor importance; and we were,
therefore, married without any publication of bans, or
any other disagreeable formality and delay.

"In the count's private chapel the ceremony took place,
and the Dean himself, in his quality of Vicar general
of the diocese, did us the honour of officiating. Never

3

was a couple more happy than we were. Every day, our love seemed to increase, and the old count, with his brother, blessed a hundred times the happy marriage which promised peace and contentment to their old age; but our felicity was disturbed by a cause we had the least reason to suspect. The old Bishop of Mechoacan, who had been a long time absent, at last returned; and, being informed of our marriage, was highly displeased at the authority which the Dean had arrogated during his absence. He immediately suspended him, and even would have condemned him to a severe penance, had not the whole chapter interceded in his behalf. He also declared our marriage null and void, and the spiritual court issued a mandate for our separation.

"The family of Letinez obliged me to abscond; but, as the Bishop was informed that I still continued to visit my wife in secret, he caused her to be shut up in the convent of St. Clair, and it was only at the end of seven months, when her advanced pregnancy rendered it absolutely impossible she should any longer continue amongst the nuns, that she obtained leave to return to her father's. Once at liberty, she was the first to propose to me to take her to the United States. Our intention was to send a messenger to her father, in order to inform him of the place of our retreat, as soon as we should reach the frontiers of Louisiana, and she doubted not but he and her uncle would come to join us. That hope rendered the moment of her departure less bitter than it would otherwise have been; but now, that the period of her confinement has overtaken her in the middle of our journey, the fear of being pursued by her father and the emissaries of the Bishop has excited a paroxysm of terror, and I anticipate the most fatal consequences.

"Now, father," continued the stranger, "I have briefly imparted to you the history of my marriage. Under the sacred pledge of secrecy, I have made this confidence. I am afraid that my wife's misgivings are but too well founded, and that we are pursued. If we are overtaken at this juncture, the fright will be fatal. Could *she* be but removed to some convenient place, at a distance from the high road, my fears would be less excruciating. If you can aid us by your counsel, and influence over the villagers' mind; oh, I beseech you, in the name of that religion of which you are so worthy a minister, take compassion upon an innocent woman, most wantonly persecuted."

The good clergyman was moved, even to tears, by the stranger's supplications, and promised to do every thing in his power. He entered upon the discharge of his promise by endeavouring to reconcile Tia Rachela with her task. The reader may remember that this worthy matron had set out on the present errand with great reluctance, and the priest was afraid if she were not soothed, and her suspicions lulled asleep, she might acquit herself of her functions in so careless a manner as to endanger the lady's welfare. He, therefore, translated, for the midwife's edification, a part of the stranger's communication, and left her completely sat isfied that the person she was called to assist was no Jewess, but a Christian, and a count's daughter to boot. He, moreover, became security that she should be well paid for her trouble, particularly if the safety of the lady and her child was the result of her attention and skilful deportment. Tia Rachela, who had, till then, manifested her displeasure by a very sulky demeanour, condescended to illumine her countenance with a cer tain sunshine of satisfaction, which proclaimed that her former suspicions were entirely dissipated.

In the mean time, they were drawing near to the village of Larza—for they had been driven with the ut most speed—and, upon their arrival, Mr. Faring, alight ing from the coach, begged the clergyman, with Tia Rachela, to await his return, and entered the *jacal*, or cabin in which his wife was lodged, in order to pre pare her for the interview. Far from being impressed with any sentiment of awe, at the idea of the priest's visit, she manifested an earnest desire to see him, be cause, being persuaded that her death was drawing nigh, she earnestly wished to receive the last sacra ments of the church.

When the good clergyman entered the cabin, he was

shocked to see the absolute want of comfort in that
miserable habitation, in which a lady of her high birth
had been reduced to take shelter. There was not a
single bedstead; and, had it not been for a mattress
which the travellers had brought with them, she would
have been necessitated to lie on the bare earth. Two
or three low stools supplied the place of chairs, and
some pieces of dried gourds, that of crockery ware.
The priest, after having received the humble saluta-
tions of the inmates of the cabin, who kissed his hand
with reverence, directed them all to withdraw, in order that he might hear the sick person's confession, during which he administered not only spiritual comfort,
but also all the other consolations which her present
state seemed to require. He told her that if her situation would allow her to be removed to the town of
Phelipa, he would procure for her a convenient house,
with proper furniture and attentive servants, and added,
that he would protect her against the attempts of any
one sent in pursuit of her, in order to carry her back to
Mechoacan. He, moreover, assured her that her marriage was valid and legal, and that she had no longer
any thing to fear from the Bishop of Valladolid, since
his mandates could have no force out of his own Diocese; and concluded by holding up to her hopes the
pleasing prospect of a happy termination of her journey, when she would find, in her husband's love, an
indemnity for her present sufferings.

The good man's representations soothed her mind to
comparative calmness; and, when he had exhausted all
that his benevolent heart and Christian charity could
suggest, he recalled the company, and they all sat
down in expectation of the moment fixed by Nature
for the lady's delivery. Tia Rachela, not only reconciled with the idea of attending on her, but even highly
interested in her behalf, by her beauty, youth, and piety,
selected from among the oldest and most prudent women of the neighbouring cabins, those by whom she
desired to be assisted in her functions, and every thing
promised a happy issue, when, unfortunately, a considerable noise was heard in the street, before the *jacal,*

and the news that a party of armed men had come in from Phelipa, though only whispered in the priest's ear, reached the Lady's also, and caused the catastrophe which we will attempt to describe in the following chapter.

CHAPTER III.

The commander of the little party of the civic guard, which had, at the instance of Dona Salas, been sent towards Larza in order to watch over the priest's safety, rode hard with his men, and arrived at the *rancho*, shortly after the carriage. Their arrival did not fail to create a kind of alarm in the village, and its indiscreet announcement within the lady's hearing induced her to believe that her worst fears were verified, and that her pursuers had, at last, overtaken her. Seized with consternation, and uttering a loud shriek, she fell into hysterics, which brought on a premature crisis. Thereupon, Tia Rachela gave the signal for all the men to withdraw, who, in consequence, retired to a neighbouring cabin, where, after two hours anxious expectation, it was announced to Mr. Faring that he was the father of a fine boy; but that the mother was in the utmost danger.

Aroused by this fatal news from a kind of stupor into which he had fallen, he hastily entered the cabin where his wife lay; and, drawing near to the bed, gave vent to his feelings by a flood of tears. Taking one of her hands, that lay motionless on the pillow, he kissed it, while she cast upon him a look, in which the tenderness of love and grief were mingled in an inexpressible manner. That kiss seemed to reanimate her sinking frame; and, summoning all her remaining strength, she addressed him in the fervid and impassioned tone of the daughters of the South. "*Esposo de mi corazon y de mi alma*," said she; "I must leave thee!—oh, my well beloved and the only beloved upon earth, what wilt thou do deprived of me?—Alas, that our happiness has been of so short duration!—That I have known thee but to be separated from thee in so cruel a manner!—Thou weepest!—Bend down thy face to mine and kiss me, before I die, and bathe my face with the tears thou sheddest: they will be as a balsam to me in my grave——"

Her husband having assented to her wishes, she

continued, "Our loves have been reciprocal—I leave thee a precious deposit—swear to me, dearest, that thou wilt bring him up in his mother's faith. I must see him made a Christian before I die, and the padre must baptize him under my eyes. I cannot die in peace without it."

Her husband interrupted her in order to give his most solemn promise that the child should be brought up as she desired; but was unable to allay the torrent of feeling, or soothe the state of excitement that could only accelerate her dissolution. The priest felt great scruples at the idea of baptizing the child in a private cabin, it being in no manner of danger, and the rubrics of the church prescribing that, unless in the case of impending death, that sacrament should be administered only in consecrated places of worship; yet, thinking that the ceremony might have a soothing effect upon her mind, he overcame his own repugnance. Every thing was, therefore, quickly prepared for the administration of that ordinance; and though the utensils made use of to hold the baptismal water, the blessed salt, and other requisites, were of the poorest description, yet the solemnity and devotion with which the minister performed the service of the ritual, hallowed the ceremony with a dignity which it would not perhaps have possessed, had the child been christened at the baptismal font of the cathedral of Valladolid, with all the pomp suited to the heir of the house of Letinez.

The mother beheld the whole in silence and with great self possession; but when, after the ceremony, they presented the child to her, she again broke forth into a torrent of impassioned expressions, which all the efforts of those who surrounded her could not repress. The mental excitement to which she had abandoned herself increased her weakness; and, feeling her strength giving way, she took out of her bosom a very small miniature painting, representing the virgin of Guadelupe, and hung it round the child's neck by means of a light gold chain, to which it was appended. Having made her husband promise that he would cause the child to wear it always in remembrance of his

mother, she next caused Tia Rachela to cut two of
the long beautiful tresses of her hair, which she handed
to her husband, requesting that he should keep one for
himself, and send the other to her father.

Mr. Faring, during this interval, endeavoured, by
gentle admonitions, to prevent the manifestations of her
awful forebodings; but when he saw her removing her
wedding ring, and presenting it to him with the solemn
words "Adios! and never bring my child under the
empire of a step-mother!" he was no longer master of
himself. He threw himself on his knees before the
lowly couch and said, in accents of despair, "Maria,
what art thou doing?—Thou art hastening thy own
death!—Wilt thou leave me to despair?—Oh, I beseech
thee, calm these transports. For my sake, for the sake
of thy child!—Have mercy upon us all."

To these endearments of her husband she answered
not ; but lay speechless and without motion. The efforts she had made seemed to have exhausted her frame,
and it was evident that Death was on the point of com-
pleting his work. Tia Rachela, who, (to her honour be
it said,) had, during this moving scene, shed abundan'
tears, no sooner saw her fainting away, than, judging
that swoon would be her last, she called upon the padre
to administer extreme unction. The husband was, by
force, removed from the bed side, and the preparations
for the administration of the last sacrament were
quickly made.

Whatever may, by various classes of Christians, be
thought of the spiritual efficacy of this rite, there is in
it a moving simplicity and a kind of patriarchal
grandeur which are eminently calculated to impress
the beholders with lively sentiments of faith, and to
excite in the patient deep feelings of repentance. In
the present instance, the interest might, to a vulgar
eye, have been diminished, by the absence of all that
pomp and glitter which generally are its accompani-
ments in so wealthy a country as Mexico; but, to a man
of feeling, it would have been heightened by the dignity
and solemn fervour with which the worthy clergyman
graced the ceremony. Truly did he appear an angel

of mercy, when, robed in his white flowing surplice
and purple stole, he drew near to the little altar,
erected by the dying lady's bed-side, and, stretching
forth his right hand over her head, according to the
rubrics, he called upon God, in the words of the ritual:
"Look down, we beseech thee, O Lord, upon thy hand-
maid whose strength is failing fast, and take compassion
upon a soul whom thou hast created. Holy God,
Father Almighty, who, by infusing the grace of thy
blessing into the suffering bodies of thy faithful, vouch-
safest to restore thy creatures to the enjoyment of
health; hearken unto the invocation of thy holy name,
strengthen her by the help of thy right hand, fortify
her by thy virtue and defend her by thy might."

The cabin in which the ceremony was taking place,
though poor and destitute of every kind of ornament,
save some clumsy images of saints, was full of sincere
worshipers, whose sympathies condoled with the
husband's grief. There was not a dry eye amongst
them, and their tears were mingled with their prayers,
as they bent, in breathless anxiety towards the *Tata
padre*. They were only poor Indians, hardly half
civilized; yet, in their poverty, every one had found
the means of procuring a slender wax taper, which he
now held lighted in his hand, in order to honour the
last breath of a sister in the faith. Those tapers had
been blessed on the festival day of *Nuestra Senora de
la candelaria*, and there was a virtue in them, to smooth
the passage of a departing soul into the nether world,
and though the *blessing* had cost two shillings, they did
not begrudge it to the strange Lady! This might be
superstition, but it was charity.

The priest went on.—The holy oil was applied to
her eyes, and they were shut to the light.—The sign
of the cross was signed over her lips, and they were
closed,—closed for ever:—She had breathed her last,
murmuring the name of her husband!

The administration of the solemn rite was suspended—the supplications for the living soul ceased—and
the priest, kneeling down, put on the black stole, and
began the prayers for the dead.

Mr. Faring was too deeply affected to take any of the measures necessary in the present circumstances; therefore the worthy clergyman, after having scrupulously recited all the prayers prescribed by the ceremonial of his church, kindly took upon himself the office of undertaker. A coffin was out of the question—that being a luxury in which none, in Mexico, can indulge, except in large towns—plank being too scarce, in many parts of the interior, to obtain it for that purpose. A fair piece of linen was however procured, in which the Count de Letinez's daughter was shrouded with decency by Tia Rachela, and the body deposited upon a high table. where it lay, the remainder of the day, in a kind of mock state, with the face uncovered, a blessed candle burning at each corner of the table, and a vase of holy water at the feet. The corpse was visited by the villagers, every one of whom, in his turn, piously sprinkled it out of the vase and then signed it with the sign of the cross, reciting, at the same time, a fervent prayer, either a *Salve regina*, or a *De-profundis*.

The next day, a sufficient number of men was engaged to carry the body on the common bier appertaining to the village, from Larza to the town of Phelipa; where it was to be interred, and the order of the funeral procession was arranged, when there arose a dispute between Tia Rachela, and some of the women of the Rancho, about the kind of dress in which the corpse should be arrayed.

In order to make our readers understand the drift and importance of this dispute; we must premise some few observations on certain monastic institutions extant in Mexico The mendicant orders, being, by their very spirit, debarred from the right of possessing real property, and reduced to live on alms, in past times, obtained, from the holy see, certain graces and privileges, which, in point of spiritual wealth, raised them far above the rest of the clergy. These were granted them as a kind of indemnity for their renunciation of temporal blessings; but it was still necessary to devise some means of quickening the charity of the faithful, which had, in process of time, grown too lukewarm;

therefore, they obtained the faculty of granting the indulgences peculiar to their order, to such of the laity as they might think proper.

The Franciscans, the eldest of the mendicant friars, eager to enhance the right conferred, and to derive therefrom the utmost advantage, instituted what was technically called the *third order* of *St. Francis*, that is to say, a confraternity of lay persons, entirely distinct from the friars and nuns. The members of this brotherhood live in the world, or even enjoy a married life, if they choose; and yet, upon their wearing a little badge of the order, and reciting a few additional prayers, they participate in all the merits of the friars and nuns. Though the acquisition of so much grace, at so cheap a rate, be a capital speculation in spirituals, still, such is the supineness and negligence of the people that many would have foregone the immense advantage, during their life time, had not a means of extending it to them after their death been piously found out. This is done by burying the body in the gown and hood of the order! In the middle ages, it was usual to put them on the dying person, before expiring, and that was called *"mori in Domino,"* or dying in the Lord; but now, it is sufficient, if performed after death.

The order of St. Francis, that acquired a vast influence in Mexico, extended this pious practice all over the country, and even, to this day, few persons are buried in the interior of the republic, without this formality. The Franciscans do not, however, enjoy a monopoly; for, the other orders, seeing the great advantages derived from it, imitated the practice. The Carmelites procured for the *Scapular* so great a reputation, that even the other religious orders saw themselves obliged to don it over their own conventual garments. The Dominicans, also, extended far and wide the credit of their white tunic, and though they never could cope with the Franciscans, still they proved dangerous rivals. This multiplicity of blessed garments for the dead, and the difficulty of making a choice agreeable to all the relations of the deceased, not unfrequently occasions unpleasant debates in a Mexican family, and has often changed the grief incident to the death of a relative, into bitterness against the living. In the present instance, it brought about a ridiculous squabble between Tia Rachela and two of the comadres of the rancho of Larza.

The old midwife, who was a very zealous devotee of the order of St. Francis, had, immediately after the lady's death, sent a courier to Phelipa, in order to bring a *mortaja* of her own choice; but when the aforesaid funeral garment was unfolded, the two old women, who had assisted her to lay out the body, vehemently exclaimed against the choice she had made.

Dona Juana Merino was the first to raise the outcry. "And what," said she; "is it in this *mortaja* of the nuns of St. Clair you intend to bury a lady of her rank? —A count's daughter!—Pshaw!—when I lived in Guadalajara, all the ladies who died were buried in the fair white gown of the Dominican nuns. It was a pleasing sight to see them in that dress. Ah, many a one I have helped to lay out!—The hood was always made of the finest English flannel, lined with white silk and trimmed with Flanders' lace. When a lady was fixed in this trim, with her hands meekly crossed on her breast and a gold rosary between her fingers, it was a sight for the Lord Bishop himself, though it was seldom that his most illustrious Lordship would take the trouble to pronounce the blessing upon the *mortaja*, except when it belonged to people of distinction."

"Hold your peace, woman," replied Tia Rachela. "Do you think that all the lace and silk which you ever saw in Guadalajara are worth a share in the suffrages of the order of our *father St. Francis*, in which this unfortunate lady will participate, by our putting on her this mortaja; besides a plenary induigence, applicable to her soul, by way of Suffragio, on the festival of our blessed lady of the *portiuncula?*—Talk like a Christian and cease your palaver about white silk and Flanders' lace."

"Talk like a Christian!" replied Juana Merino incensed; "that is to say, then, that I talk like a heretic,

or a Comanche Indian!—And what do you mean, yourself, by despising the mortaja of St. Dominic?—The
Dominicans are something better than your Franciscans,
I trow. Had you seen as much of the world as I have,
you would know, that, while the king of Spain held his
own, undisturbed, in this kingdom, *they* had the inquisition under their direction, and could shut up in their
dungeons the Viceroy himself, or even the Archbishop
of Mexico. And as for indulgences, I wish to know
whether the Dominican habit be inferior to the Franciscan?—Go to, Tia; you know nothing. Why, there
is a three hundred years indulgence for the mere kissing
of the hem of the habit of a Dominican friar. Show me
the same, among the Franciscans. Ay, you may bring
together the *Guadelupanos* of Zacatecas and the *cruci-
feros* of Queretaro, and I defy you to show the same."

"Dona Juana is in the right," interrupted the other
matron, whose name was Rita de Marfil; "and I am of
opinion that we must give to the lady a white mortaja
of St. Dominic. My daughter-in-law has one which
was blessed, in Quatorce, by a holy preacher, five years
ago. We can get it. I dare say she will charge very
little above prime cost, and the widowed gentleman is
rich enough to pay for it."

"Ah," replied Tia Rachela, "you come out plainly,
now; and I have found you out. You have a mortaja
to sell, have you?—And that is the reason why you
prefer St. Dominic's; but, as my name is Rachela, the
lady shall be buried in the one I have sent for from
Phelipa, and if you do not want to help me, you may go
about your business and I will inform the Tata padre of
your charitable intention."

The threats which Tia Rachela had thrown out immediately dissipated the opposition of the two matrons,
who submitted to the midwife's directions. The dead
body was, therefore, soon deposited on the bier, and the
funeral procession proceeded towards Phelipa. The
march was opened by the coach, in which rode the
priest, Tia Rachela, Mr. Faring, and a woman of the
rancho, whom they had engaged to suckle the infant,
until a regular nurse could be provided. Next, came

4

the corpse, borne on the shoulders of four men, followed by eight more, who were to act as relays in the
road; for it is accounted indecorous, in Mexico, to
convey the bodies of *Christians* to their grave, in vehi-
cles drawn by animals; a piece of funeral etiquette
which reigns also in some parts of the South of France.
Lastly, came all the servants, with the sumpter mules
which had accompanied Mr. Faring in his journey, the
priest having directed the former to pack up all their
master's equipage and to follow. The march was
closed by the armed men that had come from Phelipa,
at the instigation of Dona Salas, and who, having found
their expedition a work of supererrogation, had, nevertheless, remained at Larza, in order to accompany the
Tata padre back to his house, and give to themselves, in
the eyes of their fellow citizens, the merit of having
been of some service to him.

The march lasted five hours, and the procession entered Phelipa just before twilight. The greatest part of
the population came out to behold their entrance, but
the priest addressing them a few words, in reprehension
of their indiscreet curiosity, they immediately disper-
sed, and the corpse was carried to the church, where it
was deposited until the next day, when the funeral
obsequies were to take place. After complying with
those pious duties, the clergyman turned his attention
to the present forlorn state of the stranger, whom circumstances had thus thrown upon his protection. He
immediately sought out a nurse for the infant, and, for-
tunately succeeding, he placed her and her young
charge in the house of a respectable lady, who, reveren-
cing the *padre*, gladly undertook to watch over both.
Mr. Faring and his servants were lodged in the priest's
house, and the best part of the night was devoted by the
latter to the consolation of his guest.

The motives usually suggested to the grieving mind,
in order to assuage its sorrow, appear, at first, to make
but little impression upon it, and many, on this account,
are for leaving nature to take her course, as they call it,
and abandon the distressed in heart to the bitterness
of their own thoughts. This is, however, nothing but

a specious cloak to conceal the egotism which makes them indifferent to the sufferings of a fellow creature. Surely, though the consolations bestowed upon the unfortunate should not prove efficacious to heal sorrow, the manifestation of the tender sympathy of a feeling heart cannot fail to lighten the weight which, like an incubus, oppresses the sufferer. By appearing to participate in his grief, we help him to bear its burden.

Up to this rule did the charitable priest act. There was no consolatory motive, whether drawn from religion, or from the contemplation of terrene things, which he did not repeatedly press upon Mr. Faring's consideration; and although his efforts had no visible effect upon his guest's mind, still he knew they would not altogether be unavailing. These charitable cares were interrupted by sleep, to which a very small portion of the night was allotted, as, on the next morning, the body of the unfortunate Maria del Carmen was to be committed to the grave. The widowed husband could not be persuaded to remain in the house, but insisted upon attending the funeral, which was performed with all the magnificence that could be afforded in so remote a place as Phelipa.

The parish priest himself officiated, attended by a deacon and sub-deacon. The *catafalque*, or mausoleum, in the middle of the nave, was five steps high, adorned with a profusion of mourning escutcheons and wax lights; the very altar was hung with black, and the singing boys were in deep mourning; while the incessant tolling of the numerous bells published to a great distance that a funeral, *con lujo y pompa*, seldom beheld in that place, was being celebrated.

The service to which this outward exhibition served as an accompaniment is eminently beautiful, and probably the most sublime portion of the ritual of the church of Rome. It begins by the ninety-fourth Psalm, sung very high, in a plaintive tone, by a single voice, which, for the sake of effect, is always a *contralto*, where it can be got; while, at the end of every verse, the whole choir responds, in a low solemn bass voice, as though it proceeded from the very bosom of the grave. The lessons, taken from the book of Job, are read in a recitative tone, intermingled with solemn pauses, when a death-like silence prevails, and the whole is crowned by the grand dirge "libera me, Domine," &c. with a harmony and power so piercingly stirring as to be almost too affecting for the human heart. It is a perfect *Onomatopeia* of purgatory, wherein are imitated, with the utmost perfection, the low and humble entreaties for mercy, the suppressed groans of the suffering souls below;—nay their very shrieks of woe and their writhing under the chastising hand of God. It had, in this instance, a powerful effect upon the stranger, who, being a Protestant, had never before witnessed such a spectacle. He fainted before mass began, and the good clergyman, his friend, had to disrobe himself, in order to attend him home, whilst the service was continued and concluded by his vicar.

Mr. Faring was immediately put to bed. The priest found it very difficult to recover him from his swoon, and when, at last, he was restored to the use of his senses, the expressions he uttered showed that he was delirious. Greatly alarmed, and fearing the most fatal consequences, the clergyman would not trust to his own knowledge of the medical art; but immediately sent for the two physicians, neither of whom was yet returned. Forced, therefore, to rely upon his own individual skill, the priest ordered bleeding and a blister plaster, which had a favourable result, and caused a revulsion from the head. The two physicians, however, arrived before the end of the day, and relieved the worthy ecclesiastic from the anxiety to which he had been a prey, by assuring him that they did not consider the state of the patient as dangerous. They chiefly prescribed mild remedies, and rather directed their efforts to what the Frenchman called "*un traitement moral*" than a pharmaceutical one. For that purpose, they prescribed that the child should be frequently brought to his father's bed-side, and that the latter should be indulged in bestowing upon him his parental caresses.

This had the desired effect. Though Mr. Faring

shed tears the first time the child was presented, yet
he felt there was something to fill the vacuum which
his wife's death had left in his heart. His affection
began again to expand, and in a few days he was able to
rise from his bed. Little by little, his health continued
to improve, and, at the end of six weeks, thinking himself strong enough to undertake his journey, he broached the subject to his kind host, who, by this time, had
conceived a strong attachment for him, and could not
think of a separation without regret. The worthy
clergyman had been, at first, greatly interested in his
behalf, by the frank confidence with which the stranger
intrusted to him his wife's condition and the ecclesiastical persecution to which she was exposed in consequence of her marriage. Then, the various proofs of
the tender love which he had manifested towards her
showed that his heart was animated by the noblest
feelings. Lastly, the priest had found out his guest to
be a man well versed in literature, to which he was
himself passionately addicted. He made it the subject of the many conversations, which, during Mr.
Faring's convalescence, he held with him, in order to
divert his mind from the consideration of his late loss;
and thus became fonder of his society, in proportion as
he discovered the extent of his knowledge. There are
no bonds so pleasant as those which this kind of intimacy forms between men of learning. The mutual
enjoyments which they communicate to each other in
their intercourse may be compared to the effect of
friction, in physics, which produces both heat and light;
and it is with no less precision than sublimity, that a
great English poet has, in one short sentence of the
deepest meaning, styled them "the feast of reason and
the flow of soul." The unexpected points of view under
which one is brought to consider a subject, by the novel
reflections which are elicited, and the peculiar tinge that
each idea contracts in a kindred mind, when its posses-
sor, in the full confidence of friendship, permits one to
dive into its recesses,—the zest of the quick repartie,
in conversation, when unobscured by the stiff and
formal veil of worldly etiquette;—the brilliancy of the

4 *

sally, resulting, like a spark, from collision; all these
are the delicate and refined enjoyments with which a
kind providence rewards, here below, the cultivation
of the mind. All this, ennobled by self-respect and
mutual esteem, generally enriches and adorns the
friendship of men of genius and makes it durable.

The parish priest of Phelipa began to realize the charm
we have attempted to describe, in Mr. Faring's conversa
tion, and was desirous of insuring to himself its contin
uation. During a long series of years, the only pleas
ure he had known was that of reading; but what is
reading, if one is condemned to a perpetual silence
about the works one peruses?—It is true, as we have
already said, that the Alcalde and some other worthies
of Phelipa had received a collegiate education; but
then their knowledge went no further than the dog latin
into which the metaphysics of Aristotle have been
translated by father Goudin, and a few scraps from
Spanish writers of the sixteenth century, such as the
Araucana and the everlasting Don Quixote. The conversation of those literati could not fill up the void in
the priest's mind, and it was with as much truth, as
wit, that he said, once, in speaking with a brother clergyman who seemed to envy his situation—that he was
"*damnatus ad bestias.*"

He, therefore, pertinaciously insisted upon Mr. Faring's settling in Phelipa, laying before him, in detail,
all the advantages he might derive from commerce on
an extensive scale, in a place, where, for hundreds of
miles around, he would have to fear no competition;
but the resolution of his guest was not to be shaken.
He could not forego the hopes and inducements which
his rank, standing and instruction held out to him in
Maryland, to settle in a country where the manners
were strange and dissimilar to any thing found in more
civilized regions. He could not think of embracing
the religion of the country, without which there was but
little personal security; and, lastly, he was aware that
his friend, though liberal and well bred, aimed, nevertheless, at his conversion, and the attempts he foresaw
he would not fail to make for its accomplishment would

engender bickerings between them, and diminish that friendship, which he really thought it an honour to himself to have inspired in so good a man. He, of course, persisted in his determination.

When the priest saw that he could not detain the father, he earnestly begged that he might, at least, be permitted to retain the little child, and bring it up. He could not think of the length of Mr. Faring's journey, and the dangers incident to it, without fearing that it would prove fatal to the little creature. He dreaded, besides, that he should not be educated in the Catholic faith, and the mere thought was intolerable to the good man. As he had baptized him, he believed himself answerable to God for his salvation.

It was, in fact, impossible for Mr. Faring to carry the infant with him, and he was glad to grant, as a boon, what he would, otherwise, have been obliged to beg as a favour. He knew the worthy man well enough to be sure that his child would be as tenderly taken care of as if his own mother were still alive. It was, then, agreed that the babe should be left in the hands of the nurse to whom he had been entrusted, under the superintendence of the lady in whose house both had been placed; but that, as soon as he should be able to walk, he should remove to the priest's house, where the old *ama de llaves*, a very snug and motherly Indian woman, who had served the priest, in quality of house-keeper, more than twenty years, would take care of him.

Mr. Faring generously paid the nurse beforehand, made very valuable presents to the lady in whose house the child lived, and would also have bestowed proofs of his liberality on the clergyman's house-keeper, but she would accept nothing, save a small painting of *Nuestra Senora de los dolores*, which was precious in her eyes, because the Bishops of Durango and Monterrey had conceded an indulgence of forty days for every pious look that any one of the faithful should cast upon it. This painting, which had no other merit than the one just now mentioned, was brought by the deceased lady, and had been an heir-loom in the family of Letinez, and though the priest had especially forbidden his house-

keeper to accept any thing, he was not sorry when he
found out that it had been secured from the profana
tion it might have incurred by being carried into a
heathenish country, such as the United States were
supposed to be.

CHAPTER IV.

All things being now arranged, to the mutual satisfaction of all parties, and Mr. Faring's preparations
being made, he took his departure from his kind host,
with the promise of returning, if practicable, at the end
of three years, for his child; and, tearing himself from
the latter, set forward on his route. He rode alone, in
his coach, armed to the teeth, and accompanied by six
servants, who drove ten sumpter mules, loaded with
trunks, a bed, provisions and a tent. Taverns, or inns,
there are none in the country, and even the villagers are
so scantily supplied with *comforts*, that, unless a traveller be disposed to live in an Indian fashion, he must go
provided with the necessary equipage, down to the very
cooking utensils. It is true that the owners of cabins
in the ranchos generally grant permission to travellers
to sleep in their dwellings; but these, from the scanti-
ness of the population, are not always to be reached, and,
even when reached, it is commonly found preferable,
from the uncleanliness and narrow dimensions of those
buildings, to sleep out of doors. All travellers, therefore, *bivouac*, as they go, unless they chance to have
letters of introduction to wealthy families, who can
afford the luxury of a large *sala*, for the purposes of
hospitality.

Mr. Faring's journey was a sample of the manner in
which the better sort of people perform their travels in
Mexico. The march was opened by three servants on
horseback, each armed with a long sword, and a short
musket suspended from his saddle bow, whilst a dagger,
called *belduque*, was stuck in the leather wrappers which
served him for boots. Each carried, besides, a pair of
holster pistols and the lasso, indispensable for catching
their mules, after feeding, and which might, in case of
necessity, be used as an offensive weapon, and one, too,
of the most dangerous description. Next, followed the
coach, drawn by four mules, with outrider, and the
remainder of the men, armed and equiped like the
foremost ones, brought up the rear.

In this way, they rode forty or fifty miles every day,
under the direction of a trusty guide, whom they had
engaged at Phelipa, as Mr. Faring's servants were strangers to that part of the country, and, of course, unacquainted with the roads. This one acted also in the
capacity of cook, and it was his business to provide
fresh meat and other provisions, on the way, from the
ranchos through which they passed, or from the shep-
herds whom they happened to encounter on their road.
For that purpose, he would frequently leave the party
and strike to the right, or left, through thickets of *nopal*,
or *cardenche*, so thorny and closely interwoven together,
that a foreigner would have judged them absolutely
intransitable for any human being. Thoroughly en-
cased in a leathern dress, he, nevertheless, acquitted
himself with little or no damage to his skin. The
same feat was frequently performed by others among
the servants, when in pursuit of any capricious mule
that chose to leave the main road.

In fact, the character of the Mexican Indians seems
peculiarly adapted to the management of the horse
species. There is no mule, how fractious soever, which
they cannot tame in three hours; and their sobriety and
tough powers of endurance are a match for those of the
animal. Whilst the mule can, after trotting the whole
day, under a burning sun, bearing a burden of three
hundred weight, fare sumptuously, at night, upon the
dry grass which may be picked up amongst the bushes
and briars, in regions where, frequently, there does not
fall a drop of rain for six months; the Indian can lie
down contentedly, beside his pack-saddle, after swal-
lowing a scanty allowance of *frijoles* and some *tortillas*,
with a burning sauce of red pepper as a condiment.
With this regimen, both the animal and man resist the
most prolonged fatigues, and with no other provisions,
they undertake the longest journeys.

The country through which our present party were
travelling soon lost the smiling aspect of the fertile
Oasis we have described in the beginning of this work,
and they entered upon a lonely waste of some fifty
leagues in extent, destitute of vegetation, and in which

space only one single house is to be found. At a great
distance to the right, they could descry a chain of
mountains running parallel to their road, but from
which flowed neither brook nor rivulet to relieve the
dreariness of the scene. It was necessary to carry water for their use, in small kegs, with which they were
provided, and the last time they crossed the Rio Nasas,
every gourd, bottle and vessel in their possession had
been carefully filled. When, at night, they came to
the encamping place, the mules were driven to a muddy puddle, (spanice, aguage,) two leagues off, whilst the
men husbanded what the kegs contained with the greatest economy.

The night scene was picturesque, and presented a
spectacle analagous to the patriarchal times. As soon
as the mules were unloaded, the servants erected a
kind of rampart, with the pack-saddles and loads, and
pitched the portable dwelling of Mr. Faring in the centre of that species of fortification. Of strong canvass,
and firmly secured with ropes and wooden pegs driven
into the ground, it was comfortable enough, in a country where there are no dews and seldom any cold. In
this tent, were spread mats, on which the cloth was
laid by the servants; though, afterwards, a trunk was
used as a table. At the further end, was placed the
bed, so that Mr. Faring might, with an eye to greater
security, cause his servant to sleep under the same
roof, in case he apprehended any danger. There, he
could also read, write, take his supper and breakfast
with a certain degree of comfort, and enjoy cleanliness,
by no means the distinguishing characteristic of the cabins, at the ranchoz, or in the haciendas; where the fleas,
and, not unfrequently, something worse, are found a
complete preventive of repose.

While the cook prepared the supper at a fire made a
few steps from the tent, the rest of the men, after driving the mules to water, hobbled them for the night,
and turned them amongst the bushes, to graze upon the
few blades of grass which had escaped the heats of the
summer, or the voracious tooth of the great, immense

flocks of which constitute the wealth of the proprietors
of the soil in those parts.

The morning scene was still more lively, and had a
peculiar air of bustle. While Mr. Faring was drinking
his cup of chocolate and strengthening his stomach with
some of the cold relics of the supper of the preceding
evening, the men were collecting the mules, and when
these were driven together, the *lassoing* began. Taking
in his hand the rope at the end of which was the running noose, and forming it into large coils, each man,
with unerring aim, threw it over the head of the mule
he had selected, though at a considerable distance; nor
were the restiveness, and quick movements of the animal obstacles to the precision of the *arriero's coup d'-
œuil.* The mule being thus caught, the rope was, with
similar promptitude, adjusted, in the form of a halter,
and the animal led away to be saddled. The whole
operation was generally performed in five minutes, and
two men were sufficient to put on, and secure a load by
tight girthing. The whole baggage thus loaded, two or
three of the *peones* proceeded with the sumpter mules,
whilst the remainder prepared the carriage, which, being promptly ready, set off with great rapidity, and,
soon overtaking the vanguard, caused them to fall to the
rear in their turn.

In this manner, did Mr. Faring journey on, until he
reached Parras, a considerable town, in the state of
Cohahuila. This place—which has, since the epoch to
which we allude, acquired a certain fame on account of
considerable establishments in the manufacturing line,
undertaken by a wealthy English banker—is situated
in the middle of a frightful wilderness and owes its existence to the ancient Mexican Jesuits. In the centre
of that desert, at the foot of one of the spurs of granite
mountains, that stretch into the arid plain, abundant
springs of the purest and most wholesome water gush
out and fertilize a few leagues of a soil, which would,
otherwise, have remained condemned to perpetual ster-
ility. It is a situation like that of Tadmor. The reverend fathers who were the pioneers of civilization, in

those remote regions, soon brought under their spiritual empire a certain number of Indians; and, having obtained from the king of Spain permission to cultivate the grape-vine, formed, here, a splendid *hacienda.* A town grew round their conventual establishment, consisting altogether of their dependants and laborers, for the fathers did not easily admit strangers amongst their converts, lest they should corrupt their morals. Some of their enemies have, since, pretended that this jealous and exclusive spirit had for its object to keep their neophytes in more complete subjection; but, whatever may have been the cause, the effect, in the North of Mexico, resulted in the introduction of an improved system of husbandry and a knowledge of the principal mechanical arts, among rude and ignorant savages, who, had it not been for the efforts made by the jesuits and mendicant friars, would yet, like the Lipanes and Comanches, live in a state of nature.

No doubt, some of those missionaries were actuated by selfish considerations and temporal motives. Many a friar, tired of the penances of the convent, would solicit a mission, as a measure of relief; and upon finding himself comfortably lodged in a snug parsonage house, with some hundreds of devoted Indians around him—who looked upon their Padre as a kind of Demi-God, and revered his very failings—he could not be so blind as not to prefer such a situation to the naked cell of a Franciscan friary. Such motives, probably, did frequently stimulate many of those propagators of the faith; but it must be confessed that there were also amongst them many truly apostolic men, actuated by the purest religious zeal and the most sublime philanthropy.

Even these, however, could not have taken a sufficient hold on the mind of the Indians, naturally fickle and little susceptible of permanent impressions, had not the Spanish government, whose policy, in the management of its colonies, was singularly provident and suspicious, made it a rule to send, on the steps of each missionary, a party of soldiers to erect a fort where he built a church. These soldiers protected the priest, and, by degrees, accustomed the savages to the domin-

5

ion of the whites. But where the Indians proved refractory and deaf to the missionary's instructions, the
government had recourse to a singular artifice, the origin of which is to be found in quail hunting. Just as
fowlers make use of decoy birds, in order to inveigle
wild ones into their nets, the Spanish government made
use of colonies of Tlascaltecans, in order to facilitate
the subjection of the wild Indians.

The powerful republic of Tlascala, which all the
might of Montezuma was not able to reduce under the
yoke, and with which Fernando Cortez thought himself
happy in forming an alliance, has, by such arts, dwindled away, and is now diminished to a territory of eight
leagues square. Travellers are apt to wonder at the
disappearance of this once powerful people, and to manifest a philanthropic indignation at their supposed annihilation. But the Tlascaltecans were not annihilated:
They are, probably, more numerous now than they ever
were. True, their nation has been broken up, but they
exist, like the Jews, in a scattered state.

Near all the towns of any size, in the internal provinces of Mexico, you find a large village, generally
bearing the name of Gundelupe, with a church of peculiar sanctity, in which is a statue of *Jesus Nazareno*,
more miraculous than any the white people possess in
their own places of worship. In great emergencies,
and especially in cases of drought, the whites, even the
inhabitants of the proudest cities, are obliged to go in
procession to the Indian village, and borrow their ven-
erated statue, which they carry with pomp and canticles, to their own magnificent temples, in order to obtain from heaven the favour sued for. The superior
worth and sanctity of their image engenders in these
Indians a kind of nationality: It binds them together,
and persuades them that, in some points, at least, the
whites are confessedly their inferiors. In many places
they have retained the use of their primitive language,
which was the same as the Mexican, and they distinguish themselves by a neater system of husbandry.
Their fields are better tilled, they have finer orchards;
their enclosures, in particular, are delightfully green

and similar to the live hedges of Europe. Amongst them, you may see a better distribution of water for the purposes of irrigation, more industry, more activity and life, and a certain look of independence, in the men, very different from the cringing glance of the other aborigines of that country. Such a village is a colony of Tlascaltecans, whom the cunning Spaniards settled *there*—first, in order to have the advantage of their labour; and, secondly, to make, by their example, an impression upon the wild Indians. These were *the decoy birds* made use of to inveigle new subjects under the dominion of the king of Spain!—The scheme was well planned, like all those which proceeded from the Jesuits' store, and it succeeded; but the inventors have not reaped the fruit of their labour!—They acquired millions of leagues on the earth's surface, for the Spanish crown, and that foolish government dissolved their order and exiled its members, for the sake of the trifling plunder to be got from their farms and colleges. It was, really, like killing the hen for her golden eggs! —But peace be to their manes. Perhaps they will, phenix-like, rise again from their ashes, but never more to draw the chesnuts out of the embers, for Spain or France.

It was at one of these decayed *Jesuitical* (5) villages that Mr. Faring put up, about two leagues from Parras. A large vineyard, three miles square, watered by a limpid stream and surrounded by lofty walls, flanked the village on one side. On a rising ground, stood the chapel, which, for its size and internal decorations, could vie with many of the parish churches of the country; and the habitation of the *owner* occupied a plat of level ground, by the side of the babbling brook. Having been provided with letters of introduction for the master of the house, Mr. Faring went to ask hospitality, which was granted with all the noble courtesy proper to a Spaniard of the old school.

The mode of receiving travellers in those countries is, however, so singular that our readers will not, we are sure, be sorry to peruse here a detailed account of what is, on such occasions, practised, in the first and

wealthiest families. The principal building, at the
Hacienda de abajo, (such was the name of the village,)
was a vast quadrangle, including a paved court-yard
with a well in the centre, and decorated, here and
there, with curious shrubbery. To this inner court,
there was but one entrance, by a large portal, opening
upon what might be called the public square of the
village. To it, the coach drove up, and all Mr. Faring's
baggage, when unloaded, was piled up in the entrance,
and left exposed to the curious gaze of the passer by,
while, in the same *Zaguan,* was established the temporary abode of the traveller's men, *peones,* cook and
postillion. There, they remained, day and night, when
not attending to the mules, and, for the convenience of
their class, the masons who built the house had provided two stone benches, along the walls, upon which
they might sit, or lie down, as best suited their fancy.

As for their master, he was conducted to a large hall,
round two sides of which ran a low *divan* in the Asiatic
form, but not with Asiatic luxury, for it consisted
merely of a narrow bench, covered with cushions of
coarse brown velvet. In order to prevent the clothes
of those who sat upon this estrada from being soiled by
the white-wash of the walls along which it was ranged,
a piece of shining calico, two yards wide, figured as
tapestry, which made the naked space above and below
the narrow strip, more glaringly conspicuous. Six
heavy wooden chairs, and a table of the coarsest pine
plank, unpainted and unvarnished, were all the furniture this apartment could boast. The floor was of
coarse bricks, and the windows were almost blocked
up with thick wooden bars, that served rather to exclude
the light, than to insure the safety of the inmates.

Into this *pleasaunce,* was Mr. Faring introduced with
an infinity of bows and scrapes that outvied a Frenchman's ceremonial, and there he found the Mistress of
the house, with her two daughters, gravely sitting on
the *estrada,* as stiff as if they had been cut out of a
block of marble, with an immense tortoise-shell comb
stuck on their head, and a Saltillo *rebozo,* or shawl,
hanging from the comb, and tightly wound round their

neck and shoulders, which gave to their figures as un-
gainly an appearance as if they had been prepared for
strangulation. *This* is a bad substitute for the graceful Spanish mantilla, and the Mexican ladies, who have
not lost the elegant *carriage* nor *airs de tete* of their
grand-mothers, would do well to look to it.

These three females were entirely devoid of instruction. Their acquirements were limited to reading and
writing, which last was considered as a great attainment for persons of their sex, and is, indeed, exceedingly rare; but their ideas extended not to polite
literature, nor knew they the elements of history or
geography. Their conversation was, therefore, dry
and uninteresting, and Mr. Faring felt all the weight
of dulness creep upon him, when chocolate was served.
It is customary to offer a cup of that beverage to guests,
in Mexico, whenever they happen to visit in the morning or evening, and it would be grossly impolite to
neglect this mark of hospitality. To the chocolate,
succeeds a large tumbler of clear water, after which,
cigarritos are handed round.

Mr. Faring was not fond of this luxury, still he
forced himself, in compliment to his host, to smoke
away, until he was invited to pass into the *gran sala*,
which was the most splendid apartment in the whole
mansion. The furniture of this hall was, in point of
magnificence, superior to any thing else in that section
of the country, and, as the family we are now describing was one of the most wealthy in the State of Cohahuila, it may, upon the whole, be taken as a sample of
what was then and is even yet, in the northern parts of
the Mexican republic, accounted luxury and comfort.
The pavement consisted of indurated mortar, painted
red, and as highly polished as the surface of a mirror,
which is done by a process hardly understood, or, at
least, very seldom practised in the old continent. It
looked nearly as beautiful as stucco-work. The introduction of such pavements, for ground floors, would
be a great addition to the internal decoration of our
houses, in the south of the United States. They are
easily kept clean, and possess the coolness of marble.

5 *

In this instance, however, such a piece of magnificence was not in keeping with the bareness of the walls, which were white-washed, indeed, but devoid of every ornament, save some prints in gilt frames. The windows, too, were without curtains, and the everlasting estrada itself, without the accompanying strip of calico. Along the walls, on each side, were ranged rush-bottomed chairs, painted and gilt, imported from New Orleans, and conveyed on mules from the sea board. Lastly, on a mahogany table, in a corner, were placed three small statues of saints, exquisitely carved, decorated with gems, and in full dress of gold and silver tissue. These were "los santos de la casa," the household saints. Something like the penates amongst the ancient Romans.

Our traveller, attracted by the delicacy of the sculpture, paid some attention to this, and the lady of the house, mistaking his curiosity for a religious feeling, explained, at great length, all the miracles they had performed in behalf of the family; and, in order to manifest how grateful she had been for the benefits she had received, displayed before him a complete wardrobe, which she kept, in one of the table drawers, for the use of the little figures. There were white satin gowns, with silver fringe, to be used during Christmas and Easter weeks—red, for Whitsuntide! —purple, for lent and advent; nay, black velvet ones, for holy week !—She had necklaces and ear-rings for them, and treated them just as little girls treat their dolls. From her careless prattle, he even gathered that she attributed to them human passions, and thought them accessible to vanity and resentment; for, it was not without some self complacency that she detailed how many times she had punished them, when deaf to her petitions, by taking away their finery. or stimulated them, by promises of costly ornaments.

Many of our readers will, no doubt, think the present account exaggerated; but we can assure them that, far from being overloaded, the sketch has been greatly weakened, through fear of wounding *Protestant* notions of *probability*. It is, in fact, what we have

done all along, in describing the manners of the land
of the Aztecs, and the particular features which modern civilization has assumed in that singular country;
for had we stuck to a close and rigorous description of
both, the result would have been accounted incredible.
Strange as the assertion may appear, Mexico contains
in itself all the elements of a great nation; but
they are still in embryo. The transition from a
despotical to a republican form of government has
been so sudden, that it has caused civilization, among
the upper classes, to take a leap backwards, that it
might, probably, gather more impetus, in order to
clear the intervening chasm.

But though we are resolved to soften down certain
crudities which might, if exhibited, communicate to
our work an air of improbability; we will, nevertheless,
adhere to a general faithfulness of expression, which,
without shocking our readers, will present them with
a genuine view of Mexican manners. As to the modes
of civil life, as they are of themselves indifferent, or,
at best, but remotely connected with morality, we
have made it a point to depict them with the most
scrupulous fidelity, and, in this, we think, the present
work may lay claim to some originality. For that
purpose, we must continue the journal of Mr. Faring's
return to the United States; and, should our kind readers imagine this an *hors d'œuvre*, they must forgive the
little irregularity it introduces into our story, in favour
of the instruction it conveys.

The company remained in the *gran sala*, of which
we have attempted a description, till half past ten,
when it was announced that supper was on the table.
Crossing, therefore, the court yard, they repaired to
the eating room, another hall, nearly similar in dimensions to the one we have described, and where they
found a plentiful supper spread on the table. The
viands were delicate, consisting of lamb, kid and fowls;
but the cookery was a strange mixture of the old Morisco and Indian styles. There were chickens stuffed
with almonds and raisins!—Pork stewed in a genuine
red pepper sauce, sufficient to excoriate the palate of

any European mouth, and such a profusion of garlic, as
would have turned the stomach even of a Genoese.

The means of enjoying the festive board with comfort were also somewhat scanty. Chairs, there were
none, and two long narrow benches, without the addition of cushions, supplied their places. Three knives
were accounted sufficient for nine persons, so that Mr.
Faring was, several times, obliged to resort to the im-
plements of nature as a substitute. This was not,
however, so repugnant as being constrained to drink out
of a tumbler in common; but, as there were but four
glasses on the table, he was obliged also to submit to that
inconvenience. If comfort was wanting, there was a
great display of luxury to make up for it, for every
thing that could be silver about the table was of
that metal, and no less than six servants waited upon
the guests.

As soon as supper was over, one of the waiters
recited a long grace, in praise of the blessed sacrament
of the altar, and of the immaculate conception of the
Holy Virgin, after which Mr. Faring retired to his
couch, which consisted of the *mattress and clothes he
had brought with him*, spread on the floor of the gran
sala. There we will leave him to his repose, while his
servants, stretched on their blankets, are enjoying the
benefit of the cool, bracing night air, in the open court
yard, during their slumbers.

CHAPTER V.

Mr. Faring had intended to pursue his journey on the following day; but his host was urgent to induce him to prolong his stay, and his servants represented to him that his travelling mules were much fatigued, with their few days march, and stood in need of recruiting themselves in the rich pastures of the hacienda, so that he made up his mind to tarry there a couple of days longer. Before his departure, some new travellers arrived at the hacienda. They were two Augustinian friars from Durango, bent upon a pilgrimage to the shrine of *Nuestra Senora del chorro*, in the Eastern chain of the *Sierra madre;* a place of devotion just then starting into celebrity, but whose destinies, which promised to be so brilliant, have since been blasted by the Yorkino government of the State of Tamaulipas. Of these two friars, one was lame, and the other laboured under a chronic rheumatism, and both expected to be restored to healthful vigor by the intercession of the Virgin *del chorro.*

They no sooner heard of Mr. Faring's journeying that way, than they conceived the idea of palming themselves upon him as travelling companions; persuaded that they should much more conveniently perform their journey in a vehicle than on their hard trotting mules. Communicating their wishes to our host, a man most religiously inclined to oblige any one that wore a shaven crown, he broached the subject to Mr. Faring and easily convinced him that it would be advantageous to have such travelling companions. They would, in case of assault from robbers, be a protection to the whole party; and, besides, might prove useful in the way of obtaining provisions along the road—the country people, not always disposed to sell victuals to ordinary travellers, never refusing them to clerical ones, and even dutifully presenting them, every now and then, with delicacies, without receiving any consideration. The friars' company was, therefore, willingly accepted, the more so as Mr. Faring knew that his being a heretic was a circumstance which involved no little danger; and he could not rely upon the secrecy and discretion of his servants, *these* being qualities in which the Mexican Indians are generally defective.

On the day of his departure, therefore, he mounted his coach with a greater sense of security; and, when sitting between the two friars, felt more comfortable than heretofore. On their part, the *religiosos*, though not a little disgusted at the idea of riding in the same carriage with a Protestant, either mastered or disguised that feeling, and scrupled not to entertain Mr. Faring with their conversation. He was not backward in putting to them queries, and the subject he chose was peculiarly well adapted to awaken their colloquial powers.

"Be so good, reverend fathers," said he, "as to give me some information touching the place of devotion to which you are bound. I am a foreign traveller, uninformed of the peculiarities of the country, and, as I have never, hitherto, heard that place mentioned, I would be glad to learn something about it."

"Why, Senor," said the elder of the two clergymen, "it is a sequestered *canada*, (id est, glen) on the Eastern side of the Sierra madre, some ten leagues from the city of Linares, where it has pleased the holy Virgin to manifest herself in a miraculous manner, which promises to that place, in future ages, as great a fame as it has been the lot of any other sanctuary in Mexico to acquire. I should not be surprised if it were even to become as celebrated as the collegiate church of Guadelupe. That glen, being very deep, and flanked, on either side, by steep, perpendicular marble rocks, is diversified, here and there, by deep caverns, in which are found great quantities of fine alabaster, and curious petrifactions. It happened, one day, that two masons and a sculptor, who had undertaken to erect an altar piece, in the church of the Hualawises, (a tribe of Indians, converted to catholicity by the labours of a Spanish Franciscan friar,) resorted thither, in quest of materials for that purpose. Finding a satisfactory selection somewhat difficult, and having already visited

several caves and fissures in the rock, still undeter-
mined in their choice, proceeding up the glen, they
came, at last, to a large opening, in the side of the
mountain, from which flowed a rivulet of limpid water.

"It being the dinner hour, they concluded to enter the
cave, in order to enjoy their meal in the cool shade;
and, behold! upon entering it, they found the place
incrusted with the very materials they were in quest
of, and of the finest quality—all resplendent and as
white as the driven snow! The place was perfectly
beautiful, very large and disposed like a *gran sala*, as if
it had been dug by the hand of man. At the further
extremity, a splendid cascade of water, falling from a
height of thirty feet, formed the rivulet already mentioned.

"They drew near it; but judge of their surprise, when
they saw, between the chorro of water, and the alabaster wall, the image of our blessed Lady, gracefully
hovering over them in the air. They were struck
dumb with terror, as well they might, poor sinners; for
who were they, that heaven should especially favour
them with that vision, in preference to so many priests
and religious men in the country? But so it was, and
at last, recollecting themselves, and falling down on
their knees, they devoutly crossed themselves, and
recited the litanies, not daring to look up for a long
while.

"They expected to hear some verbal revelation, but,
no voice issuing from the sacred image, they, at last,
ventured to look up again, and beheld it in the same
place; making a pleasant wavering motion, to and fro,
as it were, and with a smiling countenance, which encouraged them to approach. They even ventured to
pass between the water and the alabaster wall, which
they found brilliant and polished, to a preternatural
degree; but lo! the blessed image had become settled,
and had fixed itself on the stone, where it remains,
visible to this day—as if engraved—though, no doubt,
it was never carved—save, perhaps, by angels, in a
miraculous manner."

"Oh, Maria santissima!" piously ejaculated the other friar; "what don't we owe thee!"

"And that place, no doubt," interrupted Mr. Faring, " has, since these events have transpired, attracted considerable attention from the whole neighbourhood?"

"Indeed, you may say so," resumed the friar. "Not only from the neighbourhood, but from a vast distance, multitudes resort to it, and wonderful is the number of cures wrought there. You may judge how far the fame of the place has already extended, since brother Villamil, there, and my unworthy self have come all the way from Durango, a city more than a hundred and fifty leagues distant. We had, indeed, heard of the place, long ago, and felt a desire to perform the pilgrimage; but our prior, good man, had a notion that it was an artifice of Sathanas, and a temptation, in order to divert us from the spirit of prayer and contemplation essential to a religious life. God, however, has been pleased to take the prior to a better world, and we were very careful, in the election of his successor, to covenant, before giving him our votes, that he should grant us permission to make the pilgrimage. More than ten years I have suffered under a very severe rheumatism, so that I can very seldom attend divine service in the choir, or even preach, as I was wont, when in good health; but I hope that, at the *chorro*, the most pure and most holy queen of Heaven will cast upon me a look of compassion. And, in fact, it is, as one may say, for her own interest, that I am now travelling, as much as mine. The convent of San Augustin of Durango is of some note, and should two brothers of that house get cured of their ailments, at this new sanctuary, it will greatly increase the number of pilgrims, no less than the value of votive offerings. Durango is the country for silver and gold, and the pearls of California are adjacent! Our state could in one month furnish more *preciosidades* to the Sanctuary *del chorro*, than Tamaulipas, Nuevo Leon and Cohahuila together, in ten years. I will duly explain this to the pious anchorite, who is the keeper of the blessed cave, in order that his most fervent prayers may be addressed to the mother of God in our behalf. Oh, the special blessings bestowed upon this country, by these signal apparitions! There was, first, that of Guadelupe, near the city of Mexico, shortly after the conquest. It was especially vouchsafed to the Indians, as the miracle occurred on the identical spot where had stood the temple of their famous idol Tonantzin.* An Indian, even the pious Juan Diego, was its honoured voucher; but, now, a second witness of our immaculate faith hath risen, in our northern parts, undoubtedly to bear testimony against the heresy and unbelief which threaten to invade us from the Anglo American territory. Yea, it is, in my opinion, a sign unto *them*. And what other land can, now a days, boast the same favours and heavenly visitations! Truly, we may say, with the Psalmist, "*non fecit taliter omni nationi!*"

"Your discourse edifies me, reverend father," said Mr. Faring; "yet, methinks, before this new place of devotion can obtain as much fame and inspire as much veneration as the collegiate of Guadelupe, there are certain formalities to be undergone at Rome, and the whole history of the apparition must be approved by the holy see, before it can be admitted by the faithful."

"Are you indeed aware of that?" interrupted father Villamil. "That shows you have studied our religion, and paid some attention to the constitution of our church! But your observation is correct. The testimony respecting the apparition must be scrupulously examined at Rome, before the sacred congregation of rites; and then a special holiday appointed, and a solemn office composed. It costs as much trouble as the canonization of a saint. All these formalities are expensive. If modern times were like past ages, it would be easy to collect the money required at Rome for the expenses and fees of office incidental to the process; but, with the suppression of the holy inquisition, (6) charity has grown so cold, and the looseness of private opinions so prevalent, that, we are afraid, no

---

* Tonantzin was the Mexican Ceres, the Goddess of Maize.

efficient effort will be made. However, we have heard
that the Bishop of Monterrey has already instituted a
juridical inquest. Let us hope for the best."

Mr. Faring, who felt that the friars were taking with
his feelings, as an American, greater liberties than their
situation warranted, thought proper to change the
conversation. The two holy men had but little instruction, except in matters of divinity, and of course their
company proved uninteresting; but towards the middle
of the day, the weight of dullness was alleviated, by the
view of a splendid phenomenon unknown in Europe
and the United States.

As they drew near to a little village, of the name of
Tinaja, built at the foot of a huge mountain, which lies
perfectly insulated in the centre of an immense plain,
the most lovely prospect imaginable broke upon their
sight. There lay a beautiful lake, whose limpid waters, sparkling in the sun, extended afar their broad
expanse, till lost in the mists of the horizon, and were
diversified with elegant groups of islands, covered
with shrubs of the greenest hue. Their road conducted
them, in a direct line, towards its banks; but in proportion to their approach, the lake appeared to recede,
as though it had been a scenic illusion to tantalise the
weary travellers. The vast plain through which they
rode principally consisted of what, in Mexico, is called
barrial, that is, indurated clay, which, constantly exposed to the burning rays of the sun, almost attains the
consistency of stone. It being entirely destitute of vegetation, the charm resulting from the contrast, when
the eye, after wandering over that barren superficies,
rested on the translucent waters, was inexpressible.
Mr. Faring was delighted, and declared his intention of
remaining on the bank of the lake to take his dinner, at
which the two friars smiled, and told him that if he
were not to dine until he should reach it, he ran the
chance of fasting a long time. He thought they were
jesting, and even felt angry at the liberty they took,
until his servants affirmed the same thing, to wit, that
what he saw was no water, but merely the effect of
an optical illusion.

That recalled to his memory the *mirage* of the East,
described by several travellers, and he could well conceive that a state of the atmosphere similar to that of
Arabia might also produce this phenomenon in the
barren plains of Mexico.   The friars knew nothing of
the mirage, having read little; but they had frequently
seen the curious spectacle which excited Mr. Faring's
surprise, and one of them even undertook an explanation thereof, by referring to the laws of optics, a little
smattering of which he had acquired from the Latin
work of father Jacquier.

From the borders of that beautiful but imaginary
lake, they continued to pursue an easterly direction,
and encamped for the night, near a little hamlet called
the *Alamo mocho.* No sooner had they pitched their
tent, than a numerous company of country people was
seen approaching the place where they had put up for
the night; and, apprehensive that they were robbers,
Mr. Faring and his men seized their arms, resolved to
defend themselves; while the friars, confiding in the
influence of their sacerdotal character, walked towards
the intruders.   The latter, recognizing the sacred
habit, approached the padres with deep marks of reverence, and, upon drawing nigh, devoutly kissed their
hands, and walked bare-headed by their side.

Their business was of a singular nature. A man,
who lived at a considerable distance from the Alamo
mocho, had arrived there, the preceding night, pretending to have received a revelation that a corpse
was buried near the hamlet, at a certain spot, which
he described with such minuteness and precision, that
the villagers immediately recognised the place. The
disinterment of the corpse was not his sole object, for
he affirmed that a sum of six thousand dollars was secreted in the grave, and for the purpose of its extraction the company was now convened and marching
towards the spot. Though it seemed strange that he
had collected for that purpose so many witnesses,
whom he had promised to remunerate, for their assistance; yet this was a necessary precaution to enable

him to prove satisfactorily, when called upon, the honest acquisition of the money.

Mr. Faring listened to the story with an air of incredulity, and could not, at the conclusion, restrain his risibility ; but he was assured by one of the friars that such events were not unfrequent in Mexico, and that they were not, by the shrewd ones, accounted miraculous. Being still inclined to consider it as a hoax, or a gross instance of superstitious credulity, the friars proposed to him to accompany the stranger to the place indicated, and witness the result of the search. Assenting thereto, they soon reached the spot, a dreary looking *barranco*, thickly over-shadowed by acacia and ebony trees. At the foot of a large *palma*,* between two stones, planted upright in the ground, as if to mark a grave, the stranger, assisted by the villagers, began to dig. They had hardly penetrated a foot and a half in depth, when they discovered a corpse, not yet entirely putrefied. The sight was disgusting, and the stench so intolerable, that Mr. Faring was obliged to remove to some distance, while the assembled villagers broke forth into loud shouts of joy, calling, at the same time, upon the friars, for prayers in behalf of the deceased. Thereupon, the two *religiosos*, kneeling down, recited a miserere and a deprofundis, in which they were joined by the villagers, some of whom were charitable enough to fumble in their pockets and hand the clergymen a few sixpences, in order that they should add some *responsorios*, while the digging went on. The sum thus made up was, nevertheless, too trifling to compensate the trouble of both friars; so father Garces rose, and left father Villamil to discharge the worth of the *Jolas*, whilst the search was briskly prosecuted.

The corpse was soon extracted, removed to another spot, and the grave it had lately tenanted, ransacked and examined. In it they found money, sure enough. A few inches below the corpse, there had been secreted

---

* The plant improperly called palma, in Mexico, is a species of Yucca.

a leathern valise, which contained, not six thousand, but six hundred dollars in silver, with an ingot of gold which might be worth about five hundred more. A pair of pistols accompanied the valise, and, though rusty and damaged, Mr. Faring easily ascertained them to be real Mantons. The boots and some rags of what had been the apparel of the deceased yet remained, which convinced him that they must have belonged to a foreigner, probably a countryman of his, or an Englishman. Seized with great emotion, he conquered his repugnance and approached the corpse, which, though greatly decayed, still preserved marks of having come to its end in a foul manner. The skull had been penetrated by two balls. It was, therefore, evident that some one had been inhumanly murdered; but when, and by whom?

Suddenly the idea flashed upon Mr. Faring's mind, that the man who pretended to have had the revelation, and had come from a distance, with so exact a description of the place of interment, must have been privy to the horrid deed, or, perhaps, the perpetrator; and he immediately formed the resolution of arresting and delivering him over to the authorities of Saltillo, a city situated not far from the Alamo mocho. He, nevertheless, thought it prudent to consult the eldest of the two friars, who seemed to be possessed of more sense than his companion.

For that purpose, he took padre Garces apart and said to him, "Father, I cannot reconcile myself to the idea that this man knew the existence of such a corpse, buried in so lonely a place, by revelation! It is evidently a traveller that has been murdered, and here secreted, with his money, to be disinterred at leisure, at a time when the excitement produced amongst his friends, by his unaccountable absence, should be allayed, and in order to screen the murderer from the retribution of the law."

"Your suspicions are probably just," replied father Garces; "yet heaven has oftentimes made such revelations, either by dreams, or by unequivocal signs, to poor and worthy men, to relieve their necessities, and also

6*

that the treasure, which would, otherwise, uselessly be concealed in the bowels of the earth might benefit the poor murdered soul, by being partly spent in prayers and masses of requiem."

"Father," interrupted Mr. Faring, "though I do not pretend to deny the existence of miracles, still I cannot admit, for one single moment, that there was any thing supernatural in this affair. The fellow was too intimately acquainted with the place not to have visited it previously. Rely upon it, either *he* was the assassin, or knows who perpetrated the deed. I think public justice requires that he should be arrested and delivered over to the Alcalde of Saltillo, in order that the crime may be judicially investigated. I have a sufficient number of men to apprehend him."

"I advise you," replied the friar, "not to meddle with this man, nor to do a thing which would be accounted exceedingly foolish, and might perhaps subject you to considerable delay and great expense. Why, it would be acting the part of Don Quixotte, who went about avenging wrongs and redressing injuries! What should we come to, in this country, if it were thought necessary to apprehend all who act similar to this man? I have known in my time, that is to say, since I was a novice, no less than sixty or seventy corpses, thus disinterred, between Durango and Zacatecas, and never, before, heard that any body interfered, though, to be sure, people would sometimes smile and significantly shake the head, when a fellow returned enriched from one of those expeditions. Moreover, I think you wrong this poor man, by your suspicions; he is innocent, I dare say. He appears very mild, and is certainly exceedingly charitable, for he has bestowed forty dollars, out of six hundred, for masses to be said in behalf of the deceased. A murderer or a robber would not think of the like, I am sure."

Mr. Faring, seeing that it would be impossible to persuade the friar of the justice and propriety of his design, and aware, also, that it would be very difficult to execute it without his concurrence, gave up the idea. In the mean time, the stranger made liberal donations to the rustics who had assisted him in his search, replaced the corpse into its earthly tenement, and departed, carrying off his prey.

Our traveller spent the time that elapsed till supper, in the most uncomfortable manner, being haunted by a thousand lugubrious ideas; but the friars seemed indifferent to the melancholy spectacle they had beheld. The inhabitants of the hamlet felt honoured by their presence, and the women brought them several presents. One humbly offered a couple of chickens; another, a kid; a third one, a jar of fresh cream; and, by this means, their commons were greatly improved. Upon the whole, and despite of Mr. Faring's feelings, they spent a festive and cheerful night. Before retiring to repose, they held a consultation on the direction they should pursue the following day.

The singular topography of the table land of Mexico renders it impossible for carriages to descend from the interior to the sea coast, except by doubling the northeast range of the large chain of mountains known by the name of Sierra madre. This chain is a prolongation of the Andes of Peru, which, after entering the states of Puebla and Mexico, is divided into two distinct ranges, supporting an immense plain, emphatically styled, in the language of the country, "*la mesa de Anahuac.*"

The western range runs due North:—forming the volcanoes of Colima and Jorullo, and throwing out lateral spurs, here and there, it ultimately reaches the north-west territory of the United States, where it goes by the name of the rocky mountains. The eastern branch runs at about a distance of three hundred miles from the sea coast, following its sinuosities, in a north-east direction, until it reaches the state of Cohahuila, where it is lost in the immense plains watered by the Rio Bravo. This chain, without being so precipitous, or high, as the western one, is sufficiently so, nevertheless, to prevent any carriage from crossing the proud circumvallation with which the interior of the republic is fenced round, unless its nothern extremity be turned, which can only be effected at Saltillo. This circumstance will always secure to that city a paramount importance. From the *Camino real*, from Vera Cruz to Mexico, anciently constructed by the Spanish government, this chain of mountains, extending to Saltillo, forms, for the space of twelve hundred miles, a grand wall, or natural fortification, rendering the access into the interior exceedingly difficult and precarious.

Our travellers had, now, reached the point which has become, on that account, the great eastern thoroughfare between the high and low lands, and they had to determine what road to pursue. One, that passed through the city of Saltillo, was both shorter and more transitable, but so dreadfully infested by robbers, that it was next to a prodigy to escape being attacked by them. The other, which crossed the main ridge of the Sierra, nine leagues to the northward, was accounted more rugged, but better watered, and had not yet become the resort of banditti, being seldom frequented by travellers. Mr. Faring preferred the latter, being chiefly influenced by the opinion of his guide.

The next day, therefore, they set out early, intending to cross the gap before night, and reach the head of the valley of Nicamole, which is at least six thousand feet lower than the table land west of the Sierra. Nothing can equal the magnificence of the spectacle which, upon a nearer approach, this chain of mountains exhibits. The atmosphere of Mexico being so clear and transparent, the peculiar tints of their strata are distinguishable at a vast distance, and their colours appear as vivid as if just laid on by the pencil of a skilful artist, the various shades melting into each other by gradual transitions. Those who may chance to have seen the panorama of Mexico, as exhibited by Bullock, in the west of the United States, in the years 1834 and 1835, may form an idea of the effect which a view of those mountains produces. Nor is the singularity of the appearance a sufficient motive for discrediting the faithfulness of the representation, for New-Spain is the country where the primary formation most frequently appears upon the surface of the earth, the primitive rocks having been, there, less disturbed by subterranean commotions, than in any other part of the globe, and the grand *mineraliser* of metals, sulphur, imparting, on that account, a more brilliant tinge to the bodies with which it is combined. Though one cannot help regretting the absence of vegetation, yet the sight of the shining streaks, by which metalliferous veins are indicated, following the undulations of the various ridges in which they are imbedded, amply repays the curious observer, and promises a richer harvest to the geologist.

Shortly after leaving the village of Venadito, where they breakfasted, our travellers entered the gap of the mountain. The lofty ridge, transversally divided by a tortuous glen, towered on each side, to the height of several thousand feet above their heads, exhibiting the most fantastic shapes. Every thing was on a gigantic scale—the castellated peaks—the perpendicular precipices—the gaping caverns—yet every feature bore an air of rigidness which inspired horror and deadened that sensation of mental elevation, the natural result of the contemplation of sublime scenery. No waterfalls, to give life and animation to the landscape—no trees, waving in the breeze—no birds, warbling amongst the foliage—no shepherd's reed, attuning the surrounding echoes! The scenery was sublime, but it was the sublimity of death! Even the few plants which found a scanty supply in the crevices of the rocks were of an anomalous, and, if one may say so, of a ridiculous shape, and every one thorny!—and such thorns as are found no where else on the face of the earth—thorns that can neither be cut with a knife, nor torn from the plant without breaking it to pieces—thorns that do not participate of the nature of wood, but, rather, seem to be vegetable cock-spurs, uniting the incorruptible durability of horn, with the sharpness of steel. There, flourish in pernicious variety, the different species of *cacti,* save those which produce the cochineal, and the figs called *tunas.* The dwarfish *opuntia,* with violet-coloured leaves, spreads its useless genera through all the bottoms. The viznaga, or *cactus melo cactus,* peeps out of every cranny in the rock, affecting every hue,

from dark green to pale gray, and carpetting the surface of the trap rock and porphyry, with a tripple row
of prickles, sharp as needles; while the *cactus organum*
shoots up in singular prisms from every loamy nook,
but produces no *pytaya.** Even where a tree appears,
it is sure to be a mesquite (mimosa nilotica,) likewise
entrenched around with thorns. In a word, the vegetable kingdom seems to exhibit all its rigours, in order,
as it were, to be in keeping with the mineral one.
Through this defile, Mr. Faring had already proceeded
a considerable way, when one of his men learned from
a cowherd, that a large company of robbers lay in wait
two leagues distant.

---

* A most delicious fruit of a globular form, about the size of a
walnut. It dyes all the secretions of the body of a bright red if
eaten even in small quantities.

CHAPTER VI.

Upon receiving the unwelcome intelligence mentioned in the preceding chapter, the whole caravan halted,
and a consultation was held upon the measures most
proper to be pursued in such an emergency. It was
proposed, first, boldly to proceed and defend themselves,
sure that the banditti would prove pusillanimous, and
that, as soon as two or three of their number should
fall, the rest would retreat; but the friars decidedly
opposed such a plan. They believed that the robbers,
upon a near approach, would respect their habit; but
they were not equally certain that the bullets of their
guns, fired from a distance, would show the same discrimination. They were, therefore, for proceeding in a
pacific manner; but Mr. Faring did not relish exposing
his effects to pillage out of zeal for peace; neither did
he anticipate much danger from resistance, as he had a
considerable number of men, all of whom were well
armed. The question was, whether the latter would
face the robbers and support their master.

Assembling together his *peones*, he communicated to
them his resolution, and in an inspiriting tone, commanded them to form in the order best calculated to
render their resistance effectual; but his measures were
thwarted by father Garces, who insinuated that a pas-
sive conduct was likely to prove their best safeguard.
He succeeded in his design, for notwithstanding the
show of bravery Mr. Faring's servants had evinced,
they were in great trepidation, and manifested a wonderful docility in following the padre's counsels. This
was a serious vexation to poor Mr. Faring, who bitterly
repented having allowed the pusillanimous friars to
travel in his company. There appeared, however, no
other means of extricating himself from the present
difficulty, than by retracing his steps, and proceeding
to Saltillo, where he inwardly made a vow to deposit
the two children of St. Augustine. Accordingly, he
gave orders to return.

Upon learning his resolution, and seeing the obstina-

cy of the friars, the guide informed the company that
he knew a secret path over the brow of the hill, by
which loaded mules might reach Nicamole, without in-
curring the danger of an attack, although they would
be exposed to risks of another kind, from the extreme
narrowness of the road and the precipices along side
of which it ran. The path is called " *El paso de los an-
geles*," not from its pleasantness, as the inexperienced
reader might imagine, but because it had originally
been supposed intransitable by any one except beings
of an ethereal nature. Now, the guide proposed to drive
the mules that way, accompanied by the *peones*, while the
coach and friars should continue on the common route,
and if they should encounter the banditti, he argued,
that, provided no resistance were made, the carriage
would run very little danger of being detained, and
they would reach in safety their destination. Mr.
Faring did not perfectly approve of this arrangement;
yet it appeared to be, under the circumstances, the most
prudent plan he could adopt. He, therefore, determined to accompany the mules, and trust the vehicle
to the guidance and management of the two friars.
Every valuable article he had in the carriage was transferred to the back of a spare beast, and, recommending
himself to the prayers of the two holy men, he left
them to provide for their safety, in the best way they
could, promising to rejoin them, early the next morning,
at the head of the valley of Nicamole.

The guide led him back about a league, up the glen,
and then, leaving the beaten track, began to ascend the
side of the rocky ridge, which appeared so precipitous,
that, at a distance, one would have judged the path
hardly practicable for a goat. But the mule is a
wonderful animal, no less sagacious than inured to
fatigue, and especially serviceable in mountainous and
rocky countries. Still, notwithstanding all the confidence that Mr. Faring reposed in the instinct of the one
he rode, he had not proceeded three hundred yards,
when he became alarmed, and, overcome by dizziness,
he declared that he should prefer continuing the journey on foot, to undergoing so imminent a danger.—

Alighting, therefore, he walked the remainder of the way, with a gun in his hand, to the great surprise of his servants. After severe fatigues, they crossed the ridge; and, marching until the afternoon of the following day, they reached the valley of Nicamole, where they were surprised to receive no intelligence of the friars.

The poor *religiosos* had met with signal misfortunes, and the reliance they had placed upon the highwaymen's reverence for the habit of St. Augustine had been most awfully disappointed. After their separation from Mr. Faring, ordering the postillion to drive as quickly as possible, they hoped to be enabled to pass the suspicious ground with such rapidity as to elude the watchfulness of the robbers, who were posted at a narrow pass, above a mineral spring, bearing the name of "*los Amargos.*" But the sight of a travelling carriage, at that time a rare occurrence in those parts, was, of itself, sufficient to awake the attention of the highwaymen, and make them anticipate a rich booty. As soon, therefore, as the postillion was within hearing distance, they bid him stop at his peril, threatening, with a volley of curses, to blow out his brains if he refused. The poor postillion, perceiving a numerous gang obstructing the passage, was forced to obey, and the robbers, coming up, soon surrounded the coach, and took possession of the two mules rode by the servants.

The captain of the banditti was the first to open the door of the vehicle, where he expected, no doubt, to find some family of distinction, well provided with cash; but great was his surprise to behold, instead, the two friars, whom fear had almost deprived of the power of speech.

"What have we here?" said he, in the discontented tone of a disappointed man. "Padres, who are you, and where are you going?"

"Alas, senor," answered father Garces, trembling with fright, "we are two unworthy brothers of the order of the Heremites of St. Augustine, of the convent of Durango, bound for the sanctuary of the Virgin " del chorro,"" in the mountains of Tamaulipas. We are

7

both priests, and, of course, under the special protection
of the ecclesiastical law, which prohibits, under pain of
excommunication, *latæ sententiæ*, the offering of violence
to a person in holy orders."

"Are you, indeed, friars ?" replied the outlaw, with
a look of incredulity, either real or affected. "Many
persons put on a religious habit, now a days, in travelling, in order to fare better on the road, or to deceive
gentlemen of our profession."

"Indeed we are," replied father Garces, still more
alarmed ; "and if you will not believe our habit, you
may well credit our letters of ordination, and the letters *of obedience* from our worthy prior, by which we
are recommended to the charity of the faithful, whether
laymen or ecclesiastics." At the same time, he put
his hand into a pocket, concealed in the large sleeve
of his gown and opening under his armpit, and drew
out two large pieces of writing, that looked much like
notarial acts, having the appendage of a huge seal, and
presented them to the robber.

The highwayman, who knew not how to read, was,
nevertheless, ashamed to own his ignorance, and, looking over the papers, pretended to examine their purport ; after which, folding them up, and returning them
to the friar, he said : "Well, well, that will do well
enough. You are privileged men, and we will not do
you any bodily harm. God forbid that we should draw
down upon us the curse of an excommunication. We
will treat you with all civility ; but come, it is necessary to speed the matter as quickly as possible, for we
expect new travellers every moment, and two jobs at
once might prove embarrassing."

"Well," replied the friar, "you can despatch us in a
trice. Be kind enough to return the two mules to our
servants, and the matter is all sped. We will not long
cumber your grounds with our presence, and yet we
will not fail to pray for you."

"How is this ? *Padre mio*," resumed the robber;
"you want that I should return your servants' mules!
Voto a Dios, you are a most unreasonable man. I think
you might consider yourself lucky, to escape with your

life, and thank our delicacy of conscience, which makes
us unwilling as good Christians, to shed the blood of
anointed clergymen. But make haste, for it answers
no purpose to be thus uselessly parleying, and my
company are growing impatient."

"Upon my honour," replied the clergyman, (who,
thinking now that he had nothing to fear for his life,
was growing bolder,) " I never was more desirous to
make haste than I am at :his present moment. Since
you do not want to return the mules, keep them, in
God's name, and let us go."

" Oh, *Padre! Padre!!*" said the robber, "is it possible that you do not understand me! Do you think
we can let this coach proceed, without previous search ?
People of your profession seldom travel without a
handsome provision of doubloons ; therefore, alight
from the coach, reverend fathers—we would b) sorry
to have to resort to force."

The two clergymen obeyed, reluctantly enough ; yet
without any fear of a discovery on the part of the robbers, not having secreted any money in the vehicle.
They viewed, therefore, with perfect indifference the
search prosecuted most minutely and in the strictest
manner, but which produced no favourable result. Not
a little displeased at his want of success, the captain
muttered, glancing towards the friars—"If you were
common folks, a little twine, twisted round your thumbs,
would soon make you *sing out*, and we would be saved
all this trouble ; but we must reverence you, forsooth,
and handle you as nicely as we would delicate China-
ware ! Still you must have *it* some where, and since it
is not deposited in the coach, it must be secreted about
your persons. Come, I will commence with you, who
are the younger," addressing himself to father Villamil ; "sit down upon this block of stone, and allow me
to pull off your sandals."

Upon receiving this polite injunction, father Villamil
raised the outcry: " How now !" said he ; " bethink
you that this is bodily violence, and comes precisely
within the canonical provision of the council of Trent.
By such a conduct, you incur excommunication in the

same manner as if you were to maltreat, or even murder me."

"Padre," replied the robber, sternly, "I beseech
you, make no resistance. Our patience is somewhat of
the shortest, and if our excommunication is certain at
all events, as you say, we may be tempted to enhance
its worth, by treating you more roughly. If you behave
yourself mildly, as a worthy son of St. Augustine, we
are willing to do the handsome thing by you. Come,
we will not fleece you to the quick. Only throw off
your sandals—and, also, if you have no objection, I
will help you to disrobe yourself of this cumbersome
black gown, which is probably too heavy for your paternity. We will see whether we cannot lighten it a
little. There are many curious little seams about those
gowns of yours, and many a *pescta* of gold can remain
concealed in the padding of the cowl."

So saying, he pulled off father Villamil's sandals, and,
notwithstanding some resistance on his part, two other
robbers divested him of his gown. The captain found
nothing concealed between the two pieces of sole leather of which the conventual *calceamenta* of the friar
were composed ; but his lieutenant was more fortunate.
Sewed in the lining of the hood, or *cucula*, were no less
than nine doubloons. This discovery was hailed with
loud shouts by the robbers, who now turned their
greedy eyes towards father Garces. This worthy,
upon seeing in what manner they were proceeding with
his companion, was seized with a violent fit of the
cholic, and earnestly requested not to be searched,
proffering, at the same time, six doubloons, which he
said, were all he possessed. The highwaymen diverted
themselves at the sight of the curious grimaces he kept
making, in order to persuade them that he was really
suffering horrid pains ; but his shallow stratagem availed
him nothing. He was searched as well as his fellow
traveller, and every seam of his gown which contained
any metallic, ripped open.

By the time the robbers had examined, to their
satisfaction, the apparel of the two holy men, they
found themselves possessed of a sum of nineteen doub-

loons in gold, and a fair string of pearls, destined for *Nuestra senora del chorro;* but which they sacrilegiously appropriated to themselves. The poor friars wrapped themselves in their black gowns again, which, having been ripped in so many places, presented a ludicrous appearance. The pieces dangled about, in so strange a fashion, that one would have supposed the good fathers were acting some shrove tide mummery at the expense of the religious orders. Their sandals having been cut open also, of course they remained barefooted, and their destitute situation moved the compassion of the very robbers, whose captain proposed to restore four doubloons, out of the nineteen of which they had robbed them, to which the whole company assented. They abstained also from appropriating to themselves the mules that drew the carriage, and, replacing the friars in it, dismissed them without any further molestation. The servants who accompanied them, lost their riding beasts, however, and were obliged to mount the vehicle with the padres.

They continued their journey along the *gap* in the uncomfortable plight we have described; but, as misfortunes seldom come single, they had hardly proceeded two leagues, when the coach was overturned, by which accident one of the forewheels was broken, and the night setting in very dark, the whole company were obliged to remain where they were, without any thing to satisfy hunger, except some raw *tassajo,* or jerked beef.

When the day dawned, they contrived to bind up together the broken wheel, with leathern thongs, and, dragging the carriage along, the whole company walked on foot, save the postillion. In this guise, they arrived late in the evening at the spot where Mr. Faring was awaiting them, but the deplorable plight in which they got there precluded all idea of continuing their journey, before the coach should be repaired. The nearest place which boasted a wheelright was Pesqueria, more than ten leagues distant. Thither, therefore, they had to despatch an express; by whom the two friars conveyed to the parish priest of the place a

7 *

written account of their melancholy adventure, suppli-
cating the loan of clerical garments, in order that they
might enter the town in a condition suitable to persons
of their order. That clergyman immediately sent them
two cassoks, with an invitation to come and lodge at
his house. With the messenger who brought this token
of brotherly feeling, came also a wheelright, with tools
and materials to repair the broken wheel, and, in five
hours, the caravan was ready to pursue its march.

They happened to enter Pesqueria, precisely on holy
Wednesday, and, as the three following days form a
season of great solemnity, devoted, in Catholic countries, to religious exercises, the friars were very importunate with Mr. Faring to remain during Easter, so
that, partly to oblige them, but, principally, to rest his
mules, which had greatly suffered in the passage of the
Sierra; he concluded to prolong his stay, till the following Tuesday. For that purpose, he rented a house
with a spacious court-yard for the use of his animals,
and in less than two hours, his bed and furniture were
arranged in order, and he had made for himself a kind
of temporary *home.*

The two friars were very useful to the parish priest,
in the church ceremonies and processions with which
the latter part of holy week is overcrowded, while Mr.
Faring, who had nothing to do, sauntered about, from
the church to the market place, and from the market place to a little spruce *Sanctuario,* newly erected
in honour of the Virgin of Guadelupe, the great patron-
ess of Mexico.

He amused himself, as well as he could, in witness-
ing the various exercises of religion by which these
people solemnise our Saviour's passion ; and we will
detail some particulars, which, from their singularity,
were the peculiar object of his attention. Maunday
Thursday is, in Mexico, as in all other Catholic countries,
distinguished by a solemn high mass in the morning
but, *there,* the Alcalde and Ayuntamiento, that is to
say, the Mayor and board of Aldermen, officially assist
at it, in great ceremony, and receive the communion,
after which, the chief magistrate of the town, kneeling

at the foot of the altar, receives the key of the tabernacle, from the hands of the parish priest, and wears it the whole day, suspended from his neck, by a ribbon adorned with splendid embroidery. This is accounted a great honour, and a high privilege, which costs the church very little, and wonderfully flatters the vanity of these people.

In the afternoon, all the magistrates assist also at the pediluvium and bear a part therein. Twelve poor men are seated, in two rows, in the middle of the church, and the parish priest, with his whole clergy, robed in white, washes their right foot, while one of the Alcaldes pours the water mixed with wine, and another wipes it off with a towel, after which, the foot is devoutly kissed by the whole board of Aldermen. This, when performed with gravity, is impressive, and, though the kissing of the feet should be *now* dispensed with, as no longer in accordance with the modern sense of propriety, it is at all events, a practical lesson of Christian humility, and of civil equality.

Late in the evening of the same day, a procession is made round the town, in which a crucifix of gigantic dimensions is carried, in a reclining posture, by eight men; but this exhibition is rendered shocking and repulsive, by *penitentes*, who walk at the head of the *cortege*, naked from the waist upwards, and bare-legged, tottering under the weight of a huge piece of timber, to which their arms are fastened, in the form of a cross, and having their faces covered with a black veil. As they are generally Indians who perform this part, the deep, dark hue of their skin increases the disgust which such an instance of barbarism is calculated to inspire; yet this is the share of the ceremony most admired, and the procession is accounted more or less splendid, in proportion to the greater or lesser number of penitentes that appear therein. This mummery is closed by a sermon, and the church is left open all night, during which a crowd of devotees fill the chapel where the sacrament is *exposed* to the adoration of the faithful.

The ceremonies of the following day are far more complicated, for new and multifarious processions and

exhibitions succeed each other in such rapidity as to
leave the clergy scarcely time to breathe. In the
morning, a large statue of Christ bearing his cross is
carried out. He is represented dressed in purple velvet, and goes by the name of *Jesus Nazareno.* Another
figure, as large as life, representing the Virgin Mary,
in deep mourning, yet with a profusion of sparkling
jewels about her neck, ears and head, immediately follows the statue of her son, and is pathetically called
la madre dolorosa. After leaving the church, the two
statues separate, and each is made to perambulate an
alloted circuit, followed by a numerous retinue; after
which, meeting, by previous appointment, in some
plaza, a kind of tragic pantomime is acted, when the
two images are made to salute each other, and condole
upon their mutual grief, while the people sing mournful versicles.

Returning to the church in company, hardly have
they arrived, when a new procession must set out. It
is a repetition of that of Maunday Thursday, in which
a gigantic crucifix is borne on men's shoulders.

On concluding this ceremony, a third spectacle is
exhibited for the purpose of representing the dead body
of our Saviour, inclosed in a bier and embellished with
every kind of ornament the place can afford. This
recumbent statue bears the name of *Jesus muerto,* and
the exhibition is prolonged till long after twilight, to
honour Christ's sepulture. These performances are
intermingled with sermons, exhortations and canticles
of a mournful description, thus employing the whole
day in religious *exercises,* to the exclusion of every other
occupation.

On holy Saturday, the mass is prolonged all the
morning, but so soon as the blessed fire is lighted, an
immense quantity of rockets are fired, in token of
spiritual joy—a manner of evincing their religious feelings so congenial to the character of the Mexican Indians, that there is no pious ceremony, without excepting even the funerals of little children, in which it is
not practised.

At the conclusion of these solemnities, Mr. Faring

prepared to pursue his journey; but, being earnestly requested to remain another day, in order to witness the commencement, or opening of the fair, which is held in Easter week, he consented to gratify the friars' curiosity.

There was, in Spanish times, in the North of Mexico, but one great fair, which was held at Saltillo, in the month of September; and, being an affair of the utmost importance, not only to the inhabitants of that city in particular, but also to those of a wide spread district, who resorted in great numbers to this emporium of commerce, to barter their productions for the wares and commodities of Europe—it was thought proper to solemnise its commencement with religious ceremonies of a most splendid description. A banner, blessed with pomp by the highest ecclesiastical dignitary of the place, was carried about; an immense quantity of rockets was fired, and maskers and mummers perambulated the streets in wild glee. Since the beginning of the revolution, every town of any pretensions, in the three or four surrounding provinces, becoming anxious to enjoy the same privilege, the various sovereign legislatures, intoxicated by the first draught of supreme power, granted their petitions with thoughtless facility. The town of Pesqueria grande had, consequently, its fair, and the solemnities with which it was opened were in imitation of those of Saltillo. We will not weary our readers with a description of the blessing of the banner, nor of the firing of rockets, in which there was nothing remarkable, save the waste of holy water and gunpowder; but an Indian dance, which formed a leading feature of the revels, may prove of greater interest, inasmuch as it is a remnant of the old system of policy, practised in Montezuma's empire, before the conquest, and serves to illustrate the primordial manners of the aborigines. We allude to the dance of the *Matachines*, which was, originally, a sacred performance, emblematical of the old Mexican system of astronomy, and of the manner in which this ingenious people had regulated their calendar, but which Montezuma, who, though a barbarian, possessed a truly kingly

genius, found means to turn to his own honour and
exaltation, by becoming the chief performer therein,
and making himself and his bride the object of the
adorations which were, before, paid to the sun and
moon. (7)

Some time previous to the arrival of Cortez in
Mexico, that monarch married the daughter of the old
king of Tezcucco ; and, in order to solemnise his wedding with greater pomp, ordered that this dance should
be holden at his court, at stated intervals, when
he would himself, dressed in his imperial robes, per-
sonate the sun, and his bride, the moon; while the rest
of the performers, consisting of the principal caciques
and tributary kings, would represent the stars.

The attitudes and figures have nothing remarkable,
being evidently of Tartaric origin, and limited to hop-
ping alternately upon each foot; but the postures exhibit, or, rather, are emblematic of the most cringing
servility—a refined self abasement hardly credible in
a semi-barbarous people.

The dance is opened by the boy who personates
Montezuma, accompanied by his bride, who bears the
name of *Malinche.* The former, dressed gaudily in
silks and ribbands, with a splendid crown on his head,
hops down the apartment, while his spouse walks by
his side, with a grave and reserved demeanor, continually moving a rattle, held in her hand, which emits a
gentle noise. The dancers follow their monarch and
imitate his motions. Proceeding in two parallel lines,
they reach the goal and return to the starting point,
one line wheeling to the right and the other to the left,
so that there are four rows of dancers moving in contrary directions. A man in a hideous mask, personating
the evil genius, with a whip in his hand, rules the
dance, and not unfrequently applies the lash to the
caciques and grandees ; the Monarch and his malinche
being alone exempt from his jurisdiction.

At stated intervals, the Emperor and his bride sit
down in two arm chairs, and the whole party, in two
rows, kneel and make low prostrations before their
majesties. Their obeisance is the most servile imagi-

nable, bending slowly till their foreheads touch the
dust, then raising themselves, all the time waving their
rattles. In advancing towards the throne, this ceremony is repeated nine times and the same number in receding from it; but, as they retire, they punctiliously
avoid turning their backs upon royalty, and walk
backwards, which increases the ludicrous effect of the
scene. Neither the *salams* of the East Indians, nor the
prostrations of the cardinals before the Pope, on the
day of his enthroning, manifest so deep a sense of humiliation from man to man. Still this dance has a
wonderful attraction for the Indians of New Spain, and
inspires them with an air of exultation, for which it is
difficult to account, except, perhaps, on the supposition
that its symbols awaken in their mind the remembrance
of a nationality now irrevocably lost, and shed a kind
of faint halo round the traditions of the past glories of
their race. The name of Montezuma is to them typical of every thing that was honourable to the Aztecs;
and, singular as it may appear, the northern Indians,
whose progenitors never knew that name—nay, the
Tlascaltecans, who were its bitter enemies, have caught
the infection.*

This exhibition would have had but little interest
for our traveller, had not the parish priest, a man tolerably well acquainted with Mexican antiquities, explained to him that those eighteen low prostrations
were typical of the eighteen months of the old Mexican
year, and that certain irregular steps, by which they
were followed, represented the five intercallary days,
which the Aztecs ingeniously added to their months,
to make their civil year agree with the Solar revolution.
He also named the constellation that each dancer re-

---

* From the profound veneration with which the memory of Montezuma is still cherished by the Indian race, from Tehuantepec to
New Mexico, it may be inferred that he must have possessed a
splendid and inventive genius. He had greatly advanced the civilization of his empire. His character was a compound of that of
Buonaparte and Gregory VII., with a little spice of that of Ro-
bespierre.

84   MEXICO VERSUS TEXAS.

presented, and pointed out all the references to the
ancient calendar.

Mr. Faring, happily endowed with a philosophical
cast of mind, was not sorry to have been detained, because he had thus been enabled to witness this genuine remnant of ancient Aztec manners, and he felt
grateful to the friars for having, though unconsciously,
procured him that additional stock to his information.
These worthies, having nothing else to do in Pesqueria,
and finding themselves pretty well rewarded by the
parish priest for the little assistance they had rendered,
were anxious to continue their journey; and, on that
account, Mr. Faring immediately set out for Monterrey,
the metropolis of the State of Nuevo Leon, which the
Spaniards had dignified with the title of kingdom.

This little city, which is a Bishop's see, boasts a population of about fourteen thousand souls, and is built
at the foot of a very high mountain, whose jagged summit gives it some resemblance to a mitre, and from
whose sides flow numerous rivulets of limpid wholesome
water, which spread fertility through the plain below.
The style of building is the Morisco, as throughout the
rest of Mexico; that is to say, the houses are almost
universally one story high, with flat terrace roofs, and
very few windows to the street. They are most frequently built in the form of a quadrangle, round a small
square court-yard, decorated with evergreens and en-
livened by a small fountain, or a little stream of water,
which is a refinement the present Mexicans have derived from their Andalusian conquerors. The houses
of the poor are, however, nothing but miserable hovels,
built of reeds and plastered with clay.

Having already mentioned some remnant of Morisco
taste still lingering among this people, I must, in order
to corroborate this statement, inform my readers that
the same is to be traced in their style of dress. The
men seem to regret the turban, and avail themselves of
every trifling pretence, either a little wind, or a slight
head-ache, in order to wrap round their head, a white
linen handkerchief, or some piece of showy silk. You
may even, sometimes, see priests, in their ecclesiastical

functions, or military men, on parade, decorated with this strange kind of commode. The low people are also extravagantly fond of the broad Turkish trousers, and, in imitation, their *calzoneras* are slit at the sides, from the hip, down to the foot, and the broad white drawers, allowed to float in the air, which is as strange a fashion as any invented since the *souliers a la poulaine*, and impedes as much their walk.

In the North of Mexico, the whites are much more numerous, proportionably speaking, than in the South of the republic; yet not so much so as stated by Humboldt, in his political essay on New Spain. This great writer has, on this subject, as well as on some others, been induced into error, by those upon whose testimony he relied, for he never visited that part of the country, and the descendants of the European race do not certainly amount to a fifth part of the population of Durango, Chihuahua, Cohahuila, Nuevo Leon, and Tamaulipas, nor to the seventh of that of Sonora and California. They are a very handsome people, even fair complexioned, stout and well made, and superior, in physical qualifications, to the Spaniards, from whom they are descended; but they have, to a certain degree, contracted the habits of the Indians, which has greatly helped to weaken that moral fortitude, constancy and fixedness of purpose for which the Castillian character is so eminently distinguished. One would also be tempted to suppose that a great share of Indian timidity has crept into the hearts of the whites, from the very manner in which they use the Castillian language. The Spanish *LL*, as if too hard for their palate, has been softened into *Y*, and the elegant *Z* has dwindled into a common *S*. They have also generally adopted the custom of using all substantives in the diminutive form, which was a token of servile submission, enjoined upon the old Mexicans, when addressing their superiors, and which renders the conversation of the low people, among the modern ones, intolerably ridiculous. But I do not perceive that I am wandering off! Alas, a writer is often like a cook, who, in order to make a respecta-

8

ble looking dish, out of small materials, has to eke it out
with some sauce, into which are admitted different in-
gredients, that could never have figured by themselves.
Pity me, therefore, dear reader, and pursue with benignity the history of Mr. Faring's journey.

CHAPTER VII.

At Monterrey, the two Augustinian friars separated from Mr. Faring, for they were now to travel in a southerly direction, while his route lay due east. He, therefore, after visiting the few curiosities which the metropolis of Nuevo Leon contains, continued his journey alone in his coach, until he reached El Refugio, (at the mouth of the Rio Bravo,) which was *then* hardly more than a large rancho, but, from its situation, began already to attract considerable attention. That place having, since, become a large and populous city, its name has been changed to that of Matamoros, in honour of one of the most distinguished heroes of the revolution; and its locality will, in spite of the sand bar which renders the entrance of the harbour so difficult, make it, in times to come, the principal seaport of the Mexican republic, and secure for it an extensive inland trade.

The Rio Bravo has a course of sixteen hundred miles, being, like the Mississipi, subject to periodical inundations, and flowing in a variable estuary, which has formed in many places shallow lakes, similar, though on a smaller scale, to those which are so conspicuous in the delta of Louisiana. Rising in the mountains of Taos, a country fertile in wheat, and abundantly timbered, it receives the Rio Conchos, an important stream, by which the mineral riches of Chihuahua could be transported to its mouth, in steam boats of a light draught of water. The river San Juan, to which most of the creeks that flow from the glens of the eastern range of the Sierra Madre are tributary, disembogues also into the Bravo, and its waters could be rendered available for the exportation of the surplus produce of two states, already abundant in sugar, and the soil of which is well adapted to the cultivation of cotton and the grape vine.

A rapid but comprehensive glance enabled Mr. Faring, who was endowed with a peculiar turn for commercial speculation, to remark all these natural facilities, and many a splendid plan of future enterprise was then conceived; but he reckoned, as one may say, without his host, for the Rio Bravo has remained till now a *Virgin* river, and though a population of no less than nine hundred thousand souls might be benefited by its stream, in the exportation, by this means, of their surplus produce; yet, neither the oar nor the sail have disturbed its tranquil surface. A steam boat has, indeed, made its appearance in the port of Matamoros, but has been considered as an intolerable nuisance, having a tendency to ruin the interesting land carriage by means of mules, now in general use, nor is there any probability of the like encroachment, on the part of any designing foreigner, being tolerated a second time. But this by the by.

At the epoch of Mr. Faring's arrival at Refugio, one or two schooners used to perform occasional trips, between that place and New Orleans, and in one of them he designed to engage his passage for the United States, for he had given up the project of continuing his journey by land. In order not to trespass upon our reader's patience, we will abstain from enumerating all the formalities our traveller had to comply with, to obtain his passport and a clearance for his trunks and baggage; and, taking a temporary leave of him, we will suffer him to embark for his father's home, in Maryland, from whence he had been absent more than three years, and return to the hero of our story, whom we have left in charge of the parish priest of Phelipa.

The servants and *Peones*, who had accompanied Mr. Faring on his journey, being dismissed, followed, on their return home, the same route they had pursued with him, and did not fail, on passing through Phelipa, to call upon the priest. To him Mr. Faring had addressed a letter (accompanied by some presents of value) informing him of the deep regret he had felt in parting with his child, and that he should have been tempted to recall his word, had he not reflected, that, if the little boy were carried out of the country, that circumstance might, in after times, endanger his right to the inheritance of the house of Letinez, whose preperty was of immense value. He, therefore, besought the priest to open a correspondence with the old count, or his brother, and to give them frequent intelligence of the child's state and welfare. This was a very unwelcome petition to the excellent Don Fernando. He did not set the least value upon riches, and could not understand how he would be confering any benefit on his ward in trying to secure for him his grandfather's wealth. On the other hand, he was apprehensive that the family of Letinez would take the child away, if they once knew where he was. He felt, therefore, considerable perplexity as to what course he should pursue. His innate sense of justice, nevertheless, at length prevailed over all selfish views and private affections, and he gave to the servants, who were returning to the state of Mechoacan, the following letter, addressed to Count Letinez, together with the official certificate of his daughter's death, and of her child's baptism, which latter document was, according to the laws of the country, to secure the little boy's legal rights.

"*Eccelentissimo Senor*,

"As it becomes the pious Christian to be prepared for all the losses with which it may please Almighty God to visit him; I doubt not but your excellency will receive with resignation the afflicting intelligence which I have to communicate. Your heart had, no doubt, been deeply afflicted by the untoward events that obliged your daughter and son-in-law to seek for safety in a removal to the United States. That separation, though only temporary, must have been keenly felt by your excellency; yet it has pleased heaven, to send you, now, a far heavier trial; and circumstances over which I have had no controul, render it my duty to inform you of your loss. Your excellent, your accomplished daughter has been called to a better life, where she *now* is, undoubtedly, interceding for the welfare of her temporal father. Her death was truly edifying, and after receiving the sacraments of the church with the greatest piety and resignation, she left for you a *token*, which the bearer of the present letter will hand

8*

to your excellency. Your worthy son-in-law was so
affected by her decease, that a dangerous sickness was
the consequence; and, after his convalescence, which
was tedious and painful, he has thought proper to continue his journey for his native country, from whence
it is his intention to return in three years. He has
entrusted to my care his little son, (for whom I have
procured an excellent nurse) and who, I rejoice to say,
is in good health and highly interesting. It was not
without great difficulty that I could obtain your son-
in-law's permission that the infant should remain with
me; but having, previous to your daughter's demise,
pledged to her my word, that the child should be
brought up in the Catholic faith, I was resolved to carry
this point. I send you by the bearer an authentic certificate of your daughter's death, and of your grandchild's baptism, of which I beg your excellency to acknowledge the reception.

"I remain, with great respect, your Excellency's
humble servant and *devoted chaplain*, and I *kiss your
Excellency's hands*, &c. &c."

In six weeks' time, the parish priest of Phelipa received an answer from the count of Letinez, in which
that nobleman thanked him, with deep expressions of
gratitude, for the services he had rendered his daughter,
and gave him to understand that he would take charge
of the child, as he could not think of the heir of his
family being reared amongst strangers, as if he were a
foundling. He did not state precisely when he intended to send for the boy, but the priest gathered from
some of his expressions that it would be as soon as the
grief, resulting from the unexpected news of his daughter's death, should be a little assuaged. He, therefore,
concluded that he should not be permitted to retain his
ward much longer.

How wealthy and powerful soever the Count might
be, the priest had no mind to deliver up to him his
charge. He had received the little boy from his father,
whose natural right to dispose of his son was unques-
tionable, and no law could possibly oblige him to re-

sign the deposit to any one, without the consent or order of Mr. Faring. He, therefore, in a letter written in a polite, but manly tone, imparted his resolution to the Count, beseeching his excellency not to put him to the necessity of refusing his messenger. Old Senor de Letinez and his brother were, nevertheless, resolved that their intentions should not be frustrated, and scrupled not, if milder means should prove ineffectual, to resort to coercive measures to obtain their object; yet, before recurring to force, the family were desirous to employ the conciliatory interposition and persuasions of Abbatte Letinez, who consented to take a journey to Phelipa for that purpose. It was an arduous undertaking on the part of the good ecclesiastic, and it required all the love he bore his family, now centered in the only scion left by his niece, to induce him to venture upon so hard a task.

When this projected journey to the State of Durango became known to the family of Letinez, all the servants were put in commotion, and the report of such an extraordinary circumstance, being spread through the city of Pasquaro, became the subject of general conversation. In the mean time, preparations were made for the expedition, on such a scale, that one would have supposed it was question of providing for a small army. The grand family coach, a vehicle large enough to answer the purposes of a room, was furbished anew, its elaborate decorations of sculptured wood were regilt, the seats, in the inside, were restuffed, and its ponderous wheels strengthened, by having their spokes wrapped round with tough thongs of untanned hide, and the whole wooden frame plentifully watered twice a day. (8) The most trusty and skilful servants, from the several *haciendas* of the Count, were directed to select the best travelling mules from the immense herds belonging to the family, and the cooks, employed in preparing provisions of the best quality—*fiambres*—Estramadura sausages—venison tasajo—chocolate perfumed with vanilla, and what not? At last, the day of departure arrived, and the whole party went to church to hear a mass *pro itinerantibus,* which was

celebrated by the Abbatte himself, after which he bid
adieu to his brother, but not without many embraces
and tears, and set out on his journey.

The upper classes of the Mexican population are
distinguished by a certain helplessness, or, rather, femi-
nine langour, which renders them averse to the least
fatigue. Wages being exceedingly low and the common people fond of servitude—which saves them the
trouble of providing for themselves—wealthy houses
generally retain a number of domestics which would,
in Europe, be accounted out of all proportion. In
this respect, Mexico is comparable to the East Indies,
where people keep a servant for every species of domestic work, and where each menial confines his cares
to his specific occupation. Children being, from their
most tender age, surrounded with so many attendants,
are, of course, much indulged and flattered—they contract a habit of calling upon their servants even for the
most trifling wants, and consider the performance of
any little service for themselves, as unbecoming persons of genteel standing, and as an intolerable hardship.
No idea can be formed, from the servility of the negro
slaves, in the south of the United States, of that of the
low classes, in Mexico ; for the negro, while he crouches
before his master, does it with an air of fear and visible
signs of terror, which show his humiliation to be *extorted*—and this, naturally, disgusts a man of sensibility—
whereas the Mexican Indian fawns upon his master
with a look of *love*, which seems to be spontaneous,
and there is in him an appearance of devotedness superior to any thing I have ever beheld, in free servants
—something like the Clannish attachment of the ancient Scotch Highlanders to their Chiefs—and though
partly feigned, yet it is not altogether without sincerity,
and is undoubtedly founded on the Idiosincracy of this
people.

Now, with these premonitory remarks on the peculiarities of the serving classes before their eyes, our
readers may imagine the deep reverence, the tender
care and minute attention of which Abbatte Latinez
was the object during his journey. No less than fifteen

servants, or *mozos de mulas* waited upon him, all proud
of their charge, and never failing, when passing through
a rancho, to inform the villagers, in a whisper, of the
quality of their patron, and to add some slight hints
on the object of his expedition. Whenever the good
ecclesiastic alighted from his coach, no less than five
or six of the servants would run to help him down. It
seemed as if they thought the wind committed a sacrilege by blowing upon his person, and the earth was too
much honoured in being trodden on by his feet!

Notwithstanding all the tender officiousness of the
servants, and the good cheer daily provided for him,
father Letinez felt horridly fatigued, after the first five
days ride, and was obliged to rest some days at the
house of the parish priest of Temejuatlan, who had been
a scholar of his, while he taught metaphysics in the
University of Guadalaxara. At that clergyman's, he
was informed that a part of the *bajio*, through which
his road lay, was in a most deplorable state of civil
commotion, that fertile country being, then, overrun by
different parties of insurgent Chiefs, on the one hand,
and of the troops of the King of Spain on the other;
and that the prosecuting of his journey would, perhaps,
endanger his life. This piece of intelligence greatly
alarmed our worthy ecclesiastic, and he was, several
times, tempted to retrace his steps; still he felt ashamed
to return without accomplishing the object he had in
view, and, after long reflections *pro and con*, he resolved
upon the affirmative.

Having imparted his final resolution to his friend,
the latter told him, that, since his mind was absolutely
made up, he would try how far his safety could be in-
sured by giving him a passport, which would prove of
some service, in case he should fall into the hands of
certain parties of insurgents with whom he confessed
that he was secretly connected. Father Letinez was,
however, alarmed at the idea of a passport, and told his
friend that prudence would not permit him to accept
his offer, for, it might prove as dangerous, should he encounter the royal troops, as serviceable with the insurgents. To this, the other replied that his objection

would be removed, upon a view of the instrument provided for his security; and, so saying, he opened a clos-
et, from which he brought out a bundle of walking
sticks, every one of which had a small figure of a mon-
key carved on the handle.

"These," said he, presenting his friend with two of
them, "will insure your safe passage through my parish,
which extends twenty leagues to the north east of this
place, and even procure you any help my parishioners
can afford; but, beyond the limits of my jurisdiction,
they will, I am afraid, prove of little value; though,
perhaps, some few of my *lambs* may be wandering a
little farther. At all events, keep one in your left
hand, in the coach, and give the other to the leader of
your caravan, and let him also remember to carry it in
his left hand, in order that it may be easily perceived
by any one you may chance to meet."

"Have you, then, so much credit with the insurgents,"
interrupted father Letinez, "that they will reverence
to such a degree a cane coming from you?"

"Credit amongst them!" replied the other, laughing;
"Ay, who should, if I had not?—I can tell you, under
the rose, that it is I, who direct their movements, and
while I sit here snuggly in my parsonage house, they
stir nowhere without my directions; and yet, I frequently receive the royalists officers, when passing this
way. Oh, had the rattle-brained fellow of Dolores
known as well as I, how to keep the match burning,
without letting the smoke escape, he might be still
quiet in his cure, or, perhaps, have obtained a little bit
of a yellow cap, wherewith to cover his tonsure. (9)
But my empire does not extend far, as I have told you;
and that is the misery of those who do not come out
boldly. I am horribly cramped by the wild *armadillo*
of the rocks. By my *santiguada*, you must beware of
him. Should you fall into his hands, there is an end
of your journey, I assure you."

"And who is he?" inquired father Letinez.

"Padre Torrez," replied the other in a whisper, and
putting his lips close to his guest's ear, as if afraid to
be overheard.

" Yet, you would not imply that he would murder a fellow clergyman, or offer him personal violence ?" resumed he of Mechoacan.

" Murder, no :—at least, I hope not," replied he of Temejuatlan ; "but he will fleece you, if you fall into his hands. He would fleece you were you the holy father himself."

These communications did not tend to allay our traveller's fears ; yet, on the next day, he continued his journey, carefully conforming to his friend's instructions, and commanding the leader of the party to do the same. It was well he did so, for they had not proceeded fifteen leagues, when, in the middle of a thick *palmar,* (id est, a grove of palm trees,) they were assaulted by a large gang of ragged ruffians, who, rushing towards them, cried out " *Viva nuestra Senora de Guadelupe, y mueran los gachupines.*"*

Not perceiving at first the mysterious abacus, in the hands of the leader, they were beginning to beat some of the arrieros and to pillage their loads ; when he of the talismanic truncheon rushed in amongst them, flourishing the little monkey-headed stick, and calling out ; "miren aqui, senores, miren aqui !" (look here, gentlemen, look here ;) whereupon, the marauders immediately stopped, and, taking off their hats, respectfully inquired who occupied the coach. Upon being informed, that it was a *Padre* and a friend of the parish priest of Temejuatlan, they begged his pardon, kissed his hand and even escorted him a little distance, until he emerged from the woods.

The next day, at noon, they crossed the limits of that parish, and entered a territory under a different jurisdiction, where it was expected that the mysterious cane would lose its virtue ; still they met, every now and then, with some solitary ranchero, who would pull off his hat at the sight of it.

Aware that they were now within the district over which Padre Torres claimed a sort of right, from its

* Long live the Virgin of Guadelupe and death to the Spaniards.

being frequently scoured by his troops, they sought, by
a circuitous route, to escape, if possible, his marauding
parties; but the country became more broken as they
proceeded, and, consequently, retarded their progress.
Frequently, their road lay in some of the many *barran-
cos*, by which the plains are intersected, when the carriage had to be slowly dragged along over the shingles,
brought down from the mountains by the summer
torrents, which rendered its motion irregular and exceedingly painful to father Letinez. At times, too,
those ravines, winding down steep descents, and bordered, on either hand, by high banks, in the form of
perpendicular cliffs, precluded all possibility of flight,
or of defence, in case the traveller should be attacked.
This was a melancholy prospect, which they were
afraid to see realised at every moment, nor were their
anticipations without just foundation; for, at a short
turn of one of those ravines, known by the name of *los
Berrendos*, along the narrow bed of which they had
been marching for about one hour, without having
reached the place of egress, they were assailed by a
party of troops belonging to the formidable corps of
father Torres.

A gun was fired as a signal, and immediately the
banks, above their heads, were crowned by armed men,
some with muskets, some with lances, and others with
nothing but long sticks, at the extremity of which they
had fastened their knives. Their sudden appearance
was accompanied by the well known cry of "long live
the Virgin of Guadelupe and death to the Spaniards."
In vain did the guide flourish his Temejuatlan stick,
the assailants paid it no manner of reverence, and insisted that the travellers should throw down their
arms.

Upon seeing their obduracy, the guide began to expostulate with tears. "For the love of God, senores,"
said he; "and of the holy Virgin, do not offer any indignity to the only brother of the count of Letinez.
He is a Padre, senores, and we are his servants."

He was, however, interrupted by some of the marauders who had let themselves down the steep banks, and, now, with a gentle degree of coercion, obliged the guide and his fellow servants to alight from their mules. After taking possession of the animals, and binding the men with cords, they took padre Letinez out of the coach. Nevertheless, upon seeing, round his neck, the black stock, edged with blue, the distinctive mark of the clerical order, in Mexico, they felt abashed, and abstained from offering him any insult. This did not prevent them from insisting upon carrying him to the place where their chief resided. In vain did Padre Letinez persuade them to let him continue his journey; they were deaf to his intreaties, and, although, upon his earnest request, they unloosed his men, still they marched them all with their mules and baggage towards a range of high conical hills, called *Los Remedios*, which towered aloft, at the distance of fifteen leagues to the eastward.

It was on the highest summit of these mountains that their chief, surrounded by barbaric pride and luxury, held a kind of royal court. Our travellers did not reach the entrance of the deep glen that gave access to it, till the afternoon of the following day, and they were astonished to see the natural strength of the place. Immense precipices surrounded it on every side, and rendered an approach impossible, except by following the bed of a torrent, which wound round the base of a large steep hill, commanded by perpendicular rocks, on the right hand, whence a handful of men could have easily arrested the progress of a whole army. The bed of the torrent itself was carefully fortified by intrenchments, on which were mounted some light pieces of artillery; and, even after clearing all those external works of defence, one encountered, before reaching the level plain, on the summit, a *barranco*, of more than twenty feet in breadth, which entirely precluded all access beyond, and could be crossed only by means of a drawbridge. On the other side of the ravine, the top of the mountain was perfectly level, and produced excellent grass and in sufficient quanti-

9

ty to maintain a stock of cattle for provisions, in case
of a siege; while there was also a sufficient supply of
water from a well. There, Padre Torres, the ecclesiastical chieftain, had established his head quarters,
from whence he directed the movements of no less than
seven thousand men.

CHAPTER VIII.

The dreaded clergyman, who, from the summit of this mountain, like an eagle from his eyry, domineered over the surrounding plains, had, by the insurgents, been raised to the rank of *Mariscal de campo*, and had divided the considerable extent of country under his command into districts, at the head of which it was a singular feature of his policy to place none but men whose gross ignorance was likely to make them always subservient to his own will. He was not unskilful in the arts necessary to ingratiate himself into the favourable opinion of these officers, and, as long as they conformed to his instructions, he did not care for their conduct. Thus, sure of impunity, provided they should not contradict the orders, or stand against the interests of their chief, these commandants became petty tyrants in their districts, and made no scruple of pillaging the friends as well as the enemies of the independence of their country. Many of the patriots, therefore, dreaded falling into their hands, as much as into those of the royalists, and it was not without great terror that father Letinez saw himself about to be presented to the strange and capricious being whom circumstances had rendered master of his fate.

In the middle of the plain to which the drawbridge gave admittance, was a collection of huts, towards which our good ecclesiastic was obliged to march on foot, for he had been forced to leave his coach at the entrance of the glen, below, and his horse, on the other side of the ravine.

As he drew near to that species of village, he could distinguish a house, or, rather, cabin, of more elegant construction than the rest ; and, soon after, hear two or three cracked female voices singing a curious ditty, in praise of the great warlike achievements of the chieftain.

From time to time, the melody already mentioned was interrupted by loud peals of laughter, which seemed to proceed from a very strong pair of lungs :—it

was the Mariscal de campo himself, listening to the re-
hearsal of his own exploits, and manifesting his heart-
felt satisfaction by those noisy cachinnations.

Our traveller, being introduced into the presence of
this personage, was no less surprised than disappointed,
when, instead of receiving him, at least, with the common marks of civility, Padre Torres did not even
vouchsafe to rise from the bed upon which he was
stretched.   There he lay, surrounded by military officers and women, some of whom fanned him, and others
rubbed his feet, while others administered the grossest
and most fulsome adulation, which he would interrupt
every now and then, by crying out, " I am the chief of
all the world !"

"Alas, for the independence of my country!"
thought father Letinez, within himself, " if it must be
secured by such men as these ;" but he was, nevertheless, very cautious not to manifest his disgust by any
outward sign, and stood at a respectful distance, waiting to be interrogated by the mighty chief of *Los Remedios.*

The latter, after listening to some information, whispered into his ears by the officer who had headed the
capturing party, vouchsafed, at last, to address father
Letinez, in the following words :—" So, I find you are
travelling northward, with a large retinue, and a splendid coach !—And where may you be going ?—towards
Monterrey, probably, with some message for Arredondo ;—the *gachupines* must pay you well, man, to enable you to maintain such state.—Oh, the wretches!
The Spanish tyrant affords them the means of travelling in this style :—while, here, we think ourselves
happy, if we can procure a *mesteno,* (10) or a broken
down mule to ride."

" May it please your excellency," replied father Letinez, " I have no relation with Arredondo, neither am
I opposed to the independence of my country :—on
the contrary, I do all I can in reason for its accomplishment."

" In reason !" replied the other, " Ay, that is the
word !—that is the cant !—And *that* reason would not

prevent your accepting a mitre from the Spanish tyrant, if you could get it, as some of your betters have
done."

"Padre," returned Senor de Letinez, who, though
constitutionally timorous, had a proper sense of his
dignity, and had no mind to suffer himself to be insulted; "I am a Mexican and a clergyman, as well as
you; and as you are *now* at the head of a large share
of the forces who are fighting for the liberties of your
country, no doubt, you will conceive it is your duty
to protect, and not to oppress, a peaceable fellow citi-
zen. I can refer you to the parish priest of Temejuatlan, who, I know, is one of the secret leaders of the
partizans, in the *bajio :*—I am a friend of his. This
puts me above suspicion. I am now bound on a journey
to the state of Durango, in the success of which the
welfare and honour of our family are deeply concerned; and it would be a great misfortune for us if I were
prevented from continuing my route. Therefore, I
hope you will not detain me, and, in order to prove to
you that I am well affected to your cause, I will give,
towards the equipment of your soldiers, the sum of one
thousand dollars. I will leave you an order upon my
brother, at Pasquaro, and it will be paid at sight."

"Umph!" replied Padre Torres, "it is a great way
hence to Pasquaro, and who knows whether your brother would honour the order?—We want money, sure
enough, but to let you go is not the means to provide
for our necessities. I cannot take upon myself to decide in an affair of so much importance;—it must be
referred to *congress* and *they* will decree what they
please."

"And where does congress sit?" inquired father
Letinez. "I will go, myself, to lay my case before
them."

"At Jauxilla, twenty leagues distant from this place,"
replied Torres. "But you are not to leave Los Remedios without permission. I will send them a statement
of your case, and you must await their resolution."

At these words, father Letinez lost patience; and,
forgetting his timidity, broke forth into a volley of ob-

jurgations which stunned Padre Torres, declaring that
he would set out, and daring any of the Chieftain's
myrmidons to lay his hands on him in order to hinder
his departure. None of them, in fact, dared to do so,
being prevented by respect for his ecclesiastical character; but, alas! his servants did not enjoy the same
privilege, and these were soon secured, so that, although
father Letinez was left free, and might roam at large,
yet he found no body to wait upon him, and was, consequently, as much a prisoner, as if he had been confined in irons.

He went about, complaining of the treatment he received from Padre Torres, till the latter began, at last,
to fear lest he should make, upon the minds of his fol-
lowers, an impression unfavourable to his authority,
and sent him a soothing message, informing him that
he had despatched one of his officers to Jauxilla, and
that he would soon be informed of the resolution of
congress, which would, he trusted, prove favourable to
the continuation of his journey. Upon receiving this
intelligence, father Letinez determined to wait with
patience. Nothing definitive, however, was known
till the afternoon of the next day, when the officer, who
had been despatched to Jauxilla, returned with the
news that congress were coming to Los Remedios, in
order to have an interview with Padre Torres. This
was very surprising to father Letinez, who could hardly
believe it possible that a legislative assembly should so
far forget their dignity as to condescend to wait upon
one of their officers, instead of obliging him to wait on
them; but he did not know what kind of an assembly
that congress was, nor of what they were capable.

Towards evening, they arrived, sure enough—the
whole congress on horseback! It consisted of a president and two members, whose names have been im-
mortalised in history. At the entrance of the village,
they were received with military honours by the ragged garrison; and Padre Torres vouchsafed to rise
from his bed of repose, to invite them into his own
house, where an extraordinary session was immediately
opened.

They sat with closed doors, and, after a quarter of an hour, despatched no less a personage than a *general of brigade* to summon father Letinez to their presence. This officer condoled with the good clergyman upon the treatment he had experienced, and, out of reverence for his character, condescended to communicate a slight hint of what had been resolved in congress, in relation to him, and moreover imparted some advice which, he assured him, would prove exceedingly advantageous, if followed.

"What a pity!" said he, "what a scandal, to treat a reverend gentleman like you, in the way they have done! An ancient professor of philosophy! The light of the university of Guadalajara, at its most brilliant period! But, Padre, you know what Tully says, "inter leges silent arma,"—no—it is "inter arma, silent leges," I should say. The fact is, reverend father, that we are hard pushed for money, and, though his excellency and· the general congress are inclined to treat you with all possible lenity, yet they dare not dismiss you without—ransom—I mean without something to stop the clamours of our men, who have not received one single *jola* for three months past. It is merely to prevent their murmurs—you understand me, Padre. But what you have offered is not enough for one week's pay for the garrison of this fortress. Now, should you make it three thousand, instead of one, it would, perhaps, suffice for immediate relief, and terminate the grumbling of our soldiers; for, as to us, no portion of it will come into our pockets, much less into those of the members of the sovereign congress, who, God bless them, exercise their charge out of mere zeal for liberty and hatred to the Gachupines. There is also another little thing which might help you mightily; but I hardly dare to hint it, unless you should promise me strict secrecy."

"And what is it?" interrupted father Letinez. "You may rely upon my discretion."

"Why," resumed the other, "Padre Torres went down, last night, to look at your coach, and was greatly pleased with it. He has nothing to ride in, but a poor

gig, which is somewhat out of repair, and he says it is
a shame for a Mariscal de Campo to make use of so
paltry a kind of chariot. I think he would be glad to
effect an exchange, and, no doubt, would cover the trifling difference, to make odds meet."

"Our family coach! He wants to swindle me out of
that, too!" exclaimed father Letinez, incensed.

"Well," resumed the officer, "you can do as you
please; I only give you friendly advice, and show you
how to make a protector of the padre."

They had, by this time, got to the door of the chieftain's house, and our traveller was soon admitted before
the congress. Padre Torres was sitting at the head of
the table, having the president of the sovereign assembly, on his right hand, and the two members who composed that legislative body, on his left. There were
cigarritos on the table and a bottle of brandy, with
glasses, which showed that these worthies did not perform their work *dry lipped.* Father Letinez was invited to sit down, after which the president imparted to
him the resolution they had taken, in the following
words.

"His excellency, our Mariscal de campo, has, communicated to us the generous offer you have made for
the equipment of the brave soldiers who are fighting
for the liberties of *Anahuac,* and as we do not suppose,
nor believe that you are a disaffected person, nor can,
in any wise, be dangerous to our cause—but, on the contrary, a well wisher to the same—we have agreed to accept your proposal, yet, at the same time, to remonstrate
with you on the small amount to which you have limited your offers, inviting you, in the name of your country,
(de la patria,) to make it *three* thousand. You may
send as many of your servants as you please, to Pasquaro, to fetch the silver, and, in the mean time,
remain as hostage, here. As soon as the money arrives,
you shall be left at liberty to continue your route."

To this, father Letinez answered, that he could, on
no account, consent to prolong his stay, because the object he had in view, in the journey he had undertaken,
was urgent, and a delay might cause its failure. They

had, therefore, nothing to expect from him, unless he should be permitted immediately to continue his route. This was his firm and unalterable determination.

Neither the congress, nor the Mariscal de campo expected to find so much firmness in their unwilling guest, and they were not a little stunned by his resolution. They thought, however, that it would be proper to take some time for reflection, previous to granting the liberation of so important a prisoner, and, remanding him for the present, they gave him to understand that he would be again summoned, the next morning, to appear in their presence. There was a secret reason that prompted their accession to his terms, of which father Letinez could not be informed, and which had been the principal motive of the congress coming down from Jauxilla, to consult with padre Torres.

Some time previous, the celebrated Spanish chief, Mina, had gained a considerable victory over the royalists, at San Juan de los Llanos, and all the party of the patriots was anxious that Torres and his troops should cooperate with him, and that Mina, as a man of greater military talents, should act as generalissimo; doubting not, but, under so skilful a chief, the Mexican cause would prosper. Padre Torres did not relish a plan by which he was to be reduced to act a secondary part, and had hitherto opposed it; but solely by secret manœuvres and intrigues, without openly showing his disinclination. His party, and the very commandants he had placed at the head of the various districts under his jurisdiction, became, however, so clamorous, that he was necessitated to sacrifice his private feelings and to appoint an interview with the European chieftain, at the fort of Sombrero. The day was at hand, and Torres was to leave los Remedios the following Tuesday. Taking with him his principal officers, he feared lest, during his absence, father Letinez should avail himself of the influence of his sacerdotal character, to obtain his release, and that of his servants and property; which was not at all improbable, considering the great reverence which the insurgents entertained for their native clergy. Torres would, in that case, be deprived of his prey. On the other hand, he dared not, before setting out, confine the father in prison, the only effectual means of preventing his escape; for, it would have been an abominable scandal for his whole party, and might have proved dangerous to the stability of his authority. Torres resolved, therefore, to accept the draft, and liberate his fellow clergyman, and it was for him the most easy thing in the world to obtain the sanction of his congress.

On the following morning, it, was, of course, announced to father Letinez that, upon his signing the draft, he would be permitted to depart. He, very joyfully, availed himself of the permission thus unexpectedly obtained, and, to his unspeakable comfort, saw himself, after a few hours bustling about on the part of his servants, at the head of his caravan, on his way to Phelipa. The provisions which had been so liberally made for his journey, were, nevertheless, sadly diminished, and when they stopped at night, the guide had a long and woful account to impart of the felonious abstraction of whole boxes of chocolate and delicate *fiambres*, of which the officers of the garrison of los Remedios had been guilty.

We will pass over the inconveniences which resulted to father Letinez, from the scarcity of his travel-
ing provisions, as well as from the fatigues he under-
went during the remainder of his journey, and, at one
single bound, transfer our reader to Phelipa, that he
may witness the first interview between the Mechoa-
con priest, and Don Fernando de Larribal.

It happened that when father Letinez alighted from
his coach, before Don Fernando's parsonage house,
there was no one at home besides the housekeeper,
who was not a little bewildered at the sight of this
numerous retinue. Her first thoughts were about the
slender stock in her larder, which the new comers
were likely to leave in a desolate state, should the parish priest, as was his custom, insist on entertaining
the servants as well as their master. This did not,
however, prevent her from showing a proper degree
of civility to the strange ecclesiastic, whom she introduced into the *gran sala*, and begged to consider
himself at home, till the return of her master, who
had gone to a neighbouring village to visit the sick.

Father Letinez, availing himself of the housekeeper's loquacity, inquired about the state of Mr.
Faring's child, and, no sooner manifested a desire to
see him, than, glad of an opportunity to oblige an
ecclesiastical visitor, who had condescended to enter
into conversation with her, the old woman summoned Tio Pedro, who was working in the *hueria,*
and ordered him to fetch the infant. Tio Pedro did
not set out upon his errand so briskly, but that he
found time to take a peep at Father Letinez, his
grand carriage and his numerous servants, and was
not a little puzzled to imagine what kind of visitor
he could be, for he had never seen so much magnificence in all his life, nor so much gilding as the
stranger's coach displayed, except at the altar of St.
Mathew, the patron saint of the parish:—Even the
Bishop of Durango, (God bless his most illustrious
Lordship,) was not attended by so great a

number of servants, when travelling through his diocese to give confirmation! Nor were they so richly
dressed, nor their mules so handsome!" He went,
nevertheless, to acquit himself of his errand, and,
shortly after, returned with the nurse and child.

As soon as father Letinez saw the little babe, he
took him into his arms and burst into tears. A thousand tender recollections of his niece, whom he had so
tenderly loved, rushed upon his mind,—all her fond-
ness and dutiful respect towards her father and himself were brought back to his memory,—and the idea
that she had died far from her family, in a state of
distress, and perhaps in consequence of the ecclesiastical persecution she had suffered, made him feel such
an anguish of mind, as he had hardly ever before experienced. Yet, there was a consolation. Though Maria
was dead, there was a remnant left of the ancient and
noble house of Letinez,—the beautiful and sweet-look-
ing babe who was innocently smiling upon him!

In this child were *now* centered all his brother's
hopes as well as his own :—upon this infant, depended
the consolation of their old age;—but he was still in
strange hands, and it was doubtful whether they should
be successful in obtaining his release from the parish
priest of Phelipa. Since father Letinez had entered
the state of Durango, he had acquired a better knowledge of the situation of the northern provinces, and
convinced himself, that, should Don Fernando de Larribal resist his entreaties, there was but little chance
to use forcible means; because the Spanish power was
yet unshaken in those parts, and the officers of Ferdi-
nand VII. could not fail to side with one of their own
countrymen in the determination of any legal claims,
against the best of Mexican creoles. He plainly perceived, therefore, that the attainment of his object,
depended entirely on the generosity of the Spanish
priest; and, fully convinced of the inutility of other
measures, resolved to appeal to his feelings, hoping
that this mode of proceeding would be conducive to
success.

He was not mistaken :—Don Fernando de Larribal

was endowed with a noble, elevated soul, inaccessible
to fear and incapable of being bullied into any conces-
sion through timidity. All the Biscayan energy and
spirit of independence burned in his bosom; yet he
was compassionate to excess, and unable to resist supplications for the relief of any distress which it was in
his power to relieve. The sensibility of his mind was
so exquisite, as to degenerate into a kind of weakness;
and, to this foible did father Letinez owe the ultimate
success of the suit he had come to urge.

When the parish priest returned home, he was not
a little surprised to see the splendid vehicle in his
court-yard; but, upon entering his parlour, and beholding the strange clergyman, who still held the child
in his arms, he immediately understood who he was
and the purport of his visit.

Advancing towards him, he said, with rather a cold,
but civil air, " I need not, I suppose, fear being mistaken in saluting my guest as Senor de Letinez:—no
one else could take such an interest in *this* child. But
I can tell him, in one single word, and in order to
prevent all necessity of further explanation, that, if
his object is to separate me from my charge, his intention will be frustrated. I received him from his father,
to whom alone I am accountable; and to him alone
am I bound to deliver the child. I am sorry to be
obliged to appear thus harsh with a reverend guest,
but it is better fully to understand each other from the
beginning."

Father Letinez was rather confounded by this address—with an admirable presence of mind, nevertheless, and a nice tact of good breeding, which was an
indirect reproof of his host's bluntness, he replied:
" My dear sir, I am so much delighted to see my grand
nephew—the only remaining scion of our house—in
such good health, and to become acquainted with the
noble hearted man to whom our family is so much indebted, that I do not feel inclined to grumble at any
resolution he may have taken, much less, to quarrel
with him, should he even deprive us of what we conceive to be our just right. Let us, therefore," added

10

he, tenderly embracing Don Fernando, "make *this*
pledge of friendship, the first step to our further acquaintance."

The parish priest of Phelipa, who, to quick feelings,
united nice powers of discrimination, felt rebuked and
somewhat abashed on receiving the embraces of Senor
de Letinez. Thus, the latter had already obtained
some advantage, which he was very careful not to lose.
He turned the conversation on his niece and the various circumstances that had attended her death, which
he wished to hear detailed by Don Fernando, personally.

After hearing, from his host, the melancholy history,
he did not fail to tender anew his thanks, and there
was in his language a certain warmth and unction,
which manifested that his heart sincerely felt what his
lips expressed. His powers of conversation were of
the first order, and Don Fernando could not help
thinking that he had seldom seen a man of such a pleasing address. He, nevertheless, kept on the reserve,
being rather dubious as to the object the stranger had
in view, and was incessantly on the watch, in order to
seize upon any expression that might afford him the
least chance of entering new protestations against re-
signing his young ward to the family of Letinez. His
precautions were, however, futile ; for the Mechoacan
clergyman, who did not lack a certain knowledge of
the human heart, and had

———————— " skill
To rule and warp the human will,"

abstained, during the rest of the day, from broaching
the subject, and thought proper to study his host's temper, before treading again upon such delicate ground.

Having announced to Don Fernando his intention to
prolong his stay at Phelipa, during some days, he rented a house for the use of his servants ; and, though the
parish priest strongly insisted upon entertaining the
whole party, father Letinez would by no means consent to impose such a burden upon a man who made so

benevolent a use of his income. He did accept his hospitality for himself; but his servants kept house apart, at his expense, under the direction of one of their number, who acted as steward.

Having thus temporarily become a member of Don Fernando's family, father Letinez insisted upon assisting him in his ministerial duties. He preached repeatedly in the parish church, and spoke with so much eloquence, that all the parishioners, as well as the priest himself, were delighted. There was no talk, through the whole country, but of the famous *Padre*, from Mechoacan, who was so pathetic in the pulpit, that he could almost draw tears from a rock! Father Letinez was, moreover, generous, and, as he had plenty of money at his disposal, his charities were even more extensive than those of the parish priest; so that all the inhabitants of Phelipa, rich and poor, sang his praises. With any other clergyman, besides Don Fernando, so much popularity, so rapidly acquired, might have begotten jealousy and aversion; but the worthy man was such a stranger to these vile passions, that he became more attached to his guest, in proportion as the latter recommended himself more extensively to the public; and loved him, as much for the advantage he thought his parishioners derived from his labours, as he himself admired his talents.

When father Letinez saw that he had made a deep impression on the public mind, he proposed to his host to give to his parishioners a course of religious exercises, such as are delivered in the house of St. Philip, of Neri, in the city of Mexico. (11) We must, here, state, for the information of our Protestant readers, that these exercises, which are calculated to produce what is, in the United States, denominated *a revival of religion*, were originally invented by St. Ignatius of Loyola, the founder of the Jesuits; and that they are, on a reduced scale, synonimous to what, in the *Wesleyan economy*, is termed the plan of salvation. From the book of St. Ignatius, did Wesley literally steal *his plan;* but he had the great merit of modelling it anew, on an extended scale, which enabled him to affect large

masses of hearers. Thus, what was done by the Jesu·
its, in the private halls of their colleges, with a small
crucifix, and reduced means, and which could be brought
to bear only upon a few scores of people, at a time,
was, by the patriarch of Methodism, attempted in broad
plains, or in the green wood, electrifying thousands, at
once, and giving the widest sweep to supernal grace.

Such were the spiritual exercises, the benefit of which
father Letinez was desirous to impart to the parishioners
of Phelipa. We must do him the justice to say that he
was urged by no fanatical, or knavish object; yet we
cannot but confess, that he was, in some measure, moved
by selfish considerations; for, while he expected that the
exercises would be the means of conveying spiritual grace
to many obdurate sinners, he flattered himself, also, that
they would procure to him the mastery of Don Fernando's conscience. He had, in a few days, become thoroughly acquainted with his host's character, and found
he was a man of religious scruples, exceedingly fearful
of the judgments of God, and, in a word, one over
whom a ghostly director might exercise the greatest
authority. Upon this knowledge, he formed his plan
of action, which, though it savoured of *finesse*, had certainly nothing criminal in its nature, since he wished
to obtain that mastery, merely for an object which was
not only lawful, but, even, to his notion, a matter of
strict justice.

The exercises to which we allude, and which enjoy
great reputation, in Mexico, consist of a series of prayers, familiar exhortations, and sermons, digested in a
methodical order, and calculated to work a strong
commotion in the soul, leading her on, from the tremendous paroxysms of the fear of death and hell, to a
desire of forgiveness, and a tormenting anxiety about
the uncertainty of its attainment. From that state,
which, in the Wesleyan vocabulary, constitutes the
throes of the new birth, the smitten sinner is led to
the perspective of hope—reconciliation is presented as
within his reach; and then comes the master stroke of
justification, which, among Methodists, is wrought in-
stantaneously, and physically felt; but, among Roman

Catholics, is attained, in a more quiet manner, by means of confession, and absolution. It was to this, father Letinez trusted. "Let me but see you kneeling at my feet, in quality of a penitent, my dear Don Fernando," thought he within himself, "and I will make you accede to my own notions of justice." The method he took, to compass his purpose, was uncommon, but sure; and the only one he could possibly employ, or think of, in the circumstances in which he found himself placed.

It was, therefore, announced, from the pulpit of the parish church of Phelipa, that exercises similar to those of the *Professa*, in Mexico, would be given to the public, and that all, who felt inclined, for the benefit of their conscience, to avail themselves of the opportunity, should give in their names. There were no less than two hundred applicants, and one of them was the parish priest himself, who thought proper to set this good example to his parishioners.

A kind of prospectus, containing the order of the exercises, and the rules of conduct to be observed by the applicants, was distributed, and the first sermon preached, in which the Mechoacan clergyman so far surpassed himself, that there was not a dry eye among the audience. So auspicious a beginning was followed by the most flattering results, for in less than five days, more than one hundred and fifty persons entered themselves on the penitent list and took father Letinez for their confessor. The parish priest was in the number, and thus his guest had the satisfaction of seeing his efforts crowned with the most complete success. When sitting, in the secret tribunal, as an interposer between God and his penitent host, he might assume a tone of authority, which he could not possibly avail himself of elsewhere; nor was there any appeal from the decisions he gave, as a spiritual judge. As the task, however, had a spice of selfishness, we must do him the justice to say, that, in his admonitions to Don Fernando, he reasoned the case with him upon its intrinsic merit, abstractedly from all personal interest, begging him, at the same time, to consult skilful divines, in case he should doubt the correctness of his

10*

own decision. In fact, the reasons he gave were irresistible. "By detaining the child," said he, "you expose him to lose his grandfather's fortune, for, in the
present distracted state of Mexico, when it is impossible to foresee what party will ultimately triumph, or
what political measure will, after the end of the contest, be adopted by the victors, with respect to the
conquered, it is not improbable that the boy may, if
unknown in the country, at the time of the count's demise, be deprived of the family estates, or be impeded,
by insuperable obstacles, from obtaining possession of
his property, should it once fall into the hands of government. Moreover, though his grandfather is well
disposed towards him at present, yet he may feel so
much offended at your refusal, which he will probably
ascribe to his son-in-law's instructions, as to conceive
some ideas of revenge, of which the child may be the victim. There are collateral branches of our family, now
seeking to worm themselves into my brother's affections, and nothing but the little boy's presence is able
to counteract their secret machinations. Will you, for
the gratification of your own individual feelings, detain
him, and, by so doing, expose him to the loss of so brilliant a fortune? You may despise wealth for yourself,
—it is heroical;—but you have no right to despise it
in behalf of others, who cannot exercise their own
judgment. Were the infant exposed to any spiritual
danger, from the fear of an heretical education, you
might be justifiable in the detention; but in his grandfather's house, and under my superintendence, you
cannot possibly have the least motive of fear."

In a word, the reasons which Senor de Letinez gave
to the parish priest, delivered with all the authority of
a ghostly director, triumphed over the latter's repugnance, and he consented to the separation, whereupon,
he received absolution from his father confessor, and
sang, the next morning, a high mass, to conclude the
religious exercises; but it was the saddest mass he
ever celebrated. Well has the wise man said, "Musica
in luctu, importuna narratio!" Poor Don Fernando's
heart was ready to burst, when he intoned the preface,

and, having, peradventure, cast his eyes upon the child, who was in his nurse's arms, near the railing, he could not refrain from tears.

Our Protestant readers may think this childish, and too improbable for credulity to believe; but we can assure them that it would not appear to them to involve any improbability, did they but know what feelings are apt to be engendered in the soul of a Roman Catholic clergyman, who religiously adheres to his vow of celibacy, particularly, if separated from those who are connected with him by the ties of blood.

In gloomy solitude, without any family endearment, or any kindred soul, to whom he can recur in his troubles in order to unbosom his thoughts, his heart is apt to form attachments, which, to the common run of mankind, would appear puerile. Restrained by severe laws and the constant fear of future judgment, from any indulgence which might bring him nearer to a sex made to adorn the world—but which he considers as the most dangerous enemy of his salvation—and yet, urged by his unconquerable nature, which incessantly yearns after mental expansion and love, his affections are, not unfrequently, turned towards any insignificant object which attracts his care, and that attachment becomes a passion! Thus, an animal, or a plant—a cat, a bird, or a flower, will sometimes engross all the feelings of a heart which, had they been turned into a different channel, might have secured the happiness of a family of rational beings.

Thus it was with Don Fernando de Larribal. Separated from his relations, by the broad Atlantic, placed in the midst of a nation that was now learning to execrate the Spanish name, without any bosom friend, he had already become passionately attached to the child of the foreigner, whom chance had thrown upon his protection, and had made a thousand visionary plans of future happiness, founded on the gratitude of the boy, whom he intended to bring up with all the tenderness of a father. To be, now, obliged to part with him was the most cruel stroke which could be inflicted. He resigned himself, however, since it was the will of God, and, two days after the conclusion of the religious exercises, father Letinez departed, with the little boy and his nurse, who was, by the hope of a large reward, prevailed upon to follow him to Mechoacan.

With them, we will take leave of the honest parish priest of Phelipa, who, though conscious that he had acted up to his duty, in relinquishing all claim over the child, felt, every now and then, something like sentiments of rancour against father Letinez, and personal vexation, as though he had suffered himself to be outwitted.

CHAPTER X.

Father Letinez arrived at Pasquaro, with his grand
nephew, in perfect good health. The old count's satisfaction at the sight of the child was inexpressible, and
the transports of joy with which the latter was received
by the servants, unbounded—formerly attached to his
mother, even to a degree of enthusiasm seldom felt by
those of the Indian race, they now transferred a portion of that love to her son.

It is not, however, our intention to follow our hero
through the protracted period of infancy and youth, nor
to describe every petty incident connected with his
education. Be it sufficient to state, generally, that he
was brought up in the most careful manner imaginable,
under the immediate superintendence of father Letinez,
who, though rather too much addicted to metaphysics,
was, really, a man of literary taste and considerable
erudition. Neither will we dwell on three different visits his father paid him, from the United States; nor on
the repeated attempts of the latter at abduction, which
could not be effected, in consequence of the vigilant
watchfulness and jealousy of the child's grandfather;
nor on the trip he made, when grown to the age of reason, under the guidance of a trusty servant, to the
state of Durango, in order personally to become acquainted with the good clergyman who had tended him
at his birth.

But let us, dear reader, suppose eighteen years to
have elapsed, and present him, a second time, under
the form of a tall, handsome, young man, with a pair
of epaulettes, and at the head of a company of cavalry,
under the command of Urrea. The corps to which he
belonged was winding down a long steep hill, on the
eastern side of the *rancho de la Manteca*, a few leagues
after crossing the nameless river which flows through
the village of *Capadero*. These troops were the flower
of the Mexican army. The common soldiers, clad in
a fine uniform of red and blue, having on their heads
brazen helmets of perfectly antique form, and which

shone in the sun, like burnished gold; bore in their hands long lances, adorned with little tricoloured streamers, after the fashion of the ancient knights. They were preceded by a numerous and glorious band of music, consisting of the finest looking men imaginable, in a brilliant scarlet dress, with red and white plumes in their caps; who, every now and then, made the distant hills resound with warlike melody.

These warriors were going to fight the battles of their country, against men whom they had been taught to consider as a horde of treacherous foreigners,—mortal enemies to their religion and independence,—the insidious colonists of Texas, who, not only had set at defiance the popular chief, whom the Mexican nation had placed at their head; but had, even, carried their ingratitude so far as to declare themselves independent, and attempt to deprive of the most fertile portion of their territory, the people who had so generously cherished them in their bosom.

The gallant army, entrusted with the care of wiping off this stain from the national escutcheon, was marching in two divisions, towards what was imagined would prove an easy conquest—the northern corps being under the command of the chief magistrate of the nation in person; and the southern, under the conduct of Urrea, an officer of tried courage, and considerable experience in the art of war. Though captain Letinez, (for he bore his grandfather's name,) did not, properly speaking, belong to the staff; yet the influence of his family, and his gallant bearing, together with his intelligence, so far superior to that of his comrades, had rendered him a kind of favourite with the general, who frequently honoured him with h , conversation.

They were riding together, surrounded by a knot of officers, a little in advance of the first regiment of lancers, when they were overtaken by a courier who seemed to have been riding with great speed. He brought important despatches for the general, and, whilst the latter was perusing them, the messenger, interrogated by some of our hero's military companions, informed them that he had been sent from Mier,

(a town of some importance, on the Rio Bravo, eighty
leagues above its mouth;)—that that place had been
invaded by a party favourable to the Texian cause,
aided by a large swarm of Indians, who were spreading desolation on the left bank of the river, and that
his mission was to implore speedy succour.

When the general had made himself acquainted with
the contents of the despatches; commanding a halt,
he summoned a council of the ablest among his officers, and, confirming the tidings which the messenger
had already imparted, added many other particulars
which had been concealed from the bearer of the news.
One of the principal federalists of the state of Durango,
who, at the time of the downfall of the administration
of the Ex-Vice-President, Farias, succeeded in making
his escape into Texas, had, it seems, assembled a little
band of adventurers, and formed the plan of penetrating into the heart of the *provincias internas*, in order
to re-establish the constitution of 1824. His force
amounted, at most, to ninety men, and with so small a
number, he, now, found himself within reach of Santa
Anna's army, which was marching from Saltillo, eight
thousand strong, for the purpose of invading Texas.
The bold fellow, who had thus taken possession of the
town of Mier, though he could not possibly dream of
resisting the Mexican forces, yet maintained his ground
and issued proclamations, lording it over the district
of country immediately adjacent, and endeavouring to
excite a rising of the people.

Some of the magistrates of that parish, annoyed by
his measures, had despatched this express, to beg a
speedy succour, which Urrea granted on the spot; and,
in order to furnish our hero with an occasion of distinguishing himself, he selected him to command the expedition. By his order, therefore, captain Letinez,
placing himself at the head of a hundred lances, proceeded towards Mier. He expected to be able to enter
the place unperceived, under cover of night, and, thus,
to surprise the Texian force; but their commander
had, some how or other, been apprised of his approach,
and had time to cross the Rio Bravo, staving the ferry

boat, after his passage; so that it became impossible for our hero to continue the pursuit, until some means of crossing the river should be devised. The Mexican force could, in the mean time, from the right bank, perceive their enemies' fires, on the opposite side, and when day had dawned, were tantalized with their gestures of contempt and provocation. The sight so much enraged captain Letinez's soldiery, that several men requested permission to swim the river upon their horses, to chastise the insolence of the Texians; but their commander, considering it as rash and fool hardy, refused his consent.

He had recourse to stratagem, in order to surprise the invaders; and, leaving thirty of his men, on the river bank, with a certain number of the citizens of Mier, disguised in soldiers' uniform, he gave orders to amuse the enemies, by firing at them, from time to time, a small four pounder, which, in the hurry of flight, they had forgotten, and to make a show of building a raft. In the mean time, he led the remainder of his troop, to a ford, six leagues up the river, which he crossed, before twelve o'clock, with all his force. As soon as the soldiers had dried their equipments, he set forward on his march, his guide having promised to conduct him within two hundred yards of the enemy, unperceived. Captain Letinez ordered his men to ride slowly, until within sight of the Texians, when they were to rush impetuously to the attack. As it was very difficult to wield the lance with effect, in the *nopalera*, (thicket of prickly pear,) in which the enemy was encamped, the Mexicans were directed to lay aside that weapon and to depend on the *lasso*; every soldier selecting his opponent, and abstaining from firing his pistols, except in case he should miss entangling his foe in the noose.

We must state, in praise of captain Letinez, that it was with repugnance he gave orders to use the *lasso*, considering it as a mode of warfare hardly worthy of a civilized nation; but his aim was rather to frighten the invaders, than to use them barbarously, for he gave strict commands to his soldiers to grant quarter, and, by no means to drag their victims to any distance, whereby their limbs might be seriously injured and lacerated. He knew, that, by this mildness, he was disobeying general orders; but was, nevertheless, determined not to swerve, for the fear of any man, from the rules of civilized warfare, be the consequences what they might.

The Mexicans rode so slowly, that the sun was setting when they arrived at the place where the Texians were encamped. Around it, they formed, in a semicircle, each man holding the coiled rope in his hand, and waiting, in the greatest silence, for the signal of attack; which was no sooner given, than they rushed forward, with the impetuosity of lightning. The enemy was taken by surprise, and, in a few seconds, more than thirty men were caught, like wild animals, some by the neck, others by an arm, or leg, and dragged through the thicket of overgrown prickly pear, with all the rapidity of a Mexican steed. Then arrose the most piteous cries and supplications for mercy! Limbs and faces were mangled by thorns, and the ground was streaked with gore! Several Texians had already lost an eye, some had dislocated an arm, or broken a leg; and others had fainted through fright, or loss of blood, by the time captain Letinez gave the signal to put an end to the bloody race. Of those who were not taken prisoners at the onset, five were killed by the discharge of fire arms, and their chief only, with six privates, succeeded in making his escape, while the remainder surrendered at discretion.

On alighting, to take care of the wounded, the most melancholy, and, at the same time, ludicrous spectacle imaginable offered itself to the view of the victors. Many of the Texians were so ignorant of the manners and peculiarities of the Mexican race, that, although they still felt the running noose round their body, they were not able to conceive by what means they had been captured, and much less could they account for the extraordinary violence with which they had been dragged along. A hale and vigorous Kentuckian, who had not suffered any serious bodily harm, but whose fine new coat was literally torn into shreds, off his back, swore

11

that this was the oddest way of fighting he had ever
heard of, and cursed the *fellows*, for mean cowardly
wretches, for not coming forward openly, and making
use of their fists, if they were scarce of gun-powder.
He would rather be *gouged*, than noosed like a pig!

A negro slave, who had followed his master, all the
way from the river Brazos, thought the assailants were
demons, who had thus triumphed by supernatural art,
and entreated the Kentuckian to read a pocket testament he carried about him, in order to break the spell;
but when he stood up and perceived that the complexion of many of the Mexican soldiers was nearly as black
as his own, he changed his opinion, and got into the notion that they were runaway slaves, who fought for
their liberty. Aware that there exists, in Louisiana,
many a settlement of negroes, who, having fled from their
masters, live independent, in the unexplored recesses of
the swamps, with which that country abounds, he supposed such to be the kind of assailants by whom the party to which he belonged had been so roughly handled.
Entranced by the prospect of liberty, now dawning upon
his imagination, he addressed himself, in raptures, to a
common soldier, and, heartily shaking him by the hand,
he exclaimed, " Thankee, thankee, my good feller! Me
free man, now! Oh, if only me had my Sally, along
with me, and the childer. But me go and show you
how to steal them, my good feller. But white massa
here, alive !" added he, in surprise, happening to cast
his eyes upon his master,—" you no kill him. He not
so bad a massa! Give plenty to eat, and no workee on
the Sabbath. And his Missis. She very good Missis!
Give blanket for winter, and take care of my Sally, when
she sick. Lets us go to meeting, also, once a month,
when the Rev. Zorobabbel Windhowl comes round;
while Massa he not so willing, bekase he says that them
things of the Gospel and t'other world spoil negroes
and open their eyes too much. So, not kill Massa, my
good feller; for Missis she cry too much, if he be killed."

Captain Letinez, who understood English perfectly
well, and spoke it with fluency, could not help smiling,
when he heard the negro's address ; and, drawing near

to him, assured him that he might consider his liberty
as perfectly secure during the remainder of his life,
and even might rely upon the attainment of the enjoying of civil rights, if he would settle in Mexico.

The negro felt his joy somewhat abated, upon perceiving that he who addressed him and acted as chief
of the capturing party was a white man, and could not
help manifesting the fear it inspired. "How be this,
Massa? You, white man, I declare! As white as my
young Missis, God bless her, who was the most beau-
tifulest soul I ever seed. And you commander of these
here niggers?"

"Why, they are not negroes," replied Senor de Letinez. "They are Mexicans as well as myself. I am
their captain, and we have taken you prisoners, and
that is all. But *you*, in particular, shall be immediately
put at liberty, provided you promise not to return to
Texas."

"Return to Texas!" exclaimed the black, "you
may trust me for that—there is no danger of it, Massa.
But you, Mexican, and them, Mexican, also! And yet
you be a white man, and them is niggers, or, at best,
mulattoes. How is that, Massa?"

"Why, you blockhead," replied the captain, a little
nettled, "they are not negroes—they are Indians.
You take too much liberty. Remember that, though I
have been thus idly talking to you, it was out of pure
philanthropy, and there is a certain distance between
us."

The poor negro's apprehensions were by no means
allayed by being informed that his captors were Indians ; for he could not suppose that Indians were susceptible of civilization, and he wished himself once
more in the cotton fields of the river Brazos. The
captain, however, being anxious to continue the pursuit of the savages, who had spread devastation on the
left bank of the Rio Bravo, caused the ferry boat to
be repaired, as well as circumstances admitted, and,
crossing over to the town of Mier, left his prisoners
under the guard of the citizens of the place, with strict
injunctions to take care of the wounded, after which

he recrossed the river with all his force, in search of a large body of Comanches, who, he had been informed, were scouring the plains, on both sides of the San Antonio, and spreading desolation far and wide.

The Comanches, one of the most remarkable Indian tribes of North America, are the best horsemen in the world, being as far superior to the Mexicans, in the art of riding, as these are to the western nations of Europe. It was, therefore, no easy matter for captain Letinez to overtake them, in case they should happen to receive intelligence of the pursuit. This was an expedition which he undertook upon his individual responsibility, and merely to appease the complaints of the inhabitants of Mier and Camargo, whose flocks had been, in part, carried away by those marauders.

He travelled with his party till he came to the river Nueces, a sluggish stream, which derives its name from the great quantity of pecan trees found on its banks. The country extending hence to the Rio Bravo is a level plain, producing fine grass, and immense thickets of prickly pear, which grows to a gigantic size; but there is no wood of any account except on the immediate banks of the streams, where flourish groves of tall saplings, meandering with the water courses, and rarely extending a mile in breadth. About fifty leagues above the mouth of the Nueces, a large creek, called Rio Frio, disembogues into it, from the east, after fertilising a bolder and more romantic country, somewhat similar, in its features, to the central parts of Kentucky. Ledges of fine granite intersect and diversify the plains, stretching across the water courses, in every direction, damming up the streams, in the form of petty lakes, and affording excellent localities for the establishment of mills, at the yet untenanted falls, over which the cristalline waters force their rapid way. This district, being better watered, is perfectly well wooded, and still haunted by the Lipanes and Carankaway Indians, who have the reputation of being cannibals.

In these fastnesses, did captain Letinez imagine that the party he was in pursuit of had probably taken

shelter, and he resolved to penetrate into them, in order
to recover, if possible, the booty they had carried away.

Those he wished to overtake, however, eluded his
vengeance, but he had the satisfaction of encountering
another company of Comanches, who had been on a
pillaging expedition towards the Trinidad, and were,
now, on their way home, loaded with plunder. When
he came up with them, he found them encamped on
the banks of a rivulet, quite unconscious of danger, so
that, he was nearly upon them, before they could put
themselves in a posture of defence. On perceiving the
Mexican troops, however, they quickly mounted their
horses and gave signs of resisting their invaders. But
the first discharge of fire arms so much thinned their
ranks, that they abandoned their booty and fled.

They were not pursued, so eager were captain Letinez's soldiers to seize upon the plunder so fortuitously
obtained. Besides a considerable number of horses and
horned cattle, they found, in the enemy's camp, various
kinds of furniture, which the Indians had stolen from
the American settlers on the Trinidad; and the Mexican
soldiers, very little acquainted with the tools of modern husbandry, or the refinements of northern luxury,
viewed with the utmost surprise, many articles, of which
they could not understand the use.

There was one who imagined he had made a prize of
immense value in a log chain, for, he had never seen so
much iron together in his life; and actually hung it
round his neck, and declared that he would carry it to
Mier, a distance of two hundred and fifty miles, which
he accomplished on foot.*

Another, having opened a band box, and found a lady's bonnet, adorned with a wreath of artificial flowers,
was unable to discover for what it was intended;
whereupon, having consulted some of his fellow soldiers,
one of them was of opinion, that it was a Texian cap of
liberty, and intended to be used by the rebels, as a military standard. It was, of course, considered as a very
honourable spoil, and the fellow who owned it resolved

---

* A fact.

to offer it to the church of Mier, by way of *spolia opima.*
In the mean time, it was placed on the top of a lance,
and many a jest, at the expense of the Texian republic,
was elicited at the sight.

Another, having got hold of a pocket book, found in
it some bank notes, and imagined that they were
pictures of saints, with printed indulgences, mistaking
English for Latin; whereby he was greatly edified,
supposing from this circumstance, that all the Texians
were not Heathens, or Jews, as he had been led to believe; but that there were some Christians amongst
them. The poor fellow was, however, wofully unde-
ceived, when he returned to Mier, for he, then, found
out that *these pictures* were worth five or ten dollars
a piece; but he had unhappily exchanged them, for a
silver medal, with a fellow soldier, who, now, sold them
to an Italian merchant of that place, for their full
value.

What, however, chiefly attracted the attention of the
men, and principally of the captain, was a gig, closely
covered with buffalo robes, which the Indians made
their utmost efforts to carry off, but were obliged to re-
linquish. Towards it, captain Letinez, accompanied
by some officers, rode with all possible speed, and was
the first to tear down the skins by which the interior
of the gig was concealed, when a most melancholy
spectacle presented itself to his view:—It was a young
lady, of about sixteen years of age and extraordinary
beauty, strongly bound to the carriage with cords.

CHAPTER XI.

How reluctant soever we may be to shock our readers' feelings, by the exhibition of a scene of inhumanity, practised upon an innocent and interesting female, still the truth of our history forces us to lay before them the sufferings of one who is, in the sequel, to play a conspicuous part. We beg, therefore, that it be not attributed to a vain desire of producing an effect, because, far from aiming at that species of interest, which results from the description of physical pain ; we are persuaded, on the contrary, that it evinces but literary merit of the lowest order, in the writer who is obliged to have recourse to such means, to move human sensibilities. Indeed we are so averse to that *literary charlatanisme*, that, had it been possible for us to continue the narrative of our hero's adventures, without adverting to this female's misfortunes, and the cruel treatment inflicted upon her, by her Indian captors, we would gladly have availed ourselves of the chance ; but, however, though we should be unable to render ourselves intelligible, were we to omit it, we will soften the picture, as much as the general connexion of events will permit; for we know, by experience, how delicate are the nerves of our gallant Americans.

The young lady whom captain Letinez found in the vehicle was so far exhausted, that, although judging from the report of musketry, there had been a conflict and she had, probably, changed masters, she was unable to manifest her feelings, except by some faint moans. Her deliverers found her half reclining on the hind seat of the carriage. The dreadful state of debility to which she was reduced preventing her from retaining an upright position, she appeared perfectly motionless, her head drooping on her left shoulder—her arms forcibly outstretched, and her hands strongly tied to the sides of the gig. Her wrists were swollen and bleeding from the chafing of the ropes :—her habiliments, that had originally been costly and elegant, were soiled, her complexion, pallid, and she was, from weakness, entirely incapable of motion; yet so regular and beautiful were her features that it was impossible to behold her without admiration.

When the ropes with which she had been bound were cut away, and she was lifted out of the carriage, the captain was shocked with horror at the sight, and there was none, even amongst the rough and uncultivated Mexican dragoons, there present, who did not vent his indignation against the barbarians, who had treated fragile beauty with so much cruelty.

The captain immediately directed some of his soldiers to erect a kind of tent with their blankets, in order to shelter her from the burning rays of the sun, and, as soon as it was ready, placed her under it, on a pallet, made of the buffalo robes which had served for her previous concealment. This posture, more favourable to rest, and the administration of some cordials, soon restored her to the use of speech, and the first words she uttered were expressive of gratitude to those who had effected her deliverance.

She expressed herself in English, and, as the captain was the only one present who understood that language, this, necessarily, obliged him to remain in close attendance upon the fair captive. She had no idea that she owed her rescue to an advanced party of the Mexican army; but imagined that she had been recaptured by a company of Texians, sent in pursuit of the Indians, and, although she beheld around her many dusky faces, she supposed them to be friendly Tankaways, who had assisted in her deliverance. Addressing herself, therefore, to the captain, she inquired, with much solicitude, about her father; to which, our hero replied, in good English, but with an accent that betrayed his foreign extraction: "I am sorry that I am unable to give you any information respecting your father: I have not the honour of his acquaintance, nor, indeed, did we perceive any white man among the Comanches."

"It is not probable that he is among them," interrupted the captive. "They would hardly have brought him so far. I have reason to believe he escaped, when our house, on the Trinidad, was burned; and, as I supposec you came from the Brazos, I hoped that you might inform me of his subsequent fate; but you are a foreigner! Tell me to whom am I indebted for my safety, and to what part of the country have I been conveyed. Seven days have elapsed since I have been allowed to behold the light of heaven."

"Madam," replied the captain, "rest assured that you are in perfect safety, protected by Christians, well acquainted with the honourable treatment due to your sex and rank; and who will do all in their power to alleviate your sufferings. It will, perhaps, be repugnant to your delicacy to travel with a company of soldiers; but, as their captain, I pledge my honour that you shall be treated as respectfully as if we were united by the ties of fraternity—I wish only that your recent sufferings may not incapacitate you for bearing the fatigues of the march, for we cannot remain here longer than to-morrow morning. My force is small:—we might be surprised.—Feeble as you are, you cannot possibly ride in the gig. If you have no objection, a covered hand-litter shall be constructed by my soldiers, and by that means you can be carried more comfortably."

"Alas, sir," answered the young lady, with tears, "my dependence is entirely upon you, and I confide in your honor. Great God, am I forlorn and abandoned, in the hands of utter strangers, and these strangers, soldiers! Oh, thou, Father of Heaven, be my protector! —Young gentleman," added she, suddenly addressing the captain, with a fervour which manifested how great was her apprehension, "the profession you have embraced hardens the heart, and makes light of profligacy; yet, there is that in your countenance which gives better hopes:—do not deceive them. I beseech you, by all that is sacred, to protect me and restore me to my father,—Oh my poor father—what uneasiness must he suffer on my account!"

"Madam," replied the captain, "your suspicions are unjust, yet I forgive them:—they are but too natural in your situation. I will take immediate measures to inform your father of your rescue and safety; nevertheless, the small party under my command cannot

venture into the heart of Texas. Were the Trinidad
nearer, I would send a flag of truce; but present circumstances render it impracticable. Duty compels me
to return to Mier. I see no alternative for you. You
shall be escorted to Matamoros in all honour and safety;
and there, embark for New Orleans. Nothing shall be
done without your concurrence; but it would be madness, in you, to prefer perishing in this desert. Can you
doubt the sincerity of a Mexican officer, who protests in
the face of heaven that he would rather forfeit his existence, than permit the least insult to misfortune?"

The mention of " Matamoros," and a " Mexican officer" augmented the fair captive's distress and redoubled
her tears. The captain, much moved, endeavoured to
console her by repeated assurances; but, seeing his
efforts were unavailable, he thought it would perhaps
be better to leave her to the aid of reflection, during
some hours. In the interval, he went to hasten the necessary preparations for marching back to Mier.

After a tolerable long absence, he returned to the
young lady's tent, and found her more resigned. She
assented to the measures proposed, on condition that
the captain himself would constantly watch over her
safety. The next morning, therefore, the party began
their march. It was opened by twenty men on horseback, with their lances couched, in case of an attack.
To these, succeeded the litter, borne by four men, and,
immediately behind it, captain Letinez, followed by
the rest of his soldiers, in close column, to guard against
surprise.

Their fears proved groundless: their march was,
nevertheless, interrupted by a flag of truce, despatched
by the chief of the defeated Indian party, charged with
a petition of a most singular nature. It was no less
than a request that the Mexicans should exchange the
white lady whom they had taken, for a number of
horses and mules, of which the Indians had rendered
themselves masters in their various marauding expeditions, through the states of Chihuahua and Durango.
The warrior who commanded the party of Comanches,
one of the principal men of the nation, had become so

great an admirer of his captive's charms, that he had
resolved to take her for his wife; and, lest his tribe
should grumble at his choice, as well as in order to interest them in the success of his scheme, had given
out that it had been revealed to him in a dream, that,
from this white female's marriage with him, should
spring up a famous warrior, who would avenge upon
the Mexicans, all the injuries the Indian race had received, and reconquer the country through which their
forefathers roamed, as far as the *Huasteca*.[*]

As this worthy united the character of a prophet to
that of warlike chief, his desires were implicitly submitted to by the whole tribe, who thought the future
glory of their race intimately connected with their ful-
filment, and they were now ready to sacrifice all their
booty, in order to repossess themselves of *her* who was
to be the mother of this great chieftain. That an Indian be susceptible of such a sentiment as love may be
questioned by some of our readers; but, we will answer, that beauty, like omnipotence, works in a thousand wonderful ways; and, if it has been supposed
capable of softening the wild beasts of the forest, it in-
volves, we are sure, no absurdity to suppose it able to
soften the heart of an Indian.

Be our reader's opinion what it may, the fact is that
Shaw-co-naw-taw, the warlike chief to whom we allude, had, at the sight of this young lady, suddenly
experienced a sentiment hitherto unknown to him,
which prompted him to save her from the flames, when
her father's plantation, on the river Trinidad, was destroyed; and induced him carefully to convey her
away in the family gig. He used her, to be sure, in a
manner that, to a civilized man, must appear barbarous
and cruel; but his cruelty was the effect of precaution,
to prevent her escape; and her captor, so far from intending to treat her with harshness, had, on the con-

---

[*] The *Huastecapan* of Montezuma's empire, the paradise of the
Northern Indians and the most fertile district in Mexico, and, probably, in the world.

trary, a notion of having been rather too indulgent towards one, who was, after all, nothing but a *squaw!*

An Indian warrior's idea of love, whenever he happens to experience it, is very different from the sentiment a white man entertains of that passion. The
former looks upon it as a weakness, which unmans
him, and is, therefore, very careful to conceal his flame.
The extravagance of Shaw-co-naw-taw's attachment
to this white damsel would certainly have ruined his
character in the minds of the warriors who accompanied him, had he not subtly brought his spiritual influence to favour his plan, and rendered it, thereby, an
affair of state, in which the whole tribe were interested.
This was the reason why his comrades agreed to make
the sacrifice of all their plunder, for the redemption of
his intended bride.

It may be supposed that the proposal of which the
flag of truce was the bearer was refused by captain Letinez, who was too polite to afflict the young lady by
informing her of the purport of the message. After
this strange incident, nothing of importance occurred
to disturb the security of their march, and they entered
Mier on the ninth day after leaving Rio Frio.

General Urrea had pursued his way towards Matamoros, and left orders to captain Letinez to follow with
all possible despatch; but the noble hearted young
man found himself greatly embarrassed by his fair
prize, for whom he began to experience sentiments of
tenderness, which he had never hitherto entertained
for the fair sex. To leave her in Mier, amongst utter
strangers, without a protector, appeared unnatural—to
induce her to travel in his company, was exposing her
reputation, by giving her the appearance of a " *Light
o' love.*" His perplexity was so great that he resolved
to consult the parish priest of the place, an elderly
man, who enjoyed a reputation for prudence and benevolence.

The clergyman, after hearing an exposition of the
case, was clearly of opinion that the young lady, having
a vehicle of her own, and captain Letinez being willing to defray all necessary expenses, *she* might, with-

out any breach of propriety, continue her journey towards Matamoros, provided she were accompanied by some respectable elderly female, who would appear in the character of her protectress. It very luckily happened that the same Italian merchant, of whom we have already made mention, was on the point of setting out for the same place, with his wife, an aged matron, for whose respectability the priest was willing to vouch, and these people would probably be delighted with the idea of travelling in a carriage. They might, by the way, enjoy the benefit of a military escort, by keeping within sight of the lancers, whom captain Letinez commanded, and *he* would be able to watch over their safety, without appearing to take, in their welfare, a higher interest than might be ascribed to common courtesy.

In this manner, the clergyman thought Miss Linton, (such was the young lady's name,) might reach the sea coast without awakening suspicion, or the captain's benevolence being exposed to misconstruction. The plan which the old man devised being plausible, and of easy execution, it was, of course, followed; and the Italian merchant's wife having, on the parish priest's recommendation, undertaken to act as chaperon for the *senorita Americana;* they all set out, under the escort of the lancers and safely arrived at Matamoros, after a journey of eleven days.

It was peculiarly lucky for the Italian, thus to travel under the safeguard of soldiers; for a portion of the road, west of Matamoros, may be accounted nearly the most perilous upon the face of the earth. The poor merchant crossed himself, at the rate of twenty times an hour, and shuddered, as he went along; the way being bordered with *crosses,* set up in memory of some murdered traveller or other; and, as our Italian carried with him a large sum of money, he doubted not that, had it not been for captain Letinez's protection, he would have shared the same fate, as had been the lot of so many unfortunate wayfarers.

12

CHAPTER XII.

At Matamoros, our young lady continued the guest of the Italian merchant, who, intending to remain two or three weeks in the place, immediately upon his arrival, rented a house and furnished it after a temporary fashion. Though this sea port be now a city of sixteen thousand souls, inhabited by a considerable number of foreigners, yet it is one of the blessed results of the Mexican system of civilization, that it does not possess a single hotel, inn, or boarding house, where a bed can be got for one single night. Every new comer, should he have no acquaintance willing to give him hospitality, must rent a room, as soon as he arrives, or go to lodge, under the canopy of heaven, in a public square, situate at the northwest extremity of the city, and appropriated to that hospitable destination, by the munificence of the *Ayuntamiento*. As for beds and furniture, they are still more difficult to obtain than lodgings, so that imprudent or ignorant foreigners, who neglect bringing them along, are indeed in no enviable situation.

In such a state of things, it would have been truly unfortunate for our young lady, to be abandoned to her own exertions to procure the absolute necessaries of life. She clung, therefore, to the Italian merchant's wife, with all the affection of one who feels grateful for past benefits, and for whom the price of present protection is enhanced by the prospect of future deprivation. The Mier lady—under whose matronly authority she enjoyed, in a strange place, a degree of security which could not, otherwise, have been obtained—was far from being a woman of education, refinement or elegance of manners; but she was motherly, good hearted and of unimpeachable moral character.

She had already contracted a great affection for the young *Americana*, as she called her, and, being childless and without hope of future offspring, entertained the notion of adopting her, and waited but for a favourable opportunity in order to propose it to her husband. For some days succeeding their arrival, her multifarious occupations rendered her too busy to think about the matter. She had to instruct a female cook in the particular manner in which she wished Indian corn to be ground for her *tortillas,**—a filtering machine was indispensably requisite to clarify the river water before she could use it,—a cooking hearth must be constructed out of doors; for, a *French* fire-place, as she called it, was her aversion, and she was affected in a peculiar manner, at the sight of houses adorned with chimneys; a fashion that had already been introduced into Matamoros, from the north, and which she, on that account, looked upon as akin to heresy.

But when, at last, all those bustling cares were over, her imagination recurred to her favorite plan, and to revolve the means of insuring success. Her ward, if we may designate her by that title, was already restored to perfect health. The joy of being freed from the Indians, and the hope of being soon restored to her father, had wrought wonders, and her face became the very picture of health and animation. Captain Letinez visited her twice or thrice every day, under pretence of serving as an interpreter between her and the old matron, but he was conscious to himself that another sentiment was his prime mover. Though he had never seen so handsome a woman, yet it was not mere physical beauty which attracted him; it was, rather, her graceful and dignified demeanor, equally free from prudery and coquetish airs, her sprightly conversation and well informed mind, and her superior wit, tempered with prudence, which commanded his admiration.

The merchant's wife, proud of having a man of Letinez's rank, as a visiter, encouraged him, and bethought herself of making use of his influence, to further the accomplishment of her schemes. She perceived he was in love, and supposed that, by fanning his flame, of the honourable nature of which she entertained no doubt, she would be most likely to succeed in her views. It became, therefore, her object, to engage the captain in many little parties of pleasure, where she

---

* A species of cakes, the common food of Mexicans.

expected her *proteges* to shine conspicuously. One
night, he was invited to escort them to the *Tertulia* of
Dona Catalina de M * * *, one of the first ladies in
the city, where the young Americana had been requested to display her musical talents on the piano. The
next day, he was in requisition to give them an airing in
the carriage, after the *Siesta*, for the senorita was lan-
guid, in consequence of confinement. He accompanied
them to church, or in their shopping excursions, and
was often invited to partake of chocolate with them; to
all which calls and invitations, the young man was, as
may be supposed, exceedingly punctual. In a word, the
old merchant's wife, though untutored, and actuated
only by female instinct, was as perfect in her manœuvres, as if she had been brought up amongst the first
circles of English nobility.

The young captain's person and mental and bodily
accomplishments were as conspicuous in his own sex,
as the fair stranger's, in hers; and it was not improbable that the impression made upon his heart might be
reciprocated. True love, however, is never presumptuous; it rather blushes and trembles in the presence of
the beloved object, and captain Letinez, who was endowed with all the delicacy which a refined education
can impart, was impressed with a profound respect for
her he loved. Still, his flame was betrayed by a thousand
nameless circumstances, which escape even the most
discreet, and the young lady, also, began to be sensible of his merit, as her involuntary blushes would sometimes betray.

When the old matron thought that things were sufficiently matured to render a discovery of her views
expedient, she, in a confidential conversation, broke the
matter to the captain. "Now, senor de Letinez," said
she, "what do you think of our *Americanita?* Is it
not a pity to suffer one so fair and interesting, to return to Texas, probably to be driven back into the
United States, with her kindred, when our triumphant
troops shall chase away the rebels?—How much it
hurts my feelings that so rare a beauty should be a vessel of heresy.—Does it not behove us, who enjoy a

knowledge of the Christian religion, to teach the true
doctrine to those poor stray children?—Oh, how much
I wish that I could get her baptized and made a Christian!—To you, captain, I will communicate an idea,
which, I believe, God our Lord, and the Virgin of Guadelupe have inspired me with:—it is, that I and my
husband should adopt her. We have no children, and
are amply provided with worldly goods:—what better
use can we make of our fortune than in gaining a soul
to the true church?—I know, my husband is fond of his
relations, who have never paid any attention to him,
when young, and would not give the parings of their
nails to relieve him, if he were in distress, and I am
afraid, on account of that foolish family attachment, he
will oppose my ideas. Therefore, I want you to use
your influence over his mind, and hint it to him. We
are both old, captain,—that is to say, my husband, at
least, and he may slip off when least expected. Now,
what will become of me, in my widowhood, without
any affectionate person about me, for, I am past all
thoughts of marrying again, and my relations hate me
for having married a foreigner. But here is this *pobre
Americanita* who, I am sure, loves me, and has so wound
herself round my heart, that I cannot think of parting
with her."

Gladly would the captain have lent his aid to the
furtherance of any plan tending to obtain the young
lady's consent to remaining in Mexico; but he had
tact enough to understand that neither the town of
Mier, nor the city of Matamoros afforded a state of
society to which a female of her breeding could con-
form; much less did he suppose that she would abandon the thought of returning to her father, in order to
throw herself into the old woman's arms. Her con-
tinuance in Matamoros, he well knew, was occasioned
by the absence of the vessels accustomed to trade to
New Orleans, and that, notwithstanding all her gratitude towards her benefactress, she was as anxious as
ever to leave the country.

Had the captain been unprincipled, he might have
thought the present circumstance would afford him a

fair chance of playing off his stratagems, in favour of
his passion; but he was too generous and upright to
have recourse to mean cunning. He, therefore, answered the merchant's wife, that he thought her plan
impracticable, and that, notwithstanding her husband
might be brought to consent to the measure, he was
sure the young lady would not accept her offers. "At
all events," added he, "it is but prudent to ascertain
her sentiments, before you hazard a proposal to your
husband."

This was a difficulty which had not occurred to the
old woman's mind, for she was as shallow as good natured. She agreed, however, to the expediency of the
captain's suggestions, and it was mutually arranged
that she should have an explanation with her *Americanita*—Senor de Letinez acting as interpreter.

The result was such as our hero had anticipated.
The young lady answered, she could not possibly think
of remaining among strangers, and that, however gratitude might attach her to those who had so generously
extended their protection to her; still she could not act
so unnatural a part as to renounce her own parents.
From thence, she took occasion to beseech the captain
to do all in his power to accelerate her departure, for
she knew what grief her absence and the uncertainty
of her fate must cause to her father.

Our hero promised to comply with her wishes, and,
thinking this a favourable opportunity for declaring his
sentiments, assured her that he could never be happy,
if deprived of the hope of being, at some future period,
blessed with her hand. "I know, madam," said he,
"that, in your present situation, it may be considered
worse than uncourteous in me, to press my suit, and
that my declaration may expose me to the suspicion of
indelicacy; but the idea of your leaving this country,
without being informed of the profound impression
which your charms, your accomplishments, and your
noble mind, have made on me, would be beyond endurance. Forgive my boldness—I am prompted by an
irresistible sentiment. A new existence dawned upon
me, from the first moment I beheld you;—I am so

longer master of my heart: it is bound to you in an
irrevocable manner, and from your lips I await the sentence of my eternal happiness or misery."

The young lady, thus addressed, far from manifesting a surprise which she did not experience, replied
with dignity and composure: "For having saved me
from the greatest misfortunes, I shall always feel the
most lively and fervent gratitude towards you, and
that is, for the present, all I can impart. You are
yourself aware that my dependence upon you does not
permit me to receive a declaration of the nature of the
one you have avowed. Act generously to the last, and
abstain from a renewal of your suit, while I am still
under your protection. I demand it of you; and your
acquiescence will strengthen your claims to my gratitude. In so short an acquaintance as ours, the character can scarcely be developed, so as to enable one
party to form a correct estimate of the congeniality
and dispositions of the other. Moreover, there is such
a difference between us, in point of religion, of political feeling, and prejudices of education, as would, perhaps, render a union a source of misery. I am a Protestant, and my father belongs to Texas,—Texas has
declared herself, and now the die is cast:—with her,
he will stand or fall. Your duty to your own country
obliges you to fight against his cause! See under what
auspices our promises would be exchanged, were I so
weak as to listen to your protestations!"

"Deprive me not of hope, madam," replied the captain. "Let me still hope, I beseech you. The difference of country is nothing. Virtue belongs to all countries. As for your religion, I have already told you
that my father was a Protestant. I shall never love
him the less for his belief, though I will faithfully follow my own. As for the present war with Texas—one
short campaign, madam! and it will return under the
obedience of Mexico. We will then both belong to the
same country."

"Return under the obedience of Mexico!" replied
she, with a vivacity that surprised her lover; "never,
sir, never! You knew not the mettle of those you are

going to attack. But cease your importunity. Under present circumstances, I cannot listen to it with the dignity becoming an American maiden. Your heart is endowed with sufficient nobleness to understand *this.* Obey its nobler feelings and be deaf to the selfishness of passion. I will hear no more of it, and, by *my de-pendence upon you,* I conjure you to be silent."

" Yes! I understand you—and am worthy of under-standing you—thou noble minded woman!" answer-ed he, imprinting a kiss upon her hand, (which she withdrew with the rapidity of lightning, but not in an-ger;) " my heart is worthy of you, and you shall be obeyed."

Their dialogue, the meaning of which, though it was held within the old woman's hearing, had, from her ig-norance of the English language, remained a perfect blank to her, was, here, interrupted by her exclaiming *" Ave Maria, purissima!* the little dove will be a Countess yet. But, lo! how she takes the least trifle to heart! One would have thought, from the rapidity with which she withdrew her hand, that a black snake was crawling over it. But what does she say? What does she answer to your suit, captain? It seems you have been more earnest in pleading for yourself, than for me!"

"Indeed, Madam," replied Senor de Letinez, "I have not been more successful in urging my own peti-tion, than yours. The young lady is determined to go, and we must engage her passage in the first vessel sail-ing from the *Brazo de Santiago.*"

At this information, the Mier lady set up a pitiful lamentation. " *Y me dejas, querida alma mia!*" ex-claimed she, adding many other honied expressions, which the captain did not stay to interpret. He went out, to inquire from the principal merchants of the place whether there was any vessel shortly expected to leave the port, for New Orleans; but he was stopped by an officer of artillery, who, knowing his intimacy with the Mier merchant, wished to complain of an af-front, the latter had offered to the corps to which he be-longed. The long and short of it was, that the merchant had, during his morning ramble, visited the park of artillery, and, upon discovering that the bombs and obuses, and even the canister shot, were of copper,* had enjoyed a hearty laugh, at the expense of the officers, and, thereby, wounded the feelings of the troop. "Would you believe it, Letinez," said this worthy, " he has, in bitter irony, told us that no civilized nation would commit such a blunder, as we could have iron balls manufactured in any quantity at the works, near Durango, or at the Amilpas mines, not far from Mexico, for the tenth part of the price of the copper ones; or, even, that we could exchange these, here, at the sea port, for ten times their number of iron ones, which would answer us well, to kill the Texians. *Voto a Dios!* I could not help being angry, particularly when he added, by way of taunt, ' Your enemies will be, certainly, much obliged to you, for such an unexampled generosity! Blessed are the towns which you will bombard! Oh, that one of your battles might be fought on a plantation of mine! It would make a rich man of me.' I have a great mind to call him out, for I understand he has been a military man; but there is, I think, an excommunication, fulminated by the council of Trent against duelling, and *that* staggers me. I would not like to die excommunicated."

"Never mind the excommunication and the duel, my dear fellow," replied captain Letinez. "The man is right enough. It is an unpardonable oversight, in our government; but our republic is young yet, and she will learn wisdom from misfortune. You would be very foolish to fight for such a thing. But come along with me, and help me to make preparations for a trip to the *Brazo*."

"How?—Are you going to sea?—But I see how it is: you have received some secret commission?"

"Not I, indeed," returned Letinez; " I am only to accompany thither a young lady, who is going to New Orleans."

* Founded on fact.

"What! Not that jewel, you rescued from the hands of the Comanches, I hope?"

"Even the same," sadly resumed captain Letinez.

"Is it possible you let her escape, young and beautiful as she is?" exclaimed the other. "But I understand how it is; she is not willing to be baptized, and become a Christian: That is an insuperable barrier, indeed. What a pity! It must be confessed that those women of the northern people are handsomer than ours, and somewhat better bred. What a complexion! What regularity of features! But then, they are no better than animals, you know, being unbaptized. A Christian could not possibly think of such, as long as they remain obdurate."

"Abominable blockhead!" thought Letinez, within himself. By this time, however, he had arrived at the counting-room of one of the principal importing merchants of the town, who informed him, that a fine schooner, with decent accommodations for female passengers, had just arrived at the mouth of the river, and that, in ten days, at the latest, she would be ready to sail for New Orleans.

He ran back to impart the welcome intelligence to the young lady, who immediately began to make her preparations; and when the time of her departure had come, was escorted by captain Letinez, the Mier merchant and his wife, to the place of embarkation. Many were the tears of the latter, when the separation took place, but though captain Letinez tried to stifle his grief, he felt it still more acutely.

We will now take leave of the Mexican party, in order to follow the young lady in her navigation, the doleful narrative of which will become the subject of the following chapter.

CHAPTER XIII.

Though the Rio Bravo is the largest river of the Mexican republic, yet the bar, at its mouth, prevents vessels of a certain size from entering it, and even those which do not draw so much water as to be unable to succeed in it, have, sometimes, to wait two or three weeks, for high tides, and to ride at anchor, in sight of the port, without being able to effect their entrance. The same may be said of the various bays by which the coast of Texas is indented. When southerly winds prevail with violence, they cause a great flow of the sea into the lagunes, which raises the water on the bars, at their mouths; thus enabling ships of larger burthen to cross them, while, at other seasons, they are sure to perish, should they attempt it. In a word, there is no coast in the whole world, where the depth of water is so capriciously variable, and where the nautical art can place so little reliance on preceding soundings and experience.

This, which has been the cause of numerous shipwrecks, proved detrimental to the success of the voyage of the schooner upon which our fair traveller was embarked. The vessel had not yet lost sight of land, when there arose a furious south-east wind, which drove her with irresistible fury towards the long and narrow sandy island which extends all the way from the Brazo de Santiago, near the mouth of the Rio Bravo, to the mouth of St. Bernard's bay. That long strip of sand is intersected by three principal passes, whereof the middle one, called *Corpus Christi*, is almost opposite to the mouth of the river Nueces.

The captain of the schooner, despairing of his ability to ride the gale, thought to put his vessel in security by entering the above mentioned pass; but it unfortunately happened, that, having no pilot on board, and being himself but imperfectly acquainted with the entrance; he managed his ship so unskilfully, that she stuck fast on the bar, and, the storm increasing, it was evident she would go to pieces. In that emergency, no

other resource remained but to take to the long boat,
and if the crew and passengers could but cross the bar
in safety, they would, afterwards, easily reach the
coast of the main land.

After infinite fatigues, the captain succeeded in landing all his people, consisting of nine persons, amongst
whom were three females, at a point about thirty-five
miles distant from the village of St. Patricio, a little
colony of Irish people, on the left bank of the river
Nueces. This village had been founded five or six
years previous, and promised to become an interesting
settlement, because its original inhabitants were tolerably orderly. They had with them a priest of their own
nation, and magistrates selected from among themselves, and, though they lived under the allegiance of
the Mexican government, being protected by a garrison
of soldiers, at Lepantitlan, only two miles distant,
they hardly felt the hand of their civil superiors and
rather bore the appearance of an independent commu-
nity. "the world forgetting, and by the world forgot."

Our poor shipwrecked people had no other resource,
after the loss of their vessel, than to take shelter in this
village, where they arrived, in their boat, after a labo-
rious journey up the river Nueces. The whole village
came out to look at them, when they landed; and, as
the Irish are, above all things, distinguished by their
hospitality, every one of the new comers was quickly
invited into a house, and rendered as comfortable as a
warm heart and a warm potatoe could make him.

The Alcalde, a man of some judgment, exercised his
prudence in billeting the new comers according to the
rules of propriety, and he assigned our young lady, to a
widow woman of great respectability in point of moral
conduct, and of such a strength of character, that she
was considered by the whole village as a she dragon of
virtue. Her physical qualifications corresponded perfectly well with the energy of her mind; for she was
a figure about five feet ten inches, with a rotundity of
corpulency quite proportionate to such a height. Her
bodily strength, though she was now forty years old,
was so great, that she could break a wild horse, having

actually made the experiment; and she was in the
daily habit of handling the axe, in chopping down trees,
for fire wood or for making her fences. She had refused to marry a second time, albeit a square league of
excellent land, with an indisputable title, and a *labor**
of one hundred and forty acres, which she owned in
fee simple, near the town, had procured her proposals
from many a needy adventurer.

This remarkable female, who might be compared to
the strong woman of the old testament, and in whom
were combined the characters of Judith and Deborah,
did not want a certain coarse dignity, with which she
tempered her coarse hospitality, and, as she took the
hand of the young lady, consigned to her care by the
prudence of the Alcalde of the village, in order to
pilot her home, as she quaintly expressed it, said to
her, with a strong Irish accent and a look of great benevolence, "Come now, my swate young lady. Sure,
Mr. Smasher, the Alcald, (that is his honor, the Mayor
of the town, hinney, as we would call the loike of him
in ould Ireland, for, may be, you don't know what an
Alcald is, in this country.) Well, my swate jewel,
Mr. Smasher could not have done better than to place
you with me. You shall be well taken care of, for there
is plenty to ate in my house, which is not the case
every where in this town; for, taters have failed, this
year, and this is not a good country for taters, no how,
save for their swate taters, which the Mexican paple
call *camotes:* And you shall have plenty of milk, chaze
and butter, hinney. And don't be afeard of the Texians, they will not hurt the loike of you. They were
here in great force, the other day, but did not do any
damage, hinney, bekase there was nothing, to pillage
in our church. They could not do, here, as they did
in Goliad, where they took the pictures of the saints
out of the church, and picked out their eyes for sport—
cutting the blessed vestments into shreds—and their

* Besides a square league of land to every settler, the Mexican
government generally granted a lot, near the town, to make a huerta
and for other purposes.

13

officer men took all the goold lace, to make epalets out of. Och! murdher, to hear and see the loike of it! And then they took the grand crucifix from off the altar—that is the image of our Saviour, hinney; that was all painted with goold—and picked out its eyes— then put an old hat on its head, and fired at it, for their diversion. The unhappy wretches that they are, who cry out liberty of conscience! liberty of conscience— and then, to fire at our Saviour, hinney! The captain who was here swore that they would clare the country of priestcraft, and swaipe all superstition away from the land; oh, hinney, that swaiping was a lucky job for him, for he got all the siller chalices and pix of Labahia, and the candlestics that were on the altar; besides the precious stones that were around the re- monstrance, hinney! As good as twenty-seven pounds of siller, together with pearls, toparzes and roobies! Och, some judgment will fall on them, and God forgive me for saying so. The Mexican Gineral will soon be here, with his lancers, and will give them another kind of swaiping, I trow; but you need not fare any thing. Though I am a poor lone woman, I'll defend you, hin- ney."

By the time she put an end to this characteristic harangue, they had reached her house, which was only a log cabin, divided in two by a partition of reeds; but remarkable for its cleanliness, and two small win- dows, with glazed sashes, the greatest piece of luxury about the whole village.

"Now, hinney," said the old woman, when they had entered it, "you must be far spent with hunger. Rest yourself, after changing your clothes, while I cook some *villles* for you to ate. There are some clane clothes that used to belong to my daghter, that was—but now she is dead, and is with God, I hope. They will be somewhat too large for you, for she was a stout crature of her years; but, manewhile, I will wash and iron your own, hinney. They shall be ready to-morrow. So, now, pass into that inner room, and do as I tell you, while I fry some eggs for you, bekase to-day is Friday. Och! there goes a swate crature."

The sweet creature stood in need of rest, indeed; and, of course, gladly followed her kind hostess' directions, while the latter went to borrow some tea and sugar, for she was out of those commodities. She found none, except at the parsonage, and, even there, she could not get it, without entering into a long conversation with the housekeeper, a very singular woman, half nun and half servant, who could not help manifesting her surprise at her neighbour's request.

"How, now, Mrs. Jordan," said she, "something very strange must have taken place in your house, that you should want tea and sugar! Why, woman, I have not known you to buy these articles for the last six months. You know that when I got the milk cow from you, father Supplegrowl wanted to pay you in coffee and sugar, but you declared you would have the silver."

"Och! bless your swate face, Miss Parimoy, the loike of it is not for me," answered Mrs. Jordan. "You knows how I loike milk, best, or even buttermilk; but the Alcald has given me one of the poor shipwrecked cratures that got stranded at Loive-oak point, and she seems such a dainty lady, that I can do no less, sure, than to get her some tay. I will pay you in butter. You knows that father Supplegrowl likes my butter of all things, Miss Parimoy."

"Ah, ah," resumed the priest's housekeeper, "is it for the like of them you put yourself to such an expense? I thought you were more careful of your own. However, I will let you have half a pound, but you must furnish me with all the butter I may want in passion week, which is shortly coming on."

"Och, never fare, Miss Parimoy; you shall be satisfied," replied Mrs. Jordan; "and father Supplegrowl, also. I will bring you such butter! As yellow as the purest goold, and so swate, that you will hardly feel it melting in your mouth. Let me alone for churning! Many is the woman that is come from ould Donegal, Miss Parimoy; but this I dare say, that none can bate Peggy Jordan in making butter, or spinning flax; though it is but little of the latter I got, here, to spin, unless I

148   MEXICO VERSUS TEXAS.

should go out into the prary, and pull up the wild, yellow-bloomed flax, which Mr. Dogberty says is the same
as grows in New Zealand,* and makes better thread
thau that of ould Ireland. Sorrow upon him for saying
so."

"New Zealand! May be it is New Holland, he
means, he, he, he!" interrupted Miss Parimoy, laughing at her own joke, which she meant as a cutting sar-
casm against Mr. Dogberty, who was no favourite of
hers, nor of father Supplegrowl, by whom he had been
excommunicated five or six times, and anathematised
from the altar, with " *bell, book, and candlelight.*"
"But how long, Mrs. Jordan, are you going to keep
this young woman, and who is she?"

" Alas!" replied the old lady, "I don't know, I am
sure, Miss Parimoy. And, plase God, she is welcome
to stay, until she can hare from her own paple, who
live in Texas, somewhere about the Trinidad."

" Ah, it will be some time, before she hears from
them," resumed the house-keeper. " The Mexican general will be here, by and by, and will slash the Texians,
I warrant you. Your young lady will have very little
chance to return to her parents.—She may be a burden
on your hands for a long time to come."

"Well, well," replied honest Mrs. Jordan, "she may
be a burden as long as it shall plase God:—I will not
drive her away, as long as I have a mouthful to divide
with her. Sure, Miss Parimoy, you have redde a
grate dale, and are a larned woman, seeing that you
have all them books of father Supplegrowl under your
hand, save the Latin ones, out of which he says mass;
but you never saw, nor redde that any one became
poorer, by giving some help to a forlorn shipwrecked
crature. But, Lord! it is getting late, and I am here,
chattering like a magpie, and the swate young crature,

* We beg leave to state that Mr. Dogberty was entirely mistaken
in his assertion. The flax to which honest Mrs. Jordan alludes, is a
variety of the *linum sativum*; whereas, that of New Zealand, is the
phormium tenax. The species frequently met with in the prairies
of Texas hardly ever rises above eight or nine inches.

at home, is so hungry. So, Miss Parimoy, give me the
tay and sugar, if you plase: I long to return home."

Having received the provisions she stood in need of,
for the comfort of her guest, Mrs. Jordan returned
home and soon made her cabin reek with the steam of
a savoury dish of fried eggs and onions, and, having laid
the table with a cleanliness which one could hardly
have expected, under so humble a roof, awoke the
young lady, to invite her to partake of her good cheer.
"Come, now, to ate a mouthful," said she, " there are
new laid eggs and fresh butter, hinney, of my own
churning. The eggs would have been better, had I put
in them some rashers of bacon, to make them more richer. And if I had, may be, you would have aten the
mate, being as you come from the Trinidad, you will
not keep Fridays in lent. But father Supplegrowl
would have found it out, and redde my name from the
altar. And, besides, hinney, I had no bacon; being, as
I sold the five hams that remained, to ould Hardgrasp,
for a calico gown."

Her fair guest assured her that she was perfectly
well satisfied with her cheer, and did not crave any
thing better. Her meal was, however, light, for her
heart was too full to permit her to enjoy the comforts of
the table. When it was over, she inquired from her
hostess, whether there was any means to get herself
conveyed as far as the Trinidad, or, at least, as far as
Matagorda, where her father had some acquaintances,
who would furnish her with facilities for continuing her
journey by land, or taking a passage to New Orleans,
where she had relations.

To her inquiries, the old woman answered that she
was not herself acquainted with the state of the roads,
in the present circumstances; but did not think any
one in the village, could be prevailed upon to undertake
it. She added, however, that she would inquire from
the Alcalde, who, being better informed, would be able
to give the most prudent advice.

At her return, she brought the unwelcome news that
there was no possibility of travelling in an eastern direction, as all the roads from Goliad, great ways up to

the north, were occupied by the Texian forces, and no
body would run the risk of being fired upon by their
picquets. She added that the corps of general Urrea
was momentarily expected, and that the Alcalde was of
opinion some action of consequence would take place
between San Patricio and Goliad.

This was sad news for our young lady. To find
herself, thus, in the midst of war, far from her kindred
and natural protectors, with no other dependence than
what could be placed in a lonely woman, entirely unknown to her, made her shudder, and she could not refrain from melting into tears. This excited the sympathy of her hostess, who endeavoured to console her,
saying, with her characteristic kindness, " Well now,
hinney, you need not take on so. Them Mexican
soldiers will not hurt you. They will protect the loike
of us, here. The Alcald and Mr. Dogberty have been
writing to the gineral, underhandedly ; and them dragoons and lancers are not to do any damage in San
Patricio. Then, there is father Supplegrowl, our clargy,
who will spake a kind word for the town, hinney ; and
for his own paple, that belongs to the true church.
Them Mexicans have a great reverence for the clargy,
you know. So, so, don't take it so much to heart."

In that doleful occupation of grief manifested by
tears, on one side, and well meant, but awkward consolation, on the other, they spent the five following days,
and the sixth morning opened a new scene, which we
will endeavour to portray in the next chapter.

CHAPTER XIV.

On the twenty-sixth of February, at day-break, the inhabitants of San Patricio were startled from their beds by a tremendous report of musquetry, which was followed by distressing cries, proceeding from some wounded persons. There were three houses in the village, in which a small detachment of Texians was lodged, and, as they slept quite unconcerned, without advanced *vedettes*, or scouts, they were surprised by Urrea's troop, who came on, with the greatest secrecy. Some of the Texians fled by a back door, and succeeded in making their escape, while fifteen of their number became the victims of their carelessness, being killed on the spot, and twenty-one remained prisoners. All the inhabitants of the village, as may be supposed, were up in a moment; but, as many of them were indiscreetly popping out their heads, at the doors or windows of their houses, and even venturing into the streets, certain well-meaning Mexican officers ran about, exhorting them to keep themselves quiet in their dwellings, lest their soldiers, in the first pride and confusion of success, should misuse them.

One of those who thus ventured out was our valiant Irish amazon, who planted herself at her door, with an axe, that she brandished with great resolution, ready to defend the entrance of her premises. A gallant young officer, mounted on a superbly caparisoned horse, seeing this strange figure, in hostile attitude, and afraid lest, perhaps, some of his soldiers should fire at her, rode up, to give her assurance of protection, and exhorted her to keep herself within her walls. He had hardly exchanged a few words with the old woman, when the young lady, who had risen and was already dressed, recognized the voice of our hero.

In her present confusion, when she thought the village was actually being sacked, she could not help calling upon him for protection, though, in any other circumstance, she would have rather chosen to remain exposed to the greatest inconveniences, than to press her-

self, in this manner, upon her lover's observation. " Oh,
Captain Letinez," did she cry out, " it is heaven itself
that sends you here. For God's sake, protect this poor
woman." She could not go so far as to implore protection for herself; but though she had no time to reflect upon the wording of her petition, yet it was the
instinct of true love, which, at that instant, directed
her tongue, and such a reticence was more significant
than she was aware of.

" Heavens !" exclaimed the captain, " is it your
voice I hear, Miss Linton ? Is it possible you are here?
And by what chance did you come to this place ?" At
the same time, alighting from his horse, and giving the
bridle to a soldier that was in attendance, he entered
the cabin, the old woman courtseying low, as he crossed her threshold, and shouldering her axe, in token of
honour, and in imitation of a soldier presenting arms.
Before *he* had time to present his respects to the young
lady, the old matron opened her battery of congratula-
tions upon the latter.

" Sure, hinney," said she, " you need not have been
afeard, knowing you had such acquaintances in the
army of them paple. Being as how his honor, this here
captain, is your friend, you should not have taken it so
to heart. Och, captain ! your honour ! Had you but
seen the swate crature crying and wailing for share
fright, it would have melted your heart. It would
have made a four year ould cry, captain !"

Senor de Letinez, nevertheless, paid little attention
to the old lady's address, and, altogether engrossed by
Miss Linton's presence, said to her, in a tone of deep
respect, " What happiness for me to meet with you
again, under circumstances which enable me to render
you new services. Oh, be assured, this is the greatest
enjoyment I can possibly feel. This moment alone amply repays me for all the fatigues of the campaign,
whether past or to come."

" Captain Letinez," replied Miss Linton, in a tone
in which melancholy and playfulness were blended,
" there would be something peculiarly ungenteel, in
urging your suit, in this place and at this time ; when

we are under martial law, and altogether in the power of the military. I hope, therefore, you will not be less generous, *now*, than you were at Matamoros, and continue faithful to the promises you then made me."

"Any thing to please you, Miss Linton," replied the captain; "and to obtain your esteem. Yet let me hope that, when this war is over, and all parties are reconciled, you will receive my addresses with more indulgence. Sorry as I am for the accident that brought you hither, still, I cannot help giving thanks to heaven, for meeting with you again, and finding the occasion of making a new tender of my services. All I am afraid of is, that I shall not long have the pleasure of enjoying your company; for I believe we are to march towards Goliad, in two or three days."

"What a pity," returned the young lady, "that this unhappy contest cannot be terminated by pacific measures, and that so beautiful a country as this, should be crimsoned by so much human blood. My father, I am afraid, will be amongst the foremost, and God knows whether his courage will not carry him too far."

To this, the captain would have replied by words of consolation, but he was interrupted by a sergeant, who came to inform him that the general wanted him. He, of course, took his leave of the young lady; but not without earnestly recommending her to the care of her hostess, and promising to send a guard of soldiers, to protect the house against any attempt at pilfering on the part of the military.

He wished to afford Miss Linton pecuniary aid; but dared not offer it himself, for fear of wounding her sensibility. In order, therefore, to relieve her, without alarming her delicacy, he had no sooner waited on the general, than he went to the parish priest's and begged him to take charge of a considerable sum of money, with instructions to give it to the old woman at whose house Miss Linton lodged, for the young lady's benefit; but to preserve the strictest secrecy, in relation to the giver, and rather let her believe that it had been received from Texas, in order that her suspicions might not light upon him.

This parish priest, whom we have already introduced to the reader, under his own euphonic name of Supplegrowl, was a man of some information, but one who lacked common sense, and who, having run over a great part of the world without finding any place fit for him to live in, had, as his last resource, established himself in San Patricio. With his inferiors, he was insolent; but awkwardly cringing with his superiors, and he had, besides, the unfortunate knack of mistaking any extraordinary marks of respect paid him by unknown persons, for a token of inferiority, and a willing acknowledgment of it, on their part. As he had lived, for several years, secluded from any thing like polished society, lording it over a number of Irish, who used to tremble at the very sight of him ; his self conceit had so far increased, that it bordered on folly, and, had he exhibited his spiritual freaks in any other country than the wilderness of Texas, he would have been in no little danger of visiting a mad house.

When captain Letinez, with all imaginable politeness, laid his request before him, our hollow-brained friar conceived the idea that this species of charity was a cloak for some mystery ; being probably intended to conceal an amorous intrigue, and his delicay, which, in one of his order, was rather squeamish, took the alarm. He began to moralise, in broken Spanish, with Senor de Lotinez, and, in a harsh style, and with a consequential air, represented to him the wickedness of military men, and, moreover, manifested his indignation at the idea of our hero having sought to make him a *go between.*

The captain, whose love for Miss Linton was as pure as it was disinterested, was roused to anger by the suspicions of father Supplegrowl, and treated him so cavalierly, that the clergyman resolved to be revenged upon him, and, for that purpose, had recourse to his spiritual weapons. Miscalculating the influence of his order, in Mexico, and as lofty, as if he lived in the days of Gregory VII. he bore himself with the greatest haughtiness ; but he had reckoned without his host, for, notwithstanding the external respect which is still

paid, there, to the ceremonies of religion, the high
classes have really very little reverence for the clergy,
whom it is becoming a mark of *bon ton* to despise, and
father Supplegrowl found it so, to his bitter disappointment, as well as the great diversion of Urrea's staff.

The young officer had no sooner left the clergyman's
house, than the latter, full of holy wrath, trudged to the
general's, to inform him, that, the majesty of the church
having been offended in his person, it became his painful duty to punish the guilty by spiritual censures, and
that, of course, he would, on the following Sunday,
proceed to the solemn excommunication of captain Letinez. "I am," said he, in a doleful, canting tone,
"very sorry to be, thus, obliged to deliver a guilty soul
to Sathanas; but it is in *interitum carnis*, as St. Paul
has it, General, and to the building up of the spirit.
A door of entrance is always left to the repenting sinner, and, as soon as the captain aforesaid comes to
throw himself at my feet, I will be ready to receive
him, as a tender father receiveth a penitent son, and reconcile him with the church. Do not believe that, in
acting thus, I am carried away by my resentment
against the culprit, for having insulted me. No: It is
out of pure zeal for Christian discipline, and merely
for the discharge of my duty, I thus use the spiritual
sword of St. Peter."

This address, as may be imagined, surprised Urrea,
as well as the superior officers who surrounded him :—
Some thought father Supplegrowl was mad; others,
quite indignant at his impertinence, were for driving
him away with ignominy, but one, who was a wag, after
winking to his comrades, feigned to be frightened by
his threats, and began to excuse captain Letinez and
sue for mercy in his behalf.

Father Supplegrowl did not fail to imagine, from this,
that his menaces had made the desired impression, and
that showing himself inexorable would tend to enhance
his dignity. He, of course, resisted those feigned ap-
plications for mercy, until, at last, the *wag* bethought
himself, in order to prolong the farce, to remind him
that, before excommunication, three canonical *monitions*,

on three different days, are required by the ecclesiastical law, and requested the clergyman to go through this form, in order to give his friend time to repent and offer satisfaction.

This was a request father Supplegrowl could not refuse. In consequence, he consented, though with a bad grace, to go through the formality, and prepared to make the first monition *instanter.* The captain, however, was not present to receive the spiritual summons; but the wag, who was carrying on the joke, having given the wink to his comrades; and the general, not unwilling to be amused, having granted his consent by a cunning smile, he undertook to bring the culprit in presence of his ecclesiastical judge, and immediately went out to look for him.

He soon met with the captain, but found some difficulty in engaging him to act his part, in this strange frolic. By dint of importunity, however, he prevailed, and the culprit soon appeared before the assembled officers and father Supplegrowl.

As soon as the latter perceived him at the door, even before he entered the apartment, he opened upon him, at the highest pitch of his voice, like a public crier, in the streets, without giving him time to say any thing in his defence; and thundered out his admonition, in broken Spanish, which we will translate into English, for the benefit of our readers at large. "In the name of the most holy and undivided Trinity, I, an unworthy brother of the order of preaching friars, commonly known by the name of Dominicans, make known unto thee, Ambrosio de Letinez, captain of cavalry, in the Mexican troops, now in actual service in the army of operation against Texas; that, having received from thee a most gross and flagrant insult, in my own house, this very day, I have, as ecclesiastical judge, duly appointed for this parish, declared and decreed, and, by these presents, do declare and decree, that thou shalt be cut off from the bosom of the Holy, Catholic, Apostolic and Roman church, by the spiritual sword of *major excommunication,* unless thou come to resipiscence, by publicly asking pardon of me, the offended party : and this

thou shalt do, by appearing at the door of my house,
and kneeling bare-headed, before me, holding, in thy
right hand, a waxen torch of two pounds weight, without sword by thy side, or gloves on thy hands; and,
this doing, thou shalt save thy own soul."

After delivering this pretty formula of canonical
eloquence, father Supplegrowl bolted right off, with
the greatest precipitation, for fear the captain should
manifest his repentance on the spot, and preclude him
from handling his spiritual thunder. The whole company were so much surprised, that it was some time before they could recover themselves sufficiently to enjoy
the joke. They did so, at last, and, after a hearty
laugh, insisted upon captain Letinez going through
the repenting scene, in order to quizz the *padres;* but
he absolutely refused, because he thought it would be
carrying mockery too far, and bordering on sacrilege.

This was hardly over, when another Irish figure,
quite as original, in his kind, as father Supplegrowl,
presented himself, *craving* an interview with the general, in order to lay before him a plan for the campaign,
which, he said, he would permit him to use, *whole* or
in part, just as his " *excellency*" would " *most vouchsafe
to think fit.*" As Urrea was not acquainted with the
English language, our hero was requested to serve as
interpreter.

The communications which this new applicant had to
make were prefaced by a long tale of the many subjects
of disgust he had received from the government of the
United States, whereby he had been induced to leave
" *that people.*" Amongst the grievances he enumerated,
were the pamphlets, daily published against the Catholic church, and the burning of the Ursuline nunnery, in
Boston, whereby the chartered rights of Roman Catholics had been so grossly violated, that he assured the
general *they* would all emigrate to Texas, as soon as
the Mexicans could effect the conquest. He had, himself, come *ahead,* to help, by his advice, for he possessed
a considerable experience in the art of war, having
served under Wellington, in Spain; and he doubted
not of Santa Anna's ultimate success, because the Mex-

14

icans were the children "of the true church, with which Christ had promised to be, until the end of the world;—and that the gates of hell should not prevail against it," &c. &c.

After such a Catholic preamble, of which we have only given the substance to our readers, sparing them many texts of Scripture, as well as many complaints against the Orangemen of Ireland, with which it was interlarded, he proceeded to unfold his military plan. It was pretty much of a piece with the one which Buonaparte, in his memoirs, attributes to general Cartaux, at the siege of Toulon; id est, "to march in three divisions, fight against the enemies, and *beat* them;" but the most curious particular of his communications was a drawing of a ponton of his invention, for crossing rivers. The boats were to be anchored side ways, as well as up stream, and he had provided a kind of wooden grate to stop the drift wood!—It was evident the man had seen a flying bridge of boats some where, but had not understood its use; for some of his whimsical ideas were predicated on the supposition of its being stationary. Though Urrea could not penetrate all the absurdity of the plan thus offered to his acceptance, yet he was astonished at the man's assurance, and inquired what grade he had held in Wellington's army, to which our Irishman candidly answered that he had been a sergeant.

On hearing this, a smile was exchanged by the officers there present, and the general could not help telling them, in Spanish, "I am afraid these people take us for such fools as to imagine any thing will go down with us. We are too ready to give credit to foreigners for superior information, and this induces them to believe that the meanest amongst them can instruct us. Only think of a petty sergeant drawing up a plan of a campaign, for an army he has never seen, and whose very language is unknown to him. *Santa Maria!* It requires the greatest patience to stand it!" Though Urrea spoke thus, he did not manifest to the man what he thought of his plan, and, so far from letting him know the contempt he entertained for his ideas, he, on the contrary, gave him hopes that he would examine them more carefully, when at leisure; and excused himself from so doing, at the present moment, under the pretence of a pressure of business. It often happens that the concealing of an unpleasant truth, for fear of giving pain to those whom it may concern, is a real act of cruelty; and, by a necessary recoil, exposes the weak minded man, who thus indulges his cowardice at the expense of veracity, to considerable vexations. It is what befell general Urrea in this instance. For, not having had the resolution to tell the Irishman what he thought of his plans, he induced him to conceive hopes of causing them to be admitted, made him lose five months in useless attendance, and brought upon himself the infliction of twenty importunate visits and prosing explanations, to which he never gave a more explicit answer.

The defect here alluded to, which proceeds from mental debility, is generally prevalent amongst the Mexican gentry, who have got a notion that it is a part of true politeness. They are excessive in demonstrations of cordiality and offers of service, where they do not feel the least interest, and even will frequently insist, with obstreperous violence, upon the acceptance of favours, which they have not the remotest idea of confering.

Urrea made a very short stay in San Patricio, for, seeing with what carelessness and ignorance the portion of the Texian forces, opposed to him, acted, when on the defensive; he rightly judged that it would be easy to pursue his advantage. He had left the main body of his troops, with all his infantry, eight days march behind, and had advanced merely with one hundred men. Of these, he took forty eight with him, leaving the remainder to garrison the village, and went in pursuit of Dr. Grant, who was amusing himself in collecting horses, and had scattered his men about for that interesting purpose. The doctor and his soldiers paid the forfeit of their folly, and, in five days time, Urrea returned to St. Patricio in triumph. In the mean while, however, an event had occurred in the village, which filled our hero's heart with grief.

The general, to whom he had been especially recommended, and who, in consequence, wished to afford him occasions of distinguishing himself, took him along, when he went in pursuit of Dr. Grant, and the summons was so sudden and unexpected, that our hero had barely time to take leave of Miss Linton, but without making any disposition to insure her safety, during his absence.

Immediately after his return, his first care was to visit old Mrs. Jordan's house; but judge of his surprise, when he found that Miss Linton was gone, and was informed that her father had sent for her. "Gone to her father's," did he exclaim, in the utmost amazement; "it is impossible! Her father did not know where she was; moreover, she could not have gone that way, without meeting some of our scouts. No—this is an awkward invention! An idle tale, set up to delude me! But tell me where she is, for I will know. She cannot possibly have fled from me. No, Miss Linton cannot be afraid of me. Perhaps she is the victim of some infamous plot, to bring her into danger.—Woman, you are a party to it—but do not dally with me, or play false; for, if you do, dearly shall you rue it. By all that is sacred in Heaven and upon earth, if you have betrayed her, I will be revenged. Tell me at once, where is she?" continued he with violence, and drawing his sword, "or, by the living God, you might as well dally with the honour of my own mother."

The poor woman, frightened and trembling like a leaf, replied, "Sure, captain, I don't know. Though I were, at this blessed moment, to appear before God and Saint Patrick, I could not tell you more, your honour. You may kill a poor lone woman, if you choose, particularly as I have no arms, about the house, but it will not be much to your credit."

The captain, brought to himself by these words, and ashamed of his own violence, put back his sword, into its scabbard, and looked confused, whilst the old woman went on. "Two days after you were gone, there came three men riding upon three horses, and leading a fourth one, that was a mare, with a handsome side saddle on her back, for a woman to ride. They alighted before my house, and inquired if a young lady, so and so, was not lodged with me. I told them she was, your honour—Well, then, says one of them, we have a letter for her, from her father. Thereupon, Miss Linton, who heard the whole conversation from within, came out to spake with the men, and when she redde the letter; this is not my father's hand writing, says she. No, Madam, says one of the men. Your father could not write, bekase he was sick, a bed; but he made the doctor that tended him write the letter, in his name, and he sent us to pilot you home, which we will do, in all safety, for we knows all the by-roads and secret paths, and are not afeard of the Indians, and we have got a pass from the Mexican commander. But how did my father know I was here, says Miss Linton, for she was wary and purdent, your honour. Och! Madam, says the other, he was told of it by one of the men who got shipwrecked with you, in the Lively Sally, in *Corpus Christi* bay; and procured a horse with a saddle and bridle from a Mexican ranchero, and rode, in five days, to Mr. Pierson's plantation, where your father is now living. The old gentleman is very sick, Madam, not expected to last long, and is incessantly inquiring whether you are come. Thereupon, Miss Linton, began to wape, your honour, at the idea of her father's dying; and she said she would go with the men. I told her how dingerous it was to venture out through them praries and woods, your honour; but it would not do. She said she could not bear the idea of her father's dying, and her being absent. Happily for the dare crature, I had half a keg of hard biscuits and two good chazes, which I gave her, though them men said she should want for nothing on the way; but they took them, for all that."

"And did she go in the company of men, she was not acquainted with?" exclaimed captain Letinez, with bitter sorrow painted on his countenance. "An un-

14*

protected female, all alone! Good God! what an imprudence!"

"Och, your honour, I told her it was a monstrous
cruel thing, thus, to travel, that long route, on horseback; but she would not be advised, and said no danger
nor fatigue should detain her: she must see her father,
before his death, and see him she would. But, sure,
captain, she is in no dinger from them men. They
all spake English, your honour. I'll warrant you they
are Americans. The loike of them is not going to injure
a lone woman. 'Tis not as with Mexicans, captain;—
but may be you don't know the difference!"

"Tut, tut; don't tell me about your Americans,"
interrupted the captain; "a parcel of robbers and out-
laws!—Oh, heavens! whither have they carried her?—
But this must be some deeply laid scheme of villany.
I must to the general, beg a company of soldiers, and
instantly go in pursuit of the wretches."

So saying, he left Mrs. Jordan's house with precipitation, but had not proceeded a hundred yards, when
he was met by father Supplegrowl, who had been on
the look out for him, in order to pounce upon him with
his second *canonical admonition*. He had, during the
five days of the captain's absence, been on thorns, for
fear he should pass over into another parish; and, thus,
escape his jurisdiction. As soon, therefore, as he was
informed of his return, he hastened to execute what he
called a "painful duty." He could not have selected
a more inauspicious moment, the captain being, *then*,
wrought up to the highest pitch of anger, and breath-
ing nothing but vengeance against the villains who had
carried off Miss Linton.

Father Supplegrowl, therefore, had no sooner drawn
near, and begun to utter the above cited formula, "In
the name of the most holy and undivided Trinity,"
&c., than captain Lotinez, seizing him by the collar of
his coat, and squeezing him sufficiently tight to oblige
him to loll out his tongue, told him: "Father Supplegrowl, Father Supplefool;—I am not, now, in humour
to carry on a joke. I forbid you to continue your fool-
eries at my expense, and if you do, my cane will be-

come acquainted with your back." So saying, he pushed him off, with so much violence as sent him reeling
to twelve paces distance, and went his way.

From what our reader has been told touching father
Supplegrowl's temper, he might be inclined to imagine,
that, after being thus handled by our hero, he would
have displayed against him all the terrors of the law
of which he was the interpreter, but the fact is that he
cooled off, as if by enchantment. Father Supplegrowl
was a spiritual bully, and the *argumentum baculinum*
is the only one that has any influence upon these kind
of people. He peaceably withdrew to his own house,
and, in token of peace, indited a letter to the general,
by which he begged him to act as mediator between
the captain and himself.

In the mean time, our hero, having obtained a sufficient number of soldiers, from Urrea, began the pursuit
of the wretches who had carried off Miss Linton. He
took with him three *rancheros* from the vicinity, a class
of people so skilful in tracing, by the prints of horses'
feet, the direction of any one who has preceded them
on a road, no matter how often he *cuts, turns*, and *winds
about*, that, in some cases, their abilities appear almost
supernatural. These skilful *pilots*, after carefully examining the shape of the horse-shoes, the marks of which
were still visible about the old woman's premises, declared that they were not of Mexican manufacture,
and that the animals must be strangers to that part of
the country.

The footprints led them to about twenty leagues east
of San Patricio, where they bivouacked the first night
near a marsh of considerable extension, which those
they were in pursuit of seemed to have crossed. There
they were afraid they would lose the *scent*; but one
of the party being of opinion that probably it had been
done by way of stratagem, the whole company spread
themselves about, following the banks of the *laguna*,
and looking for the *track*, which they found again, and
in such a spot, as really manifested some design on the
part of the fugitives.

After wading through the marsh the distance of half

a league, the latter had retraced their steps, and taken a westerly direction, crossing a tremendous thicket of prickly pear, by which both horses and riders must have suffered cruelly. Captain Letinez's heart bled within himself, when, upon an inspection of the road they had held, he saw to what sufferings Miss Linton must have been exposed; and the desire of avenging her wrongs was a new incitement to hasten his march. The guides briskly led on, animated by the promise of a considerable reward, in case they should make any discovery; but when they reached the river Nueces again, the captain began to despair of success, and told them they must have been mistaken. They still insisted they were on the *track*, and that the men they were pursuing had certainly crossed the river.

How repugnant soever to believe them, the captain, who knew he was now near San Patricio, thought it prudent to accompany them until they should give up the undertaking themselves. They crossed the river, therefore, and, following its right bank, down stream, soon arrived at Lepantitlan. This was a fort the Mexican government had built, about two miles from San Patricio, in order to protect the colonists, and of which the Texians had taken possession, at the same time they occupied the Irish village. Before the gate, which was carefully shut, though the fort seemed abandoned, the guides stopped, declaring that the young lady must be secreted within. Their assertion appeared extravagant, and captain Letinez was on the point of giving up the search in despair; but the rancheros were so positive, that he, at last, consented to demand admittance, and repeatedly knocked at the gate, but without receiving any answer. He knew that the place, after having been retaken upon the Texians, had not been garrisoned by Urrea; Of course, he could not account for the portal being so scrupulously locked inside.

CHAPTER XV.

Seeing, after repeated efforts, that nobody heeded their summons, they forced the entrance, and the guides had no sooner crossed the threshold, than they declared they could perceive the same foot prints by which they had been, till then, directed. This considerably raised the hopes of the captain, who, now, began to visit the buildings. A strong log house, of large dimensions, which had been used as barracks, was in a sad state of dilapidation; yet, it seemed, from the relics of a recent carousal, to have been, very lately, the resort of some convivial party. This discovery increased the ardor of the search, and, soon after, one of the guides espied a man softly stealing over the palisades, whereupon he gave the alarm and started in pursuit of the fugitive.

The fellow was, nevertheless, too nimble for his pursuer, and, at one single leap, from the top of the stockade, cleared the ditch that ran round the fort, and made towards the thick woods, on the margin of the river, where he succeeded in concealing himself, before the captain's men could come round by the gate and intercept his flight. Some of the party continued the chase, while others, amongst whom was our hero, returned to the fort, to pursue their researches. They tried to enter a small building, which had been used as a powder magazine, but found it locked. As they shook the door, they were startled by hearing some faint moans proceeding from the interior, whereupon one of the guides triumphantly exclaimed, " *Aqui la tenemos—aqui esta!*" (here she is.) " *Animo! senores,* we have succeeded." Captain Letinez, nearly delirious with joy, yet dreading lest the fright, at seeing the door broken by main force, should prove fatal to Miss Linton, from whom he new judged the wailing moans proceeded, called out to her, through the key hole, that it was himself, who had traced her to her place of imprisonment, and had come to set her free. An exclamation of joy, followed by loud sobs, informed him that these good tidings had reached her ear; but still he found considerable difficulty in effecting his purpose. The door was strong, covered with thick plates of iron, and studded with large nails. In vain they tried to raise it off its hinges, by means of a long lever, or to break it, by repeated knocks, with a large beam of timber; their efforts proved useless, and, after half an hour's severe labour, it still remained fast on its hinges, and precluded all entrance. The young lady, from within, encouraged them with a faint voice, and suggested the idea of getting in, by the roof, in case they should not be able to break open the door.

"By the virgin *de los dolores*, she is right," exclaimed one of the *rancheros*, "and it is a shame for us not to have thought of it. The roof is strongly terraced; but, for all that, I will soon have dug a hole through it. Here, Juan Dolos, let me climb on thy shoulders, man!—now hand me that sharp ebony handspike, and let one or two more get up here, to help me."

No sooner said than done. In less than half an hour, a portion of the roof was off; yet as the young lady would not consent to be lifted up through this sky hole, they continued their work until they had made a gap in the wall, which was no difficult task; the stones, though quarried and massy, being badly cemented, and, of course, easily removed, when once the superstratum of the roof was thrown down.

Miss Linton, at last, came out of her prison, but almost fainting, and nearly as weak as when she was first rescued from the hands of the Comanches. The first words she uttered were addressed to her lover. "Blame me not, captain Letinez," said she; "I was unworthily deceived. Alas, I was made to believe that my father was dying, and earnestly desired to see me. Could I, then, listen to pusillanimous suspicions, and remain unconcerned?"

"I know it," replied the captain: "Mrs. Jordan has given me a faithful account. But tell me, my dear Miss Linton;—who was the author of this infamous deception? I need not inquire about the vile motives by which he was impelled."

"Indeed, captain," returned Miss Linton, "the man is a Mexican, to all certainty; and an officer of high rank, if I may judge from his military costume; but I don't know his name. After leaving St. Patricio, I was made to travel two days, till we came to a large pond, through which we waded. Then, after crossing the most frightful thicket of prickly pear I ever saw, in two days more, we reached this place, which my guide made me believe was a Texian fort, on the Guadalupe river; and that we should remain here until a carriage should come for me, which he expected every minute. In about two hours time, there arrived, instead of a carriage, the officer already mentioned. He spoke English very imperfectly, but sufficiently to make me the vilest proposals, confessing that he was the author of my abduction, and that I was in the hands of persons entirely devoted to him. I treated him with all the contempt he deserved; and, irritated to the last degree by my reproaches, he caused me to be shut up in the loathsome dungeon whence you have freed me. Since I have been imprisoned in it, he has himself come twice, to bring me food, and has renewed his efforts to shake my resolution."

"Then," resumed the captain, "it must be some one of the principal officers of the southern division of the army, for you are here in the old fort of Lepantitlan, not above half a league from St. Patricio. But where could he have previously seen you, and who are the men of whose help he has availed himself, to execute his execrable purpose?—Mrs. Jordan told me that they spoke English perfectly well, and she took them for Texians."

"The wretched man," replied Miss Linton, "must have seen me at the chapel, in St. Patricio, on the Sunday I went to mass with Mrs. Jordan. As for the agents of his villany, two of them, I believe, are Scotchmen, as well as I can judge from their pronunciation, and the third one struck me as having about him some of the peculiarities of the coloured race of Louisiana. At all events, he knows French, and speaks it as Creole negroes do,—but where my persecutor had found them passes my comprehension."

"Oh," returned the captain, "there are so many adventurers following our army, in order to partake of the
spoils, in case of success, that it is not difficult to
account for his finding such vile tools, quite at hand.
But what are we to do, now, that you are free?—It is
difficult or rather impossible, to provide against the am-
bushes of a secret and powerful enemy, and, by returning to St. Patricio, you will, perhaps, be exposed to
new persecutions.—Could I be continually present, to
watch over your safety, there would be no great danger,
but we are shortly to march towards Labahia, and the
Irish village will be left unprotected. Resolve, Miss
Linton,—what are we to do?

"Alas!" replied she, "I see no alternative. Surely,
you would not wish me to follow the army?"

"Dear Miss Linton," resumed the captain, "I am
aware it would look improper, if we were in ordinary
circumstances; but reflect, that necessity has no law.
There are some of our officers' wives, who are women
of virtue, standing and good breeding, and have female
servants with them. Might you not, without any great
breach of propriety, travel in company with some one
of them, until we reach the Brazos; when a flag of
truce shall be sent to the enemy, and you shall be conveyed to your friends, in all honour and safety?"

"Indeed," returned Miss Linton, "I cannot do so!
The ladies you speak of may be very honourable,
but their ways and customs differ so much from what I
have been used to, that I cannot help thinking they
border upon licentiousness. I do not, however, condemn them. Every country has its peculiar sense
of propriety. But familiarity with them, I would consider as a committing of my own principles. Better
for me to return to my good natured hostess, and wait
until the campaign is more advanced."

"Well, then," said the captain, "since such is your
resolution, we may begin our march for St. Patricio,
immediately. We have found here a side saddle, probably the same on which you rode, when you left the village, and if you feel yourself sufficiently strong to ride,
we will leave this wretched abode."

Miss Linton having consented, every thing was quickly made ready, and they set out for St. Patricio. The three men who had gone in pursuit of the young lady's jailor, returned, as the rest of the party were leaving the fort, and informed them that the villain, after leading them a race of two miles, up the river, had, at length, escaped, by swimming over to the opposite side, and mounting a horse, which it seems, was ready at that place, having been left hobbled, in case he were wanted. Sadly did captain Letinez regret that they had not taken him, for he had expected to discover, by his means, the author of the foul outrage, which he had, now, very little hopes to effect.

In about three quarters of an hour, they arrived at the Irish village, where old Mrs. Jordan was delighted to see Miss Linton, in the middle of the cavalcade which stopped before her door. "Och, och!" did she exclaim, "what a blessing, hinney, that you are found again. By my troth, my jewel, the dear captain would have gone beside himself, I think!—But you are wellcum home, for, I declare to goodness, I have been in the fidgets, ever since you went. Them praries are so dingerous to travel!—They are full of *painters*, hinney. And the sarpents :—The rattle-snakes, the black vipers, and the mocasins; besides the scorpions, that crape about the grass, and are so apt to get among ones bed clothes at night!—And the Tarentulas!—Och, we have none of them things, in ould Ireland,—blessed be St. Patrick, for it!—But alight, hinney,—you must be fatigued and hungry. And how did you like the two chazes that I gave you, and the crackers?—But, I dare say, you hardly tasted them, and them monstrous cratures, who carried you off, ate the best share of them."

Miss Linton was soon established again in the little room she had previously occupied, and her lover obtained leave from general Urrea to place a guard of two soldiers at the old woman's door, in order to watch over the young lady's safety. He also made his utmost efforts to discover who could have been guilty of her abduction; but the general showed a considerable unwillingness to favour his researches. "It can be no other," said he, " than some one of the superior officers, and, if discovered, it might be dangerous to attempt punishing him. During a campaign as arduous as the one we have undertaken, it is impossible to prevent every misdemeanor of the kind. It is one of the sad consequences of war, that many acts of licentiousness, which, in time of peace, would be severely chastised, must be suffered to pass unnoticed." This was but a poor satisfaction for captain Letinez ; but, as he had no means of obtaining redress, he was obliged to put up with it.

About a week after this occurrence, general Urrea began his march towards Labahia, otherwise called Goliad. There was, on the way, a considerable settlement of foreigners, chiefly Irish people, at a village bearing the quaint name of *the Mission*, of which the Texians had taken possession, and from whence, the Mexican commander judged necessary to dislodge them. For that purpose, he detatched a portion of his troops, who found the enemy fortified in the church, where they made an unexpected resistance. The Mexicans having, nevertheless, begun to batter the building, with a piece of artillery, the besieged surrendered. Some of them, however, refusing to trust their enemies, made their escape; whilst those who became prisoners of war had no reason to anticipate the dreadful fate which was reserved for them, as they were treated with a kind of carelessness unusual in border warfare.

After the taking of the Mission, the forces which had been detached for that service rejoined the main body, and advanced, full of animation, towards Goliad. They had the mortification to find the place destroyed, and the Texians in full retreat. Excited by that appearance of fear, on the part of the enemy, Urrea pursued Fanning, and found him in the middle of a plain, awkwardly intrenched with a narrow ditch and some wagons. The Texian commander had neither the knowledge to fight, nor the discretion to retreat; for there was a thick and large wood at a short distance, on his rear, in which it would have been easy for him to fortify himself in an inexpugnable manner. He al-

together neglected the chances of escape which this
might have afforded, and yet did not avail himself of
his superiority in point of numbers and artillery to
make his resistance good.

Urrea, on the other hand, showed very little less indiscretion and fool hardiness, for he advanced to the
attack of Fanning's intrenched camp, with so scanty a
supply of ammunition, that, a short time after dusk,
his soldiers were obliged to suspend firing for want of
cartridges. He had left his artillery with all his *ma-
teriel*, at a great distance behind; and, had the Texian
commander attacked him, at this critical moment, and
improved the occasion, Urrea's total discomfiture would
have been the inevitable result; but Fanning kept
himself quiet within his camp, while the Mexican, commanding his soldiers to lie flat on the ground, amused
the Texians by feigned demonstrations, which he made
with his music and drums, in various directions, round
their intrenchments; thus gaining time to send for his
ammunition and two pieces of cannon.

Having suffered the precious occasion to escape,
Fanning, when attacked, the following morning, by all
the forces of Urrea, surrendered with a facility which
can have been atoned for only by the fortitude and
sangfroid with which he met an unjust and barbarous
death.

As it is not, however, our object to expatiate, in this
place, on the tragical and ever to be lamented events
that disgraced the war with which our hero's history
happens to be connected, nor to work upon our readers'
feelings by a pathetic description of the horrors of the
violation of Fanning's capitulation, we beg to be excused, if we cursorily run over the surrender of his
corps, to return to captain Letinez's private affairs.
When he saw the Texians surrendering, though they
had every means of resistance, he could not help, in
his heart, accusing them of cowardice. He knew that
the orders to refuse quarter to every one taken with
arms in his hands, were peremptory; but he had not
the least suspicion that they would be enforced against
such as surrendered, and, in consequence, put them-

selves out of that category—much less could he anticipate that a solemn capitulation, granted and signed with due reflection, would be violated in a manner that has no precedent in modern warfare. Of course, he was not uneasy about the prisoners' fate, and availed himself of his knowledge of the English language, to mix among them, and become acquainted with their officers. He chiefly remarked a middle aged man, of good appearance, though seemingly oppressed by sorrow, whom he heard some one call major Linton. It immediately occurred to him that he might be a relation of the young lady to whom he had become attached in the manner already related, and he inquired from one of the Texians whether his suspicions were well founded or not. He soon discovered that he was *her* father. Drawing near, therefore, he introduced himself to him, saying, with that proper degree of civility which a courteous victor never forgets with a vanquished foe, " I rejoice, sir, that it is in my power to alleviate the chagrin which you must naturally feel in finding yourself a prisoner, by announcing to you the most happy news."

" Alas, young gentleman," sadly returned the major, " what happy news can you, possibly, announce to a man that has lost all. Property and child, all is gone, and I am myself a prisoner !"

" But, sir," resumed the captain ; " it is about your daughter."

" My daughter !—what of my daughter ?—For God's sake, tell me, immediately," replied the major, taking hold of captain Letinez's hands, and pressing them to his bosom, with an ardour that brought tears to his eyes. " Do you know where she is ?"

" Yes, sir," returned the captain ; " but be master of yourself.—Your daughter is in perfect safety, and not far from this place ; yet I doubt whether I should communicate what you seem, in your present state, hardly able to bear."

" Able to bear !" resumed the major. " You know not the heart of a father. Oh, for the sake of humanity, tell me all. Incertitude is beyond my powers of endurance. I was prepared to hear the most awful accounts, shall I not be able to hear glad tidings? Proceed, young gentleman; in the name of heaven, proceed. Where is my daughter—where is my child?"

"Well, sir," returned the captain, "Miss Linton is, as I have already told you, in a place of safety. Having casually fallen in with a party of Comanches, who were carrying her off, I had the happiness of becoming the instrument of her deliverance." Thereupon, he gave him a brief history of the young lady's journey to Matamoros, of her embarcation and subsequent shipwreck, as well as of her landing at St. Patricio, which, in order not to go twice over the same tale, we will abstain from repeating. Be it sufficient to state that the father, delighted at the idea that his daughter was safe, and not far from him, manifested to captain Letinez his gratitude, by the most lively and sincere expressions.

The latter, anxious to show the major all the civility in his power, and desirous that he should be treated with more indulgence than the rest of the prisoners, went to the general, over whose mind he possessed great influence, and begged him to permit him to take major Linton to his tent, laying before him, in an ingenuous manner, the motives that actuated him; but he found a great difficulty in obtaining leave.—Although it appeared to our hero a matter of little importance, Urrea believed, or affected to believe, that it might displease the commander in-chief. The captain was, nevertheless, so importunate, that, at last, he carried his point, and major Linton found, in the Mexican's tent, the refreshments he stood so much in need of, and part of his own clothes and linen, which had been pillaged by the lancers, but which Senor de Letinez had redeemed at his own expense.

Several other officers availed themselves of the example set them by our hero, to show civilities to certain prisoners, with whom they had previously been acquainted; but the most moving instance was that of a young lieutenant of *cazadores*, who found, amongst the Texians, a dear friend with whom he had received his

15*

education, at a Catholic college, in Kentucky.—This
officer's name was Marinez. He had no sooner cast
his eyes upon young Brashears, than he rushed towards him, and, tenderly locking him in his arms, cried
out: "O, my dear, dear friend!—Is it possible that we
have been arrayed in arms against each other, and that
I have been exposed to the danger of piercing the bosom of him I love best upon earth!—Cursed be war,
with the ambition and arts of politicians!—Hadst thou
perished, I would not have survived thee; but now, thou
art safe, my Brashears:—as safe as if thou wert my
own brother. With thee, will I divide the bread I eat,
and the narrow tent under which I sleep. Remember-
est thou the day when thou savedst my life, by venturing thine, in the Ohio river, when I was drowning?—
Oh, what a happiness to see the again!" While Marinez was thus addressing his friend, he wept aloud, and
though this flow of gratitude was rather a strange spectacle for the Texians, and seemed to them to border
on the ridiculous, it appeared natural to the Mexicans,
who, by their looks, manifested that they approved of it,
though evinced towards an enemy of their nation and a
professed heretic; for, to do them justice, in spite of
their many vices, they reverence and practise the virtue
of gratitude, to a degree which ought to put to the blush
certain nations far more illustrated than they.

After obtaining the necessary permission from his
superior officers, Marinez led away his friend, and,
along with him, another young man of the name of Duval, from whom Brashears refused to be separated, and
treated them with all the tenderness which the strongest friendship can inspire.

We do not, however, intend to dwell on the interest,
which might be derived from this episode; but return
in haste to our main story, in order to show to our
reader major Linton, in captain Letinez's tent, in close
deliberation with him, on the practicability and propriety of sending for his daughter. "And she is in St.
Patricio, you say, captain;—only seventy miles from
this place!" did he exclaim;—"But are vou sure of it?
—Is there no possibility of your being mistaken?—It

would be the most cruel thing for me to be induced to conceive ill founded hopes."

"My dear sir," replied the captain, "I cannot possibly, be mistaken. I would as soon suppose that I can be deceived in believing you to be major Linton, although I have the testimony of all your acquaintances for it, as to refuse to admit that the young lady I am speaking of is your daughter. Her name, the circumstance of her having been carried off by the Comanches, the place where she resided, when taken prisoner ;—all is an evident proof of my being in the right. Surely, there were not, on the Trinidad, two majors, nor two young ladies of the same name, age, and features !"

"You are right, captain," resumed Mr. Linton ;—"I was a fool to start these doubts; but a father's feelings turn a gray head crazy. It must be my daughter. It is herself. Oh, what do I not owe you for having saved her honour and life. But we must send for her immediately, unless you can obtain leave for me to go to St. Patricio. I must see her, and relieve the painful anxiety which she must feel on my account."

"It would be impossible to obtain leave for you to go," resumed Senor de Letinez. "From our general's present temper, I judge that the mere proposal would appear to him an absurdity. Nothing remains, therefore, but to send for your daughter. She will not refuse to come, when she is informed that you are here. Captain Alvarez, a friend of mine, has a gig, for the use of his lady :—I will obtain the loan of it, and I do not despair to prevail upon Mrs. Alvarez herself to go for Miss Linton. I know she took a great interest in her, and she is obliging even to a degree bordering on enthusiasm. Write a letter to your daughter, while I am going to bespeak my friend's gig, and you will soon have the pleasure of beholding her."

"Well, my dear friend," replied the major, "I am going to write. I will exactly follow your instructions; but it hurts my feelings, not to be able to reward the poor Irish widow, that has behaved so generously towards her."

"As to that," answered the captain, "make your mind easy:—It has been cared for. Nay, do not look so serious," added he, at the sight of a little flush of displeasure, which appeared on the major's countenance; "I could not possibly suffer that poor old woman to feel her hospitality as a burthen; but it was money which I advanced in *your* name:—I consider it as a debt, for which I have a right to call upon you."

Thereupon, the old man's rigidity of features relaxed into a smile, and the captain, leaving him to write his letter, went to look for his friend, Alvarez; but, in the mean time, some deliberations of dreadful import were going on, amongst the principal officers of Urrea's staff. These particularities could not, however, figure in the present chapter, without lengthening it out of all just proportion.

CHAPTER XVI.

Under a large marquee, seven officers of high rank were sitting in various attitudes, upon trunks containing the general's baggage, while he lay himself, half reclining, on his camp bed, smoking a *cigarrito*. Though apparently in a mood of great *nonchalance*, there was a sombre look spread over his countenance, which indicated that highly unpleasant thoughts occupied his mind. " By the virgin *de los remedios*," (12) exclaimed he, addressing a middle aged man, who was sitting at the foot of the bed, " all this embarrassment arises from your having granted *them* such advantageous terms."

"Indeed," replied the person thus addressed, " I cannot be blamed, without your excellency participating in it; for, you saw the articles and approved of them. I acted only as *your deputy*."

"Oh, I saw the articles!—To be sure, I did," resumed Urrea; "but my intention was only to take *the birds in*, (agarrar los pajaros.) I wanted to prevent the effusion of Mexican blood. Those devils were so curiously intrenched with a double row of wagons, that our cavalry could not open a way to itself,—you know, we tried it. And to be thundering at them, from afar, with our artillery, was a work of time and a great waste of gunpowder. Besides I did not like to expose ourselves to the chances that might have turned up in favour of the confounded rascals, had we refused them terms, and rendered them desperate. But now, what are we to do ?—Major Farialega, have you seen Fanning, and told him what I said ?"

"I have been with him," answered Farialega. " He maintains his right to be treated as a prisoner of war, according to the uses and laws of civilized nations, and says, that, whatever may be the point of view, under which the Mexican government looks upon the Texians, a capitulation is like a solemn treaty, and that the terms which were granted them cannot be violated without a breach of faith, which will leave an everlasting stigma upon the Mexican General who shall be guilty of such an enormity."

" *Voto a Dios !*" exclaimed Urrea, interrupting him; " a solemn treaty, with a parcel of rebels, and ungrateful colonists ! They are no nation, and have no right to be treated like one."

" Certainly, they are no nation," replied Farialega; " but still they are men."

" Men ! confound them," returned Urrea, " a parcel of heretics, who want to introduce Protestantism into the republic ! If they were Christians, they might have some plea ; but as things are . . . . However, gentlemen, let every one of you openly say what he thinks. I have convoked you, in order to get your advice. You, colonel Bebe-Sangre, what is your opinion ?"

" Oh, my opinion is soon expressed, and my advice soon given," said Bebe-Sangre. " They are rebels, taken with arms in their hands, and the *Senor Presidente's* orders are express. The sooner they are made away with, the better. Provisions are rather growing scarce with us, and what is the use to permit them to consume a portion of them to no purpose ?"

" And you, Don Prudento Miralejos," interrupted Urrea, " what do you say ?"

" For my part," answered the officer thus interpelled, " if I am free to express what I think, I must say that this appears to me a weighty affair, which should be viewed in all its bearings. It should be considered with an eye to future contingents. If we treat our prisoners in the manner Senor Bebe-Sangre seems to wish, we expose ourselves to retaliation, in case any misfortune befall our army. Gentlemen may consider the success we have obtained with too partial an eye. In my poor judgment it is not decisive. I have had some acquaintance with the Anglo-Americans. They are cold and apathetic ; but by no means cowardly. It always takes two or three defeats to put them in motion and warm their blood. They lose ground in the beginning of every war they undertake ; but triumph in the end. You may be sure that, after our two victories, we are in greater danger than ever. As to this Fanning, you are undoubtedly aware that he is no deacon of his trade; otherwise, the poor thing would have remained in the fort of Goliad and sustained a siege. It would have taken us two months, at least, to force him to surrender."

"Well, now, hush, Miralejos," interrupted Urrea. "Did I not consider thee as more crazy than Fanning, I would be angry with thee. Two victories brought us into greater danger than we were in before! *Santo Dios!* What art thou saying, man? Thinkest thou that we are in the season of *Carnes tollendas*, (shrove tide) to play the bufoon?"

"May it please your excellency, I am rather afraid that we are near *Passion week*," replied Miralejos, with some asperity.

"Gentlemen," resumed the general, "our consultation will never come to an end, if it degenerate into an altercation, and the two bottles of choice Burgundy, which are cooling for us, in the *jarro*,* will lose their relish, if we drink them after exciting feelings of bitterness amongst us. Come, Milagros, tell us what you think. You, who are my *aid-de-camp*, will be of my opinion, I know."

In spite of this broad hint, Milagros took the liberty of differing from his general. "I could not think," said he, "of shooting them, according to the President's orders, even had they surrendered at discretion, but that was not the case. They laid down their arms on certain specified conditions; and if we violate them, we trample upon our military honour; we defile our own glory. There is but one line of conduct for me—it is the line of duty. Here, however, expediency persuades us to the same course; for, if we treat them mildly, and keep faith with them, it will induce others to surrender, and Texas will soon be cleared of them."

"You have perfectly well expressed my sentiments," said colonel Maccana, addressing Milagros, "and since the general left it to the majority, I believe, his excellency may now be satisfied."

* Jarro, earthen jar.

"So am I, gentlemen," interrupted Urrea, with a forced smile; "I am quite satisfied that you are nearly all for throwing the responsibility upon me, in the eyes of the world. You know the President's orders strictly forbid giving quarter to any one of the rebels taken, arms in hand, and still you are afraid to vote for their execution. But if you wash your hands of it, so do I—Urrea is something of a fox, I assure you—I will not, in this business, act by myself. Now—the consultation is over, gentlemen; but let us have the wine. Here, boy—Pedro! Bring drinking glasses and the two bottles which are in the *Jarro*. I drink to you, gentlemen of the staff. By the holy cross of Queretaro,* this is excellent. What a taste! It is superior to the best Champaign I ever sucked. Well, thanks to Fanning's officers! They have taken good care to provide for us. Won't you take a little bit of this Bologna sausage? Won't you taste these French *sardines*, or this *pate de truffes?* Long live Texas, I say! we found no such dainties, after the battle of Zacatecas, though our President found ore enough."

The wine was drunk, and all the officers who had assisted at this strange consultation departed, except an intimate counsellor of the general, with whom he held the following dialogue: "I am sadly disappointed.—This cursed consultation, to which you advised me to have recourse, does not turn out as well as you expected. Had they all voted like Bebe-Cangre, they would have taken the odium of the job off my shoulders; but, now, what shall we do? The articles of Fanning's capitulation, or surrender, or whatever it may be called, are public; and I was the fool who published them, and sent a copy to Matamoros! On the other hand, Santa Anna's orders are too strict to be trifled with.—I know his temper. One might as well dally with an African hyena, as to attempt soothing his mind.—It were as much as my head is worth, or, at least, my post.—By the Virgin of Guadelupe, I am well nigh bewildered!—What am I to do?'"

---

* A convent of Franciscan Missionaries, of celebrity.

"I'll tell you," replied the other; "send a courier to Santa Anna, to consult him. You know, beforehand, what will be his answer; but you can be absent when the messenger returns."

"An admirable idea! This is well contrived," exclaimed Urrea: "It extricates me from my difficulties. But whom shall we find to execute the *job?*— It is a cursed dirty piece of work."

"Whom shall we find, you ask?" replied the other: "Why, you have forty—fifty persons, who will gladly undertake it. But, I think Garrafon deserves the preference. He will do it without flinching, I warrant you."

This being settled, Urrea's *ame damnee* (as the French call it) departed, leaving him to write his despatches to Santa Anna, who was then at San Antonio de Bejar, the principal inland town in Texas.

Whilst these things were going on in the general's tent, our hero was looking for captain Alvarez, a man whose name deserves to be transmitted to the latest posterity; not for the small part he plays in our story, but for having, at his own imminent peril, and against the general feeling of his countrymen, saved the lives of about one hundred prisoners, who were taken after Fanning's surrender; and who, by *his heroical exertions and those of his noble-minded wife*, escaped being massacred. In the midst of the confusion and bustle incident to such times and circumstances, captain Alvarez was not easily found; but, when at last, our hero lighted upon him, and begged him to lend him his gig, Alvarez answered: "My dear friend, I am sorry to refuse you; but really, my wife is on the point of being confined, and I am obliged to send her away to some place where she may enjoy more quiet than is to be found in a military camp."

"Why," replied Letinez, "I did not suppose Mrs. Alvarez was so near her term. I had a thought of begging her to go along with the gig, in order to bring hither a young lady, whose father turns out to be an officer of rank among the prisoners, and is ardently desirous of seeing her.—She was carried off by the

16

Comanches, and I had the happiness to rescue her.—
Now, she is at St. Patricio, without a protector, and
probably in great danger.—Along with her father, she
would be safe. Alvarez, you must not refuse me. I
know your wife is more humane than you; I will speak
with her."

"Hey day!" replied Alvarez, "what an heroical
squire of distressed damsels you are become! *Tandem
homo factus est!*"

"Hush, for God's sake, dear Alvarez," resumed our
hero, "nothing of that. The lady I am speaking of is
a woman of high rank, education, and unblemished
character. The slightest joke, at her expense, might
hurt me seriously."

"Oh, sits the wind in that quarter!" cried out Alvarez. "Real love, matrimony, and all that!—Well,
well, I am no spoiler of fair play. Go to my wife; I
dare say she will undertake the expedition. Even if she
were sure to be overtaken by the pains of *accouchement,*
in the midst of a nopalera, she will go; for females
are wonderfully heroical, when it is a question of alleviating the sorrows of one of their sex."

"Having thus obtained his friend's consent, our hero
went to the lady, who, after much supplication, suffered
herself to be persuaded to oblige him. She took half a
day to make her preparations, and, at last, set out for
St. Patricio, escorted by a corporal and two soldiers
of her husband's company, and provided with ample
credentials from major Linton and captain Letinez.
The latter was anxious to go along with her, but having
received strict orders from the general to hold himself
in readiness for an expedition towards the Guadelupe
river, he could not obey his inclination.

Soon after Mrs. Alvarez's departure, Urrea began
his march, eastward, leaving the prisoners, and a large
body of troops to guard them, under the command of
colonel Garrafon, with instructions to receive and open
all the despatches that might come from Bejar, directed
to him, and to execute with punctuality whatever orders
they might contain. Our hero, quite unsuspicious of
what was to happen, for, none besides the superior offi-

cers had been entrusted with the secret, left major
Linton in possession of his tent, and strictly directed
his servant to wait upon him with all possible attention.　He, also, recommended him to captain Alvarez,
and some other friends, and set out, quite unconcerned,
not doubting, but, at his return, he would enjoy the
satisfaction of seeing both father and daughter, happy
in the company of each other.

While our hero is marching towards the Guadelup
river, at the head of his company, in immediate attendance on his general; we will transfer the scene to St.
Patricio in order to make our readers witness what
passes between Miss Linton and captain Alvarez's
lady.　The latter, not understanding English, had no
sooner got to the village, than she repaired to the
priest's house, in order to beg him to accompany her
to Mrs. Jordan's, and act as interpreter.　The clergyman rendered wiser, or, at least, more condescending,
by his preceding altercation with Senor Letinez, dared
not refuse the favour asked by Senora Alvarez, and
both were soon in the young lady's presence.

Mrs. Alvarez, who had previously had a slight acquaintance with her, introduced herself with graceful
politeness, and father Supplegrowl, who could, when
he pleased, be as civil as any man, and was not devoid
of an elegant flow of language, addressed Miss Linton,
saying—"It gives me great pleasure, Madam, to be the
interpreter of the happy news this lady brings you.
Your father is alive and in good health.　It is true, he
is in the number of the prisoners who were taken on
the other side of Goliad; nevertheless, being now under the care of captain Letinez, there is no doubt every
attention will be paid to him.　But the letters which
this lady brings will inform you of those particularities
more in detail."

Upon hearing that her father was alive, Miss Linton, who had already heard of the skirmishes, or battles, as they were called, fought against the Texians,
and who had feared the worst; was seized with universal tremor, and, in spite of all her efforts to master
her emotion, shed tears of joy.　She raised her eyes

up to heaven, while her tears were trickling down her face, and seemed, for a moment, absorbed in mental prayer; after which, she read her father's letter with comparative composure.

Whilst she was perusing it, the company were silent; but as soon as it was over, Mrs. Jordan, who already anticipated her departure, and felt chagrined at the idea of losing her company, told her, "Now, hinney, you will be for laving the ould woman, I am afeard, and for going to your father; but, mind me, though I am glad he is safe and sound, yet I don't know how I shall be able to live without you, after being used to the loike. Och, dare! You were to me loike my own daghter, who died last fall; save that you could not work in the tater garden, as she did; for she was a stout crature of her years—God be merciful to her soul and the blessed St. Patrick. And now, I will be alone—all alone; with no body at all to keep me company, about the house—except the brindled cow—her that is so tame, you know. Och, och, but this is a sad hour for Peggy Jordan!"

"I must go to rejoin my father, indeed," said Miss Linton; "yet, my dear Mrs. Jordan, I hope to see you again, before long. Trust me, I will never forget the kindness with which I have been treated under your hospitable roof. I wish it were, at this time, in my power to offer you a just remuneration for it; but what I cannot do *now*, I hope to be shortly able to effect."

"The dare!" cried out Mrs. Jordan. "You spake of recompense to me! Is it money you mane, hinney? I want none from you, I am sure; but if you would do the poor Irish widow a favour, she could name a thing that would be quite asy for you, hinney!"

"It is granted, ere it is named," returned Miss Linton. "What is it?—It shall be done immediately."

"Well, I will tell you in your ear," resumed Mrs. Jordan, "for it is not for every body's hearing." Thereupon, she whispered to her guest:—" Be kind to young captain Letinez. He is a good lad, and well-favoured, and loves you dearer than the very drops of his heart.—The poor crature!—He wept, when he found you gone;—when them monstrous chates carried you off to Lopantitlan.—Yes, he cried for love!—Now, only think! a man loike him to wape!—You will break his heart, if you don't have him." Miss Linton coloured up to her ears, and gently pushed her hostess from her, interrupting her, at the same time, by informing senora Alvarez that she was ready to set out.

The latter lady could not help manifesting her surprise at the sight of so much readiness, and inquired whether she had no trunk to take along, to which Miss Linton answered by a smile, and said that her baggage was limited to so few articles, that she could easily pack them all in a reticule. "Inform this good lady," said she to father Supplegrowl, "that the Comanches left me but little, and *that* little was still diminished, when I fell into the hands of the Mexican soldiery; and, lastly, our shipwreck, in Corpus Christi bay, left me without a stich. In fact, my wardrobe has been kept up, here, at the expense of good Mrs. Jordan."

When this was translated to senora Alvarez, she manifested her feelings of compassion, by a string of pathetic exclamations, such as "*Pobre muchacha!—Que lastima!—Valga me Dios!*" But, as there was nothing to wait for, they both immediately set out, accompanied by their military retinue.

16*

CHAPTER XVII.

Our two female travellers proceeded towards Labahia with great rapidity, and were already within three
miles of the place, when they stopped under a wide-
spreading poplar, or cotton-tree, as some would call
it, to take their breakfast. It was on Palm Sunday
morning; and Mrs. Alvarez, in allusion to the religious
solemnity of the day—which is one of peculiar sanctity
among Roman Catholics—tore a green bough from the
tree under which they were sitting, and gave the young
lady, partly by signs, and partly in broken English, to
understand, that palms were, on that holy day, consecrated, in sign of spiritual joy, and carried about in
procession; and then, in a playful mood, twined a verdant crown, which she placed on Miss Linton's head,
signifying to her that she found some coincidence between the festival of the day and her present situation.
The sentiments which, in her disjointed mode of
utterance, she manifested, might, if translated into
English, have amounted to this : "After so many difficulties and dangers, from which Divine Providence has
delivered you, you are going to meet your father, therefore rejoice in God, and give him your sincere thanks."
Miss Linton, who understood her meaning, could not
help being moved, and in a silent, but impressive manner, pressed upon her bosom the hand which had just
been crowning her, when, at that moment, both were
startled by the sound of horses' feet.

They arose in surprise, which was soon changed
into terror, upon Mrs. Alvarez recognizing her husband's favourite servant, and Miss Linton that of captain Letinez, riding in haste, with the deepest consternation painted on their countenance. The two servants, in the extraordinary hurry of their march, liked
to have passed by the ladies without perceiving them;
but Mrs. Alvarez hailing them, they reined up their
horses, and manifested the greatest astonishment at
finding them in that spot.

This very brief pause was, however, soon followed by an explanation which increased the alarm of the ladies. "For God's sake, Madam," said captain Alvarez's servant, "mount and ride,—ride on, as fast as you can:—It is for life or death.—They are going to shoot the prisoners!—They have marched them out, under pretence of embarking them for Louisiana, according to the capitulation; but it was merely in order that none should remain concealed. Captain Letinez is absent, and my master has done all he could to save the life of that major, who is his friend; but he can obtain nothing. The American begs to see his daughter before his death.—Only one hour is granted him.—Oh, ride on,—ride on,—for Heaven's sake!"

Luckily for Miss Linton, her fortitude did not abandon her. Without shedding a tear, or making any useless lamentation, she was soon seated in the gig. Nature, however, could not long withstand the shock given to her feelings; and, in less than a minute after resuming their march, she fainted away on Mrs. Alvarez's bosom. The latter did not think proper to stop, whilst the old major's life was in danger; but, though she abated nothing of the rapidity of their march, she so successfully exerted herself with her smelling-bottle, that Miss Linton recovered her senses just as they approached the place whither the first lot of prisoners had been led to suffer death.

A double row of soldiers surrounded an empty space, and permitted no person to penetrate into it. In the middle, the Texian commander was sitting on a low stool, while the Mexican colonel, who presided at the execution, addressed him with a degree of asperity highly unbecoming. The address being concluded, Fanning took out his watch and a purse of gold, which he offered to the Mexican officer; but the latter had decency enough to refuse accepting it; whereupon, the Texian martyr, calling up to him some poor women, who were near, distributed the money amongst them. In the mean time, one of the soldiers appointed to shoot him, impelled by a kind of cruel impatience, came up, in order to lay his bosom bare, and Fanning, guessing at his intention, opened his coat and vest, and, silently pointing to his heart, with his right hand, looked upon his executioners, with a magnanimity, of which they cannot, to this day, speak without admiration. Now, the hour of his death had come. The Mexican colonel raised his sword on high, the drums gave the signal, the guards who attended formed into a long hollow square; the spectators, like a mighty wave receding from the foot of a cliff, with a sudden recoil, withdrew from the fatal spot, and the word was given. There! Fanning welters in his gore. Four bullets, with fatal aim, are lodged in his heart, and, while his limbs are yet palpitating and the muscles of his face quivering; his executioners rush forwards to divide his spoils. His clothes become an object of contention among them, and they

> " Hold o'er the dead their carnival,
> Gorging and growling o'er carcass and limb!"

But what was Miss Linton doing during this horrid scene?—She had espied her father, in the midst of a knot of prisoners, surrounded by dragoons, who kept their arms levelled at them, and in spite of all her efforts, tears and supplications, had not been able to open to herself a passage through their ranks; but when Fanning fell, there was a remissness of attention on their part, and Miss Linton, availing herself of it in order to cross the double file, flew towards her father. She threw herself on his neck, crying out: "Father, father!—I will die with you. No ball will reach you but after having pierced my bosom. Oh, Heavens, must we meet, merely to die in each other's embrace!"

Mrs. Alvarez, however, from whose arms Miss Linton had escaped, had sought out the commanding officer, and thrown herself at his knees, which she embraced, beseeching him, with the eloquence of true humanity, to spare major Linton. "See, yonder, colonel," did she say; "his daughter holds him locked in her arms: —you cannot reach *his* breast without slaughtering her. Will you shed the blood of so innocent and beautiful a creature?—will the most heroical filial piety ever seen meet with no better recompense from a Mexican officer, than cold blooded murder?—Have mercy, colonel, as you will, one day, wish for mercy yourself in presence of the everlasting God."

"Women are the devil," brutally interrupted colonel Garrafon:—"This one would make me weep, I believe." Thereupon, Alvarez himself coming up, he called out to him: "Here, captain,—here, Alvarez:—govern this wife of yours, man. She won't let me go about my duty."

"Oh, noble colonel," replied Alvarez: "I join my prayers to hers!—I call again upon you to spare this man. If you do not, his daughter will die along with him, and she is my friend Letinez's promised bride. He will not survive the loss of her!—And you know, he is the general favourite of the army. Save him, oh save him!—Here, I kneel to you!—I, who never knelt to man before;" and, suiting the action to the speech, he sank upon one knee, before Garrafon, and, seizing one of his hands, pressed it to his lips and bedewed it with his tears.

"You are all mad," replied the colonel, "and make me as mad as yourselves!—By heaven, I venture my post and perhaps my life!—But get up, Alvarez;—I cannot bear to see thee weeping. Take the man out, with his daughter. And, hark thee; carry him to the hospital, and let him turn physician. Be sure to let him know the necessity of this measure. You understand!—The *major* must go to the devil!—He must be dead and buried. Hey! you take my meaning."

Thereupon, drawing near the double line of dragoons, who surrounded the prisoners, he commanded them to open a passage for Alvarez, who led away major Linton, thus suddenly transformed into a physician, without his own concurrence or knowledge, and soon installed him in his new employ, giving him short instructions on the part he was to act.

They were interrupted, in their conversation, by the firing of the soldiers, who continued their murderous day's work. The unfortunate prisoners were shot by

fifty or sixty at a time; and those whom the gun miss-
ed, or only crippled, were, afterwards, despatched with
the bayonet or the lance.

In the second lot, were ten or twelve *Catholic* Irish-
men, from St. Patricio, who called for a priest; but
were not permitted to enjoy the consolation. There
was a clergyman of their own church, within a short
distance, who might have been sent for:—a short respite
was sufficient; but their cries were not listened to. It
was, according to the belief of their executioners, con-
signing them to the everlasting flames of hell; and yet
it was done!—The cries, and prayers, and calls of the
unhappy men, who died unshriven and unabsolved,
melted even the rough Mexican troopers; but were
drowned by the beating of drums, and the awful work
went on, until the whole number of the prisoners,
amounting to five hundred and twenty, had been sacrificed! Seven or eight only were saved, chiefly under
the plea of being physicians.

In the last lot, came two Baptist preachers, who went
on, exhorting their comrades. When they had arrived at the place where they were to suffer, the eldest
called upon his companions to join him in prayer.—
Not one refused.—Even many of the Mexicans, though
unable to understand the language he used, fell on
their knees, in imitation of the Texians. Then, with
an enthusiasm of which none but an eye-witness can
form an idea, the *elder* called upon God, saying: " We
return unto thee, O Almighty Being, who, from high
heaven, directest all things for thy greater glory. This
body, which thou gavest us, is now going to fall a sacrifice to the rights of mankind, and the liberty of thy
holy gospel; but, oh! vouchsafe, thou, to receive our
spirit in thy bosom; and grant true freedom to this
land, which has drunk the blood of our companions in
arms. Deliver it from the darkness and superstition
that overshadow it, and inspire the people with sentiments of repentance for their deeds of cruelty. *Thy
martyrs we are; but lay it not to their charge.—We,
who bleed beneath their knife, beg it of thee!—En-*

lighten that obdurate priesthood, who have thirsted for
our blood."

Here, he was interrupted by the voice of the commander, who, in a rage, called out: "*Fuego, fuego!
Acabad con ellos.*" But yet, as the bullets whistled,
and his companions fell around him, the preacher lifted up to heaven both his arms, reddened with gore,
and cried: "We come, we come, O Lord!—In thee
we die."

He had no time to continue, for, one of the dragoons, running up to him, cleft his head, at a single
stroke, and was followed by his comrades, who fright-
fully hacked the dying and the dead, and soon achieved what their guns had left unfinished.

With the two preachers, perished young Brashears
and Duval, whom Marinez, the officer we have already honourably mentioned, had promised to protect.
He would certainly have saved their lives had he been
present; but care had been taken to send him upon a
remote expedition, and, when he returned, he found
his friend already dead.

Dear, unfortunate young men! May the tear which
bedews this page, prove to your manes how beloved
you were by one who had trod the same academic
groves with you; and, whilst your bones are bleaching
on the grassy plains of Goliad, may these few lines,
consecrated to your memory, convey to the heart of
every one who reads them, sentiments of detestation for
the act of cruelty, of which you were the victims. In
you, Kentucky lost two gallant sons; still, the remembrance of your death will nerve many of your valiant
fellow-citizens to fight for that freedom which was
cemented by your blood. Land of Kentucky! country
of my youth, *these* have extended thy moral empire!—
These have concurred to found a new home, in the
South, for thy numerous progeny.—Oh, forget them not
in thy records of fame!

A LAMENT ON THE GOLIAD MASSACRE.

I.

O'er Goliad's plain had swept the night
And Sabbath rose in purple light,
　When thund'ring drum and clarion bright
Arous'd the captive from his lowly bed
And by the perjur'd victor he was led,
　　　　Unconscious, to the field of slaughter.

II.

With wanton jest and smiling glance
The murd'rous bands hail their advance :—
　In sign of gladness waves each lance,
While, circling their devoted victims round,
They close, with serried files, the fatal ground
　　　　Where blood in streams shall flow like water.

III.

The chief on high hath rais'd his sword
And to his soldiers giv'n the word :—
　Their heart no mercy can afford ;
And, slaying, they rejoice ; and o'er the slain
Triumphing, they exult in proud disdain,
　　　　And rest as from a deed of glory.

IV.

There died the good, there died the brave,
That of priests would not be the slave ;—
　His bones shall bleach without a grave,
The wild dog gnaw'd his heart and lapp'd his blood,
And they of Rome the crimson'd spot have trod,
　　　　To consecrate with hymns *their victory !*

CHAPTER XVIII.

The march of Urrea's division through the south-
west portion of Texas, was like the passage of an army
of Cossacks. Every thing of a moveable nature, was
pillaged. Flocks of horned cattle, of which that country
contained, at the time of the invasion, a quantity sufficient to support the Mexican army five or six years,
were every night, slaughtered, in wanton prodigality;
a fat bullock being frequently killed for the sake of a
favourite piece of meat, for which some of the officers
happened to have a craving, and the rest of the carcass
being left to rot, without benefitting any body. Forget-
ful that, soon or late, they would be obliged to return
the same way, and miss, then, the provisions they were
now wasting, they proceeded, destroying every thing
they could not use, and laying the country bare.

In proportion as they advanced eastwardly and drew
nearer to the American settlements, they found articles
of furniture with the use of which they were totally unacquainted, and which piqued their curiosity, no less
than they awakened their avarice. At the Mission,
even before reaching Goliad, they saw some frame
houses belonging to Irish settlers, with glass windows
and painted venetian blinds, and this struck the minds
of the common soldiers, as the *ne plus ultra* of magnificence; but when they came to the town of Victoria, on
the Guadalupe river, their expectations rose still higher, at the sight of brick buildings of three stories in
height, and their covetousness was excited by the opening of some large stores full of merchandise.

The general, however, and his officers took care to
have the picking of the choicest, and the soldiers, though
possessed of the best will in the world, obtained but
poor gleanings after them, being obliged to put up with
coarse, unwieldy, or frail articles. To them was abandoned the iron and crockery ware, as well as the most
part of the glass furniture, and with such goods as these,
they loaded their wives, and the sumpter mules which

17

they secretly appropriated to themselves. The immense number of women who followed the army, in fact, diminished the necessity of beasts of burden. Every one of them, immediately upon getting what she considered a valuable lot, would return to Matamoros, sometimes on horseback, sometimes in an ox cart; but, more frequently, on foot, tottering under the load she carried.

Then, also, began the desertions. Men would shave their upper lip, and put on female apparel, the costume of Mexican women, which admits of a shawl being partly drawn over the face, favouring the deception; and the style of features being nearly as coarse in one sex as in the other. Thus, dozens of tender couples, in disguise, would pass through the outposts, in the character of females, returning from a rag fair, and loaded with trumpery. One man was seen with a load of smoothing irons, walking with an elastic step and a joyous countenance, as though he had been carrying away all the riches of Louisiana; while his wife, at his side, sweated under a burden of crockery ware, exclusively consiting of tea-pots!—Another had seized upon two kegs of hog's lard and a box of spermacetti candles, which he expected to sell at a high price, in Monterrey, a city more than nine hundred miles distant. A fourth one had loaded the massive feet of a billiard table upon a mule he had stolen, and put a parcel of empty bottles, on the top, in order to complete his cargo!—But the most ludicrous spectacle was afforded by a fellow who carried on his back a large yankee clock, the weights of which were dangling down, even to the calf of his legs, against which they thumped, at every step he fetched, keeping time, as he went along. Vexed beyond measure, the trooper kept swearing at the weights, but durst not throw them away, thinking that they were an essential part of the curious machine of which he had possessed himself. The smartest, however, at this kind of work was Urrea himself, who, though acting on a larger scale, fell, sometimes, into no less ludicrous mistakes.

He had no sooner crossed the Guadelupe river, and

rifled the town of Victoria, than he resolved to wait a
while for the troops he had left behind, at Goliad.
Whilst waiting for them, he sent his scouts about, to
sweep the country, and one of these soon returned with
the strange information that he had found a breed of
hornless cows, which gave an immense quantity of
milk. As the general had never before heard of this
hornless breed of cattle, he was rather dubious of the
truth of the information, and one of his officers warned
him against the artifices of those Jews, the *Colonists*,
who, probably, had dealings with Sathanas, and might
have contrived this, in order to entrap him. Being,
however, what the Spaniards denominate *un espiritu
fuerte*, (anglice, an unbeliever,) Urrea made it a point
to see with his own eyes, and commanded some of the
above mentioned cows to be brought into his presence.
The cows came, and after he had felt their foreheads,
and convinced himself they never had horns, and that
there was no deception in the case, he was delighted
with this *phenomenon*, in natural history, (as he termed
it,) and seized upon forty of those highly privileged animals, which he sent, under a strong escort, to the state
of Sonora, a distance of no less than seventeen hundred
miles, to stock his *hacienda*.

The country about the Guadelupe river is the most
fertile it is possible to imagine; but, being somewhat
swampy, it is inferior in point of salubrity to the district about Bejar and the river San Anton, which may
be considered as the paradise of the new world. To
the most salubrious climate, it unites the most varied
and enchanting scenery, consisting of an elegant mixture of hill and dale, watered by large springs, which
furnish abundant supplies for irrigation. The temperature is such that winters are hardly felt, and two yearly
crops of Indian corn are the regular tribute of husbandry. The sugar cane lasts eight years, and a certain species of cotton, three; their product being superior in quality to what is grown in Louisiana. To
all these advantages, is to be added the facility of raising cattle, the wild grass being so excellent and abundant, that they multiply without any care on the part

of their owners. And then, the fruits! From the orange
and *chirimoya* of the south, to the apple and pear of
northern climates, the immense variety of Pomona's
realm embellishes that land, and enriches the husband-
man. The most delightful districts of the south of
France, with all the wealth and refinements which ages
of civilization have accumulated, do not deserve to be
compared with this blessed spot, such as it is, even
now, when its natural resources have hardly begun to
be developed, nor could the island of Calypso itself,
in the fabled description of Fenelon, enter into competition.

Through the southern parts of this district, did Urrea's troops, now, spread themselves, rioting in wild
exultation, and the mass of plunder they had got together, by the time they reached the Rio Colorado,
was so considerable, that the general's share alone
loaded fifteen wagons, of those he had taken from Fanning. Them he was careful to send, betimes, to the
city of Durango, under the superintendence of a trusty
servant, and what could not be appropriated to the
decoration of his own house was sold for a large sum
of money.

He met, however, with some singular disappoint-
ments in his attempts at removing objects which he
considered as valuable, and one of these, in particular,
is so ludicrous, that we cannot resist the temptation of
relating it. A little marauding party, consisting of
five soldiers, having strayed to some distance, up a
creek called "*La Reservada*," rejoined the main body,
in great alarm, bearing upon their shoulders one of
their companions, sadly wounded, with a gash, that had
penetrated the nose and frontal bone. Upon being
questioned about the cause of this accident, they described a monstrous piece of machinery, which, they
shrewdly conjectured, had been set up by the Colonists,
for the express purpose of injuring the Mexican army.
They represented it as an immense knife, of solid
steel, moving perpendicularly, with the swiftness of
lightning, and connected with various wheels; the
whole, so complicated, that they had not been able to

discover the principle of motion. "The entire machine, Senor," said the corporal who commanded the party, "was at rest, when we got there, and entered the lofty shed, under which it is erected. We proceeded to examine every corner, thinking some of the rebels might be concealed in some nook or other, when, suddenly, upon Juan Ferdajo pushing aside a piece of wood, that dangled from the roof, the whole machine was put in motion, and at a most tremendous rate! Wheels began to whirl; levers, to creak; iron chains, to drag ponderous logs; and the knife that I told you of, to saw, up and down, with such a velocity, that the eye could not follow its motion. We fled for our lives, being frightened; I mean, we *retreated*, thinking it might be some stratagem of the enemy, but Juan Dolos had drawn too close to the treacherous *knife* to escape unhurt, and it cut him in the way your excellency beholds. The poor fellow followed us about a hundred yards, calling for help, and crying out that he was losing all his blood, whereupon, seeing we were not pursued, I turned back to take him up. Now, it is my firm belief that this *invention* was contrived by those heretics, those infernal Jews, in order to cut us off. And they deal in the black art, for, how could they, without the help of the devil, have invented such a thing? Oh! what a pity we have no chaplain with us. Had we but one of the Franciscans of Zacatecas, he could, in an instant, dispel this *brujeria*; but so it is! we are poorly provided. Not half a pint of holy water in the whole division! There is but one chaplain for so large an army, and the Senor Presidente keeps him with himself!"

Urrea was not superstitious; of course, he feared not the supernatural powers attributed to the Texians; yet, from the strange description he heard, he conceived some dread of an ambush, or some other stratagem, and resolved to go himself a-reconnoitering, at the head of four hundred chosen men.

His orders were immediately issued, and the party were soon on their march. They approached the place in the greatest silence, with their arms ready; and,

17*

upon drawing near, were startled by the noise of the machine, at the sight of which, not a few of the soldiers crossed themselves, and cried out: " *Valga me Dios!*" and "*Ave, Maria, purissima!*" but were immediately disturbed, in their devotional feelings, by a broad peal of laughter, which proceeded from a Hungarian, a lieutenant in the regiment of Tampico. This officer, being questioned upon the cause of this scandalous cachinnation, could not help answering that their present expedition reminded him of the adventure of Don Quixotte and the fulling-mills; for, what they beheld, was neither more nor less than a saw-mill!

Upon receiving this information, Urrea, though mortified, acted like a gentleman, and joined in the laughter; but, though he, thus, in good taste, gave vent to his mirth, he did not lose sight of his interest; and, after having examined the machine, seen it work, and admired its ingenuity, resolved to send it to his own farm, in the state of Durango. The execution of this order, however, found insuperable difficulties in the unwieldiness of the pieces of which the mill consisted; and the general was forced, much to his sorrow, to renounce his project.

The Mexican commander continued his march towards the Brazos, without meeting with any considerable difficulty; but, before reaching Brazoria, finding himself under the necessity of sending a trusty officer to Santa Anna, in order to communicate to him certain alterations he wished to make in the plan of operations which had been sketched out for his division, he selected our hero, as the most intelligent person he could find.

Young captain Letinez, therefore, came in contact with the President of the republic; and, though the latter was accustomed to browbeat and treat with brutality any one of his inferiors who ventured upon opposing his plans, yet the young officer behaved with so much independence, and argued in favour of Urrea's ideas, with so much perspicuity and force of reasoning, that he carried his point, and the general-in-chief assented to the proposed alterations.

Whilst captain Letinez was vindicating the correctness of his general's views, with the President of the republic, he knew so well how to temper his resistance by demonstrations of respect, and his military frankness was so well set off by gentlemanly courtesy, as could not fail to charm one, who, though not well bred himself, was peculiarly pleased with elegance of manners in his inferiors; and the young man's information appeared so important to the general-in-chief, that he became desirous of securing his immediate attendance about his person. Captain Letinez, therefore, received an official order to join the main body of the army, and was appointed aid-de-camp to the President, whilst another officer was despatched to carry an answer to Urrea.

Our hero being, by such an unforeseen series of events, prevented from hearing any thing about Miss Linton and her father, or providing for their welfare, in person, had no other resource than to write to Alvarez and several other friends, to recommend his *proteges* to their attention; and he doubted not that, from their attachment to him, they would comply with his request.

It is not our intention to follow him through the various military movements in which he participated. The fool-hardiness of Santa Anna, who, after having seen a thousand of his soldiers killed, at the storming of Bejar, by two hundred backwoodsmen, still persisted in the notion that the Texians were inferior in bravery and intelligence, to the peasantry of his own country, prompted him to rush headlong, with his vanguard, into the very snare prepared for him; and the fatal twenty-first of April taught him the difference between the two races.

The action of San Jacinto has been sufficiently celebrated through the world to render a description of it, in this book, a work of supererogation; but it is not likely that its results have been yet justly estimated by any one not intimately acquainted with Mexico. What that battle made Texas, it will remain, at least, for ages to come. (14) In twenty-five minutes, a country larger than France and Italy, was

lost to the Mexican republic, and an opening made for
the Anglo-American race, to the immense mineral
wealth of Chihuahua, the far greater part of which is
yet unexplored. The Texians, after the first heat of
the battle was over, generously gave quarter to the
vanquished, though they would have been justifiable by
the laws of war, in retaliating upon them; and it was
to this merciful conduct, on their part, our hero owed
the prolongation of his life.

When he beheld the whole Mexican vanguard thrown
into sudden disorder, he and some other officers tried
in vain to rally their men. Having seen one of their
own captains killed by his soldiers, whom he attempted
by blows, to force against the enemies, they became
convinced that the defeat was irretrievable, and that
they had nothing better to do than to follow the stream
of those who fled. They found, however, their retreat
cut off, by the destruction of the bridge, beyond which
they had incautiously advanced, and, after dispersing
themselves in confusion, and skulking for some time
in the woods, being hunted down by the riflemen, they
all yielded themselves prisoners.

Now, our hero enjoyed a great advantage in being
able to speak the language of his captors. A Texian
officer of rank, to whom he had surrendered, prejudiced
in his favour by his noble mien and his elegant manner
of expressing himself, took him under his protection,
and exercised, with military frankness, such rites of
hospitality as his own distressed condition left in his
power.

Great was the surprise of the victors to see amongst
their prisoners a number of officers of gentlemanly appearance and good breeding, for, judging from the ex-
cesses their army had committed on its passage, they
thought them so many monsters, insatiable with human
blood. The fact is, however, that the Mexican race is
remarkable for its mildness. They are, indeed, susceptible of sudden mental exaltation, and, whilst under the empire of political phrenzy, they will, sometimes, forget their character, yet, in general, they are
neither cruel, nor ferocious. It is true, the number of

assassinations by highway robbers is considerable; but we make bold to assert, that any portion of Europe, suddenly placed under the empire of the same political circumstances as Mexico, would soon present a greater number.

In the western parts of the old continent, now most distinguished for their morality and intelligence, Scotland, for example, murder and theft have been, within the memory of man, of more frequent occurrence than they are, at this day, in Mexico; yet, how soon was a wholesome reformation introduced into that country, by a strict execution of the laws? The same would take place in the land of *Anahuac*, by a rigorous administration of justice, for, we repeat it, the people are docile, and easily receive impressions from their civil rulers.

In fact, instead of being surprised at the sight of the immorality they exhibit, we should, rather, wonder that they have not fallen into utter confusion and absolute barbarism. Moral instruction is almost null in the country. The priests are in too small number even to discharge the *mechanical* duties of their religion, hardly sufficient for the administration of baptism, marriage, and the celebration of masses and funeral rites; so that, even if they would, they have no time to instruct the people. Their parishes are too large, averaging, at least, sixty miles in extent, which prevents the most of the peasantry from repairing to church above once or twice a year. The mass of the clergy, moreover, are grossly ignorant, most of the *vicars*, or labouring priests, hardly understanding the Latin of their own breviary; and where a bright exception occurs, either in point of knowledge, or morality, (which is more frequently the case, amongst parish priests, than is believed abroad,) the subject thus distinguished generally lacks zeal and that *Esprit de corps* which renders the French clergy so efficient.

To this capital defect, of absolute ignorance in the people, is joined a complete perversion of justice, in the tribunals of the country. In *civil* affairs, the magistrates are as accessible to bribery as Turkish Cadis, and, in the cognizance of crimes, as nobody pays them to be severe, they, of course, give way to the mildness of human nature, and almost always suffer the guilty to escape. Will it be believed that in the large state of Cohahuila, famous, throughout all the North, for murders and robberies, no capital punishment has been awarded, but once, in the space of ten years, and then, merely, because the murder had been committed in a church, during the night, and upon the person of a friar? In the organization of the courts of *first instance,* all the rules of common sense seem to have been put at defiance. Every parish is governed by three or four Alcaldes, concentrating in their hands all powers, (except the military and ecclesiastical,) and obliged to labour incessantly in the administration of justice, or management of the municipal concerns of the people, without any emoluments from fees of office, or the public treasury; so that these posts would become intolerable burdens and ruinous to the incumbents, were it not for the bribes the latter receive. This causes all honest men to shun them, and when they happen to be elected, they must be forced to accept, by the fear of heavy fines. Moreover, the Alcaldes are seldom professional men, acquainted with the laws they undertake to administer. Even, when they happen to be honest, they act without any other rule than common sense, and, concentrating in their body, powers which are every where else, carefully kept separate, it is not surprising that they continually fall into the arbitrary. Add to this, that the clergy and military are exempt from the common jurisdiction of the judges of the land, even in civil causes, and can be sued, the former, only before the spiritual courts, and the latter before their superior officers, and you can form an approximative idea of the confusion and want of justice which this country exhibits. Moral ignorance in the people, general bribery in the administration of civil justice, and impunity in criminal cases joined to the extravagant privileges of the priests and soldiers; have done much to demoralize this nation; but it is truly wonderful that they have not done more.

CHAPTER XIX.

Our hero, now brought into contact with a foreign race, and a people of a different religion and modes of life, had new chances of enlarging the sphere of his ideas upon civil government, and human nature. He saw, with his own eyes, a moral phenomenon, which had never, till then, taken place in christendom, and shall not, probably, happen a second time:—a *nation* of twenty-five thousand people, resisting one of seven millions, and, by means of coolness and public spirit, making their resistance good. His mind was not mature enough, nor his experience of the world sufficiently enlarged, to enable him justly to estimate the causes which had produced so strange a result. Neither would his patriotic feelings have permitted him to allow them their just weight, had he been clear-sighted enough to discover them; but yet he was eager to study the Texians, supposing that, in them, he would see a sample of the Anglo-Americans, whom, on account of his father, he was rather inclined to esteem.

He first directed his attention to their religious tenets; for, this is a subject, which, with a Mexican, whether pious, or impious, is always uppermost; but captain Letinez could not realise, amongst them, any thing bearing the semblance of religion. He saw no images in their tents,—no beads about the men,—nor pious medals hanging from their necks:—They never made the sign of the cross,—nor prayed,—nor had they any thing like a religious service on Sundays; so that, although convinced they must have a worship, he was at a loss to guess what it might be.

The notions he had conceived of religion, (which will appear strange to our American readers,) were, that, no matter in what its speculative tenets might consist, its *external* part should be fixed and formal. In Mexico, Catholicity, though of a more *plastic* nature than is generally supposed by Protestants, has put on the peculiar rigidity and inflexibility of the an-

cient religion of the Aztecs. The barrenness of invention, and propensity to servile imitation, which are
the distinguishing characteristics of the mass of the
people, probably have had a considerable influence in
bringing about this result; but, whatever may have
been the cause, the ceremonial of the church of Rome
admits, there, of fewer local differences, than in any
other part of the world, not even excepting the Pope's
dominions. There is not, through the vast extent of
Mexico, the least variation in the ritual. From the
frontiers of Guatemala, to Santa Fe, the churches are,
everywhere, scrupulously built upon the same plan,—
the same number of bells, suspended in every steeple,
—the statues of the holy family, carved in the same
posture, with the same inflexible rigidity of features,
and dressed exactly in the same style,—the same processions are performed at the same hours, and the same
cut of ecclesiastical furniture is preserved.

Imbued with ideas of religion, such as the state we
have been describing is likely to inspire, our hero could
not help wondering at the total want of formality, in
this important matter, amongst the Texians; and,
though afraid to offend, he inquired from his host in
what Protestantism consisted.

His entertainer happened to be a man of education
and philosophical cast of mind, noways hampered by
blind adherence to any peculiar creed; and, in order
to enlighten our hero on the subject, answered him that
the Protestant religion consisted rather of *negatives:*—
"Catholicity," said he, "is like a figure dressed up for
winter, with cloak and cape, and linings of fur.—Protestantism is like a young fellow in his summer disha-
bille. It may be called Christianity in *roundabout.*
Our creed sits upon us as light as summer-air: it is of
a most plastic nature, suffering itself to be moulded
into any form or shape. There is but one single point
in it which can be considered as unalterable, and in
which we all agree: it is to *protest.*—Hence comes our
name! To be serious with you, my dear friend," continued he, "we are now divided into so many petty
schisms and parties, that the whole is well nigh reduced

to an impalpable powder, having lost all the original leaven and savour. It will be necessary that some strong genius arise, to *knead that dust*, and fashion it anew into shape. Such an event is not, probably, far distant: North America is ready for it; but he must be an original and powerful mind, indeed, that will undertake to effect the moral conquest of such a people.

"As for *us*, here, in Texas, you may be sure that we are noways particular about religion, since we reported ourselves as Roman Catholics, though mortal enemies to that system of faith; yet think not that we deny the necessary articles which constitute the basis of all religions, such as the existence of a Supreme Being, the spirituality of the soul, and a future state of rewards and punishments. We hold fast that indispensable substratum, without which, not even civil government could be maintained. I must say, also, however harsh it may sound in your ears, and deprecating all ideas of offending you, that we are pure in morals, at least, far more so than your people. There are no highway robberies amongst us, nor thefts, except what proceeds from negroes. Whenever we feel tempted to wrong our fellow-citizens, we go about it in a mild, peaceable manner, under *cover of law!*— The party attacked is in no bodily fear; he can foresee and take his measures! In point of chastity, also, the most important and influential qualification of Northern nations, we are infinitely superior to you.— Lust is, with us, hateful and shameful: with you, it is a matter of indifference. *This* is the chief curse of the South: the leprosy which unnerves both body and mind. It is what caused the Roman empire to sink under the assaults of the Northern barbarians. Notwithstanding all the science, policy, and refinement of the *Queen of the earth*, she was struck, as with a moral consumption, by this vice; and all her strength was swept away by a deluge from the North. A mighty wave is again starting from the same point, and it will sweep even to the Equator. The Southern races must be renewed, and the United States are the *officina gen-*

18

tium for the New Continent. Your country cannot
withstand the shock, nor your people resist. How
could they?—Who is there to rouse them and direct
them?—Your priests?—Are they not sunk into gross
immorality and ignorance?—What will a sacrilegious
priesthood, loaded with concubines and bastards, do for
you?—Are they not polluted to their heart's core?—
Have they not introduced a pestilent distinction between morality and religion? It is not so with Protestantism. Christianity is, with *us*, one and the same
thing with morality, or, at least, we never attempt to
separate them. There are, undoubtedly, hypocrites
amongst us also; but, I would say, comparatively few;
and they know that they are cheats and condemned.
They cannot trust in outward rites, as possessing any
value of themselves, in order to lay a deceitful "*unction*" to their souls. Your religion, I know, possesses
in itself all the rules of morality, and the most efficient means of spiritually enforcing the practice of
virtue; and those who assert the contrary, utter an
abominable calumny; but the kings of Spain *modified
it*, for the use of their colonies, and warped it to their
purpose, and your statesmen are not likely to succeed
in purifying it. Catholicity, with you, receives a
strange hue, from your system of civilization, which
is, in the main, too much a-kin to the Morisco."

Captain Letinez, who was not endowed with a great
stock of patience, could bear no more without retaliating upon his entertainer, and interrupted him, exclaiming, "And tell me, if you please, how does it happen
that so moral and chaste a people have so many mulattoes amongst them?—You may travel the whole extent
of Mexico, without meeting so many individuals of
mongrel breed, though, amongst us, marriages between
the various casts are neither prohibited by law, nor
stigmatised by public opinion. And your slavery!—
what have you to say to that?"

"Ah, ah," replied the other; "there, you think you
have embarrassed me; but I can produce good arguments
to prove that negroes are an inferior race, made pur-
posely to be hewers of wood and drawers of water to

the whites. Do you wish scripture authority?—I can quote the curse of Noah against one of his sons and his posterity, and nothing prevents us from supposing that our negroes are descended from Ham. In that case, we do nothing more than fulfilling the scripture, you know. Do you wish for philosophical proofs?—Dissect a black man, and you will find the internal structure of his body somewhat different from that of the whites. It is some-where about the lumbary regions, anatomists say! does not this make my assertion good, and prove them to be intended by nature to serve us as playthings?—If you want metaphysical arguments, we can show that negroes are inferior to us in judgment, and though some of their fanatical friends represent them as naturally superior in warmth of fancy and quickness of imagination, we are not bound to acknowledge the truth of the fact. But let us drop this subject. It is dangerous to treat of it, even in the coolest manner. My neighbours might mistake you for an abolitionist, and in that case you would become hateful. The suspicion of abolitionism operates like the plague here."

In conformity with his entertainer's wishes, they turned the conversation on another topic,—the progress of the mechanical arts in the United States; and our hero was lost in amaze when the great revolution in-troduced into the civilized world by the application of steam to machinery was explained to him. Steamers, locomotive engines and power looms were the subject of his wonder! He had indeed, before, heard of these things, but had no idea that they were applied on so ex-tensive a scale to the purposes of social life. He had been under a vague impression that these inventions were, rather, philosophical playthings, calculated to show forth the ingenuity of their authors, but not to be-come popular, much less had he suspected that they were destined to change, one day, the face of christen-dom, and increase the comforts of mankind to such a degree, that, before many years have elapsed, a com-mon labourer, among the decendants of the Celtic race, shall partake of more enjoyments, than the wealthiest nobleman did, five hundred years ago, in the most powerful monarchies of Europe.

Now, that his curiosity was awakened, he bitterly lamented having lost his liberty, for he anxiously desired to travel through the countries where those prodigies are met with at every step; but, though a prisoner, along with his fellow soldiers, he found the rigors of his captivity softened by his love of reading, and the interest he had created in the breast of his captor.

Filisola, having agreed to obey the instructions which Santa Anna, after falling into the power of the Texians, had sent him; the latter abstained from avenging on their prisoners the massacre of Goliad; while the old Italian fox appeared to grant, as a matter of favour, and in order to save the President's life, a retreat, which necessity imperiously demanded of him, and without which his army would have been entirely lost.

A portion of the Texian forces followed Filisola in his march, through swamps and thickets, while the rest of Houston's troops were dismissed; a part of the prisoners being previously secured in various *depots*, and some being distributed amongst the farmers, in order to be supported with more facility on their different plantations.

Under this new arrangement, it was not difficult, for the gentleman who had been our hero's captor, to obtain leave to take him to his farm, which was situated a few leagues west of the Sabine river.

Once there, captain Letinez had greater facility for studying the domestic habits and modes of life of the Anglo-Americans; things which, though seldom descanted upon by writers on morality or legislation, have a far greater influence on the political existence of nations than is generally supposed. He saw in the Texian yeomanry, a bold, undaunted race, of an outward bearing, bordering on the profane, which one might have easily mistaken for ferocity; yet, at bottom, humane, hospitable and generous. He was peculiarly struck with the noble liberty with which, in the more refined circles, the sexes commune and converse together;

whilst, in his own country, the least communication between them is looked upon as suspicious, and sufficient
to ruin the character of the most respectable female.
The process of husbandry, also, appeared to him to have
attained a high degree of improvement. He admired
the American plough, and wondered that the Mexicans
were still content to put up with the rude *aratrum* of
barbarous ages. The extent to which female in-door
industry is carried, excited no less his attention, being
not a little supprised to see the spinning wheel and the
common loom in operation, in every family, whereas, in
Mexico, the like is never found, except in extensive
manufactories; the weaving process being carried on,
amongst the poor farmers, by a rough portative instrument, similar to the one used by the wild Arabs, in the
great desert of Zaara, as described by captain Ryley;
whilst the good wives' method of spinning has not even
yet reached the dignity of the distaff.

We will not enter into any further details, relative
to the remarks our hero passed on the more advanced
state of civilization enjoyed by the Anglo-American
race, whether political, moral, economical or religious;
fearing, even, that what we have said should be thought
irrelevant in such a work as this; the greater number
of our readers being probably rather inclined to look,
in a novel, for emotions and amusement, than for instruction. Nevertheless, as usefulness is the main object we have in view, we hope to be excused for having
introduced into our history so many details, hitherto,
hardly ever mentioned by novelists. Mexico is behind
hand, by at least three centuries, in politics, religion,
and civil economy. It is now, by a series of strange
circumstances, effectually brought to wrestle against
all the weight of modern civilization, and the glare of
modern lights. The portraiture of the *contest* cannot
help being interesting to the reflecting mind, and
though we are far from believing ourselves adequate
to the task, yet we would think ourselves happy,
should we obtain the praise of having "started the
game."

18*

CHAPTER XX.

With a sufficient share of tranquility and comfort
would our hero have spent his time on his friend's
plantation, every day's occurrence having for him the
zest and piquancy of novelty; and his pursuit after
knowledge being diversified by bodily exercises most
fitted to his age, such as hunting, fishing and riding;
had not his heart been prayed upon by gloomy and distressing thoughts. The uncertainty of Miss Linton
and her father's fate incessantly occupied his mind,
and the absolute ignorance in which he was of the
movements of the southern division of the Mexican
army, since he had himself joined Santa Anna, made
him fear the worst for the dear object of his affection.

He had heard from the Texians the history of the
massacre at Labahia, and though he believed it exaggerated, yet he dreaded lest Mr. Linton's life should have
been sacrificed, in which case, he doubted not, the
young lady would not survive him. Even, should the
major's life have been spared, in what situation could
he and his daughter find themselves, in the midst of an
army forced to retreat in confusion, through a ruined
and deserted country, where, at the time of their tri-
umphal advance, the necessaries of life were doled out
to the soldiers with a sparing hand? To think that
Miss Linton, so delicately brought up, should, after
having already experienced such heavy calamities, be
exposed to fatigues and deprivations of every kind,
and, perhaps, to the horrors of famine, in the midst of
a disorganised army, where the bands of discipline
could no longer repress the licentiousness of the soldiery, and where unprincipled officers might be tempted to take advantage of the general disorder, to insult
her, was for him the bitterest mental torment he had
ever felt. Every day his grief grew more intense, and
its ravages became visible on his countenance. In vain
did his friend try to dissipate his sorrow; his efforts
proved unavailing. At last, providence offered him

the facility of regaining his liberty, when he the least expected it.

On a plantation, adjoining that of his captor, lived a wealthy physician, who had, amongst his servants, a quarteroon, of so light a complexion, that, in many a country, he might have easily passed for a white man. This slave was rather a favourite with his master, who employed him chiefly in hunting, in order to provide game for his larder. Our hero had, frequently, met him in the woods, and, by chance, exchanged a few words, but never paid a serious attention to him, until the following circumstance awakened his curiosity.

He, one day, found the quarteroon, reclined at the foot of a tree, fast asleep, with his gun by his side, and a book on his knees. Not a little surprised that one of his condition should know how to read, our hero gently took up the volume; but, his astonishment grew when he found it was Milton's Paradise Lost! While he was turning the leaves, looking for a favourite passage, the slave awoke, and, seeing captain Letinez with his book in his hand, started up in dismay, and, with an air of supplication, exclaimed, "for God's sake, sir, do not betray me to my master."

"Betray you to your master," replied the Mexican, "and for what? But, I understand! you have stolen the book?"

"Oh, no, sir. Not so bad as that, neither," resumed the quarteroon. "The book is my lawful property; but I meant to beseech you to keep secret the discovery that you have just now made,—that I know how to read. Were it to come to my master's knowledge, it would prove the greatest of misfortunes for me, and cause him to sell me, probably, to some planter of Louisiana. I hope, sir, you will not refuse to listen to my prayer. Being yourself acquainted with misfortune, you will bear a compassionate heart."

Captain Letinez thought within himself, this was a pretty close hit at the famous verse of Virgil,

"Non ignora mali, miseris succurrere disco,"

and he was moved by the elegance of the sentiment expressed by the slave, still more than by his tone of supplication, to condescend to promise secrecy, which his suppliant thought of so much importance to himself.

The latter thanked him with the truest effusion of gratitude for what he considered as an act of extraordinary condescension, and both began to converse on literary subjects, with which the quarteroon was tolerably well acquainted. He possessed a small collection of the modern classics, which he kept carefully concealed, and in the reading of which he frequently indulged, during his hunting rambles, and sometimes also, he would borrow a volume from his master's library, while the latter was absent, which happened oftentimes, on account of his extensive practice in the exercise of the medical profession.

In the stolen enjoyment of this mental luxury, our hero had it in his power to assist the slave, and he made no scruple to lend him, from time to time, all the interesting works he could obtain. Thus, they frequently met, and pity, on the one hand, and gratitude, on the other, soon gave to their intimacy, the charms of friendship.

We are afraid that, by this avowal, we will in the mind of many of our readers, ruin the character of our gallant captain, and that he shall, from henceforth, be considered as a degraded being; if many have not already turned from him with loathing, or thrown away our book in disgust; and indeed we have reflected a long time, whether it would not be better for us, to suppress altogether this part of his history, than to present the scandalous spectacle of a white man befriending a quarteroon, and serving as an accomplice in the acquisition of literary knowledge by the latter; but, as some of the most important events which follow are intimately connected with, and dependent upon, the acquaintance our hero contracted with this poor slave, the suppression of it would have maimed our history, and perhaps rendered the latter part unintelligible. Deprecating, therefore, all the evil intentions which might be attributed to us, and, merely urged by necessity, we proceed to state some of the principal events which resulted from their close intimacy.

Captain Letinez happening, in a conversation he had with Flambeau, (such was the quarteroon's name,) to learn that his master had been one of the officers who took Bejar, at the time of Cos's capitulation, and that he had himself accompanied him, in that expedition, asked him many questions on the nature of the intervening country, the difficulties of the rivers, and the possibility of procuring food in the woods; and was so minute in his inquiries, and so particular in noting down every item of information the slave gave him, that it awakened strange suspicions in the latter's mind. "Excuse me, sir," said he, when captain Letinez had made an end of his inquiries, "it is your own kindness which makes me presumptuous. From your queries, I am led to suspect that you have a mind to escape back to Mexico, but beware how you undertake it without a guide, for, if you do, you will find your death in the wilderness which you have to cross. Could you but get the company of some one previously acquainted with the country, the undertaking would be comparatively easy; but, all alone, and unaware of the dangers that strew your path, you will certainly perish with hunger, should you escape being killed by the Indians, or retaken by the Texians."

"Alas," replied our hero, "there may be a great deal of truth in what you say, but where am I to find a trusty companion? And even, how could I, with security, reveal my secret to any one, here! Yet, I can stand no longer the torture of mind I am now undergoing."

"Why, sir," replied the slave, "the confidence you have reposed in me would be ill repaid, were I not to place the same trust in you: I, also, long to be liberated from my present state of servitude, and if you will accept of my services, as pilot, in the way, I promise to take you with safety as far as Bejar. Beyond that place, I am not acquainted with the country, and am told it is, for the space of eighty leagues, a complete wilderness, without provisions, and scarce of water. It is what has hitherto prevented me from abandoning my master; for, though he has treated me with kindness, I do not think I would be guilty of injustice in leaving his service."

Captain Letinez was delighted with the quarteroon's proposals, yet, being rather suspicious, he did not accept his offers immediately, but took time for reflection. After having long considered the subject, he held new communications with the slave, and it was settled between them, that they would effect their escape in company; Flambeau binding himself to act as pilot, in the way, and to provide provisions for the journey; and the captain becoming security, that, once arrived on the Mexican territory, he would be admitted to the enjoyment of civil rights.

The quarteroon took ten days to make his preparations. He pounded dry venison and mixed it with suet, in the form of *pemican*, a composition well known in Canada, amongst the *coureurs de bois*, as affording the most sustenance under the smallest comparative volumen, and provided, besides, a quantity of ammunition in order to hunt during the journey. Mr. Letinez procured a small keg of crackers and a little runlet of whiskey; and their necessary clothes, with some few favourite volumes, belonging to the quarteroon, being made up into a bundle, the whole cargo was put on a mule, which Flambeau took from his master's pasture grounds, and, one fine moonlight night, in the end of July, they took their departure in a western direction.

They walked on foot, the mule having as much as she could do to carry their effects, and little library; but the hope of succeeding made them bear the fatigue with cheerfulness. The slave having assured his travelling companion that he was perfectly well acquainted with the woods, and that the fear of the Indians would prevent his master from pursuing him to any great distance, their dread of being overtaken diminished as they advanced. Still they were not remiss, but pushed on, with a brisk pace, in order to get out of reach; but, on the following evening, the mule being sadly tired, they were obliged to stop, in order to give her time to rest.

With a certain degree of sagacity, the quarteroon selected, for their encamping place, a secret nook, in a bend, formed by a muddy creek, with precipitous banks, where it would have been next to a miracle for any one sent in their pursuit to find them out. He would not, however, permit captain Letinez to light a fire, lest the smoke should betray their place of concealment, and of course, they had, at supper, nothing but *pemican* and dry crackers, while the mule feasted far more luxuriously on a kind of herbage superior to the *Guinea* grass, which Texas produces in abundance.

As they had long to wait before sleeping time, without any thing to occupy their leisure, captain Letinez begged the slave to relate the history of his life, and how he had become possessed of his literary knowledge, a favour which the latter granted very readily ; but, as from that narrative, the suspicion of a criminal partiality for *abolitionism* would attach to certain clergymen of high respectability, yet residing in Louisiana, by whom Flambeau had been brought up and instructed in polite learning, we will take the liberty of passing it over in silence ; for, we do not wish that the present work should be the occasion of any one being brought into jeopardy. Let our kind reader, therefore, without regret for this episode, which circumstances force us to omit, accompany our travellers in their progress through the wilderness of Texas.

CHAPTER XXI.

They slept long, and, rising the next morning, quite refreshed, pursued their journey with the same speed as on the two preceding days, and reached, at last, the Rio Colorado without accident. That river had been swelled by heavy rains, and it became for them a matter of difficulty to cross it; still the quarteroon succeeded, by his industry, in conveying the mule over to the right bank. Then, with a hatchet he had taken from his master, he cut down a number of saplings, which he bound together, with withes, in the form of a raft; and, upon it, our hero, who did not know how to swim, ventured himself, having previously seen the experiment tried, in the ferrying over of the baggage. Flambeau swam behind, to push it forward, whilst the captain, with a long pole, gave also some assistance, under his companion's directions. He was, however, so awkward, as to lose his equilibrium; and the consequence was, that he fell into the water. The slave immediately caught hold of him, but the raft getting, in the meantime, released from his grasp, and the captain embracing him so closely, as to prevent him from swimming, both were in the utmost danger. Providence afforded them relief, at the very moment when they were sinking. The efforts which the quarteroon made to disengage himself from the Mexican's grasp, at length succeeded; and his right hand being now at liberty, he took hold of a log, that happened to be floating by, while, with the left, he still supported the captain, holding him by the hair of his head. The latter, at last, grasped the log, in his turn; and his companion, thus relieved from his encumbrance, was enabled, with comparative ease, to land his cargo, and save his fellow-traveller's life.

Having put the Rio Colorado between him and his master, the quarteroon relaxed something of the precautions he had hitherto taken, and told our hero that they should now remain a few days encamped where

they were, in order to rest themselves from the fatigues
of their hurried journey, and refit, from the effects of
their ducking. The mule, also, was sadly jaded, and
needed repose, so that all concurred to render a halt
necessary.

Flambeau, who was extremely shifty, soon built up
a nice little booth, well deserving the name of cabin,
and, under its roof, secured his books and baggage.
Then, taking his rifle, he went out to look for game,
while the captain remained at home to make a fire.
Deer are so plenty in that country, that our hunter had
no need to ramble to any great distance. Within three
hundred yards from the place where they had established their abode, he killed a fat buck, which he had
great difficulty in dragging home. Once there, however,
the creature was soon hung by the hind-legs upon a
bough of a neighbouring tree, flayed and quartered, and
the richest portion of the saddle set on a wooden spit
before the fire.

While it was roasting, Flambeau, addressing his
companion, said: "Now, captain, we should have some
fresh bread to eat with our venison. I am tired of
these dry crackers."

"Fresh bread!" replied Mr, Letinez—"I wish we
had; but wishing will be of little use, unless you have
the gift of miracles, and can change stones into loaves."

"Well," resumed his companion, "I can give you
something similar to good wheaten bread, with your
meat. Is it possible that you have made the campaign
of Texas, and are still so little acquainted with the
natural resources of the country? There is here a plant,
called *Topinamboux*, by the French, and Jerusalem
artichoke, by the Americans; the root of which is fully
equal to the Irish potato, in taste and flavour. What
do you say to a dozen of them, nicely roasted under
the embers?"

"Ah!" returned the captain, "it would be a luxury,
indeed, were it but true.—But, I dare say, you are
only jesting. What pleasure can you find in tantaliz-
ing me, in this fashion?"

"A jest!" exclaimed Flambeau: "Well, I will con-

19

vince you; and, to make you more ashamed of your incredulity, I will furnish you, not only with bread, but bring you, besides, a delicious dessert of fruit."

"And what kind of a dessert, pray?" inquired the captain.

"Pacans," replied the quarteroon.

"Oh, that is true!" returned the Mexican: "I know they are to be got in abundance here. Well, do go in haste for your Jerusalem artichokes:—the meat will soon be done; and I long, in my turn, to show you au article of dessert, with which I dare say, you are not acquainted.

Away went the quarteroon, armed with a large knife, or *belduque*, to dig up the roots, and soon returned, with fifteen large ones, which he put under the embers. He brought also a handkerchief full of pacans; and, while he amused himself in cracking some of them by the fire, watching the saddle of venison, his companion went in quest of another fruit, far superior to the pacan. It was the yellow *tuna*, the produce of a variety of the *cactus opuntia*. He found them, though not in plenty; and returned in triumph to the cabin, where the slave was delighted with the taste of that production, hitherto unknown to him. The savour partakes of that of the pear and peach, and it is extremely wholesome. Our travellers were *now* enabled to make, not only a comfortable, but even a luxurious meal; and, after having satiated their appetite, they conversed upon the amazing fertility of the soil of Texas, and the singularity of this portion of the New Continent, by far the best of the whole, having remained unsettled, and almost unknown till the present time.

"The country about the Brazos," said Flambeau, "is unhealthy; but much less so than Louisiana. In the latter, the yellow fever displays its malignant influence in the summer and fall of the year. About the Brazos, it is only the ague which the settlers have to fear; but *west* of the Guadelupe river, the salubrity of the climate is perfect, and fully equal to that of Connecticut and Canada, while the fertility of the soil is superior to that of Louisiana. Two crops of Indian corn are

produced every year! The sugar-cane and cotton need
no replanting, except at long intervals; the former
lasting eight years, and the latter, three. Nearly all
the fruits of the north, with those of tropical climates,
succeed to perfection. There is a sufficiency of wholesome water, and the most luxuriant range for cattle!—
These are advantages enough to attract hither the half
of the Anglo-Saxon race, and to turn the tide of emi-
gration which is now pouring into the United States.
Should the few Americans who are already settled in
the country, make their stand good, there will, in less
than the fourth part of a century, be such an extraordinary influx from the north, as has never been seen in
the world, since the great migrations of old, that over-
threw the Roman empire."

"Now, heaven forbid," interrupted captain Letinez,
"that your anticipations should prove true."

"Indeed," answered Flambeau, "I deprecate it as
ardently as you, but I don't see how the North of
Mexico can escape being overrun by them. To use a
negro expression of great energy, though indelicate,
they breed much faster than any other set of people,
whom we have any account of, and they are far superior to your nation, or, indeed, to any other, in mental
power. There is but one means left Mexico to withstand this *Northern* blast: it is to embrace, with all
possible diligence, all modern improvements. But are
you prepared for it? Is not the public mind, amongst
you, still too much cramped? Does not the genius of
old Spain still lie upon your nation like an evil incubus?"

"I am afraid, it is but too true," replied the Mexican, with a sigh. "The Spaniards have left us their
laws, and system of civilization, in which it will be an
arduous task to introduce the necessary alterations.
But, during their domination, there was, at least, something like system and method, which we seem to have
entirely cast off, since our independence, and, for want
of it, I foresee nothing but political misfortunes for
Mexico, during a long time to come."

"Indeed," replied the quarteroon, "the transition

from absolute monarchy, to a republican form of government, was so violent and sudden, that nothing less
than a state of anarchy could have been anticipated. It
would have been better for you to admit, as had been
first designed, a prince of the Spanish branch of the
house of Bourbon, to reign over you, and to content
yourselves with a limited monarchy, which would have
been better suited to your old habits and prejudices,
and would, probably, have preserved you from the frequent revolutions and changes which have, in your
country, unhinged the political machine."

"Had the introduction of monarchy been effected in
proper time," replied captain Letinez, "it might have
been settled on a sure footing; but *now*, the chance of
applying such a remedy to our political evils is passed.
No scion of European growth would flourish in our
land. Should any one ever ascend the throne, there,
it must be one of Mexican birth."

Thus, conversing about politics, religion, and agriculture, and diversifying their conversation with hunting and reading, and faring upon choice game, our two
travellers spent four days, in a very comfortable mood,
and rested themselves from their fatigues.

At last, the time appointed for the continuation of
their journey arrived, but, before leaving their encamp-
ment, they held council about the route which it would
be most prudent for them to pursue. Should they incline too much to the south, they were in danger of
meeting with parties of Texians, either of those who
had formed a part of the corps who had accompanied
Filisola's army in his retreat, or others, who might be
prowling about the country, in the direction of Bejar.
Should they incline to the north, they might fall into
the hands of straggling parties of Comanches, or other
Indians, scarcely less formidable than the Texians.
Their perplexity, therefore, was great; but, after long
debates, they thought that steering a middle way would
be most prudent. In consequence, they took a north-
west route, towards the Rio Bravo, calculating to
leave Bejar on their left hand.

CHAPTER XXII.

In spite of the prudence with which they shaped their course, they had the misfortune of encountering a party of Comanches, whom they especially dreaded. They were just emerging from a thick *nopalera*, when they descried two Indians on horseback coming towards them. It seemed as if the latter had no design on them, for, as soon as they perceived them, they gave a loud whoop, in sign of surprise, and, with the rapidity of lightning, disappeared from the back of the animals on which they were mounted. The horses fled, retaking the way by which they had come, while there remained no vestige of the riders, nor could the poor quarteroon imagine by what leger-de-main they had vanished. He had incessantly kept his eyes on them, from the first moment he descried them, and was sure they could not have alighted, and fled on foot, without b_ing perceived; yet he could have sworn the horses were now running off without their riders. Captain Letinez amused himself for a while, to see him so much puzzled; but, at last, explained to him that the Comanches are the best riders of any people, ancient or modern; that it is very common among them, in a flight, to lie in an horizontal position on the side of their horse less exposed to the arrows of their enemies; and that they are enabled to continue a considerable time in that strange posture, by putting one leg through a loop, depending from the saddle bow, and provided for the purpose, while they hold, with their hands, by the horse's mane and neck.

"I have no doubt," continued he, "it is precisely the way in which those fellows are even now effecting their retreat; but I am afraid they are not the only ones of their nation in this vicinity, and I wish to God we may not fall in with some larger party. This neighbourhood is their favourite haunt, and probably the two that have just now fled with so much precipitation are spies sent about to make discoveries."

19*

"And what, should we encounter them ?" said Flambeau.

"It is not a thing to be trifled with," replied the Mexican; "they are exceedingly cruel, and irreconcilable enemies to my countrymen. But I have the resource of passing myself for an American, and the more easily, as I am in your company. Should we meet them, beware to make any resistance and let me manage every thing. I have heard a great deal about their ways and customs, and am more likely to succeed than you, in soothing them, or winning their favour."

The captain's forebodings proved but too true—they had hardly proceeded a league, when they saw themselves invested by a large party, consisting at least of two hundred men on horseback, many of whom were armed with lances, some with rifles; but none of whom was without a bow and arrows. Instead of manifesting any fear, Mr. Letinez, on the contrary, drew towards the nearest group, with an air of confidence, bearing a buffalo robe spread on high in the air, which, according to the notions of these tribes, answers for a flag of truce; and the Indians manifested their respect for this sign of peace, by stopping short. The captain was no sooner within speaking distance, than he began to harangue the Comanches, in English, for he supposed that in so large a number there would be some one acquainted with the language of the Americans, and able to translate the substance of his address, for the information of the others. He told them that he and his companion were Texians, sent towards the Rio Grande, as spies, and that a considerable army of their countrymen was on its way, to lay waste all the towns on the banks of that river, after which the country would be abandoned to the Indians, its ancient lords and lawful possessors. He added that he was commissioned to propose an alliance between his people and the Comanches, in order to direct their simultaneous efforts against the Mexicans.

He had not been mistaken in his suppositions. Several of the Indians understood English sufficiently to seize the meaning of his address, the various items of

which were translated by them, and commented upon,
for the information of their comrades. The topics
which the captain had treated, and the manner in which
he had touched upon them, pleased the Comanches, who
determined, by common consent, not only to abstain
doing any injury to our travellers, but even to treat
them with honour. The chief of the whole party now
advanced towards the captain, and shook hands with
him, while one, who, it was supposed, acted as interpreter general, gave him to understand that they had
resolved to exercise the rites of hospitality towards
them, and invited them, for that purpose, to their place
of residence, at the foot of the Sierra of St. Sabas, on
the head waters of the Rio Colorado.

Such an invitation was far from agreeable to our
hero, who anxiously desired to get rid of these Indians,
for fear of being discovered, for their inveteracy against
the descendants of the Spaniards is so great, that it is
next to a miracle for any Mexican to escape from
amongst them with his life. The captain, however, had
entrapped himself by pretending that he was commissioned to propose a treaty between them and Texas.
Such a commission necessarily required that he should
go to their towns, in order to hold a talk, and he could
not *now* refuse, without rendering his veracity suspected, and, perhaps, endangering his life.

On the other hand, it was a dreadful addition to the
fatigues they had already undergone, (the nearest
towns of the Comanches, at the foot of the Southern
ridge of the Sierra of St. Sabas, being, at least, two
hundred miles distant,) no less than a postponing of
the so much wished-for meeting with Miss Linton and
her father, who, he had great reasons to believe, had
followed Filisola's army to Matamoros. Pity for the
fate of the father, and the state of dereliction to
which, in consequence of it, the daughter was reduced, pleaded in his heart, with a voice almost as
powerful as that of love, to make him desire a quick
riddance of his present difficulty; and it was less
painful to venture exciting suspicions in the minds of
the Comanches, than stifling the secret whispers of

love and compassion united. He therefore intimated,
that, for the present, it was impossible for him to go so
far North, because the errand on which he chiefly was
sent, consisted in spying out the positions of the Mexicans, on the Rio Bravo, and the state of their affairs:
it being urgent that an account of it should forthwith
be placed before the Texian authorities; but that, if
they would consent, he would treat with them on the
spot.

To this, however, the Comanches refused to accede,
not being invested with the necessary powers from the
rest of the nation, and, of course, unwilling to enter
into any engagements by themselves. Though thus
disappointed of their expectations, by the captain's
false pretences, yet they lent a favourable ear to a
petition for an escort, to accompany him as far as the
Rio Bravo. He was afraid to meet with some other
party of Comanches, who might be worse disposed than
the present ones; or, perhaps, some Carankaways, who
are noted cannibals, and would not scruple feasting
upon the body of a Mexican, any more than eating a
fat yearling.

He obtained what he sued for; and no other remuneration was asked, than the hatchet which Flambeau
had purloined from his master, and the keg which had
contained their whiskey, but which, unhappily, was then
empty. As there is between Bejar and the Rio Bravo,
a desert of sixty leagues, where provisions and even
water are very scarce, our travellers and the Indians
who undertook to escort them, were under the necessity of preparing a certain quantity of *tassajo*. For
that purpose, they killed ten beeves, (cattle being
still in plenty, notwithstanding the great havoc made
amongst them by Santa Anna's army;) and, cutting the
meat into thin slices, hung it up in the sun. The atmosphere in that country is so dry, and the heat so
powerful, that the meat thus prepared is soon cured;
and proves, even in its raw state, pleasant and wholesome food. The *pemican*, pounded by Flambeau, had
already given out, so that he was not a little rejoiced
to see the tassajo, not quite so substantial, it is true, as

the Canadian preparation, but not much inferior to it
in taste.

It is not astonishing that the Comanches, who entertain a mortal hatred against the Mexicans, should have
thus treated with distinction the two pretended Texian
spies. The Indians felt a sympathy for them, and
looked upon them as their natural allies against an in-
veterate foe. Had *this* been better known to captain
Letinez, he would not have been so much afraid of
rendering himself suspected, by refusing to go to their
towns. All the Indian tribes who inhabit Texas had,
by this time, heard of the battle of San Jacinto, and
felt a sort of reverential awe for the race who had won
it. That action was a kind of backwoods Waterloo,
which, in their imagination, surrounded the new republic with a halo of glory. They were disposed, therefore, to look with a special benignity upon every thing
appertaining to it; and, in order to testify their high
regard for the two pretended spies, they resolved, before dismissing them, to give them a grand feast, according to the custom of their nation, in the plain where
they were assembled.

For that purpose, the warriors divided themselves
into various squads, say twenty-five or thirty; several
of whom went out a-hunting, in order to provide game
for the banquet, while the remainder employed themselves in building cooking-hearths for preparing their
entertainment. The country is so productive of every
kind of wild animals, considered as delicacies, in more
civilized regions, that, in very little time, they were
amply provided. One brought a fat buck—another, a
couple of turkies—a third one, a dozen of those delightful thrushes which are, in Louisiana, (and not un-
deservedly so,) looked upon as the *ne plus ultra* of an
epicure's desires. Some slaughtered *pecaris*, one of
the most remarkable animals in nature, very abundant
in the lowlands of Mexico, and the meat of which
tastes much like that of the wild boar of Europe;
while others repaired to the neighbouring brooks, for
fish and turtles. All these articles, when prepared,
though without any difference in the way of cooking,

offered such a varied cheer, as would have made a London alderman's teeth water; and the keen wind that sweeps the plains of Texas, might be considered as giving them a new relish, by sharpening the appetite of our travellers.

In spite of all these intrinsic and accidental recommendations, the captain and Flambeau shuddered, on being informed, that, in order to do honour to the good intentions of their entertainers, they were obliged to partake of every meal which had been prepared for them.

"Good God!" cried out the quarteroon, "how shall we be able to get through this tremendous job? There are no less than fifty different boards spread out. The plain is covered over with them. It would require the appetite of a *hyena*, to acquit one's self to these people's satisfaction. Oh! had I but known of this betimes, I would have fasted so rigorously, as to be now able to come up to their most refined ideas of politeness; but, after the four days we have enjoyed on the banks of the Colorado, it will be impossible for us to do here any thing worthy of men. We will certainly offend our entertainers, and endanger the respectability of the character we have assumed."

The poor quarteroon's lamentations were, however, unavailable, and the various cooking parties being ready for the reception of their honoured guests; it was again signified to them that they should perambulate the plain and eat of every meal prepared for them.

"Oh, Ciel!" exclaimed again the quarteroon, using the French language, in the excess of his grief. "Voici bien le restant de notre ecu! what is to become of us?"

"Santo Dios!" echoed the Mexican, "ahora si, que he de reventar! Oh, my dear friend," added he, recommending himself to the quarteroon, "do not fail to inform my relations of my fate, should I happen to die in this dreadful undertaking—in order that they may cause masses to be said for the repose of my poor soul." But, in the middle of their mutual condolences, the Indian who acted as master of ceremonies became urgent to usher them to the nearest banquet, which consisted

of a roasted buck, various pieces of which were served
before them, upon prickly pear leaves, which answered
for platters, and of which they ate very sparingly, re-
serving their appetite, to satisfy the numerous cooking
groups, who were impatiently awaiting their approach.

They rose from their seat, in a few minutes, and left
their entertainers highly displeased with the abruptness
of their departure. Passing on to a second board, they
did the same, and so on, to a third, and to a fourth, until at last, after having, by their sobriety, which looked
like contempt for the meats prepared for their entertainment, offended the half of the warriors there present, they were themselves ready to die with an indi-
gestion. In spite of the best will to give universal satisfaction, they were obliged to leave about twenty
boards unvisited. In vain the kind-hearted Comanches
begged, and complained of their want of civility—quar-
relled and tried to bully them into eating; a complete
physical impossibility stood in the way of the accomplishment of their wishes; so that, after much teasing,
they withdrew in high dudgeon, and the result was that
the two pretended Texian spies lost the half of their
popularity with the Comanches.

It was represented to the white men, in no very mo-
derate language, that, had they gone up to the Indian
towns, at the foot of the Sierra of St. Sabas, they would
have been invited into every tent, to partake of a meal
prepared for their reception, but that, as they could
not comply with the wishes of their good friends; these
had taken the pains of preparing for them a splendid
banquet on the spot, and they had not, however, done
to it the honour their entertainers had a right to expect,
but rather left a part of the entertainment untouched,
which was a slur thrown upon those who had prepared
the feast.

The captain and Flambeau, thus teased out of all patience, and driven to the utmost extremity, gave out,
as a last awkward excuse, that they felt sick, and this
liked to have exposed them to greater difficulties than
those from which they sought to extricate themselves;
for, the Indians immediately offered to physic them

according to their fashion. Our travellers were, however, lucky enough to make their refusal acceptable,
under the pretence that Indian medicines would not
answer for white men, and, succeeded, in the end, in
obtaining forgiveness from those whom their abstemi-
ousness had offended.

All matters being now pacified, and all differences
amicably adjusted, our hero and his friend took their
departure from the field of feasting, and shaped their
course towards the Rio Bravo, under the escort of
seventy Indians, who brought with them a sufficiency
of provisions for crossing the intervening wilderness.
They suffered sometimes for want of water, but not so
much as they had anticipated, for whenever they found
none in the *charcos*, or pools, they generally obtained
some, by digging a deep hole in the earth. Sometimes,
however, they got nothing but what was impregnated
with Epsom or Glauber salts, chemical compounds
with which it seems that the Mexican territory is con-
dimented at large, to the inmost recesses of the bowels
of the earth, and which will render the largest portion
of the republic unfit for agricultural purposes, until the
inhabitants shall have recourse to the method of collecting the rain water in artificial tanks.

In seven days, they reached the Rio Bravo, where
they dismissed their escort, intending to enter the
Mexican territory without any thing which might excite suspicion. They had struck the river, a considerable distance above Revilla, and were deliberating
on the best way of crossing it, when an unexpected
facility presented itself.

CHAPTER XXIII.

As they were sitting on the bank of the Rio Bravo, considering what means there was of conveying their mule to the opposite side, a large empty canoe offered itself to their view. It was moored in a small cove, under some spreading *sabinos*,* and afforded them not only an unexpected facility for crossing the stream, but even a very convenient way for descending it, as far as Matamoros, should they wish to escape the fatigues of a journey by land. Flambeau proposed it to the captain; but the latter, still remembering his ducking in the Rio Colorado, and the danger to which he had been exposed. made a wry face, and started various objections. The quarteroon, however, insisted with perseverance, and painted in such colours the ease and pleasantness with which a trip of that sort could be performed, on the smooth and meandering stream of the Bravo, that he conquered his companion's repugnance.

An impediment that was not so easily got over, concerned the right of ownership of the skiff. The canoe was the property of another man, and, by depriving him of it, they committed an act of injustice! To this objection, urged by the captain, the quarteroon replied that they could easily indemnify the owner, by leaving a sum of money for him, in the hands of the parish priest of the first town they should come to, and informing him of such a disposition, by a letter, left hanging on a bough of the cypress-tree, at the foot of which they had found the boat moored.

The expedient appeared reasonable, and the plea of urgent necessity seemed to justify it. In fact, they were in such a case; for, how repugnant soever senor de Letinez might feel in embarking in a canoe, and trusting his person to an element of which he was in special dread, the continuation of his journey on foot had become nearly impossible, from soreness; and

* Cypress.

the district of country they were now to cross, did not
offer the same resources as Texas, to refit themselves.
From the plain, where the mighty banquet by which
they had been so much annoyed, had been held, they
had been conveyed to the banks of the Rio Bravo, on
horses lent them by the Comanches; but *now,* should
they overlook the convenience of a canoe, they had
before them the awful prospect of a five hundred miles
journey, to be performed on foot, through countries not
altogether desert, indeed, but mostly devoid of water,
and exceedingly unsafe, on account of the great number of deserters who had taken to the highways, as the
only means of support left them by the carelessness of
government. This was more than sufficient to out-
weigh all the scruples senor Letinez might have felt at
seizing on the canoe; and we hope it will be no less
satisfactory to our reader's mind, particularly when he
considers that our gallant hero made provision for re-
imbursing the owner of the clumsy skiff, its full value.

The resolution of trusting themselves upon the river
being taken, the letter for the owner of the canoe was
written, and appended to the tree already alluded to,
the mule was unloaded and turned loose, their goods
and provisions were transferred to the skiff, over the
prow of which a little booth was constructed by Flambeau, with a few green boughs and a blanket; and, un-
mooring it, they began to descend the river. The
quarteroon took upon himself the duties of pilot, and,
with a paddle in hand, sometimes rowed, to accelerate
their progress, or get clear of the eddies; but, more
frequently, contented himself with using his oar as a
rudder, and sat motionless, merely directing the course
of the canoe.

The Rio Bravo is at all times a rapid stream, but it
was now the season of the year when it begins to rise:
for, like the Mississippi, it is subject to periodical inundations; so that the velocity of our travellers' march,
relieved the want of excitement that would otherwise
have resulted from the lack of personal motion. At
every turn and meander of the stream, a new scene
presented itself.—Here, perpendicular clay banks, se-

renty or eighty feet in height.—There, wide bottoms, indented by *bayous*, extending far inland, as having anciently formed the bed of the river. Whenever they landed, the quarteroon was amused, as well as instructed, at the sight of many plants, growing wild, which he had hitherto considered as rarities, created only for the ornament of conservatories, and the luxury of the rich. As he brushed by, whole clusters of the *mimosa sensitiva* drooped, and shut their leaves in vegetable convulsions, the rose-geranium shook its elegant perfume, and the yellow-bloomed *guisache* embalmed the air with odours equal to those of the blossoms of the grape-vine. In many places, they found the finer species of the cocheneal insect, (coccus cacti Sylvester,) at work, on the thick and mucilaginous leaves of its favourite opuntia, while every shaded spot glowed with the splendid flowrets of the red-bloomed sauge, one of the most brilliant productions of the reign of Flora. Not unfrequently, during the heat of the day, they would land, to enjoy their *siesta* under some spreading ebony-tree, the thick foliage of which perfectly screened them from the sun, while the *sinsontle* (mocking-bird) lulled them asleep by his mimickry; and sometimes they would amuse themselves in looking, among the sands and shingles, in the shallow parts of the river, for a species of muscle which produces pearls nearly as fine as those of California.

Thus varied, their journey down the stream proved no less instructive than amusing, and it possessed, besides, the invaluable advantage of affording them a perfect security, for, they were the first wayfarers who had ever travelled in such a manner in that country, and it will be long, indeed, before the robbers with which it abounds be taught to consider the greatest navigable river in the republic, as a highway.

Near Revilla, they saw immense banks of stone coal, which made Flambeau cry out in exultation, "Good Lord! what a resource for this country, where wood is so scarce! What a blessing has not Providence prepared for the population, in order to navigate this beautiful river by steam, and how strangely ignorant or apathetic must they be, to neglect availing themselves of these advantages, especially as they have the example of the North Americans before their eyes! Now, this is a continuation of that stone coal formation which pervades the north of Texas, and it, probably, extends much further west. It is calculated to furnish immense facilities for manufacturing purposes, in a country like this. When will the people open their eyes? and why do not the many foreigners settled among them enlighten them on their interests?"

" Why do not *foreigners* enlighten them on their interests?" interrupted the captain. " Ay, indeed!— the foreign merchants, who thrive amongst them, are the first to conceal the light. A few years ago, a steamboat was started on the Rio Bravo, and it was immediately exclaimed against, by the American, Irish, and French merchants of Matamoros, with as much bitterness, as by the Mexican mule-drivers and ox-cart gentry. Even at this day, if you want to make any one among them fall into a furious passion, you have but to maintain before him the *possibility* of establishing cotton factories in this country. Though there are already more than ten in a flourishing state, working, at least, two hundred power looms, and some of them as far north as the State of Durango, these foreign importers will not fail to exclaim against it, as the greatest extravagance that could ever enter the head of a reasonable creature. It is *statesmen* and *philosophers* that will enlighten us, if we are ever enlightened, but as to merchants, they are mere routine men, generally heartless and without elevation of mind, and not a bit better than the *inquisitors* of old among divines."

Our travellers stopped a short time at Revilla, to take in provisions, and settle the manner of paying for the canoe, should the owner of it call upon the parish priest, as they had, by letter, instructed him to do; after which, continuing their voyage, they soon reached the town of Mier, which had, a few months before, been the theatre of captain Letinea's first exploits, and witnessed the dawn of his military career.

The Rio Bravo, notwithstanding its rapidity, de-

scribes so many sinuosities, that it took our travellers
nine days to reach Camargo, a town of some importance, at the mouth of the river San Juan, and seventy
leagues distant from Matamoros by water. There,
Senor de Letinez resolved to leave his canoe, provided
he should be able to procure mules and servants to
terminate his journey by land. Flambeau in vain
pleaded in favour of the other mode of conveyance, as
less fatiguing and more secure; the captain was inexorable, pretending that he should become the laughing-
stock of his brother officers, should he make his entrance into Matamoros by water, and that the ridicule
which would, in consequence of it, attach to him, might
prove a stain to his military character. So unnatural
does river navigation appear to Mexicans in general.

"That is to say, then," resumed Flambeau, laughing, "that your countrymen believe rivers have been
created merely to be crossed by means of bridges or
ferry-boats!"

"Precisely," replied the other, in the same merry
tone. "Not even the Persians of old had as much ab-
horrence for navigation as we. With eighteen hundred leagues of coast, on the Pacific, we do not own
one single vessel trading to the East Indies, though the
Spaniards showed us the way long ago; and with an
extension of eight hundred leagues on the Gulf of
Mexico, I do not believe that one of our merchant
vessels has yet crossed the Atlantic. And as for our
rivers, we have three of superior importance; that of
St. Yago, the River of Mescula, and the Rio Bravo, but
for the service they do us, they might as well be dried
up."

20 *

CHAPTER XXIV.

In Camargo, the captain found several officers of cavalry, of his acquaintance, quartered in that place, with a number of horses, for the convenience of pasturage. They welcomed him with exultation, and congratulated him upon his escape, for it had been reported, he had perished in the battle of San Jacinto. From them, he easily obtained mules and servants, together with some money, and soon continued his route towards Matamoros, impatient to hear what had happened to Miss Linton, and yet fearing to learn disastrous news. Those who have never experienced love, when it rises pure and unadulterated by any selfish motive, in a virgin heart, can hardly form to themselves an idea of captain Letinez's feelings, when he approached that city. Though he had some reasons to believe that Miss Linton entertained towards him a reciprocity of sentiments, yet he had no certainty of it, and this doubt was the source of a cruel anxiety. He anticipated also a sad history of wo, in the long series of sufferings which she must have encountered, in the midst of a demoralised and broken down soldiery, during Filisola's difficult retreat. But, perhaps, even in this supposition, his thoughts carried him too far! He had no proofs that major Linton had escaped the massacre at Labahia. *His* hopes of his safety were only founded upon the confidence he reposed in his friend, captain Alvarez, and others. He doubted not they had made their efforts to save him; but had those efforts been available against the strict orders of Santa Anna? And if the father had perished, he was sure, the daughter could not have survived. Now, the cruel doubt was going to be cleared up; but as he drew nearer to the city, the anxiety of his mind grew more excruciating, and wrought upon his body like an agony of grief. He felt dizzy—unable to support himself on horseback —and was obliged to alight to rest himself, in order to give his feelings time to be calmed.

He laid himself down at the foot of a tree, and leaned on the quarteroon, who, not knowing the cause of this unexpected debility, attributed it to bodily exhaustion, and expostulated with him on the imprudence of undertaking to terminate his journey on horseback, when he was so inadequate to the task.

The captain suffered him to murmur as much as he pleased, rather than discover the state of his mind, for he was conscious that his feelings were above the comprehension of most men. It was a fever of love, buoyed up by a virginity of heart, hardly ever found in the rougher sex; but embittered by the most cruel uncertainty! Since the day when he rescued Miss Linton from the hands of the Comanches, when that pale, fainting form, lay, for a few moments, upon his bosom—beautiful beyond any thing he had ever dreamed of; the dear image had incessantly remained present to his imagination. It had accompanied him in the field, as well as in the camp; and supported him through the fatigues of war and the rigours of his captivity. Why does he now tremble? Why is his ardent desire of seeing her again mingled with an indescribable dread, the motive of which he hardly can or dares define? Is it the mere fear that perhaps she has died, which thus causes his torment? Is not there another thought, mixing its bitterness with that pang? Oh, the misery of his situation! The object of his love has, perhaps, become unworthy of his aspirations. A captive in the midst of a routed army—without protector, amongst men accustomed to laugh at every kind of excess, how can she have escaped pollution? O God, avert the tormenting idea! Heavens, distil your soothing balsam into that wounded heart, and let not the utmost of your rigour be poured upon a child of virtue!

Now, like Alp before Corinth, he

> " Passed his hand athwart his face;
> Like one in dreary musing mood,
> Declining was his attitude;
> His head was drooping on his breast,
> Fevered, throbbing, and opprest;

> And o'er his brow, so downward bent,
> Of his beating fingers went
> Hurriedly as you may see
> Your own run o'er the ivory key,
> E'er the measured tone is taken
> By the chords you would awaken."

Now, he would rise with sudden exertion, but remain rooted to the spot, listening to the mighty south wind, that lowed, and shook the gnarled boughs of the mesquites and guisaches; as if it could bring him news to calm the fever of his mind. Then, his eye, with a vacant and unconscious stare, would follow the pelican, which, from the highest verge of the sky, cleft the air with the velocity of lightning, and plunged into the blue pool at his feet, to seize upon his unsuspecting prey. Sometimes, his fingers would mechanically pluck a blossom from the adjoining bough, and scatter its leaves to the wind, without experiencing in his mind the least distraction, or even adverting to what his hands were employed in, and then again he would fall into a complete listlessness.

The quarteroon endeavoured to rouse him from that musing, which appeared to border on monomania ; but, still, judging that it might proceed from some concealed pain of the heart, he essayed to probe the wound, and said to him : " Now, sir, your soul is overburdened with some heavy weight ;—might I presume to solicit a share of your confidence ?—God is my witness, it is not through vain curiosity, but only a desire of affording you consolation, I address you this request. It is true, our acquaintance has been but short, yet I have given proofs of the utmost devotion ; and there is such a thing as a communion of feelings—an understanding between kindred spirits ! If we were in a country where the line of demarcation between your race and mine is rigorously sketched out, I would abstain from urging my petition : but a perfect civil equality prevails here; and you have been so kind to me, that I cannot suppose you lack confidence in my probity. Oh, disburden your heart into mine, and trust one who, notwithstanding

the artificial distance which separates him from you,
still dares call himself your friend!"

"You are my friend, indeed," replied captain Letinez; "neither will I, for an instant, suffer the vain prejudices of the most unnatural cupidity of a foreign
nation to control my feelings; but I hardly know how
to express the thoughts which engross my mind at this
moment. Confiding them even to an only brother,
would be excruciating. Excuse me, then, dear friend!
—My heart is bursting, it is true; yet I am conscious
there is no one that could fully understand me, or condole with me."

"And why not?" replied the quarteroon: "Think
not so meanly of one whose lot it has been, indeed, to
move in an humble sphere through life, but who is not,
however, altogether ignorant of mental sensibility, that
luxury of the soul, so apt to inflict on man exquisite
pains, but which is, nevertheless, the *seal* of *predestina-
tion* for great thoughts and noble actions. Believe that
I am able to *understand you.* Why should I not?—I
have suffered so much myself!"

Senor de Letinez was, notwithstanding his repugnance, conquered by this ardent desire of sharing in
his grief, and made the quarteroon participant of the
state of his mind. The latter had not presumed too
much on his powers of consolation. He assuaged the
captain's anxiety, reanimated his hopes, and strengthened his confidence in himself. Thus, in great measure, restored to calm and fortitude, our hero proposed
to continue their route; and he had already his foot in
the stirrup, to mount his horse, when a band of robbers
rushed upon them.

Our travellers were completely surprised, and in the
utter impossibility of making use of their arms: of
course, they were at the robbers' mercy. The latter
were beginning to pillage their effects, and, having discovered that Flambeau could not speak Spanish, began, with a volley of tremendous oaths, to curse him
for an American, and one even proposed killing him;
when the captain recognized amongst them some of the
troopers of his own company of horse.

"How, now, Pedro Tormoya?" cried he, taking a tone of authority; "is it thus you welcome your captain, after he has been so happy as to escape from among the Texians:—you, who were one of my favourite soldiers?—And you, too, Santiago Solino?—What in the world has happened, to induce you to take to this evil course?—I could have sworn you were both men of honour?"

"Y valga me Dios, senor capitan!" exclaimed Solino and Tormoya: "Who could have recognized you under the strange garb you wear?—But, blessed be the Virgin of Guadelupe and St. Corolampio, that you have escaped from the hands of the Texians!—Very sorry we attacked you!—Very sorry, indeed!—It will give you a bad opinion of us!—But really, sir, we cannot help it: we must do it, or starve. We get only half a rial a day, to procure our victuals and all other necessaries, in a place where, even a whole rial a day would not buy a sufficiency of bread for a man. Either the government makes no remittances, or they are absorbed by the generals. All the troops are perishing with want, and there is now nothing to be got in Matamoros. The half of the foreign merchants are gone."

"And who commanded the army when you left it?" interrupted Senor de Letinez.

"Valga me Dios!" replied Solino, astonished at the query, and crossing himself; "we have not left it. We are not deserters:—God forbid we should be! We can obtain leave of absence, every now and then. As our officers have so little to give us, they are indulgent; but we do not make a bad use of their kindness, and kill nobody. Even this fellow, here, a servant of yours, I suppose," added he, pointing to Flambeau, "we would not have done him any harm, although we spoke so roughly about him."

"He is not my servant," said captain Letinez:—"He is my friend, and a Christian; and I wish you to respect him, as myself."

"Oh! if he be a Christian, that is quite another thing," replied one of the robbers: "So, all the Texians are not Jews, then, as our clergy say!"

This was, by the captain, translated to Flambeau, in order to convince him how important it was, in that country, to lean on the church for protection; and the quarteroon, wittily taking the hint, corroborated the captain's statement, and confirmed the robbers in the idea of his orthodoxy, by making the sign of the cross, which dispelled any remaining doubt that might have been lurking in their mind, and charmed them so much, that two of them actually shook him cordially by the hand, in token of spiritual fellowship.

The captain inquired from Pedro Tormoya, who was endowed with intelligence above mediocrity, for news from the army, and the particularities of the disastrous retreat under Filisola; to which the other answered that it would be rather a lengthy relation, and tiresome to be told standing, (for they had all along retained that posture), but that, if his worship had no objection, they would sit down on the green sward, and he would tell all, *de pe a pa*, as it had happened.

To this Senor de Letinez assented, and, stretching themselves on the grass, Tormoya began his history, the thread of which he interrupted, every now and then, in order to drop quaint reflections of his own, on the conduct of the chiefs, or various accidents which had had an untoward influence on the result of the campaign.

CHAPTER XXV.

"Shortly after you left us," said the narrator, "we
reached Brazoria, but General Urrea found the place
so low and marshy, that he was afraid to remain in it,
for, in case of a rise in the river, the country would
be all overflowed, and our division could not but perish.
You know what repugnance we Mexicans feel for water. A single shower of rain dispirits us more than a
week's hunger and thirst. Now, that cursed country of
Texas is nothing but a swamp, at least, along the sea
shore. There is a river at every tenth league, and
such rivers as carry ships! You may judge what a
frightful prospect it was for us, who, in all the table-
land of Mexico, have no larger stream than the Rio
Nassas, and think a country well watered, if there is a
spring at every fifty miles. We left Brazoria, therefore, with all possible haste, and followed the right
bank of the stream, in order to reach an elevated spot,
where we should be safe against the fear of inundations. But in our march we had a terrible fright. We
were first alarmed by a horrid noise repeated at short
intervals, and with which the woods rung to a vast distance. We had never heard any thing similar to it; but
some thought it was the heavings of an earthquake,
whilst one from Campeachy, who had been at sea,
maintained it was the blowing of a whale. All the
corps came to a stand, and the men looked aghast, not
knowing whether to flee or stand their ground. Presently we saw a large machine, much bigger than a
ship, floating on the water, and coming towards us
with incredible rapidity. On the prow was a large
furnace, from whence volumes of flame and smoke escaped, by two big iron tubes, which towered aloft like
huge cannons, and on either side was an enormous
wheel, whirling round as if ten thousand spirits from
the bottomless pit had been lodged in it. These wheels
were armed with flapboards to put the water in motion,
and raise an artificial storm in the river, as some of

our officers conjectured, in order to prevent us from crossing to the other side. Upon that abominable *invention* drawing nearer, most of our troops were on the point of breaking loose and running off; but the very fear it inspired prevented them! In fact, we were not sure but it might overtake us on land, and we had no other resource than prayer. So, we fell upon our knees,* and called upon the Blessed Virgin of Guadelupe and Almighty God! *She* delivered us from that horrid *brujeria*, (witchcraft) and we continued our route, but sadly dispirited. How could it be otherwise? Without any priest amongst us, we were exposed to the wicked arts of those heretics and the powers of hell! Fighting for our country, yet without absolution or extreme unction, in case of death! And then to be buried like dogs, without either prayers or *suffragios* from an ecclesiastic! Oh, sir, but this was a disastrous prospect and an awful anticipation!

"We were forced to continue our march, indeed, but from that moment I augured badly of the expedition; and would to God that my forebodings had not been so well founded!—would to God that Mexico had not received the deep humiliation, the stain of which will be so difficult to blot out!

"We had already proceeded a considerable way up the river, when an extraordinary courier brought our general the news of the defeat of San Jacinto, together with an order from Filisola, who now succeeded in command, to join him in haste with his division. It was a sad and mournful meeting, and we were all afraid that the prisoners, amongst whom was nearly the whole staff, comprising several of the most distinguished generals, would be put to death by the rebels, in order to avenge the massacre of Goliad; but Santa Anna had art enough to turn the wrath of the Texians. It must be confessed, that, if he has the greatest knack in the world for falling into snares, he has also an admirable skill for getting out of them. When, at Tampico, he rushed so inconsiderately into the clutches of

* This actually happened at the sight of a steamboat.

21

Barradas, did it not, in the end, turn to his greater glory, and didn't he succeed in capturing his captor ? That very affair brought him to the presidential chair; and I have no doubt the affair of San Jacinto will, after all, turn to his profit and serve to his further elevation. He is a man whose fate it is to derive as great advantages from his defeats, as others do from their victories. He will, no doubt, find it difficult to get out of the hands of the Texians; but you will see that he will accomplish it, at last, and rise again in Mexico. Though a prisoner, his instructions and orders were obeyed by Filisola. There was a grand council of superior officers held at the house of one Madame Paoli, where a retreat was resolved upon, and where all the generals insisted on Filisola retaining the command.

" The army, disorganized as it was, could not have continued on the offensive, and had the Texians known our situation, they might have easily destroyed us. Perhaps, they were still afraid, after their victory ; for, I have, since, understood they had not above six hundred men, and, it was, upon the whole, wisely done, by Houston, to let us return; for, it is certain, this retreat has dispirited the nation as much as a complete annihilation of the army could have done. We are not the same in a foreign land, as upon our own territory. When battling, on the parent soil, against the Spaniards ; we were animated by our native clergy, who had to avenge upon the *Guchupines* the humiliation and contempt of two hundred years, things which priests never forgive! We prevailed by the weight of overwhelming masses, and, had the Spaniards been as numerous as we, it is very doubtful whether we could have succeeded. But none of those things can be brought to bear upon Texas. Our clergy would, certainly, be desirous we should drive the heretics away ; but none, amongst those who possess eloquence and can manage large masses, will take the trouble to come and inspire the minds of the soldiers, neither does the government pay any attention to this powerful mover. If, after long murmurs on the part of the army, they send us a chaplain, it is some foolish friar who can hardly read the Latin of his own breviary, and does nothing but bring religion into contempt. The race of *preaching* heroes seems to be extinct amongst us. There are no longer any Moreloses or Matamoroses to be found! Even father Belausaran appears to have turned a dolt, since they have put a mitre on his head. One would think it has addled his brain!"

"But, my dear fellow, you are straying from your narration," interrupted the captain; "I long to hear the history of your retreat, and you lose yourself in useless reflections upon political subjects which neither you nor I can amend!"

"Ah, it is true, sir," replied Tormoya. "It was my patriotism which carried me away; but let us resume. As soon as the Texians had agreed to spare the life of the president and his companions in arms, our army began its retreat. General Filisola offered again to cede the command to any one whom the other chiefs might elect, but all insisted upon his keeping it; yet, from this moment, Urrea commenced to undermine him in his correspondence with the government, and, at last, succeeded in obtaining his post.

Our march was accompanied by every dismal circumstance which can be imagined: Hunger, nakedness, violent rains, and a complete destitution of *Spiritual succours*, for the sick and dying! The generals engrossed all the wagons and beasts of burden, to convey the plunder they had seized, so that part of the necessary baggage was left behind; but it was particularly at a place called the *Atascadito* that we suffered beyond what I thought possible for humanity to bear. By a dreadful cold rain, we found ourselves in the midst of a swamp, through which the utmost progress of a day was only three miles! There seemed to be no possible means of extricating the artillery, and our officers would have left it behind, had it not been for the unparalleled exertions of Don Pedro de Ampudia, the commandant of that corps, who, by his indefatigable labours and resolution, succeeded in extricating all the guns, and prevented the soldiers from breaking the carriages to pieces, in order to get fire wood to warm themselves.

The vanguard, under Urrea's command, preceded the main body, by eight or nine days march, and, as they went along, they gleaned every thing that had escaped us in the month of February, so that, at our coming on, (for I had joined the main body) we found nothing to pick up. We were followed by certain Texian commissioners, coming under the treaty, to claim some property taken from them, and particularly negroes, who had run away, and taken refuge in Matamoros. There was, also, a small body of observation of theirs, who accompanied us a part of the way, and even did us considerable service by helping us out of some swamps, in which our artillery would have remained buried, had it not been for their assistance. For this kindness, however, they got but a poor requital, for, no sooner did their commissioners get to Matamoros, than Urrea made them prisoners, but this by the bye.

"The troops that had been left to garrison Bejar, had suffered perhaps more than the rest; so that, notwithstanding the orders of government, that the place should not be abandoned, it became impossible to hold that post.

"Before reaching the Rio Bravo, Urrea took the supreme command, and Filisola was obliged to repair to Mexico, in danger of being tried for *that* retreat. which, though disastrous, was, nevertheless, a proof of talent and generalship in him, whereby he had not only saved the President and his fellow-prisoners' lives, but even rescued the army from total destruction. No doubt, as it was a mortification for our national pride, he had to bear the odium; and, as he is a foreigner by birth, he found less sympathy: but I expect they will do him justice yet; for, notwithstanding the outcry raised against him, it is certain that affairs have gone on worse since he has resigned the command.

"When we reached the river, and were ready to cross over to Matamoros, we felt completely broken down, both in body and mind; and, since that time, deser-

tions have become so numerous, that the army hardly
amounts now to two thousand men. In the meantime,
Urrea is carrying every thing with a high hand in
Matamoros, and seems determined to make hay while
the sun shines. The campaign will be worth to him a
brilliant fortune!"

Senor de Letinez had all along expected to hear
some news of Miss Linton and her father: but his in-
former, it seems, had not noticed them; for, even to
his specific inquiries, he could answer nothing satisfactory, except that he believed seven or eight of the
colonists, taken at Goliad, had been saved, in quality
of physicians, and two of them sent to Bejar, to attend
the sick, where they had done good service. Some of
these, he added, were now at liberty in the city, and
three or four were still in confinement. As to any
young lady, he could not tell. There were so many,
young or old, who had followed the army!—The whole
town of St. Patricio had come along with the troops,
when *they* left Texas, in order to escape the wrath of
the rebels, against whom they had fought in the beginning of the campaign!—She might be among them!—
Perhaps, too, she had died on the way; but he was not
able to say.

Our hero derived, therefore, very little desirable information from the confused account of Tormoya; and
his anxiety about the fate of his fair one continued un-
relieved. He could not, however, part from the robbers, without giving them a severe rebuke for their
wickedness; and the two that belonged to his company of horse, were so sensible of their misconduct,
that they asked his pardon, and promised to change
their lives.

CHAPTER XXVI.

Our travellers, having resumed their route, soon entered Matamoros, where the first scene which presented itself to their view, greatly surprised Flambeau,
and excited his censure, as a ridiculous and unnatural
thing. It was a procession, which he judged to be of
a religious description, from a number of clergymen,
in their canonicals, accompanying it; and holden for
some joyful purpose, from the brilliant music that
played, and the great number of rockets which were
fired. Yet they were carrying the corpse of an infant;
and it was the funeral of the little creature they were
thus solemnizing!—He asked the captain an explanation of this singularity and seeming contradiction; to
which our hero answered that the Mexicans, as Roman
Catholics, not only believe that infants dying after baptism are admitted to the immediate enjoyment of heavenly bliss, but that they rigorously follow up the consequences of this consoling dogma, and actually rejoice
in the death of their children, whenever they happen
to die under age. "This music and these rockets,"
said he, "are a manifestation of gladness on the part
of the child's parents, because he is become an angel,
(angelito.) This will not be the only expression of
joy. This night, there will be a ball and carousal in
their house; and, however poor the father be, he
would not dare to omit those rejoicings, which are,
here, no less than tears and lamentations, in other
countries, accounted tokens of parental love."

"It is very strange," replied the quarteroon, "that
the strongest feeling of nature can be thus suspended,
and the purest passion of the human heart counter-
acted by a speculative consequence of one of the
minor dogmas of religion!"

"Yet, perhaps, in this instance," resumed the captain, "it is of service. It affords, at least, a harmless
consolation to the bereaved parents, and dries up tears
which would flow to no purpose."

"Such is not my opinion of this singular practice of your countrymen," returned the quarteroon. "I would not speak against the religious dogma itself upon which it is based. As a speculative tenet, it is consoling; and I would leave to the church her spiritual rejoicing at the death of the infant Christian; because her joy is grave, decent, and pious: it exhales itself in canticles of praise to the Most High. But to see rational creatures make the death of a poor innocent child an occasion of merry-making, to see parents so far hardening their hearts, as to dance on the brink of their infant's grave, is shocking and worthy of barbarians."

"Well, you may be right, for aught I know," returned the captain, "but beware how you express such an opinion to any body else, for it might give offence, and would be looked upon as right down impiety. Many other things you will see, which may appear strange and unnatural; but be cautious how you manifest your feelings before the natives, for they are jealous of foreigners, and apt to suspect of Judaism any one who gainsays their religious prejudices; and *that* may bring a man into great danger. My own father, nineteen years ago, was stabbed for much less, and, thank God, the knife glanced along one of his ribs, otherwise I would not be here to tell the story."

With these reflections, they passed by the funeral procession, and went to alight before a fine house, in Sonora Street, where the captain had been informed, in Camargo, that the *teniente* of his company of horse, who had succeeded him, was lodged. The latter was delighted to see him, and received him with the utmost civility. He did not, however, permit his guest to rest himself, before he insisted upon his dressing and shaving, in order to pay his visit to the general-in-chief. *Dressing*, in the fashionable sense of the expression, was a thing quite out of our hero's power, for he found himself in that philosophical state of existence, when he might say, with the Grecian sage, "omnia mecum porto." How humbling soever the situation, he cheerfully confessed it to his friend, who immediately offered to lend him a suit of his own. In these borrowed

clothes, therefore, our captain sallied forth, to pay his
respects to Urrea. He felt inclined to go, first, in
search of Miss Linton and her father; but his friend,
having represented to him that his first visit was in
rigour due to the general, he suffered himself to be
lead along in the hope that the interview would be of
short duration, and that he would have the remainder
of the day for his perquisitions.

Urrea received him with transports of joy, and after
inquiring the particulars of the battle of San Jacinto,
and the state of affairs among the Texians, said to him,
"Now, my dear fellow, although glad to see you, yet, I
confess, your return embarrasses me. Your company
of horse has, in your absence, been given to your friend,
here, who was once your lieutenant. We believed you
were dead, and he deserved promotion. We cannot
take it from him, to make him sink again to his former
rank, particularly after his admirable conduct during
our retreat. Yet you have yourself so much suffered,
in your country's cause, that you cannot remain without a post, and I have none to give. My army is now
dwindled away to the fourth part of what it was, when
it left Saltillo, under the President's command. What
shall we do in this case?—will you accept of the post
of colonel *graduado*? (15) It is honourable! and the
fortune of your family enables you to dispense with
the emoluments."

"Why, general," replied captain Letinez, "don't
put yourself to any trouble for me. I will be glad to
retire from the service, and, by tendering my resignation, of my own accord, I conceive, I will smoothe all
difficulties."

"Resign!—No indeed," replied Urrea,—"you shall
not. You must accept my proposal. Think how glorious, from a mere captain, to become at once a colonel!"

"There are so many *graduados*, sir!" resumed the
captain.

"It is true," said Urrea, "we have an immense number,—I dare say five and twenty generals, and sixty or
seventy colonels without exercise!—But still it is ac-

counted an honour and will be especially so in a young
man like you. Therefore I insist upon it. I will immediately write to the secretary of war, and in the
meanwhile, if you want to go to Mechoacan to see your
relations, I will give you leave of absence, and you may
take your time for your return, for it will be long before we be ready for another campaign."

Our hero consented, at last, rather in order to satisfy
the general and get rid of his importunities, than
through any desire of elevation, and, having taken leave,
went to the *cuartel*, or barracks, where he was told some
Texians were confined, in order to inquire about major
Linton. These prisoners of war had been in great
danger of being shot, and an order to that effect had
been sent by Santa Anna from Bejar; but the Irish,
American, and French merchants of Matamoros had
saved their lives, by offering a large sum of money,* and
the Mexican ladies of the same place had also presented a very eloquent petition in their behalf, for which it
is just to render to their humanity the meed of praise
it deserves. But the lives which had been saved with
so much trouble were well nigh being lost for want of
food. The Mexicans gave them nothing to eat, and,
had not the same merchants, who had already made
such generous offers, to save them from death, subscribed for their support, they would actually have been
starved. Nor is it to be supposed that, in this instance,
the Mexicans were impelled by cruelty, or special hatred to the Texians; for it is in the *same way* they
treat their own prisoners. As soon as one is under
lock and key, the government meddles no more with
his bodily wants; but abandons him to the mercy of
Providence and the charity of the faithful!—Only, in
desperate cases, when hunger grows ravenous, they will
sometimes permit him to go out and *beg* under the
guard of a soldier or two.

Captain Letinez did not find Major Linton amongst
the prisoners, but heard of his being in town, and was
directed to his house. It was a little *Jacal*, or cabin,

---

* Thirty thousand dollars were subscribed in half an hour !

built with large unburnt bricks, called *adobes*, in the
language of the country, and thatched over with *tule*,
a kind of rushes that grow in the swampy bottoms of
the Rio Bravo and are nearly incombustible. The
thatch itself had, by the effect of time, been reduced to
an earthy mass, that had shrunk into consistency, and
afforded sustenance to various parasitic plants, which,
being now in full bloom, gave it the appearance of a
flower garden. Amongst them various kinds of opun-
tias were remarkable, some with large red blossoms,
and others with pale yellow ones. The captain was
diverted by this extraordinary appearance ; but upon
entering the edifice, he was shocked at the state of
poverty the interior exhibited. The only person he
found in the house was an old female Indian servant,
who acted as drudge to the family. This was no proof
of easy circumstances, in the owners, for, ordinary servants are so cheap in that country, that almost every
house-holder keeps three or four.

The furniture consisted of a little cot, with very
coarse, though extremely clean bed clothes, a small
table, four old chairs without backs, and a mattress,
rolled up in a corner, which, being spread, at night, on
a rag carpet, served one of the inmates as a bed. Some
crockery ware, upon a shelf, a few books, on the man-
tel piece, and two trunks completed the inventory.

The aged sybil who, for the moment, acted as house
keeper, being asked where was " el Senor Linton," answered with a kind of stutter : " In the *huerta*, culling
figs, to send me to sell them through the town—or he
may be gathering dry seed of palma christi, for, he said,
last night, he would extract from it an excellent oil,
proper for many ailments, and, particularly, to purge
people when their bowels are disordered. He may afford it cheap and yet make money, according to what
he says."

" How," interrupted the captain, " going to manufacture castor oil ?"

" Oh, yes, bless your honour," replied the old woman,
"and I wish he may succeed, for it is a shame in a
Christian country, like this, to have such apothecaries

as ours. No later than two weeks ago, sir, they made me pay one dollar for a spoonful of that same oil, for my daughter, Juanita, and the poor child has not been any better for it—hardly able to crawl about, so that I saw myself obliged to call an old witch of a *curandera*, who made a remedy with Spanish brandy, of which she drank the best part—and you may believe me, sir, but she swallowed two bottles of it in five visits, and left the child as bad as ever. Then I had recourse to Dr. Laverdure, the French physician—an awful and solemn man, sir—as stiff as the statues of the blessed saints in the church—and God forgive me that I should compare Dr. Laverdure to them. He won't stir from his room, till you put a hard dollar in his paw !"

Heaven alone knows how long the old woman would have protracted her address, had not the captain given way to impatience, and plainly bid her hush her prattle and show him where Mr. Linton was. Thereupon, the old crone, not a little cut down, opened a door, made of reeds wattled together, which gave access to a little court-yard, through which she marshalled him to the gate of the huerta.

This *huerta*, (by which word, Mexicans understand a fruit garden,) was extensive, and full of fig, pomegranate, and orange trees, planted without any attention to symmetry. They were set so thick, and their foliage was so dense, as to afford a coolness extremely pleasant in that southern climate, and moreover, produced a kind of artificial night upon the vision of one, who, coming from the glare of the broad day light, entered this deep shade.

The Indian beldame having left our hero to grope his way as well as he could through this labyrinth, in search of her master, hastily returned to the house, the door of which she had left opened ; so that captain Letinez was at a loss which way to direct his steps, not knowing in what part of the garden the major might be found. His eyes having, nevertheless, in a few seconds, become used to the half light, which rested on the empty space, under the verdant canopy above his head, he distinguished, at the extremity of the garden, a little arbour, under which was a female figure in a sitting posture.

Thither our hero directed his steps, and had the inexpressible pleasure to find that it was Miss Linton herself, who was so busy sewing, as not to notice his approach. He stood at a short distance to contemplate her, whilst a variety of tender emotions rapidly succeeded each other in his mind, and caused his heart to palpitate, as though it would have burst its ligaments. He had found her again, his beloved one! The only woman he had ever loved, but loved to adoration! He had found her again, and under such circumstances as made a union certain. Her father's life had been saved by his friend's exertions! Gratitude, he thought, would combine with love, in Miss Linton's heart, and in the intoxication of his hope, he was almost sure of her consent. She and her father had lost their property.—They were now in want and poverty. He was nearly glad of it, for it would serve to prove the disinterested fervour of his affection. But she was pale!—Oh, how much she must have suffered in the midst of those scenes of war and desolation! Yes, the weight of wo had sunk her eyes and tarnished their lustre—the tears of misfortune had furrowed her cheeks! Perhaps some of those tears had been shed for him!—Yet, though suffering, how beautiful!—Even more interesting than when in the bloom of perfect health.

> " The rose" that " was upon her cheek,
> Was mellowed by a tenderer streak!"

He must advance; but, lo! he trembles like a child, his knees can hardly support his tottering frame. He, the accomplished gentleman, who can acquit himself with so much grace and elegance in the most polished circles and brightest companies, is *now* at a loss for words to hail the maid he loves. He even feels that he is blushing at the thought of this interview. Blush on, dear youth, blush on!—As Diogenes said, it is the colour of virtue. She, whom thou lovest, cannot take offence at the embarrassment thou feelest. Were thy heart less pure, thou wouldst be bolder.

The spell was at last broken by major Linton, who, till that moment, had remained busy in a remote corner of the garden; but, having now finished his task, came near his daughter, and was startled at the sight of a man standing so close to the arbour. He approached him with a threatening aspect; but, recognizing him, threw himself into his arms, crying out:— "Oh, my dear friend!" He had no time to continue, when Miss Linton raised her eyes from the work which had engrossed all her attention, saw her lover, gave a scream of surprise, sprang up from her chair, and again fell into it, like a dead corpse.

The captain and her father ran to her help, and, after considerable efforts, brought her to the use of her senses. The first manifestation she gave of her returning reason, was by a flood of tears, which alleviated a little the fulness of her heart. Her lover was behind her chair, when she first recovered her consciousness; and, missing him, she said: "Oh, father! was it a dream, or has captain Letinez really been here?"

He could no longer control himself. "Yes, my dear Miss Linton," said he, "I am here. Your own Letinez, always faithful and true. Yes, my love, I have returned more worthy of you. During my captivity, I have learned that you as much surpass your own countrywomen, in kindness of heart and generosity of disposition, as these surpass mine, in beauty and gracefulness; and, if I was thy lover before," added he, kissing her hand with ardour, "I am now thy adorer!— Here is your father, who will not refuse his consent to our mutual vows. He will become my father also," added the generous youth, "and I will glory in the adoption."

"Yes, I will," said the old man, embracing him; "and, Heaven is my witness, with what sincere joy!— I receive you as the greatest blessing God can bestow upon me. Had I selected a son-in-law among ten thousand, I could not have made a better choice. Yes, my children, you will both be happy, and crown my old age with gladness. Be not ashamed, my daughter,"

22

continued he, addressing Sophia, whose face was suf-
fused with blushes; "be not ashamed to confess your
virtuous flame, when you have your father's consent,
and the approbation of your own conscience. Consider yourselves as plighted to each other, and may the
blessing of Heaven attend you."

Miss Linton, now a little more composed, and feeling all the embarrassment of maidenly modesty, rose
to withdraw; but the captain, in an ecstacy of joy, at
seeing the object of his ardent wishes attained, and
emboldened by the father's presence, could not help
clasping her to his bosom, and stealing a kiss, as the
earnest of his future bliss.

> "Dear, wedded love!
> Which men so seldom, blameless prove;
> A harmless pair, for once, at least,
> Thy holy pleasures taste!"

Now, walking hand in hand, they returned to the
house, where major Linton and captain Letinez, in
close colloquy, made their arrangements, and took all
the measures they thought necessary for the execution
of their scheme. All parties being equally desirous to
bring it to a happy issue, they did not anticipate any
difficulty, chiefly as there was no matter of interest to
be debated, or settled. They were, however, destined
to be crossed by an unknown circumstance, which,
how trifling soever it might have appeared in another
country, is, in Mexico, a thing of the utmost importance, as the reader will see by the trouble it gave
them.

CHAPTER XXVII.

The first thing our hero inquired of major Linton, after his transports were calmed, was the history of his escape from the massacre, with which our reader is already acquainted; and the details of his journey from Goliad to Matamoros, in which there was nothing peculiarly interesting. The few prisoners who had been saved from that horrid butchery had been sent, under an escort, to the Irish village, where Miss Linton had found again her old acquaintance, honest Mrs. Jordan, and retaken possession of her little room; while her father and a few others were kept confined in an out house, belonging to the Alcalde, who treated them with humanity. They had afterwards followed the inhabitants of St. Patricio, when the latter left their village at the instigation of Urrea, who threatened, that, at his return, he would make no distinction between friend and foe; but would hang every man and burn every house. Since his arrival at Matamoros, major Linton, who had, by his practice of medicine, made several friends and protectors among the Mexican officers, had been permitted to remain in a private house, with his daughter, and had earned his livelihood by tending his garden, while the young lady helped also, by her skill in sewing and millinery.

Captain Letinez's curiosity being satisfied, the conversation naturally reverted to the intended marriage. Major Linton had no idea of the many intricacies and formalities by which a nuptial union is attended in Mexico. He thought that it would be as easy as in the United States, where there is nothing else to do than to take out a license from the clerk of the court, and go to be married by the first justice of the peace, whose office happens to be opened; but he found that the Spanish law, which still rules the Mexican republic, has thrown the greatest difficulties imaginable in the way of the most necessary thing in nature.

First, both the young lady and gentleman, being na-

tives of other dioceses than that of Monterrey, in which
Matamoros is situated, were obliged to get their *fe de
bautismo*, id est, the certificate of their baptism, and, for
that purpose, captain Letinez must write to Mechoacan,
and wait at least six weeks, before that important paper
should arrive; whilst his bride would have to wait perhaps six months, before she could get her own, from
Maryland, where she had been baptised in the church
of England.

This difficulty being once got over, they had both to
prove that they had never been married, which was being reduced to prove a negative, and might be looked
upon as physically impossible, but is, nevertheless,
strictly required by the Mexican law, and done every
day, after some fashion or other.

Thirdly, there was the article of religion. Miss Linton being a Protestant, the marriage could not be sol-
emnised without a special dispensation from the Pope,
or the bishop of Monterrey, in case the jurisdiction of
the latter should have been enlarged by the Holy See.
All this would require time, expense and powerful
friends. Expenses the captain could afford, friends he
had; but time was what he begrudged. He thought
proper, however, to explain all this to the major, in order that his own sincerity might not be suspected,
should not the marriage be accomplished as quickly as
external circumstances might induce any one not acquainted with the laws of the country to think practicable.

This subject of conversation being exhausted, our hero
took leave of the worthy major and returned to the house
of his ancient lieutenant, where he soon began to receive
the visits of his friends. As he was a general favourite
in the army, and his escape from among the Texians,
the history of which began to spread through the town,
was so romantic, every one was curious to see him.

One of the first that presented themselves was captain Alvarez, whom senor de Letinez embraced with
real transports of joy, while some tears of gratitude,
which he could not repress, bathed his cheeks, and expressed to his friend, better than the choicest words

could have done, the sincere acknowledgment of his heart, for having saved major Linton's life, and so efficiently protected the young lady to whom he was attached. Major Linton had informed him of the noble and almost heroical manner in which Alvarez had stood forth as the champion of humanity, and captain Letinez thought he could never sufficiently acknowledge such a piece of service. "Alvarez," said he, "I will not fatigue you by long protestations of gratitude; but, had you saved my own life, I could not feel more than I do. From henceforth, all I have,—my credit, and that of my family, are at your disposal."

"Dear Don Ambrosio," answered his friend, "I did no more than humanity required. Would to God I had been able to save *them* all. But, for Heaven's sake, let us drop that subject, and banish the painful recollection from our mind. It makes my blood curdle in my veins! —Let us rather talk of your marriage. Ah, lucky rogue! But you must have been born with a cawl upon your head, to light upon so much beauty and sense united! It was your good angel, no doubt, who inspired you to go on that expedition against the Comanches! We thought it the trick of a mad-cap, when we heard of it, but it will turn out a fortunate trick for you. Now, when comes the wedding?—The *sponsalia?*—I hope you will give a ball, and the thing will be done with some *eclat.* I want to be the first to open the dance with your wife. By my *santiguada*, it is my due!"

"That it is, indeed," replied Senor de Letinez, laughing; "and you shall dance as long as you please: but, I am afraid, that, notwithstanding your impatience, we shall have to wait some time yet."

"Wait!" replied Alvarez, with surprise; "and for what, pray?"

"Why," returned the captain, "I have to write to Mechoacan, for my certificate of baptism, and to get dispensation of the publication of bans, both in my own native parish and here; and the young lady has to procure her *papers* from Maryland, which is a great ways off, in the North of the United States."

"Pooh, pooh! wherefore all that?" replied Alvarez:

23*

"Don't suppose that the padre, here, is so scrupulous. No, not he, good man. He will never require such a thing from you, provided you pay him a good round sum."

"Do you think," inquired captain Letinez, "that he will violate these canons of discipline, to oblige one?"

"Canons!" resumed the other: "He has twisted more canons than you or I ever saw fired. What a babe you are!—You think every priest is like your grand-uncle, and that other good soul of Phelipa, of whom I have so often heard you speak?—Clergymen that are walking towards heaven on tiptoe!—There are not many of these, in the Mexican church."

"But then," objected Letinez, "I do not want to render my marriage null and invalid."

"Why, this will not affect it, in the least," answered his friend. "It is an impediment, to be sure; but not one that breaks the band of matrimony. There is your *impedimentum dirimens*, and your *impedimentum impediens*. The lack of publication of bans, belongs to the latter category only: you should know *that*, as you are now a courting gallant. It is the priest's business to require it of you; but, if he be willing to overlook it, it is none of yours to make him mind it."

"Well, really," replied our hero, "the thing had never been considered by me under this point of view. I stand corrected by your superior knowledge of divinity."

"So much the worse, then," said Alvarez. "In a country like ours, where the canon-law is a part and parcel of the law of the land, every *gentleman* should be something of a theologian!"

"Well," resumed captain Letinez, "since you are so knowing, I will consult you upon another difficulty. Miss Linton is a Protestant, and she will not change her religion, I know; neither do I intend proposing it to her. Will that make any difficulty with this padre?"

"Not the least, not the least," replied Alvarez: "Only be liberal with him, and you will find him the most liberal man in the world. *Ave Maria!*—He would

marry a man of your condition with a Jewess, or a
Turkish woman, if you wished, and never bogle at it.
Foreigners accuse our clergy of illiberality; but, by
my Santiguada, if they were all like padre Robinez,
they would reverse the judgment they so rashly pass
on them. Why, man, I have known this fellow to
marry a French Catholic, without previous confession,*
on a special bargain of a fifty dollars fee."

"If such be the case," said senor de Letinez, "there
will be no difficulty with me; and I will come through
easily enough!"

"You will,—you shall," resumed his friend; "and,
therefore, I hope the business will soon be over."

"Not so quick, neither," observed our hero; "for,
although there is no need of postponement, for the
sake of the publication of bans, and other formalities, yet I have to write to my grandfather and his
brother. It would be the basest ingratitude in me to
marry without informing them of it, and asking their
leave. I know their love for me will not permit them
to refuse their consent."

"As to that," said Alvarez, "it is quite a different
thing!—Certainly, it is your duty to write to them. I
would be the first to blame you, if you did not."

Thus enlightened by captain Alvarez's superior information in canonical matters, and well assured of
padre Robinez's pliability of principle, our hero felt relieved of an oppressive weight; for he had imagined, from
what he knew of the history of his father's marriage, that
the difficulties he would have to encounter would almost
prove insuperable, or, at least, put so many delays in
the way of the accomplishment of his wishes, that he,
sometimes, felt tempted to despair.

Captain Alvarez was not the only one that took a
lively interest in his fate, and future union with the
object of his love. Great many of his brother-officers
congratulated him also on the acquisition of Miss Linton's hand; and it was in the midst of those friendly

* Marrying, without confession, is a sacrilege in the Roman Catholic Church.

wishes and amicable demonstrations, he directed to the old count of Letinez and the good clergyman his brother, a letter to inform them of his engagement, and ask their permission for his marriage.

There was another person to whom he was tenderly attached, and whom he wished it had been in his power to consult. It was his father: but he was at too great a distance. Though Mr. Faring had never earnestly insisted on carrying his son away to the United States, for fear of exposing him to lose his grandfather's fortune, yet he had taken several trips to Mechoacan, in order to visit him, and made on the boy's mind an impression which time could not obliterate. The last of those visits had taken place, about three years previous to the period we are now treating of, when our hero was a lad of fifteen; and his father had then promised to return in four years, and take him to travel. This plan would be *now* defeated by the young man's marriage; but yet the latter complied with what filial respect required of him, by despatching a letter to Mr. Faring, at the same time he wrote to his grandfather.

Our hero being now wholly engrossed by his matrimonial scheme, Flambeau, who had been accustomed to live with him in the greatest familiarity, saw himself a little neglected, and, thinking rather hard of it, resolved to leave him. In vain did the captain expostulate with him, the quarteroon answered, in a melancholy manner, that he was too sensible of the distance which separated them, to expect familiarity; and that he could not, however, resolve himself to live as a menial. He had struck up a kind of acquaintance with some coloured people from Louisiana, refugees, like himself, and he was inclined to try his luck at a little commerce, he intended to establish, between the city and the mouth of the river. All the efforts of the captain could not dissuade him, and even it was with difficulty he could prevail upon him to accept a gratification, for Flambeau's heart was proud, and he thought himself offended. Our hero sincerely regretted him: but, seeing that it could not be helped, took a servant to supply the deficiency.

CHAPTER XXVIII.

We will now leave our hero to carry on his court-ship in the most approved manner known to a Mexican gallant, and beg our reader to transfer himself to the state of Mechoacan, in order to witness the scene that took place in the family of Letinez, upon their being informed of his captivity. The disaster of San Jacinto had been concealed from the Mexican people, by their government, as long as possible, and when they were, at last, obliged to publish it, they did so with every at-tenuating circumstance they could think of, never making public the number or the names of the prisoners. The count of Letinez, therefore, who knew that his grandson was in General Urrea's division, and was not informed that he had been transferred to the main body, under the President's immediate command, felt no painful anxiety about him. Having, nevertheless, re-mained a long time, without receiving any letter from him, after the return of the army to Matamoros, he wrote to Urrea, to whom the young man had been es-pecially recommended, in order to know the cause of his long silence, and was informed of the doleful truth, that his grandson was a prisoner among the Texians.

On the reception of that news, the old count and his brother, were well nigh overpowered with grief. Their child, as both called our hero, was the only scion of their noble and ancient family, the object of all their affection, endowed with talents and qualifications which promised new illustration to the name he bore, and now, he was in the hands of a horde of needy adventu-rers, who were represented as the most unprincipled and cruel of mankind. O!, how bitterly did the old count and his brother repent having permitted him to enrol himself under Santa Anna's banners! They had done so, indeed, in the idea that the expedition could not prove dangerous, and would be nothing worse than a military *paseo*, from whence the heir of the family would return adorned with fame, and improved in ex-

perience, without having been exposed to any peril.
They had, however, been deceived in their expectations, as well as many others, wiser than they, and now
they began to consult upon the means of repairing the
sad effects of their condescension. But was there any
possibility of effecting it? Would it be practicable to
rescue their beloved Ambrosio from captivity? Could
they, for this purpose, avail themselves of their influence with men high in office under the federal government? Alas, no!—Corro's administration neither held
nor permitted any correspondence with the rebellious
colonists, and would not even allow the exchange of
flags of truce.

In this sad emergency, and well nigh driven to despair, the old count took a resolution, which, in a man of
his age and weakly habits, might seem to border on
extravagance. It was to set out himself for Matamoros,
and, thence, try to get in among the Texians, by way
of New Orleans, and ransom his grandson with money.
"At all events," said he, "they are poor and needy!
Their government, if such it can be called, must be in
want of resources, and I will offer them such a sum as
will obtain *his* liberty."

His brother, however, would not consent to his departure. "No," said he, "if any one is to go, I will
be the man. You are *now* past travelling and would,
certainly, be unable to resist the fatigues of such a journey. Moreover, brother, I have more experience of
the world than you, who have always lived in retire-
ment. And if it be necessary to cross the gulf of Mexico, have I not seen the sea, from the peak of Colima,
while I lived in the state of Guadalaxara?"

It was not necessary for Abbatte Letinez to insist
with much perseverance in order to extort the count's
assent to the proposed change; for, to tell the truth,
the old man dreaded travelling beyond expression, and
nothing short of the agony of grief he felt at the loss
of his grandson could have prompted him to so strange
a resolution. Moreover, he was subject to sudden
changes of mind and seemed, at times, to be verging

towards his dotage, circumstances which incapacitated him for an undertaking like the present one.

It was, therefore, settled that the good ecclesiastic should immediately set out on his journey, towards the mouth of the Rio Bravo, a distance of more than twelve hundred miles, and the servants received orders to make the necessary preparations forthwith.

When it became known in Pasquaro that Abbatte Letinez was going to Matamoros, with the purpose of penetrating into Texas, every body was in the greatest amazement, and not a few supposed that the good man, through grief, had lost his wits. The Texians were reported to be monsters in human form, worse, if possible, than cannibals, for whom it would be a special delight to put to death any Catholic clergyman who might fall into their hands. They were said to have taken the parish priest of Goliad to Harrisburgh, and there to have burned him alive; and could it be any thing but sheer madness, which now prompted the good Abbatte to expose his life among such a people? A great number of female devotees, whose father confessor he was, moved heaven and earth, to make him alter his mind. They prayed and wept! They burned blessed candles before every image in the parish church, and caused masses to be said upon every altar, but all would not do. The day of his departure, at last, arrived, and, in spite of all their tears and supplications, he set out.

A new and splendid coach had been bought for the purpose, and no less than twenty servants were engaged to accompany him. Provisions in plenty and of the best quality, with a large and commodious tent, had also been provided, so that our good clergyman had the chance of enjoying every possible convenience on the road. But as we have already described the mode of travelling in the interior of that country, we will abstain from repeating, here, what could not but prove fastidious to the reader.

We have once hinted that the period marked by our hero's father for paying him a visit had elapsed. The great trouble to which the family of Letinez had, in

consequence of the young man's captivity, been a
prey, prevented them from resenting this want of
punctuality, as much as they would otherwise have
done; still they had several times thought of it, particularly after learning the news of the battle of San
Jacinto, for, they imagined, that, had Mr. Faring
been in the country, he might have gone to rescue
the young man, with greater probability of success,
than the Abbatte could expect.

Captain Letinez's father was, nevertheless, faithful
to his promise, and he arrived in Pasquaro shortly
after the departure of his late wife's uncle. He would
have been there sooner, and time enough to save the
old man his long journey, but he had to take Vera
Cruz and Mexico in his way, in order to transact some
commercial business for a house in New York, with
which he was connected, and this had been the cause
of his delay. His arrival, though late, was, nevertheless, hailed, with the utmost joy, by the old count:
"Welcome," said he, as he embraced him, "a thousand times welcome, my dear Faring—You will be
yet time enough to overtake the *Padre*, and assist
him in rescuing your son, if heaven have spared his
life."

"My son!" exclaimed Mr. Faring, alarmed. "Ambrosio's life is in danger!—Where, and how?—Is not
the boy here?"

"Alas, no, my dear friend," resumed the old count.
"When it was ascertained, that President Santa Anna
would march with the flower of the Mexican army,
against the rebels of Texas, the lad was seized with an
irresistible desire of joining our troops. The Padre
and myself did all in our power to prevent him, but
he so teased and besought us, that he, at last, conquered our repugnance. In fact we did not think the
Texians would make any head against our troops, im-
agining the campaign would be nothing but a military
pasco, and, that, as the boy had always lived in seclusion, he wanted some use of the world and a little
gentlemanly *desenvoltura*, which he would acquire in
his intercourse with the superior officers, to most of
whom he was especially recommended. But, *valga me*

la virgen de los dolores! The affair has turned out
contrary to our expectations, and he is now a prisoner amongst the Texians."

"Gracious heavens!" exclaimed Mr. Faring. "My
son, my poor son! Perhaps he has parished, by this
time, though innocent, in expiation of the Goliad
massacre! But are you certain that he is a prisoner,
count? Have you any official news?"

"Alas!—It is but too certain," answered the old
man, and, thereupon, he detailed all the information
he had derived from his communications with various officers, who, after surviving the campaign, had
returned to Matamoros.

The unfortunate Father, having become possessed
of all those details, immediately took his resolution,
and told the count that he would set out on the spot,
in order, if possible, to overtake the good Abbatte.

"Heaven be merciful unto us and the virgin *de Los
Remedios!*" returned the old man. "You cannot be in
a greater hurry to go, than I wish you; but, it is impossible to undertake such a journey without servants and a coach, or, at least, a gig. And wo is me, it
will take some time to make every thing ready!—The
house has been turned topsy turvy with my brother's
departure, and I don't know where to find trusty servants for you."

"Put yourself to no trouble about it," replied his
son-in-law. "I will not tarry twenty-four hours. Two
servants and a good sumpter mule will be sufficient.
I came from Mexico hither, with no larger train, and
I need very little baggage on the road. It is no time to
study my own convenience when my child's life is
perhaps in jeopardy."

"Verily, my dear," resumed the count, "I will not
permit you to expose yourself in the way you propose. Madness itself would not undertake so long a
journey, and partly through desert countries, without provisions, and a number of attendants
capable of defending you, should you be attacked. Moreover, something is due to the standing
of the family of Latinez to whom you are
so closely allied!—Consider what would be thought

should one belonging to our house travel with no more
state than the merest *ranchero.*"

"And would you," said Mr. Faring; "postpone, for
one single day, the succour I owe to my son, for the sake
of so paltry a consideration?—Oh! count, count, is it
possible that your mind can, be set upon such frivolities,
when the only scion of your house, the worldly honour
and feudal glory of which you esteem so highly, is in
danger of his life, or, at least, straitghened with want?
—No, sir; I will set out immediately. You may give
your orders to your *mayordomo,* in case you are disposed to speed me on my way. I want fresh horses, for
mine are jaded; a strong sumpter mule, and two servants of approved fidelity:—undoubtedly, your resources can command all this, in twelve hours' time. If a
proper degree of speed is used, I may yet overtake the
padre, and then travel in state, and with all the pomp
suited to the son-in-law of the count of Letinez."

It was as a kind of sweetener Mr. Faring threw in
these last words, and in order to bring the old man to
accede more freely to his proposal, for, though he had,
as yet, no idea that the weakness of intellect peculiar
to old age had begun to creep upon his mind, he knew,
of old, his vanity and pride of ancestry, and did not
think it beneath him to soothe that foible.

The bait took effect accordingly, and the count gave
immediate orders to his mayordomo to furnish his son-
in-law with what he wanted. These commands being
promptly executed, Mr. Faring took his departure
from Pasquaro, and rode with all possible speed, in
order to overtake Abbatte Letinez, which he entertained well founded hopes to compass, for he knew the
good clergyman would be slow in travelling.

His expectations were not, however, realised as soon
as he had imagined, for the old gentleman rode hard,
and had already reached the frontiers of the state of
Cohahuila, before Mr. Faring came up with him. Even,
then, he would not have been enabled to overtake him,
had not our clergyman been detained by a singular occurrence, which stopped his further progress and caus-

ed him to prolong his stay in the little mining town of
Mapimi, from which the extensive desert alluded to in
the beginning of this work derives its name. There,
Mr. Faring found him, and under such circumstances
as excited his astonishment, and required all his energy to extricate him.

CHAPTER XXIX.

The place where our reverend traveller was stopped,
though its population amounts but to four thousand
souls, ranks high among the *minerales** of Durango,
and supplies a considerable portion of the precious
metals that enrich this large and populous state. About
ten silver mines, in which the abundance of the ore
makes up for its poverty, give occupation to two thousand miners, who spend five days of the week in the
bowels of the earth, descending into the subterranean
caverns, on every Tuesday, and returning to the broad
daylight, only on Saturday evening. The silver extracted from those deep recesses is distinguished by
what is, in the language of the country, termed "*ley
de oro;*" that is to say, a portion of gold, that cannot
be separated from the less precious metal, with which
it is chemically combined, save by a long and scientific
process, hitherto practised solely at the mint, in the
city of Mexico; (16) but which a French chemist, of
the name of Bras de Fer, has lately introduced into the
casa de moneda, at Durango, and by which the profits
of the owners of the mines have been greatly increased; for they were, before, obliged to sacrifice that portion of gold, for a trifling consideration. Now, *these*
circumstances, how unconnected soever they may appear with our history, had the effect of suspending, for
some days, father Letinez's progress to the Eastward.

In order to enable our readers to understand the
connexion of events, which seem to bear no manner of
relation to each other, it is proper to premise here,
that, in consequence of such a state of things, and for
the purpose of levying an indirect tax, by means of the
acignorage, in coining the precious metals, the Mexican government has strictly prohibited the egress of
bullion. The nation is still so far from appreciating
the economical theories of Smith and Say, that they
think the greater the quantity of silver and gold they

---

* *Un mineral* means a mining district.

keep stagnating at home, the richer the country is likely to prove. For that purpose, they have also established very high duties on the exportation of specie.
But, not satisfied with this, and, as if it were not sufficient to cramp trade and industry, they have continued and augmented a transit duty, which, under the
Moorish name of *Alcavala*, existed in the Spanish
times, and prevented the circulation of bullion and
coin, from one province to another, without a permit
from the officers of government, under pain of confiscation. It is not only the precious metals which are
subject to this enactment, every kind of merchandise,
even goods manufactured in the country, being placed
under the same restriction, and debarred from passing
freely from parish to parish. Were the greatest philosophers and most ingenious statesmen of the earth to
be offered a splendid premium, for the concoction of a
system of political economy, the most inimical to the
developement of industry and commerce, and were
they all to meet in convention, and exhaust all the resources of their mind for such a purpose, they could
not possibly produce any thing worse than the present
Mexican plan of finances. The ideas by which the
leading statesmen of this nation seem to be governed,
are absolutely those of the eleventh century, when
cramping and restriction were supposed to be the best
policy, and the limits of a parish accounted sufficiently extensive for all the purposes of internal trade.

It was this very law, how absurd soever the statement may appear to our American readers, which now
occasioned our traveller's embarrassment; for, as they
may remember, the Abbatte had taken with him a large
sum of money, and, by a singular oversight, had neglected to get a *pass* from the *Alcavalero*, id est, the
custom-house officer charged with recovering the duties. Nay, he had, contrary to law, taken several bars
of silver and ingots of gold; and the purpose of his
journey being divulged by his servants, the collector
of the revenue, in Mapimi, became aware that our
ecclesiastic was carrying specie and bullion out of the
country, without permit. His office gave him the right

23 *

of examining the stranger's baggage; and, in case of
a discovery, the law awarded him a large share of the
confiscated property.

As the traveller was a priest, the revenue-officer
felt some repugnance to interfere; but the prospect of
a valuable wind-fall easily overcame those scruples.
He would not, however, proceed to the intended
search, while padre Letinez was in town, for fear of
giving scandal, as well as out of respect for the *cura*
of the place, at whose house the stranger lodged. He
said nothing, then, of the resolution he had taken; but,
having secretly summoned four guards, over whom he
had authority, he lay in wait for senor de Letinez, at
the little village of Vinagrillos, three leagues from
Mapimi; and, when the latter's caravan came on, in
the morning, his servants, as well as himself, were disagreeably surprised to see their further progress stopped by the Alcavalero, who presented his begrimmed
face at the door of the carriage, and, with a profusion
of bows and congees, called upon the padre for permission to search his baggage.

The servants were indignant that a man of their
master's quality should be treated in such a fashion,
and were ready to resist the unpleasant request; but
the Abbatte would not permit them to make use of
their arms. He relied upon the respect inspired by his
cloth, and supposed that the examination would be only
for form's sake; or, even, he thought that, at the last
extremity, he could bully the collector into terms, and
make him consent to receive a gratification.

He was, however, mistaken in his expectations, and
the Alcavalero discharged his duty with as much rigour
as if it had had for its object the meanest ranchero. "I
hope your paternity will forgive me," said he, "but
the laws of the republic prohibit the exportation of silver in bars, and it is my duty to see that none be carried eastward; therefore, I humbly beg you to rise
from your seat, in order that I may examine this carriage."

"How, now?" interrupted Senor de Letinez, "is it
thus the officers of a Christian government treat a

Catholic clergyman? Do you think we have overthrown
the impious Yorkinos, to be dealt with in this manner?
Will you dare to stop a priest of the Lord, on his journey?"

"Really, sir," replied the officer, "notwithstanding
the reverence we are bound to pay to men of your order, and which we render most willingly, I feel myself
under a consciencious obligation to follow the dictates
of the law, in every thing that concerns temporal matters. I pray you, therefore, not to think hard of me,
if I again request you to rise from your seat, and allow
me to do my duty."

"Well, be it so," replied Abbatte Letinez, "since
you are so rude. Only, I hope you will permit me to
take out my travelling chalice and other sacred vessels, these being utensils that you cannot even touch
without sacrilege, as you are a mere layman."

"Santo cielo!" exclaimed the revenue officer, "the
most important portion of what I am in search of will
escape me, after all—but I must be plain with you, sir,
I see. If I cannot touch your chalice, I may, at least,
look at it. You must, therefore, uncover it for my inspection, and it will be safe from my unhallowed grasp,
as well as the cruets, if you have brought any with
you!"

"Hear! now, how the creature is scoffing at religion," resumed Abbatte Letinez. "O seculum nequam!
That a Catholic clergyman should be stopped on his
road, by Catholic Christians, under pretence of obeying
revenue laws, and have his baggage searched, like a
vile smuggler! O shame! O abomination!"

"It is too bad, it is too bad, indeed," cried the servants, "and we cannot permit the brother of Count
Letinez to be treated in so unworthy a manner. The
Alcavalero shall not prevail. Shall we smite him, Padre?"

"For God's sake, commit no violence, my children,"
replied the pacific clergyman. "Better for me to submit, than to see blood spilt in a quarrel like this. I
command you to make no resistance. I am going to
alight. But, Juan Fades, open this box, and let me

take out my chalice and breviary, together with the
diurnal—and the box of holy oils—and my ritual also
—and my portative altar stone. The unhappy man
will not dare to put forth his sacrilegious hand to touch
these consecrated objects! If he should, I will resist
unto the death, even as the high priest resisted unto
the impious monarch of Israel, when he put forth his
hand to seize upon the censer."

So saying, he helped his servant to select the articles he had named, which, being wrapped up in many
folds of paper and linen cloth, defied scrutiny ; and, to
tell the truth, while he was fumbling about, in haste,
and throwing every thing topsy turvy, with well feigned confusion, he contrived to conceal several ingots of
gold, in the folds of the paper that served to wrap up
the chalice, ritual, breviary and diurnal, and Juan Fades, catching inspiration from his master's alertness,
secreted two *silver bars*, under pretence that it was the
altar stone—only the altar stone, folded up in consecrated linen!

But the Alcavalero was resolved not to be balked,
and insisted upon looking at that pretended altar stone,
as well as examining the smaller bundles, which they
had snatched away with so much precipitation ; and,
as they dared not offer him positive resistance, he had
the satisfaction of seizing upon more ingots of gold than
it had ever fallen to his lot to clutch at one time. A
few silver bars, also, became his prey, and the milled
dollars which the Abbatte was carrying away fared no
better, because it was without permit from the custom
house officer in Pasquaro.

By the zeal of the minister of the law, our good
clergyman was left nearly destitute, and, in the utter
impossibility of prosecuting his expedition, saw himself obliged to retrace his steps and throw himself
again upon the hospitality of the parish priest of Mapimi.

There he was, now, without funds, equally unable,
either to advance or recede, and with too numerous a
retinue, to render it tolerable for the *cura*, to keep him
in his house any length of time. The only resource

left him was to write to his brother, and send some of his men, in order to get wherewith to continue his journey; but the shame of having been the dupe of his overweening confidence made this application for money highly repugnant to his feelings. Moreover, his brother, though wealthy, was scarce of cash, and it had not been without difficulty the talegos with which he had set out had been made up, so that the count might find himself straightened to comply with his wishes. The loss of so considerable a sum as the *Alcavalero* had possessed himself of, was also no trifling cause of grief to the Abbatte, for, the amount was too large to be overlooked by any one not out of his senses.

All these reflections were bitter and galling, but regret could bring no remedy; and he, at last, saw himself obliged to write to his brother a statement of the case, and despatch four of the most trust-worthy amongst his servants, to convey to him this sad piece of intelligence, and ask for more funds.

The servants had not yet reached the frontiers of the state of Zacatecas, when they were met by Mr. Faring. The latter would have passed them unknowingly; but his *peones* recognized those of father Letinez, and, both parties having come to a stand, an explanation ensued. Our Marylander was a man of resolution, and, after a few minutes' reflection, took his determination. He directed the Abbatte's messengers to retrace their steps, and accompany him to Mapimi, promising that he would settle the difficulty, and there would be no need to trouble the count with so disagreeable a piece of news, as the confiscation of the money and bullion. The servants were indeed at a loss to imagine by what means he would recover what was in the Alcavalero's power; but they obeyed, and all pursued their march towards Mapimi, with renewed ardour.

Senor de Letinez's joy, at the sight of our American, was not a little damped by a sense of the embarrassed situation into which his neglect had brought him; but, when the latter proposed the scheme he had framed for the recovery of what had been confiscated, he became alarmed, and, for a long time, refused to give his assent. Really, the plan was excessively bold, and, in any other country than Mexico, would have exposed the perpetrator to severe penalties; but, as *Anahuac* is a republic, where any illegal act, not amounting to an enormity, can be executed with little danger from the tribunals and courts of law, Mr. Faring did not think that he ventured much, and insisted upon the old clergyman giving his consent.

He intended entering the Alcavalero's house, in broad day light, with his men fully armed, retaking possession of the money and bullion, and marching off. Should the scheme fail, he would laugh it off as a joke! But he had very little doubt of its success—for revenue-officers are generally detested—and there was no probability of any of the neighbours coming to the help of the man upon whom he wanted to make an irruption.

How strange soever it may appear to the inhabitants of more civilized countries, the plan succeeded, and was brought to a favourable issue, without the least danger. Thus, about seventeen thousand dollars, *confiscated according to law*, were, in the face of a town of four thousand souls, and in broad day light, abstracted from the house of the officer who had them in custody, without any resistance being offered; the eye-witnesses only laughing at the adventure, and applauding the precision with which it was achieved.

Mr. Faring, well knowing that it would be no part of discretion to prolong his stay, after such a feat, had been careful to have every thing in readiness, before going to the Alcavalero's. The sumpter-mules were all loaded, and waiting a little way out of town,—the coach ready,—the good Abbatte snugly seated inside, reciting his breviary, and all prepared to set off at a moment's warning, when our gallant merchant, at the head of fifteen of the servants, well armed, and guided by Juan Fades, of whom we have already made honourable mention, went to invest the dwelling of the revenue-officer. Leaving a guard of eight men at the door, he, with the remainder, proceeded to search the interior of the house, and had no need of long perquisitions, for the Alcavalero, frightened by the invaders' first threats, immediately returned the confiscated property; but Mr. Faring, not content with recovering it, and, in order to prevent a recurrence of similar accidents, forced the officer to give him a *guia*, or permit, in the most ample form.

This exploit happily achieved, our American marched off in triumph to the place where the old ecclesiastic was waiting. His men mounted their mules, the coach-driver gave the signal of departure, and all trotted off in great glee.

Soon after they had left Mapimi, however, the Alcavalero, having no longer an immediate danger before his eyes, picked up courage, and, enraged at the taunts and jests which his neighbours were showering upon him, made a formal petition to the Alcalde of the town for a party of the civic guard, to go to the rescue of the money and bullion.

Such a request the Alcalde could not refuse: in consequence, he summoned thirty of the citizens, commanded them to get horses and arms, and, when they were fully equipped, put them under the orders of the revenue-officer. The parish priest, however, who got wind of it, despatched a swift messenger, who overtook father Letinez, and gave him information of the impending danger, advising him, at the same time, of a cluster of mines, situated at about two leagues distance from his road, in a very precipitous *canada*, or glen, and the *sobresaliente* of which, being a particular friend of the cura, would afford him a secure place of concealment for his effects and money.

It may be easily imagined that this advice was received with gratitude, and the means thus offered to escape the rapacity of the revenue-officer, joyfully embraced. Leaving, therefore, the high road, they turned into the *canada*, and began to ascend the rocky acclivity, by which they were to penetrate into one of the most remarkable mining districts of the state of Durango.

The group of mountains in which those mines are

situated is called "*la Buffa de Mapimi*," by which
generic word, the inhabitants of Mexico designate any
isolated cluster, of small extension, rising abruptly in
the middle of a plain, without connection with any of
the longer and more important chains, to which they
apply the name of *sierra*. The Buffa to which we are
now alluding, about ten leagues long and five broad, is,
on all sides, surrounded by an extensive plain, and rises
abruptly, on the left side of the Rio Nassas, which,
meandering round and washing its base, environs two
thirds of its circumference. It may be considered as
an immense block of primary lime stone, cut by various deep gullies, and penetrated, to its inmost recesses,
by fissures and caverns, in which nature has lodged an
inexhaustible quantity of ores of various metals. Copper, in the state of green oxide; lead, in immense
quantities; silver and gold, gypsum, alabaster and sulphur are amongst the product of these mountains; towards the internal fastnesses of which our travellers
were now hastening,

CHAPTER XXX.

It was impossible for them to drive their coach to the appointed place of refuge. They were, therefore, obliged to leave it in a thick *palmar* situated in a nook, at the entrance of the glen, where the winter torrents had accumulated a little vegetative earth. There, they concealed also the bulkiest portion of their baggage, leaving the whole under the care of eight of their most courageous servants, with strict orders to keep themselves and their charge out of the officer's way. In the mean time, our travellers, with the remainder of their retinue, proceeded up the *canada*, on mules, a kind of conveyance exceedingly painful to the Abbate, and rendered more so, by the precipitous nature of the road. It lay mostly in the narrow bed of a torrent, now dried up, but full of large fragments of rock, that had tumbled down from the neighbouring eminences, and over which the mules had to scramble, with a pace so irregular, now sliding, now jolting their riders, that, they had hardly proceeded half a league, when the Padre declared all his bones were unhinged. "I cannot stand it, my child," said he, to Mr. Faring, for it was by this endearing title he used to address him: "I cannot stand it, any longer. I will even alight, and take it on foot. Oh blessed St. Peter of Alcantara, what a road! Oh, holy fathers, wo is me! I will never get over this. It once fell to my lot, while I was teaching metaphysics in the university of Guadalaxara, to go to exhort a poor French *Huguenot*, that had been thrice put on the rack, in the dungeons of the inquisition, and the sight of the miserable patient struck me with horror, and actually made me shed tears; but, certainly, what he had suffered was nothing to *this*. And, I think, if the inquisition had but known of this glen, they might have saved themselves the trouble and expense of the rack and other engines of torture, and sent all the French Huguenots and English Protestants whom they could have apprehended, to pace up and down this

24

canada. Three turns upon it would have brought
them to their recantation, I trow! It would convert
Barrabas himself and old Calvin to boot!"

With this, the good Padre alighted from his horse,
and began to walk, but soon gave out, so that the servants saw themselves obliged to carry him on a kind
of hand-barrow, which they made, on the spur of the
occasion, out of a strong piece of linen and some sticks.
Sometimes, their path rose on the crest of lofty eminences, when it was bordered, on either hand, with
deep precipices; sometimes, it sunk into the deepest
gullies, when towering cliffs nearly concealed the light
of day; but, which way soever they rode, they frequently crossed veins of precious ore, marked out,
even at the superficies of the ground, by a red oxide
of silver, which streaked the clefts of the rocks, as
bright as a trail of cinabar.

This spectacle entertained father Letinez, who was
something of a naturalist, and who, much relieved by
his new way of travelling, found, as he went along, leisure to indulge in various learned disquisitions. Their
guide, who had received from the parish priest of Mapimi, strict injunctions to give them all the assistance
in his power, was ready enough to amuse the Padre, by
communicating all the information he possessed, in relation to the mines which they saw at a distance. "That
opening which your paternity perceives, yonder," said
he, "at the top of that perpendicular cliff, shining with
hues as brilliant as if it had been painted with vermil-
lion, is called "*El Gato*," (the cat,) because it was originally supposed that no other animal could climb up
to it. A Gachupin, however, discovered the means to
reach it. He caused himself to be let down by means
of strong ropes, from the top of the cliff, and having
found the mineral rich enough to justify the cost, he cut
a road in the form of a cornice, through the live rock,
up to it; but, after all that expense, he found the mine
very poor in the interior of the cleft. The best speci-
mens of metal were at the mouth, and it turned out a
perfect *chasco* (disappointment.) That other gaping
cave which you perceive, a little above the *cat*, is, from

its great height, called *la Luz*, (the light.) Nature had
provided a scrambling path to reach it, but it ruined its
first owner, for all that. The way was so narrow, that
a goat would hardly have been able to tread it, and he,
without thinking, drove a large *atcjo* of mules up to the
mouth of the mine, to load them with ore; but the poor
animals could never turn round, to come down again.
He only saved a few of the hindmost ones, by blind-
folding them, and forcibly pulling them backwards, but
the greatest number, being scared, leaped down the
steep and perished."

"Friend," interrupted the Abbatte; "it is but a poor
account you have to give, I see, of the mines of this
celebrated Buffa!"

"Oh! but wait a little, senor," resumed the guide;
"and we will, presently, come to something better.
There, now, you see this deep pit, that yawns at your
feet,—it is the mine of San Juan. It has, in its time,
proved a little Potosi. It belonged to a certain padre
don Roque, who was the most determined miner in the
whole district. For seven weary years, he toiled and
sweated, running up and down the whole country,
climbing up hills and rocks, like a goat, reducing to cin-
ders every loose stone that bore any indication of metal,
and saying masses to support himself, at half a dollar
a piece, when he could get no better; until, at last, he
lighted upon this *creston*:—nay, I am wrong in saying
he lighted upon it; for it was a goat-herd, whom he assisted on his death bed, that told him of it, and by the
same token that he buried the boy, free gratis, and made
his mother a present of a gold doubloon and a green
plush petticoat!—But it was a lucky hit for the padre!
—He had not dug sixty varas when he came to a *cria-
dero*, that is, a large insulated chamber, in the rock,
which was partly filled with *polvillos*, the most precious
kind of ore we have in these parts. The padre realised ninety thousand dollars in nine months, besides
what was stolen by his workmen, for he was a careless
man."

"And what became of this padre don Roque?" in-

quired senor de Letinez. "I have not seen him amongst
the clergy of Mapimi!"

"I dare say not," replied the guide. "And good
reason there is why you should not. The man became
mad, sir. His good fortune turned his brains. He ran
into every kind of excess and rioting,—gave balls,
where, out of magnificence, he watered the floor with
French brandy, and, at last, in one of his mad frolics,
undertook to say mass with *pulque* whiskey; whereupon
the illustrissimo senor Castaniza, bishop of Durango,
caused him to be shut up in the prison of San Pedro.
Some folks thought that he should be burned alive, in
punishment of so dreadful a profanation; but the chapter of the cathedral being consulted, all the prebendaries
were of opinion that such an action could not have been
committed with full knowledge, and that it would be
more advantageous to religion to treat the padre as a
crazy man, than as a sacrilegious wretch. He was,
therefore, sent to the mad house of San Hipolito in
Mexico."

"Verily, the owners of mines, in these parts, seem
to be unlucky!" observed the Abbatte.

"Oh, senor padre," replied the guide, "you have not
seen the good ones yet, but we will presently come to
them. They are situated in a cluster, at the upper part
of that sharp crest you see, yonder, and are but ramifi-
cations of one mighty vein, which has not probably yet
been reached by the miners. Each mine occupies about
two hundred men and produces seven or eight *tejos* of
silver a week. And there is, besides, the profit on the
lead, which is immense, and the *ley de oro*, which is no
trifle."

"But do not the poor miners lead a very miserable
life, in those dark and pestilential caverns?" inquired
father Letinez.

"No, indeed," replied the guide. "They are, on the
contrary, happy and well paid. You will presently see
what buzz, what life and what gayety!—The bottom of
the *canada* is a real village, sir: the Indians laugh, and
crack their jokes, and dance!—why, the life of a miner
is one of the merriest upon earth!"

With these and several other discourses of the same
kind, did the guide contrive to beguile time and amuse
the padre, until they reached the mouth of the *Ojuela,*
where they intended to conceal their precious effects and
money. The director of the mining operations, and
the *sobresaliente,* (a kind of police officer that watches
over the conduct of the miners) being informed in a
whisper, by the guide, of the quality of the new visitors,
and the protection which the parish priest of Mapimi
extended to them, did the honours of their subterranean domains, with a courtesy which one could not
have expected in those abodes. They sent their miners to help the new comers to unload their mules
and put their effects under shelter, and prepared every
thing for the accommodation of the travellers.

The entrance into the mine of the Ojuela, is by an
horizontal gallery, of three hundred yards in length,
till one reaches the first perpendicular shaft. That
adyt is wide enough for several persons to walk abreast,
and very lofty, being originally a cleft in the rock, which
nature had filled with precious ore, but that has, long
since, been cleaned out. As all the mines, thereabouts,
are perfectly dry, the owners have saved themselves
the expenses of a *tiro general,* by which, in *wet* works,
they draw out the water, which would otherwise inun-
date them. They are, here, content to go on according
to the old imperfect method used immediately after
the conquest; and the ore is brought on men's shoulders, up steep ladders, which reach from the mouth, to
the bottom of every shaft, each of these not being
above fifty or sixty feet in depth, and receding one
from the other, in the fashion of steps, so as to afford
room for fixing and securing the timbers. By this word,
ladder, our reader is not to understand any accommodation similar to what bears this name elsewhere; but,
merely, an uncouth piece of wood, with notches cut
into it, sufficient to support the foot. Up such *ladders,*
placed almost perpendicularly, is the poor miner obliged to climb, with a load of eighty or ninety pounds
weight on his back—when his support creaks, shakes,
and bends under his feet, at every step he takes up-

24*

wards. It is particularly when the ladders are overloaded, if a great number of miners happen to be as
cending at the same time, that the danger is more imminent; and one single accident, such as a sudden
swoon, or the missing of one's footing, or the breaking
down of a beam, might be sufficient to precipitate,
sometimes, as many as three or four scores of men into
eternity. On the other hand, the spectacle is interesting, and a sense of awfulness raises it to sublimity.

Shaft succeeding shaft, in a slantwise position, and
so skilfully managed, as to permit the lights that shine
at the bottom of the last to be perceived at the mouth
of the first, even from three to four hundred feet in
depth; and a string of miners ascending those dangerous ladders, each with a candle fixed in a kind of hel-
met he wears on his head, affords a most curious subject of contemplation. It is like a telescope directed
towards the inmost recesses of nature!—And, thank
Heaven, a sense of religion is not unknown in those
places. In the midst of the dangers that accompany
their every step, the poor miners are mindful of their
Creator. " Out of the depths, they call unto him :"—
and do call in a manner worthy of Him, in a sublime
manner !—Every now and then, all join in singing the
following simple but noble rhymes:

> " Santo Dios, santo fuerte, santo imortal,
> Libra nos, sonor, de todo mal."

It is the "*Agios o Theos, agios ischiros*," &c. of the
Greek Church.—Nothing more than these few words!—
No monkish littleness, no superstitious conceit!—
When these sounds, proceeding from sixty or seventy
human beings, who, more than any other class, feel
their dependence on Providence, come out of those
rocky caverns, being reverberated by the neighbouring
echoes, they are answered by their friends and companions, on the surrounding hills, and the barren mountains become vocal with praise:—Then, the wilderness
seems to rejoice, and " the solitary place is glad !"

It was, with a singular emotion, father Letinez wit-

nessed this spectacle; and he was melted, while every
tenatero, after unloading his cargo, came to him, with a
smile of gladness, to kiss his hand, and bid him welcome to the Ojuela. The priest's visit was accounted
a great event in the annals of the little establishment,
and one which could not fail to bring down great blessings. The padre, therefore, was feasted to the poor
miners' best abilities; but he did not stay above two
days, for, having received information that the Alcavalero, with his armed force, had returned to Mapimi,
he resumed his march, and soon crossed the river
Nassas.

As our travellers entered a little town called "El
Alamo de Parras," they witnessed a curious scene between the tithe-proctor and the inhabitants. While the
Yorkinos wielded the political power of the Mexican
republic, they abolished the civil obligation of paying
tithes, and suppressed the temporal jurisdiction of the
chapters of cathedral churches, but yet left the *moral,*
or conscientious duty, existing; so that any one of the
faithful, who had a regard for his soul, was still bound
to pay over the tenth part of his produce to the bishop
and chapter. However, as the latter had no longer any
earthly tribunal to recur to, in order to see themselves
righted, the *moral* obligation, which had been left untouched, was but little regarded, and the poor canons
were nearly in a state of starvation. Their fat liv-
ings, of ten and twelve thousand dollars a year, had
been reduced to as many hundreds; and the incumbents, driven to desperation, had had recourse to excom-
munications and anathemas. The refusal to pay had
been denounced as a heresy, condemned by the ecume-
nical council of Constance; and a kind of crusade
actually preached against the wicked opinions of
Wickliff, John Huss, and Jerome of Prague, heresi-
archs, who had, in their time, endeavoured to despoil
the church of her wealth.

Strengthened, as he thought, by all the spiritual terrors that had gone forth, the proctor called upon the
villagers of the Alamo, and insisted upon their discharging, not only what was due for that year; but

even all the arrears which they had neglected to pay.
Nevertheless, the people in general proved refractory,
and, in the end, the non conformists raised a mob, in
consequence of the proctor's extravagant demand upon
an old woman, who had already paid the tithe of her
fowls and garden stuff. The collector of the holy revenue required her to pay the tenth of her *melon and
pumpkin seed*, which is, in Mexico, an object of some
importance, a most delicious beverage, called *orchata*,
being prepared with it.

"How, now, *picaro !*" cried out the old woman, when
she heard the exhorbitant request; "I have already
paid the tithe of the melons, themselves, and must I
still pay the tenth of the seed of those I have eaten ?
Who has taught you such a way of reckoning ?"

"The chapter, good woman, the chapter !" replied
the proctor. "The canons of the holy Cathedral church
of Durango have prescribed it. And you shall pay, or
be a heretic. A Jewess—you understand !—And your
portion shall be with Wikliff, Huss and Hyeronimo de
Praga, three Turks, from England, who were burned
alive, at the council of Constance, by order of the holy
inquisition and of the old king of Spain."

"I, a heretic—I, a Jewess!—And all, for three or
four handfulls of melon seed !" exclaimed the old woman, greatly incensed. "*Vaya!*—If it is so, I will, at
least, retake my own." So saying, she threw herself
upon the chickens, which the proctor still held in his
hand, and a scuffle ensued, during which the fowls
escaped his grasp, and flew off as fast as their wings
could carry them. The old woman and the proctor ran
after them, through the public square of the village,
each loudly calling for help, and showering vitupera-
tive epithets upon his antagonist, so that a large crowd
was soon gathered round them, and, as was natural,
sided with their town's woman.

The proctor had the indiscretion of facing the popu-
lace. He invoked the canons and the fathers of the
council of Constance, and waved, before the mob, a
pastoral letter of the Bishop of Durango, as if to shake
some excommunication out of it, against the insurgents,

but all would not do. They began pelting him with stones, and he ran an imminent danger when father Letinez's coach drove into the Square. This attracted the people's attention and suspended the fray, and the good Padre, being informed of the cause of the uproar, harangued the multitude and succeeded in pacifying them. He, however, seriously advised the tithe proctor to desist and leave the place, which the latter did, but not without giving the Padre to understand that he strongly suspected him of being a favourer of the pestilent heresy of John Huss and Hyeronimo de Praga.

We have related these petty incidents which befell our travellers, thinking that they might prove of some interest, as having a tendency to illustrate the manners and customs of the country; but, for fear of rendering our narrative tedious, or falling into the *puerile*, we will pass in silence over the remainder of their itinerary, and return to Matamoros, where we left our hero, with the other *personæ dramatis*, anxiously waiting for letters from his family.

CHAPTER XXXI.

Captain Letinez would have spent his time pleasantly
enough in Matamoros, had he been allowed to give
himself up to the cares of love, but the wretched condition and precarious situation of Urrea's troops, who,
however, continued to be pompously styled the *army
of operation against Texas*, kept the general in a state
of constant perplexity and embarrassment. From that
disagreeable position he sought to extricate himself, by
endeavouring to open a correspondence with, and excite movements among various tribes of Indians in the
west of the United States, and he employed our hero
in carrying on these diplomatic communications, or
methodising the various schemes he was daily hatching
to that effect.

By a strange coincidence, there was, at that time, a
general discontent prevalent among the aborigines, on
the western frontier of the union ; and, from Canada, to
Texas, they were preparing an insurrection, that would
certainly have taken place, had the Florida Indians
been able to make a decided impression on the blacks
of the neighbouring states, and given, thereby, more
importance to their contest with the whites. The rapidity with which Santa Anna had, in the beginning of
the campaign, chased the Texians from the Southern
parts of the country, had served to buoy up the hopes
of the Indians. They expected a powerful diversion
in their favour, as soon as *he* would reach the frontiers
of Louisiana, and, in that expectation, several of their
tribes sent him embassadors, who did not, however, arrive at the Mexican head quarters, till the defeat of
San Jacinto and Filisola's retreat had blasted the hopes
they might, otherwise, have entertained from that side.
Yet the Indians, who are not endowed with much
shrewdness to distinguish "the nick of time," did,
after their arrival, enter into arrangements with Urrea,
with as much confidence, as though he had been scouring the plains of Texas in triumph.

There were three Cherokee chiefs who *treated* publicly and above board, and who, in order, as they conceived, to render the treaty more binding on the Mexicans, caused themselves to be solemnly baptized.

Besides the Cherokees, there were other emissaries
sent by some of the northern tribes, who remained in
Matamoros *incognito*, but held secret communications
with Urrea, during which our hero acted as interpreter.

All diplomatical intercourse between the high con-
tracting parties being carried on in such French and
English as it had pleased God to endue the Indians
with, it formed a jargon so difficult to understand, that
captain Letinez was frequently at a loss to take their.
meaning, so that, after several mistakes which fretted
the general in chief, it was resolved to call in the aid of
one of the chaplains of the army, a clergyman who had
occupied eminent posts in the United States, and possessed considerable literary knowledge.

This worthy was an ex-jesuit, bred in one of the establishments the society possesses in Maryland; but
from which he had been dismissed, on account of an
unconquerable propensity for certain alcoholic liquids,
whereby he had frequently derrogated from the upright
standing of a child of St. Ignatius. Save this little misfortune, the chaplain was an exemplary clergyman, with
so strong a zeal for the faith, that it had prompted him
to come all the way from Louisiana, to offer his services to the Mexican army, at the time Santa Anna was
sweeping every thing before him in Texas. Unfortunately, he had reached the theatre of war too late, and,
at his arrival at St. Patricio, the news of the defeat of
San Jacinto came to dissipate certain splendid visions
of schools, colleges, Catholic settlements, and fine sugar
and cotton plantations, all intended "ad majorem Dei
gloriam."

He undertook, however, to serve the army in its retreat, inasmuch as they were nearly destitute of spiritual succour; for, Santa Anna's chaplain had been taken prisoner at San Jacinto, and the Texians had retained him to administer spiritual consolation to their
captive.

Whatever assistance our worthy priest could give to captain Letiñez, in translating and explaining the extravagant proposals of the Indian emissaries was freely bestowed, and he was in so far useful, that he made the Mexican chief understand the purport of some documents, with which those deputies had been entrusted by certain eminent divines residing in the United States, but accustomed to fish in muddy waters, and to mix politics with theology.

The first paper he perused was presented by a warrior belonging to a tribe of Indians, living in the west of the Union, and was in the Latin language. It consisted of a certificate of Catholicity in favour of the bearer, and, as our readers may be curious to know how those things are done, we will transcribe it here literally.

Nos Rodericus Von Ruse, Epps. &c, &c. &c.

Cunctis hasce nostras litteras inspecturis, fidem facimus latorem hujus, Romualdum, vulgo dictum *L'ois cau blanc*, ex Indica gente *des Otawas* oriundum, et a nobis baptizatum; esso pium sincerum que Catholicum Romanum, et auctoritatem fœderis faciendi, cum quibuslibet, quorum intercsse potest, a Sua gente accepisse, necnon fidem, ab omnibus Christi fidelibus, ei adhibendam esse.

Datum apud Prairie des chiens, in fœderatis Americæ septentrionalis provinciis; pridie idus martii. Anno Domini, MDCCCXXXVI.

†RODERICUS VON RUSE.
De Mandato Suæ Illustritatis:
Vicentius Brigandeau, secretarius.

Now, this paper appeared to Urrea an unintelligible riddle. "It would seem," said he, "to have been given by some ecclesiastical person, constituted in dignity. There is an authoritative form, and it is in good Latin; but what are these words, in italic, *l'oiseau blanc*, and *des otowas?*"

"I take it to be some nickname, by which this fellow, (this commissioner, or emissary, I mean,) is distinguished in his own country," said captain Letiñez.

"Well, that may be," replied Urrea: "But, what does it mean?—And this *Prairie des chiens!*—What is the purport of it?—It is not Latin."

"Why, Excellentissimo senor," explained the priest, "it is French:—*L'oiseau blanc*, means the white bird! —*Otowas* is the name of a powerful tribe of Indians, in North America; and *Prairie des chiens* is the name of a city, where, I suppose, the document was signed and sealed. Its literal meaning is the *dogs' meadow:*— A quaint name!—They are hard pushed, in the North, for giving names to their towns, and make any word answer the purpose."

"The Otowas!" exclaimed Urrea, "The white bird! —The dogs' meadow!—Upon my word, it looks, or, rather, sounds worse than quaint!—This fellow is quizzing us, as I take it. But, wo to him, if he be, for I will send him to a *presidio:* yet we must investigate this somewhat more deeply. Can you guess who has signed this paper, padre?—Having lived so long in the United States, you should know the clergy there."

The priest, thus interpelled, answered: "May it please your Excellency, in order to make matters plain and intelligible, I must enter into some details, seemingly bearing no manner of connexion with the subject now in hand. I fear it will be with me, as Horace says, 'Trojanum bellum gemino orditur ab ovo.' But, I will abbreviate as much as possible, and give you no reason to be tired with my prolixity, taking care, nevertheless, to inform you of all the facts necessary for a clear understanding of the purport of this paper, as well as any other, which might be presented by the same individual, or other Catholic Indians from the United States. For, otherwise, I might fall into the opposite extreme, no less to be dreaded than prolixity, according to what the same Horace says:—'Brevis esse laboro, obscurus fio.'"

"Padre," interrupted Urrea, out of patience, "If you go on at this rate, you are not likely to get through before the end of the week. Let Horace alone, man, and speak to the purpose."

25

"Well, General, I come to the point," resumed the
ex-Jesuit:—"You must know that, when the first
bishoprick was erected in the United States, by Pius
VI. of happy memory."——
"O Lord!" exclaimed Urrea, "he carries us back
to the eighteenth century:—It is intolerable."
"Well, then, at once, and in four words," returned
the chaplain, "our church, in the United States, is
divided into thirteen dioceses, though the number of
Catholics hardly amounts to half a million of people;
and the bishops, having no income to support their dignity, depend upon alms, transmitted from Europe, by
two societies established, the one in France, and the
other in Germany. These *confraternities* consist of
millions of members, and send prodigious sums to
those prelates, which they are supposed to employ for
the propagation of the faith. The German associa-
tion is under the peculiar superintendence of a deep
politician, who, thinking that the appropriation of so
much money, besides furthering the propagation of
his religion, might also be made to serve to spread
the political influence of his sovereign, has directed
that the largest share should be applied to the conversion of the Western Indians, and entrusted the execution of his plans to a little baron, of the name of
Von Ruse, a very shrewd fellow, chiefly in money matters, and well acquainted with the fashionable world,
for he served with distinction in the *Shwartz yagers*,
and was even promoted to the grade of corporal, by
the Duke of Brunswick."
"Corporal!" interrupted Urrea, with a broad peal
of laughter: "And you represent him as a man of
consequence!—Sir, your cloth gives you privileges,
by securing impunity. We will not, however, suffer
ourselves to be trifled with. Your jesting, in this manner, is in bad taste. By my Santiguada, if you were
not a priest, you would pay dear for this."
"I am not jesting, General," resumed the ex-Jesuit:
"Your Excellency is certainly the last person at whose
expense a prudent man would venture to jest. But,
had you given me time to proceed, you would have seen

that the very circumstance, which shocks you, as improbable, is perfectly credible. The Duke of Brunswick's
celebrated legion of Shwartz yagers, was exclusively
composed of noblemen of most ancient pedigree; and
the last soldier in it was, at least, a belted knight. Now,
to have been a corporal in such a regiment, might be
accounted an honour any where. But, to resume, senor:
this Von Ruse found military glory unable to satisfy
his heart; he found that the world and its vanities
were nothing but an empty sound,—*æs sonans, vel cym-
balum tinniens*,—he found the truth of what the blessed St. Augustine says, in the book of his confessions,
' *irrequietum est cor nostrum*'—"

" And I find," interrupted again Urrea, quite enraged, and violently stamping with his foot, " that you are
enough to drive any man out of his wits. Come to the
pith and marrow of the thing at once, without dragging
us through Germany and Flanders, at this rate. What
have we to do with the Duke of Brunswick and his
legion?—Tell us, if you can, what is this Von Ruse,
now?—and what is the purport of this paper?"

" Well, well," answered the chaplain, somewhat ter-
rified by Urrea's violence, " this Von Ruse is, at this
time, an ecclesiastical dignitary of high standing and
influence, who has had, several times, the honour of
officiating as train-bearer to our holy father the Pope."

" Oh, oh!" exclaimed the general in surprise:
" *Caudatario del Papa!*--That is a dignity, indeed!—
And that man, you say, is in the United States, and
carries on a correspondence with some of the principal
politicians of Europe?"

" Undoubtedly, sir. You may rely upon my information; I am perfectly well acquainted with the man,
and the history of his life."

" Well, then," returned Urrea, " he desires, probably, to enter into correspondence with us. What do
you think, captain Letinez?—Is not this certificate of
Catholicity, a hint from him?—We must not overlook
so fine an opportunity. Who knows what may turn up
in our favour, in those parts?"

"I hardly think," answered the captain, "that it would be prudent to treat with him, without knowing something more in relation to his standing and respectability; particularly when the medium of communication is an unknown Indian, who can hardly be supposed to have an adequate idea of the importance of his mission. But let us hear the father chaplain further. Perhaps he may throw some more light on the subject."

"Why, Gentlemen, certainly I can," resumed the priest. "This Von Ruse, while he appears to husband the German prince's money, according to his instructions, is really carrying on a nice little under-scheme of his own, with which his highness has nothing to do. Our little baron is filling an eligible territory, in the north-west of the United States, with settlers entirely devoted to him, whom he trains in a spirit of nationality distinct from that of the Americans. I do not know whether the little *yager* will succeed; but you may be sure, the United States will have their Texas, too. They cannot escape it,—and there are those who will plant a thorn in their side, as Tennessee and Kentucky have done with you."

"Well, we must treat with this Indian," said Urrea. "This is a good *windfall!*—By my Santiguada, it is not to be neglected. But look at this other paper which he has put in my hands. See, it is full of hyeroglyphics. Representations of various animals, I declare! —There is an eagle,—there is a turtle,—and there is an armadillo, I believe."

"An armadillo!" exclaimed the priest; "it cannot be, for there are none in the United States. It is, I suppose, an alligator. These are the signatures of the various Indian chiefs of his nation, who have given him power to treat. It is customary for them to delineate on their public instruments representations of the animals whose names they bear, and it is *this* which imparts to those papers their authenticity, just as signing and sealing does amongst civilized nations. Now, this is in French. But the orthography is so bad, that it is not easy to unravel its meaning. It must have been composed by some ignorant *courcur de bois.* From it, however, I can make out, that *L'oiseau blanc* is empowered to treat with the Mexican President, or any of the generals of the nation; and the Indian chiefs beg arms and ammunition."

"Oh, as to that," said Urrea, "it is not in my power. Our stores are too low. I cannot, without orders from the supreme government, encroach upon what remains."

"If such be your resolution," said the priest, "you need not think any longer about making a permanent treaty with them. I know their ways and habits:—you can put no reliance in whatever arrangements they may enter into, unless they be bound on their memory, by presents proportioned to the importance of their nation. The English and Americans have accustomed them to it, and the highest bidder is sure to have them for allies."

"If that be the case," replied Urrea, "they may return home, and God speed them. We are not able to buy their alliance. It is a pity, nevertheless, for a diversion on that side would have been advantageous to our cause."

"But the Cherokees who are here?"—said captain Letinez;—"They ask no presents, I believe. They only want lands in Texas. It is not very costly to grant them what they desire, and they may annoy the Texians until we be able to renew the campaign. It is, however, uncertain whether they can bring a respectable force into the country."

"The Cherokees," interrupted the clergyman, "form a very powerful nation, now half civilzied. They have already acquired the use of letters and of the mechanical arts, and should you be able to get them all over to your side, they might relieve you of the present war against the Texians; but would, in future times, prove no less dangerous neighbours. Moreover, the lands upon which they live are surrounded on all sides by establishments of white people, and they can-

25 *

not emigrate to Texas without the permission of the
United States."

"Well, then, let us even drop all thoughts of alliances and treaties with them," said Urrea. "They
may go their way. I wash my hands of them. Our
country does not buy allies with gold; but conquers
her enemies with iron!"

CHAPTER XXXII.

Urrea, who had been excessively anxious to make treaties and enter into alliances with the Indians, no sooner saw that presents were expected, than he dismissed the subject, with the levity and carelessness which the reader has seen in the preceding chapter. Thus, plans that had cost weeks of labour and consultation were, in an instant, laid aside, and our hero found himself freed from the irksome occupations which had nearly engrossed all his time.

Now, he could attend on Miss Linton with more regularity, and pay his devoirs with all the punctuality worthy of a gallant and chivalrous nation. The young lady, however, naturally fond of a retired life, was not always inclined to accept his invitations to balls and other assemblies. One night, when there was to be a grand party, given by the superior officers of the army, to which she and her father had received letters of invitation, and where it was anticipated that she would play on the piano ; she felt strongly inclined to remain at home, but her lover and her father having earnestly besought her not to disappoint her acquaintances, she was, at last, prevailed upon to accompany them.

As she entered the ball room, her unrivalled beauty attracted universal admiration, and she was so often requested to dance, that, at last, she saw herself, through weariness, obliged to refuse one of the most eminent officers. The latter felt a little piqued, but, conquering his chagrin, with perfect good breeding, he requested Miss Linton to pass into the music room, and charm the company with harmony, since it was out of her power to delight them with the gracefulness of her steps.

With this invitation she readily complied, and, while she moved, from the ball room, to the apartment where the piano and other instruments of music were placed, was followed by so great a number of gentlemen, eager to hear her, that dancing was suspended.

There was, among the men, a tall figure, muffled up
in a large brown cloak, lined with red velvet and mag-
nificently embroidered with gold lace, who had, during
the evening, attracted considerable attention and excited much curiosity, not on account of his costume, for,
in the very middle of summer, the cloak frequently
makes its appearance, in Mexico, as well as in Spain,
but from the care with which he had kept his face concealed. The question had frequently been asked, " Who
is he ?—Who can he be ?" but nobody was able to give
an answer.

Though thus rigorously preserving his incognito, he
seemed to be a great admirer of our young lady, for he
constantly kept himself in sight of her, and his eyes,
curiously peering over the part of his cloak that was
wound round his face, followed her every motion.

When she left the ball room, he was amongst the
first to follow, but still concealing his visage, and
even redoubling his precautions. Presently, Miss Linton began to play a beautiful solo from that fine opera
" La Dame Blanche," and accompanied the sounds of
the piano with so sweet a voice, that all the company
were charmed beyond expression. Her lover was on
one side, bending, in a kind of rapture, over her shoulder, and turning, with the greatest readiness, the leaves
of the music book, while her father enjoyed the delightful spectacle, with an air of reflection.

All at once, in the middle of a passage of superior
power, the cloaked unknown, forgetting himself, suffered the folds of the cloak, by which his face had been
concealed, to drop down. Miss Linton, happening to
look up at the time, cast her eyes upon him, and, notwithstanding the hurry with which he endeavoured to
shroud his features again, recognised him—uttered a
piercing cry—rose from her chair with precipitation,
and threw herself into her father's arms.

It is not necessary to describe the disorder that ensued thereupon. None but captain Letinez guessed at
the cause of the young lady's extraordinary conduct.
While her father soothed her and asked the cause of
her fright, an old matron who had brought to the ball

two daughters, whose beauty was eclipsed by Miss
Linton's, shrewdly remarked, in whispers, to three or
four old crones, who attended upon her, that those
American women were singular, with their nervous at-
tacks, and that, for her part, were she a man, she could
never admire such baby-like things, that would scream,
and throw a whole company into disorder, for nothing
in the world, but to draw the whole attention upon
themselves. Father Pafarro, the vicar of the parish,
observed that this came from admitting heretics to a
Christian ball, and that Mexicans could promise to
themselves nothing but the corruption of their morals
and the downfall of their faith, by their criminal condescension to strangers; but the principal officers
thronged around Miss Linton, in order to offer their
services against any one who might have offended her.

In the mean time, he who had given rise to this commotion had vanished. Taking advantage of the trouble
which his presence had created, he passed through the
crowd, without being observed, and when Miss Linton
got over her alarm, she was no longer exposed to encounter his odious gaze. However, she no sooner felt
her emotion subside, than she desired to be conducted
home, and left the party to their surmises, in relation
to what they termed " *el accidente de la senorita ;*" in
which they exercised the acuteness of their wit, with
no more uncharitableness than is customary in the
fashionable world.

As soon as Miss Linton, accompanied by her father
and the captain, had got home, the latter said to her :
" I need not inquire whether you have seen this man
before. I have no doubt my suspicions are well founded, and he is the villain who made the infamous attempt, at Lepantitlan !"

" He is, indeed," answered the young lady ; " but,
I beseech you, captain,—nay, I lay my strict injunction upon you, to do nothing rashly. As you
value my happiness, abstain from any attempt at
avenging what is past. I am now, here, out of all danger, and absolutely forbid that it should be made a
subject of quarrel."

"Leave that to me, my dear Miss Linton," replied our hero: "We, men, understand these matters better than your sex. I could not, without disgrace, continue to aspire to the honour of your hand, were I not to call him to an account. Only, I am afraid, he will refuse to give me satisfaction."

The young lady begged and threatened by turns, but could never shake the resolution of her lover, who, taking leave of the family, withdrew to make his dispositions for the ensuing day's encounter. He thought proper to consult the officer at whose house he lodged, and begged him to act as his second; but this one, also, endeavoured to dissuade him.

"You know," said he, "how unusual duels are amongst us. Not a single one has taken place during the whole campaign; and, in fact, I never heard of one being fought in our army. Take my word for it, it will look excessively odious—ten times more so, than if you were to pistol your man in the street. A murder, committed in cold blood, would be less prejudicial to your reputation. In a duel, if one of the combattants dies on the spot, he is deprived of Christian burial; and this, as you are probably aware, is a circumstance that affects the imagination of our people, more than any thing else. Should you prove victor, you gather upon your own head the execration of the family of the deceased, and the odium of the public. Should you die, you are deprived of the suffrages of the church; and your body is buried, like that of a horse, in unconsecrated ground, whereby your family is forever disgraced. Therefore, my dear friend, take my advice, and give up your notion. There are many ways, besides this, of disposing of your enemy. I do not mean that you should basely assassinate him; but, can you not, as we have heard that some of the northern people do, in their own country, cowhide the man in the street?—He, that wished to dishonour your promised bride, shall then be himself dishonoured, and you never the worse for it"

"Come, come," replied captain Lotinez, "all this is childish!—I, never the worse, should I cowhide him!—Why, man, he would then assassinate me, and be justified in the public opinion!—It behooves me to do every thing like a gentleman. I must punish the wretch; but it must be in a manner worthy of Miss Linton and myself. Say, at once, whether you are willing to be my second, or not."

"Your second!" exclaimed the other, "God forgive me, I will. There is, indeed, an excommunication against seconds, as well as principals; but, as I never feared man in your quarrel, so, I will not fear the devil, this bout."

"Well, then, the affair is settled," said our gallant hero: "I am going to write the challenge; and, as soon as it is day, you will carry it to the gentleman."

"I carry it!" replied captain Letinez's friend:— "Cannot a servant do the job?"

"My dear," replied our hero, "such things, among civilized nations, are always done by seconds. To send a servant, would be an act of meanness. We must not unnecessarily degrade the man we wish to fight against!"

"Well, captain," returned the other, "we are not so well informed of the rules of duelling, in this country, that you should fear any improper criticism shall be passed upon your conduct, should you fail in some trifling item of etiquette."

"Still, I must, and will insist upon every thing being done according to strict form," replied senor de Letinez.

"Very well," answered the other, "every thing shall be done in conformity to your wishes; I will start no more objections, but will be as submissive as a child. And now, don't you think it is time to go to bed?— What, with the ball, the Champaign we have drunk, or the idea of the duel which is to take place to-morrow, I am nearly bewildered, and my head is dizzy."

"Oh, stop!" resumed our hero: "We have yet a great deal to do, this night. I may be killed, and I must make my will. We must get witnesses, and send for an *Escrivano*, (notary public.)

"Good Lord!" exclaimed the other, "that will keep us up till day, and I am nearly dead with sleep. Where are we to get witnesses at this time of night? Why, you must have five men, besides the *escrivano*. Do you think people will get up from their bed, for such an uninteresting purpose?"

"Why, surely, we do not want so many persons. Two witnesses with the notary will suffice," observed captain Letinez.

"No, indeed," resumed his friend, "you must have five witnesses with the escrivano, and seven *without him!* So, you see, it is sheer extravagance to pretend to collect so many persons together, at this time of night. Wait till to-morrow. You cannot help yourself, now."

"If such be the case, indeed, I must wait," replied the captain.

"To-morrow, then," resumed the other, and they withdrew to bed,

CHAPTER XXXIII.

The next morning, our hero had no sooner risen, than, according to the preceding night's resolution, he immediately set about making his last will and testament. Thanks to the many and cumbrous formalities prescribed by the Spanish law, it could not be done without a certain degree of publicity, and he was aware that the good health he enjoyed was a circumstance that would give rise to various surmises, and perhaps excite suspicions in relation to his further intentions.

In this, however, he was mistaken; for, as duels were nearly without example in the republic, it did not enter the head of any one to suspect him of such a design. The *escrivano* and witnesses having been sent for, the instrument was drawn, signed and sealed, and, though, in less than one hour's time, it was reported all over the town that captain Letinez, being as yet in good health, had just made his will, no one guessed at the motive. Some attributed it to a whim, or caprice. Some thought he was going to undertake a journey, and had taken this precaution in case he should meet his death in the way, and others pretended, that, as he was on the point of being married, he had made his will before hand, to show that it had been done uninfluenced by his wife; but none divined the true reason.

In the mean time, our hero sent his challenge, written in polite language, to the officer who had so infamously offended Miss Linton. The latter was yet in bed, when captain Letinez's friend was introduced into his apartment; and, upon reading the note, manifested a great surprise. He understood not its meaning, and inquired from the bearer what it could be. "Captain Letinez complains of me, as I understand by this here paper," said he, "for some wrong he pretends I have done to the American young lady upon whom he was waiting, last night. To be sure, I found her very handsome! but I did not know, till lately, that she belonged to a family of distinction, though, by the bye, her father is

26

nothing but a rebel. But whatever may have taken place in St. Patricio, I don't see what right captain Letinez has to interfere. She is not his sister, nor relation. And what does he mean by desiring me to give him satisfaction? Is it money for the young lady, he asks, in order to make up for the Lepantitlan business? By St. Coralampio, I am sorry for *that*. I did not think, at the time, that she was more than a common *ranchera*. But, *vaya!* If *she* want money, money she shall have, though God knows and the virgin, it is but little I have to spare!"

"Major Firana," interrupted captain Letinez's friend. "I am sorry that you do not seize the meaning of Don Ambrosio's note. The young lady is his promised bride, and he considers any insult offered to her, as if offered to himself. In St. Patricio, she was under his protection, and you must have known it. Were he informed now of the tender of money, which you make, it would incense him still more."

"The devil it would!" replied the other. "What is it then he requires? What other satisfaction can I give?"

"Why, sir," resumed the other, "if I must be explicit with you, such offences amongst men of honour are not atoned for, without a duel. You are a soldier, and understand me, I suppose."

"A duel!" echoed major Firana, in surprise, "does the fellow mean to introduce that foolish thing amongst us? In the time of Don Quixotte, it did very well, but, now, it is *past*. It is worn out and become ridiculous. It smells too much of feudal times, to be acceptable to the children of *Anahuac*."

"You will find," resumed the other, "that the suspicion of cowardice is yet apt to light on the character of those who prove recreant, and that such a suspicion, in a military man, is equivalent to a complete disgrace."

"I cannot be suspected of cowardice," said Firana; "I made my proofs at the storming of Bejar, and you were an eye witness."

"It is true," replied the other; "and it is what now
causes my surprise at your refusal."

"But what would you have me to do, my friend?"
returned Firana. Duelling is not customary amongst
us. I don't even know how it is to be gone about.
What arms are we to use?—In what way, when, where
are we to fight?—Must I have a second, a *padrino*, as
it is called, and he, another?"

"Certainly," replied senor Letinez's messenger;
"you must appoint some one amongst your friends, to
act as your padrino. Captain Letinez has appointed
me, on his side, and when you have named your man,
he and I will regulate every thing, so that you shall
have no trouble except that of fighting."

"We shall be much obliged to the seconds for their
courtesy," replied Firana, with a sardonic grin, "in
taking so much trouble off our hands, and leaving us
nothing more to do than the trifling matter of handling
our arms. But I must have some time to get a padrino; it is not a thing to be done in the twinkling of an
eye. I cannot make my dispositions in less than one
or two days. So, tell your friend to wait patiently,
As soon as I am ready, I will answer his note."

"And what arms will you choose? for, as you are
the challenged party, it is your privilege to take your
choice," said captain Letinez's friend. "Will you
prefer the sword?"

"We will see as to that. I must reflect. But, for
heaven's sake, be not so hurried, and give one time to
breathe."

With this verbal answer, our hero's friend returned
to his principal, and faithfully related all the conversation which had taken place between Firana and himself. Captain Letinez was not a little disappointed at
the result, and began to suspect that the major sought to
shuffle off. However, he kept till night some hopes that
a sense of military honour would prompt him to accept;
but his surprise was great, when, towards sun down,
he received a summons, from the general in chief, to
repair to his house, and found there a counsel of offi-

cers, assembled to deliberate upon the challenge he had
sent to major Firana.

At his entrance into the apartment, the paper, signed
with his own hand, was put under his eyes, and he was
asked by Urrea, whether he owned it; being at the
same time reminded that the ancient ordinances of the
kings of Spain, which were, still, in those matters, the
supreme law of the land, prohibited, under severe penalties, the fighting of duels and sending of challenges,
and that this frightful evil, having, as yet, gained no
footing in the country, it became the duty of the chiefs
to see that the first attempts to introduce it should be
carefully suppressed.

Though this explanation was added to warn him not
to commit himself by owning the challenge, and the
captain perceived Urrea's intention and design; yet he
had too much honour to deny the truth. He, therefore,
boldly admitted that the note had been sent by him,
and added, by way of comment, the history of major
Firana's attempt on Miss Linton, concluding by pro-
claiming him as cowardly as beastly; since, after so
shocking an offence, against a defenceless female, he
had not the heart to face her protector; but must take
shelter under the egis of the law.

Thus confessing, without any palliation, what the
code of the country considered as criminal, and against
which it awarded a severe punishment, our hero brought
himself into danger. The officers who were present,
acting as a court of inquest, saw themselves obliged to
send him to prison, and, though every one admired his
spirit and applauded his gallantry, still a legal process
was commenced against him, for a breach of discipline,
which threatened a very disagreeable delay to his marriage, if not some danger to his person, also.

Upon learning what had befallen the captain, Miss
Linton was thrown into the utmost grief, accusing herself with having been the cause of it, by the imprudent
manifestation of her alarm, at the ball. Had she had
presence of mind to suppress it, when she, unexpectedly, beheld major Firana, her lover would have preser-

ved his liberty. But, now, entangled in a criminal
accusation, to which no speedy termination was likely
to be put, how much would he not have to suffer, and
all for her sake!—Was there any thing she could do
in his behalf?—She would go, accompanied by her
father, and throw herself at the feet of the general in
chief. She would present her supplications to the superior officers, who were to compose the court martial,
in whose hands her lover's fate was placed. But was
this compatible with female modesty?—Was it even
practicable with such men as these officers were supposed to be?—Would not such a step be considered as
a degradation of her maidenly character, of which she
was still more jealous than of her life, because she felt
it was dearer to her lover?—Alas, was there nothing
she could do?—Her father, at least, could with propriety interfere and solicit in behalf of the captain. But
who would pay attention to the prayers of a mere prisoner of war, without friends or influence in the country,
besides what he had derived from his intimacy with her
lover?—While her mind was agitated by those cruel
reflections, and her tears evinced the bitterness of her
grief; she received some consolation from a letter our
hero sent her from his prison. The tone of cheerful
playfulness with which it was fraught gave her some
hopes that there was not as much danger as she had, at
first, anticipated. It was worded as follows:

" *Dear Miss Linton :*

"As I hope you have too much sense to be seriously
alarmed at what has happened, I will not exhaust my
rhetorical powers in pouring forth the balsam of consolation. What was begun in the real tragic vein, has
dwindled down into sheer comedy. The hero of Lepantitlan has acted in perfect keeping, which I might
have foreseen. I am, however, better avenged than if
I had lodged a bullet in his brain, for he has covered
himself with ridicule; and, though duels are not much
in use amongst us, sarcasms and epigrams are by no
means strangers to our country; and, I am told they

they fall so thick upon the poor major, that he cannot
possibly stand the 'pitiless storm.' He has *brass*
enough; but yet, the shafts that are directed against
him, must penetrate to the quick. I give him but three
days to stay in town; and, in three days more, I will
be at your feet.   Yours, &c. &c."

It was exactly as the prisoner had foretold. Major
Firana became the subject of so many *pasquinades*,
that he had to leave Matamoros; and went to visit his
family, on a furlough, which Urrea gave him to understand he was welcome to render perpetual.

CHAPTER XXXIV.

After the major's departure from the city, captain Letinez did not remain long in prison, for all the army took a lively interest in his fate, and looked upon the treatment he had received, as an indignity; but, while there, he made a little acquisition, which, at the time, appeared unimportant, but had, nevertheless, some un-pleasant consequences upon his rest of mind. It consisted of a little miniature portrait, set in gold, which he bought from a soldier that had made the campaign of Texas. It attracted his attention, on account of the close similitude of the features to some one with whom he was conscious to have been acquainted, but without recollecting exactly who it was.

The portrait was bought at a low price; and our hero's interest being awakened, he considered it for a long time, endeavouring, by the closest reflection, to clear up his remembrance, in order to find out when and where he had seen the face which the portrait represented. It was the effigy of a middle-aged man, of handsome features and prepossessing aspect; but our hero in vain taxed his memory: it furnished him with no clue to unravel his confused ideas, and, though fully convinced he had been familiar with the original, whose likeness the miniature exhibited, yet he remained uncertain whether it was in Mechoacan or in Texas.

In his disappointment, he turned the portrait round and round, examining the frame with a kind of pettish impatience, till, at last, the thought occurred to him that it was rather massy, and must contain another portrait inside, or some token from the original owner, whereby he might be led to a discovery. He was not mistaken. Upon a closer scrutiny, he discovered a small spring, upon the pressing of which, the back of the portrait flew open, like the lid of a snuff-box, and discovered an elegant little design, embroidered with human hair, upon a piece of white silk set in a frame, which must probably have belonged to the person by whom the portrait had been presented.

On further examination, he perceived some words written, in diminutive characters, beneath the design, and, judge of his surprise, when he read the name of *Sophia Linton!* " Is it possible," exclaimed he, " that this portrait belongs to her!—But, there can be no doubt: here is her own name, written with her own hand. This must have been got amongst the Texas plunder. But, whose picture can it be?—I am acquainted with these features, nay, they seem those of a person with whom I have been familiar, and yet my treacherous memory cannot clear up the uncertainty!— Is it some relation of Miss Linton?—Is it not, rather, some lover, whose memory she still fondly cherishes? —Oh! if she have loved any one before me, then her heart cannot be wholly mine; and yet, how perfectly new did love appear to her!—How modest and unobtrusive has she always shown herself, even when I had the conviction that her heart was won, and pleading in my favour!—But, what, if I had mistaken gratitude for love?—Would real love be compatible with so much coolness and self-possession, as she has always manifested?—Did she not dread my presence, even at the time she owed me the greatest obligations?—Did she not always endeavour to render our interviews as short as possible, and seek for pretences to prevent me from declaring my sentiments?—Yes, I see how it is.—Her heart belongs to another, and it is merely through necessity she consents to wed me.—It is out of regard for her father, and in order to insure *his* welfare, she agrees to become my wife.—But I will not press myself upon her.—I will not build the hopes of conjugal felicity on the inspirations of mere gratitude.—I will tell her that I leave her at liberty; and her more favoured lover may claim the accomplishment of the pledges which, in more happy times, have passed between them.—And yet, can I part from Sophia Linton?—Is there another woman like her in the world?—No, there is none.—None, at least, for me.— My felicity is intimately connected with the hope of obtaining her: my soul is identified with hers; and, without Sophia Linton, life were a burden."

Thus was our hero plunged into all the torments of jealousy, and without knowing who his fancied rival could be, though he was conscious of having seen him somewhere. In vain he inquired from the soldier who had sold him the miniature, how he had come by it; he did not receive any information capable of clearing up his doubts. It had been found in a house which had been abandoned by its owners, at the approach of Urrea's corps, and was secreted, with several other valuable jewels, in a piece of furniture, which, from the soldier's description, captain Letinez concluded must have been a writing desk. This meagre account left him in the same ignorance and perplexity. He resolved, therefore, to come to an explanation with Miss Linton, for, the trouble of his mind had become so excruciating as to be perfectly intolerable.

As soon as he was liberated from confinement, his first visit, as our reader may guess, was paid to the Texian major, who received him with the greatest joy, and testified the deep concern he had felt, when informed of the danger he had incurred, in order to avenge his daughter. "But I was glad when I heard you were in prison, my dear friend," said the good old man, "for there, I knew, your life would be safe. In spite of Firana's villany, I owe him some thanks for his prudent conduct. Confess that you were too warm, and that such a scoundrel was beneath your notice."

To these felicitations and parental expressions of regard, the captain answered in a confused manner. His brow was overcast, and a heavy anxiety sat upon his mind. His conversation with Miss Linton was unmeaning, and his serious demeanor and cold address appeared unaccountable and almost offensive. He had come with the intention of presenting the miniature to the young lady and demanding an explanation; but now, when in her presence, he could not screw up his courage to the proper pitch.

The embarrassment of his manner was visible, and surprised no less than displeased Miss Linton and her

father. The latter, however, attributed it to the mortification the captain's military pride must have suffered, in his imprisonment, and proceeded to administer
well meant consolations, in the jocose strain peculiar
to him; but which sounded in the captain's ears like
so many bitter taunts.

"Come, come, cheer up," said the major. "Don't be
cast down for such a trifle. What are a few days imprisonment? All in the way of your profession, man.
And it was for an honourable cause. Although I scold-
ed, yet it rejoiced my old blood, to see you act so manly a part, and so ready to avenge my daughter. A
woman knows better the worth of a man, when she sees
him thus willing to shed his blood in her quarrel."

But notwithstanding all the major could say, and he
said much, to enliven the conversation and put the captain in spirits, he could not succeed in chasing away
the clouds of deep anxiety that overhung his brow, and
the interview ended in the same cold and embarrassed
manner it had begun.

Our hero returned to his lodgings, angry against
himself for his want of resolution; and, in order to
remedy it, made up his mind to send the miniature
with a letter; but he found it nearly as difficult to in-
dite an epistle appropriate to the circumstance, as he
had found it to make the verbal communication. He
wrote several letters, and, unable to please himself, tore
them one after another. Sometimes, he found the style
too vehement, and sometimes, it was too humble, and
did not sufficiently express the feelings of an offended
lover. Then, again, the thought would recur to his
mind that the picture was perhaps the portrait of a relation, and had been received as a token of family affection, in which case his peremptory demand of an explanation would prove the most awkward thing in the
world; but further reflections showed this supposition
was improbable, for he had never been acquainted with
any of Miss Linton's relations except her father, and
he was firm in the persuasion that he had seen the original of the portrait, though he could remember neither
when, nor where. After long debates, within himself,

and scribling over and tearing to pieces, nearly a quire of paper, he was unable to take a final resolution, and went to bed despairing to come to a conclusion.

But we must not omit informing our readers of the conversation which, after the captain had withdrawn, passed between the major and his daughter. The old man started the subject, by observing that he could never have supposed that a few days imprisonment would have such an effect upon a lad of spirit like the captain. " One would think," did he observe, " that he is quite bewildered, and has become stupid. How absent minded he was, and what foolish answers he gave to some queries you addressed him. Sophia, my dear, did you ever before remark that he was subject to such *tantrums ?* And yet, he kept his eyes constantly fixed on you! He seemed to be grieved in mind, and one would have thought you were the cause of it. Have you done any thing to wound his feelings ?"

" No, indeed, papa," replied Miss Linton ; " and I am still more surprised than you at his strange behaviour ; the more so, that I cannot imagine his imprisonment has soured him to such a degree. His manner amounted to positive rudeness !—There must be some other reason beside what you suspect. But I will know from him. I will put him in the way of making an apology ; and, should he not tender it of his own accord, I will not be in a hurry to give him further encouragements. The Lord preserve me from caprice and sourness of disposition in the person to whom I am to be united !"

" That is well said, my daughter, and is a magnanimous disposition of mind," resumed her father, playfully ; " adhere to it. Be not too rash, however, and do not take offence at trifles. You are young, and lack experience. Think that such a conquest is not to be effected every day. I speak not of his fortune, nor of his rank ; for, were he the poorest of mankind, he would still be the son of *my* choice. Believe me, child, a pure virgin heart, in a man of his years and profession, is a treasure that will never wear out, if once put in the keeping of a woman of feeling and in-

telligence. Be not rash, therefore; and, though I am
of opinion that you should maintain your maidenly dignity and pride of worth, with proper spirit, still, do it
with moderation, and beware of going too far."

"Father," replied the young lady, "I am astonished to hear you speak in such a manner. Would you
advise me, in order to secure an advantageous match,
to put up with a treatment which I conceive to be unworthy of me? I am aware of the captain's good qualities, but he must *respect* as well as love me, if he
wishes to secure my regard. Whatever you may say,
I will expect an apology from him; and, if he is not
able to appreciate *me*, it will be an easier task for me
to console myself for the loss of him."

In such a disposition of mind did Miss Linton go to
rest; so that the captain and herself might be now considered as in a state of mutual coolness and suspicion.
It was too painful to last long; and the captain being,
as he conceived, the offended party, and the one whose
anxiety of mind was greatest, was the first to break
the ice.

After spending a sleepless night, he, the next morning, took heart of grace, and paid Miss Linton a second
visit. He found her alone; and, the first greetings
being over, he took the miniature out of his pocket,
and, with a peculiar solemnity of manner, presented it
to her, saying, "Here is something that belongs to you,
madam, as I conjecture, from your name being written under this design."

At the sight of the portrait, Miss Linton manifested
the most lively joy, and exclaimed: "My uncle's miniature!—How in the world did you come by it,
captain?"

Now, the great mystery was cleared up!—Our hero's
countenance lost the dignity of offended worth, to
exchange it for an air of awkwardness, bordering on
the comical. He felt how strange his conduct, on the
preceding visit, must have appeared to Miss Linton;
and began to stammer forth an apology. The good-
natured girl did not give him the trouble to go through
it; but, interrupting him, said, with a smile, "Say no

more, say no more. I see how it is. You were jealous. It will do well enough for once, and I am disposed to overlook it; but, from henceforth, beware! You must put an implicit confidence in me, or we cannot promise ourselves any happiness. Enough of this, however. Tell me, now, how came you by the picture?"

Thereupon, the captain recounted in what manner he had bought it, and what he had learned from the seller, relative to the house where it had been found, confessing, with ingenuity, that his suspicions sprung from the consciousness of having seen, somewhere, the person whom the miniature represented.

Miss Linton was not a little surprised at this assertion. "Are you sure," said she, "that you are not mistaken? Some similarity of features may deceive you, considering, chiefly, that you do not recollect *where* you saw the individual to whom you allude. My uncle has never been in Texas, neither have I myself a perfect recollection of him, having never seen him since my infancy; for, shortly after my mother's death, my father removed from Maryland to Alabama; and, though we have, of late, kept up an amicable correspondence with her family, we have never visited. It is true, my uncle has travelled much, both through Europe and America; but you can hardly have seen him in Mexico, for, I have understood it was in his youth he visited the country, and you must have been then too young to become acquainted with him."

"Well," interrupted the captain, "if he has travelled through this country, it makes good my surmises, and shows that I was not mistaken. But pray, my dear Miss Linton, do you know what parts of Mexico your uncle visited, and at what particular time?"

"Indeed, I do not," replied she: "I have already told you all I remember about him. He was my mother's youngest brother; and there had been some estrangement between him and the rest of the family, on account of his mother's whole fortune having been settled upon him. It is only of late years, that the difference between him and my father has been made

27

up; and, in consequence of that reconciliation, he sent
me his portrait."

"May I inquire what was your mother's maiden
name?" said the captain.

"She was called Claughton," answered Miss Linton.
"My uncle, however, took his own mother's name, in
consequence of her estate being settled upon him. But
if you are anxious to know further particulars, you must
consult my father, for, I confess, my information is neither exact nor extensive on this subject."

The old major not being yet returned, all further
eclaircissement was postponed.

CHAPTER XXXV.

Miss Linton did not fail to communicate to her father what had passed between herself and the captain, and he was as much astonished as she, to hear that the latter had a notion of having been personally acquainted with her uncle, though unable to remember when, or where. The thing seemed too romantic, and he would have pronounced it absolutely incredible, had not the captain possessed all his confidence. He, therefore, impatiently awaited a second visit, in hopes, that, by imparting to him what he knew of his brother-in-law's history and peregrinations, he might, so far, refresh his memory, as to enable him to recollect whether his surmises were founded or not. Major Linton's knowledge of the particulars which the present moment presented as possessing a capital interest, was not, however, so extensive, as to induce him to believe he could throw much light upon the subject, unless, as he thought, he should happen to light upon some peculiar circumstance that might have made an indelible impression on our hero's mind, during his infancy, for he supposed, that, if he had seen his brother-in-law, at all, it must have been in a very juvenile age.

The captain, no less desirous than the major, to clear up his doubts, and tormented, besides, by an indescribable anxiety of mind, the cause of which appeared unfathomable, and seemed to portend some strange discovery, did not fail to return to Mr. Linton's, as soon as he judged it likely to find him at home, and obtained from him the following account of the Claughton family, from which the major's wife was descended.

They were the posterity of one of the original settlers of Maryland, under Lord Baltimore, and made a considerable figure in that province, until the revolutionary war, when they began insensibly to dwindle away. They had remained zealous Roman Catholics until the major's wife's mother married into the family,

who, being no less strict a Protestant, instilled her religion into the mind of her daughters and youngest son.
This bred continual quarrels between her and her husband, and, at length, she died broken hearted; yet those
amongst her children who had imbibed her religion
could never be prevailed upon to abandon their faith
to please their father, but, rather, looked upon him
with some rancour for the treatment he had caused
their mother to undergo. "In that state of things,"
continued the major, "James, the youngest son, left
the paternal house, and turned his attention to commerce, while, about the same time, I married one of
the daughters, of whom it has been my misfortune to
be deprived these nine years. My brother-in-law having publicly conformed to the church of England, it so
much exasperated his father, that he declared he would
entirely cut him off from his inheritance, and this very
circumstance was the cause of his fortune; for, his
grandmother, who was no less zealous a Protestant than
himself, settled upon him her whole estate, as an indemnity for what he had lost. His sisters, and elder
brother saw this with a jealous eye, and he was so much
vexed by their ill will, that he resolved to absent himself for a time, and obtained, from the commercial
house he served, permission to visit Mexico, where he
managed the interests of the firm with great success.
He may have, then, travelled through this country, but
it is nineteen or twenty years ago, and you cannot possibly have seen him."

"Has he never since visited the republic?" interrupted the captain.

"I am not able to tell," resumed the major, "because,
since that epoch, a great coolness reigned between us,
and I was not informed of his movements; though it is
not impossible, for he has been a great traveller, partly
for commercial purposes, and partly for information.
We are on good terms, now; the more so, that he was
the first to seek a reconciliation, though, perhaps, the
greatest share of blame was on my side."

This short account did not give to captain Letinez
any clue whereby his doubts might be cleared up. He

took the miniature in his hands, considered it again and again, muttering to himself, " Claughton, Claughton ! —Have I ever heard that name ?"

But suddenly an idea seemed to flash on his mind, and he asked major Linton, " Did you not tell me that your brother-in-law changed his name, in order to receive his grand-mother's bequest ?"

" To be sure," replied the major ; " it was one of the old lady's special conditions ; for, she was proud of her family name, and an act of the legislature of Maryland was obtained to that effect, and not without difficulty, for they are very particular in Maryland."

" And what was his own family name ?" eagerly interrupted the captain.

" Faring," answered the major.

" Faring !" exclaimed the young man, in the greatest surprise. " Great God of heaven, it is my own father !" And eagerly kissing the picture, he gave way to a flood of tears !

The major and his daughter, unable to account for this sudden emotion, kept a profound silence, exchanging, however, significant glances, as if they could have read each other's thoughts. They feared lest it should prove a fit of insanity, for, being unacquainted with the captain's history, they could not possibly conceive the cause of his tears, nor suspect the connexion, which he had just discovered.

The first burst of passion being over, our hero perceived their surprise, and became aware that his emotion must have appeared to them unaccountable. He hastened, therefore, to give them a brief history of his mother's marriage and the manner in which he had been brought up by his grand-father, the count of Letinez. He had, hitherto, put off giving them an account of his birth and family, because, expecting, from day to day, legal papers and vouchers from Mechoacan, he had thought the communications which courtesy required he should make, would be best accompanied by the written documents ; but now, when a proper occasion offered to give that information, he did it with modesty, when speaking of the wealth and rank of the house of

27 *

Letinez, and with such a tone of tenderness and filial
affection, when alluding to his father, that the old major was melted.

The latter had, nevertheless, a difficulty on his mind,
of which he asked the solution with great frankness.
It was about the captain's name. "Be not offended
with me," said he, "if I make so free;—but how does
it come that you do not bear your father's name?"

"It is usual, in this country, as well as in Spain,"
replied the captain, "for children of families of distinction to bear the mother's, as well as the father's name;
but the old count would never hear of any other preceding his own. He had retained many prejudices
of the ancient times, and considered it as a species of
degradation for the name of Letinez, to be linked by
the conjunction *and*, to a more plebian appellation, and
dragged in tow by it, as it were. There might have
been, also, some illiberality, on the score of religion.
My father being a Protestant, his name was, I believe,
considered as heretical, and would have been thought
inauspicious for me!—But the arrangement was made
with his consent, and he has never showed himself dis-
satisfied with it."

"Has your father visited you frequently in Mechoacan?" inquired the major.

"I remember to have seen him thrice, since my child-
hood," replied the captain. "He was with us four
years ago. I was then going in my fifteenth year, and
he promised to return to take me to travel; but I doubt
whether the old count and my grand-uncle could have
been brought to consent to it. It was only by protracted importunities that I extorted their permission to go
to Texas, and yet they thought the campaign would
only prove a military *paseo*, and a kind of recreation!
—Travelling abroad would appear to them fraught with
much more danger. However, I have no doubt, my
father will keep his word; and he either is, *now*, or will
soon be in Mechoacan."

"Well, captain," resumed the major, "it is you
who impart to us your own history, and, therefore, we
believe it; but were it any body else, it would strike us

as a disjointed romance. Egad! I will have many a
joke at you, for having had your father's picture in your
hands, and been unable to make out who it was, till
prompted to the name."

"It certainly looks odd," exclaimed the captain,
laughing, "but yet there have been a thousand similar
instances, when an idea, deeply engraved in the heart,
and with a perfect hold on the powers of memory, cannot be fully developed, for want of some leading circumstance, that has escaped remembrance, and is, like
the match, absolutely indispensable for setting the train
of gunpowder on fire.—Though the miniature is not well
executed," added he, looking at it, "yet the features
present the general expression of my father's face, and
I felt I had been familiar with the original; but there
was a vagueness in the impression which did not dis-
appear, till you uttered his name.—It was like a mist
suddenly rolled away. Now the whole appears so clear
and plain that I am astonished at myself for my want
of penetration."

"It is then certain," said the major, "that you and
Sophia are cousins. I give you both joy of it."

"And, I think, my *prima* should do the same," interrupted the captain, stealing a kiss; "and, from this
moment, give me leave to call her *coz.*, and call me
Ambrosio."

"Though we be cousins," replied Miss Linton, playfully, and disengaging herself, "it is no reason that
you should grow saucy and familiar. Senor capitan, I
must make you keep your distance yet, and teach you
discipline."

"Will you, indeed?" replied our hero, who was now
in a fine flow of spirits, and in a witty vein: "But,
what say you of going to a ball, this evening, at Madame Larrouie,—the French lady's house. It will eva-
porate all the remainder of ill humour against me, for
my foolish conduct of yesterday."

Miss Linton's father urging her to accept the captain's invitation, she consented; and the latter took
his leave.

As soon as he got to his friend's, this one perceived,

by his radiant countenance, and the peculiar buoyancy
of his manner, that some happy circumstance must
have turned up; but the captain did not wait till he
should inquire the cause of his joy. He broke forth,
in a tone of exultation:—"Give me your best felicitations, Troles; give me joy.—We have made an interesting discovery.—Miss Linton is my cousin!—Her
mother was my father's sister!"—And, thereupon, he
repeated the account which the major had given him of
the Claughtons, and showed in what way his own
father had come to change his family name; manifesting, at the same time, that the discovery of such a connexion, rendered Miss Linton still dearer to him.

His friend was, however, far from felicitating him
upon such a discovery. On the contrary, he told him
it was rather unlucky for him, and that he would find
it a serious obstacle to his marriage.

"An obstacle to my marriage!" exclaimed the captain:—"What do you mean, my dear Troles?"

"Why," answered the latter, "are you not aware
that this is an impediment which renders your marriage null and void, unless it be released by a previous
dispensation from the Holy See; and that such a grant
is not to be obtained without a large sum of money?—
I wonder that a man of your standing should have so
imperfect a knowledge of the laws of his country.
Yes, my dear sir, before you can marry your cousin, you
have to obtain leave from an old gentleman, that lives
ten thousand miles off. Such is the prescription of the
canon law!—You shall have to pay a good round
sum, you may be sure; but you don't mind that, I suppose. What will be less to your liking, however, will
be the postponement of your marriage. It will take
one year, at least, to send to Rome and get an
answer!"

"Is it even so?" exclaimed captain Letinez: "Then,
confound the canon law!—It is an abominable impo-
sition."

"Hush, hush:—for God's sake, my dear friend, do
not blaspheme," cried out Troles: "Why, Heaven
help us!—the canon law is to be reverenced!"

"But, what shall I do in the premises?" asked the captain.

"Why," resumed his friend, "I would advise you to pay a visit to Padre Robinez, the great canonist, of this place, who will inform you of the measures to bo taken for procuring a dispensation. He is a venal soul, and has the greatest respect for riches. You may bo sure he will smoothe the matter for you as much as possible."

"Well, then, I will go to see this Father Robinez," said the captain; "and, if money be all that is wanted, he may have cause to call this marriage one of the best windfalls he was ever blessed with." And, as there was yet a long time before the hour when he was to accompany Miss Linton to the ball, away he went to consult the above named clergyman, who was considered quite an oracle in matters of canon law, and was, moreover, ecclesiastical judge of a parish more extensive than any diocese in Europe.

CHAPTER XXXVI.

Padre Robinez, of Matamoros, with an ecclesiastical income of about ten thousand dollars per annum, was, in all things, the very reverse of the good clergyman whom we have depicted in the beginning of this work; yet he possessed that fawning address, which too many amongst the Mexicans mistake for politeness. An affectation of humility which amounted to self debasement, and a hypocrisy of benevolence that made him press his favours upon those who needed them not, accompanied by perpetual smiles, and mellifluous words, covered a heart as hollow, and a temper as wrathful as it is possible to find. This worthy was a peculiar respecter of the rich, for it was his principal aim to keep up his popularity with the upper classes. Of course, he received our hero with the utmost civility, and had no sooner been informed of his business, than he hastened to relieve him from his fears and forebodings. "It is true," said he, "that the dispensation you want for your marriage, being *in secundo gradu consanguinitatis*, is, by the canons, reserved to his Holiness; but the Pope, considering the unsettled state of the republic, has, in his fatherly mercy, sent an *indultum* to our Bishops, whereby they are enabled to grant those dispensations to their diocesans, *quando in Domino expedire videbitur;* that is the phrase. Now, there is no doubt but a gentleman of your house has a peculiar right to the favours of the church, and his most illustrious Lordship, our Bishop, will delight in having it in his power to oblige you. You must be forewarned, however, that you shall have to pay some little thing, not as a price for the dispensation, you understand, but as a *multa*, (fine) for the violation of the laws of the church, which is employed in pious works."

"Well," interrupted the captain, "this will be no difficulty with me, unless the amount should prove enormous."

"Enormous!" replied the Padre.—" No.—The Mexican church is too tender a mother. It will on the contrary, be very light:—I dare say not above a thousand dollars."

"A thousand dollars!" exclaimed the captain, in amaze, "And you call this a trifling sum?"

"Why!" said the priest, "for such a man as you, it certainly is light. Consider, Senor, that our most illustrious Lord, the Bishop of Monterrey, was a poor friar, without a *maravedi* in his pocket, and that, upon being raised to the mitre, he had to go in debt to the amount of forty thousand dollars, to furnish himself with the pontifical paraphernalia ; and, after taking possession of his see, he found his income could not even defray the expenses of his household, much less enable him to pay his debts. Now, he is reduced to live in the convent of San Francisco, in Mexico, for the sake of economy, and to apply the proceeds of those *multas* to satisfy his creditors. So, it will not be too much for you to contribute to this good work. But, take notice, that I do not include in that sum, the various fees of office, church rates, *paraguantes* to the sacristan and choristers, beadle and bell-ringer, notarial fees and my own charges for brokerage."

"For brokerage!" echoed the captain, with a smile, that was any thing but flattering for the Senor Padre.

"Ay, brokerage," resumed the priest, a little confused. "The word was perhaps ill chosen, but I meant the proper fees for my trouble and intervention in the matter. You are aware, no doubt, that the drawing of the petition to his lordship must be in Latin, that it requires no little skill and some labour to compose it, and detail the canonical reasons, which alone can prompt the church to grant the favour sued for. You do not expect these things shall be done gratuitously."

"I expect and desire nothing to be done gratuitously for me," replied the captain with haughtiness, (for, the idea of obtaining the rites of the church free gratis, or de *limosna*, as the Mexican clergy express it, in order to stimulate the pride of their parishioners, is one of the greatest humiliations they can possibly undergo.)

"I confess, however, I was not prepared for the manner in which these things are carried on. I did not expect to see an explicit contract entered into, as for the acquisition of a piece of property. I supposed it was left to the generosity of a gentleman. But, since every thing is done above board, and in a merchant-like manner, I will write to the Bishop, and send him my petition myself."

The priest, who saw he was going to lose this rich windfall, wanted to repair the effect of his indiscretion. He apologised, and said that the sum would not, probably, amount to a thousand dollars. That it was the maximum, and that he could obtain the dispensation for eight hundred, nay, perhaps, for seven. All would not do. The captain was inexorable, and, taking leave of him, returned home, where, by recalling to his remembrance various scraps of Latin he had learned in his youth, and with the help of his friend, he succeeded in composing an eloquent petition to the Bishop of Monterrey, and despatched it, that same evening, with a strong letter of recommendation, from the general, to back it,

This business being over, his mind felt at rest, for he doubted not to receive a favourable answer from Mexico, in less than a fortnight. He, therefore, thought of nothing but paying his court with assiduity to his fair cousin, and, for that purpose, was very importunate to take her to the balls and assemblies, which the people of fashion frequently gave to the superior officers.

It happened that, five days after Madame Larrouie's party, Don Gregorio Francisco de Paula Joseph Maria de Castro, with his spouse, Dona Catalina Teresa de Jesus de Meragua,—(I like to give both names at full length, because, in Mexico, the wife preserves her own, distinct from that of her husband,)—gave a splendid assembly, which, it was intended, should surpass any thing hitherto seen in Matamoros. Madame Larrouie, they confessed, had stolen a march upon them, in causing her *gran sala* to be floored with fine wrought plank, imported from New Orleans for the purpose, which was a piece of luxury, of which no body had ever thought

before, and was extolled beyond measure, on account
of the wonderful ease and grace it imparted to the
movements of the dancers.

Don Gregorio and his wife could not offer the same
convenience to their party, but still they were anxious
to outdo Madame Larrouie ; for, they held it a kind of
humiliation for the Mexican character, that a foreign
lady should know better than they, how to order these
things. To carry, therefore, their scheme into effect,
they borrowed all the fine furniture they could cram
into their hall. Four mahogany sideboards, placed at
an equal distance, two on each side, displayed an immense quantity of china, lent by an importing merchant :—Four large looking-glasses, all borrowed, decorated the walls, and afforded to the beauties of the
place, peculiar facilities for contemplating their charms
and toilette :—Sofas, of the latest fashion, filled up the
empty space between the sideboards, and afforded
superior facilities for lolling with grace and elegance ;
but, what capped the climax, and commanded the general admiration, was a cut-glass chandelier, suspended
from the centre of the ceiling !—Such a piece of furniture had never been seen in Matamoros, and was accounted the *ne plus ultra* of magnificence ; so that
Madame Larrouie was, by the unanimous voice of the
company, declared altogether distanced, and absolutely
conquered.

All the great officers of the army, and not a few of
the inferior ones were present, and participated in the
festivities of the night, appearing in a variety of cos-
tumes, which, without being either elegant, or picturesque, were sufficiently varied for the purposes of
singularity.—A colonel presented himself in the pleasant summer *neglige* of the country ;—white vest, pan-
taloon and roundabout of the same, with a bright red
silk sash round his breast :—His military rank being de-
signated only by two small embroidered strips, worn on
his shoulders, in lieu of epauletts.—A captain danced
in the cumbrous regimentals of his grade, loaded with
more gold than is, in Europe, lavished upon a general ;—every seam of his trousers covered with gold

lace—the collar, cuffs, and skirts of his coat, richly
embroidered with the same, and two epaulettes, nearly
as large as warming-pans, spreading their fringe down
to his elbows;—whilst a lieutenant appeared in a *citi-
zen's* dress, without the least insignia of his profession. There was, however, a point, in which, notwithstanding their variety of costume, they all agreed:—
It was the wearing of hats covered with oil cloth.—
An absurd fashion, in a country where it hardly ever
rains, and of which it is not easy to discover the
origin.

The ladies were no less fanciful, in their habiliments, than the gentlemen. The elegant *gala* dress of
the Spanish females, consisting of a white tunic and
mantilla, trimmed with the richest Flanders lace, at
once the most modest and coquetish of female cos-
tumes, did not, however, make its appearance. It
seems that Mexican women are insensible to its charms.
In ordinary circumstances, they use their pitiful *rebo-
zos*, to cover their heads and part of their face; but,
in their balls, they appear bareheaded, whilst their
gowns, (cut short to display their delicate ancles, on
the shape of which they deservedly pride themselves,)
are generally more gaudy than tasteful, being furbel-
lowed all over with gauze and ribbons, and not unfrequently bedizzened with spangles, like a doll's frock.
Their necks, hands, and ears, are loaded with jewels,
chiefly set with pearls; and when they move in the
mazy dance, with all those meretricious ornaments
dangling about them, and the noisy castanets in their
hands, they look rather like Indian *Bayaderes*, than
Christian females, indulging in a decent recreation.

It was in that style they were dancing at Don Gregorio Joseph Maria de Castro's; and Sophia Linton,
though she assisted at the ball with a certain repugnance, nevertheless, commanded the admiration of all
the men, by her superior beauty; while the women did
not fail to criticise the simplicity of her costume, with
all the bitterness of envy. She had just been led
down, for a *volero*, by colonel Passamonte, next to captain Letinez, the finest looking man in the army; and

all eyes had been fixed upon them; the young lady's lover enjoying, with a kind of transport, the gracefulness and elegance of her movements, and listening, with secret pride, to the praises which he heard, on all sides, lavished upon her, when two strangers entered the ball room.

They created very little sensation, for there was nothing peculiarly remarkable in their appearance; and, in fact, none, except those who sat near the door, paid any attention to them. Both wore soiled clothes, and appeared just arrived from a long journey. One was a reverend looking old man, with a mild, intelligent countenance, and silvery hair; but so weak and feeble, withal, that he needed his companion's arm to support himself. The second was a strong, fine looking man, whose countenance indicated the most vigorous health, and whose shrewd expression of features marked him out for a man of intelligence. Both of these now comers stood for awhile, gazing at the assembly, and successively fixed a scrutinizing glance on the various groupes, as if looking for some one, when, at last, the elder one suddenly sprang forwards, towards captain Letinez, who, having recognized him, met him half way, and received him in his arms.

It was his grand-uncle, from Mechoacan, who had just arrived at Matamoros, and having learned he was at liberty, had not even given himself time to change his clothes, before embracing him. Now, he pressed, on his bosom, the child of his promise, the only hope of his family, the dear pupil, whom, from the first dawn of reason, he had carried through the various stages of instruction, and fashioned according to the wish of his heart—another *himself*, as he thought—and dearer, than if he had been a real son. Now, he held him in his embraces, and there was no danger of their ever again being separated! The young man's arms were round him, to support his weak frame, while the venerable old man wept with tenderness!—" Oh, Ambrosio," said he, as soon as his emotion, a little subsided, permitted him to give vent to his feelings, " I find thee safe, at last!—Heaven be praised for all its mercies, but mostly for this last one."

The good clergyman's companion, who was, in fact,
no other than our hero's father, was more successful
than the good Abbatte in mastering his emotion, for he
was descended from a more phlegmatic race, yet a
tremor of pleasure shook his frame as he took his son's
hand in his, and his voice faultered, when he articulated
a fatherly blessing on his head. The tall, beautiful
form before him, that shone resplendent with all the
grace of youthful manliness, was his child!—O joy!—
Oh, had only his long lost Maria been alive, now, to
share with him the pleasure of contemplating the son of
their love! But yet, though he was *alone*, what did he
not feel, when the young man, in his turn, pressed him
on his bosom? The whole father *yearned* within him,
and he felt it as one of those few moments when the
soul is well nigh overpowered by a trance of bliss, and
a spasm of internal pleasure seems to reduce her to the
very brink of annihilation.

O God of Nature, condemn those who have refused
to know thee, to bodily enjoyments, and in order to
avenge thyself on them, plunge them into the degradation of sensuality, but grant me the pleasures of the
soul—grant me the delights of paternal love, which never cloy the inward taste.

When thou hadst created man, thou didst rejoice at
thy own work, and when he stood before thee, in the
beauty of manhood, paying thee his tribute of praise
and gratitude, thou didst crown him " with honour and
glory ;" but of all the privileges thou grantedst him,
none was like this one, except that of knowing thee!—
Let such be mine!—That I may, one day, behold the
son of my bosom, standing before me in the plenitude
of manhood, and smiling on me with gratitude and
filial love!—Then I will be content to lay my head in
the cold lap of the grave, for I shall have tasted the
greatest of human pleasures—the one that comes nearest to thy own unspeakable joys!

Such thoughts as these had frequently crossed Mr.
Faring's mind, especially at the sight of parents fondling
on their children, when he was reminded of his own
dear boy, far away, but *now* he saw his utmost wishes

realised. His affection for his son was probably greater than it would have been, had the latter been brought
up under his immediate inspection, for he possessed
one of those ardent and imaginative souls, for whom
the remoteness of objects lends them higher charms,
and the rarity of the enjoyment enhances its worth.

The scene which the meeting of our friends exhibited suspended the amusements of the company, who
were now gazing at them with a lively interest. A
general officer, who had been acquainted with father
Letinez approached him, to pay his respects, and begged
to introduce to him some of his young friends, but the
old clergyman, anxious to retreat out of the apartment,
besought him to put it off, and reminded Mr. Faring
of the strange figure they made in the middle of the assembly. They were going to withdraw, when our hero
told his father that he had another relation besides himself, at the ball, and immediately passed into a neighbouring room, whither Colonel Passamonte had taken
Miss Linton and her father to procure them refreshments.

The Texian major could hardly believe his ears,
when the captain informed him that his brother-in-law
had just arrived, and he made him repeat the news
twice, when, at last, he arose, muttering, "Impossible!
impossible!" took his daughter under his arm and
rushed into the ball room. The scene of recognition
between the two brothers-in-law was not so pathetic
as the one that had preceded it, for they had once
been at variance; it was, nevertheless, sufficiently cor-
dial, and after excusing themselves to the master of the
house and the assembly, they left the ball, and hastened to major Linton's house.

As they went along, they formed a joyous company:
Miss Linton, between her father and her lover, and the
old Abbatte, between the latter and Mr. Faring. And
it was such a confusion of queries and answers! "But
you are a bold and brisk traveller, Faring," said the
major, " you, *Tranche Montagne*, as your grandmother
used to call you. To pay us such an unexpected visit,
and in such a spot! After having not seen us for four-

28 *

teen years !—Ay, it does my old heart good, however, to have, before death, sealed our reconciliation, by a hearty embrace."

"I was preparing to pay you a visit in Alabama," replied Mr. Faring, "when I heard of your removal to Texas. I knew, my niece had grown up into a fine woman, and I had an interest to make in her heart for some one."

"Ah, you rogue!" interrupted the major. "There, also, you have been more lucky than wise, and *we* have done the work in your absence. But you may thank Texas, and the Comanches and a thousand strange circumstances that have concurred in bringing it about, for, without it, you might have as soon hoped to pluck the Sierra Madre from its foundation as to get your lad out of the old count's clutches, to make him take an airing through the world. But, Lord! I have not asked you when did you land, nor by what vessel you came."

"Oh," replied Mr. Faring, "I have not landed at this port. I come from the interior. It is now more than two months since I landed at Vera Cruz, and after visiting the old count, from whom I learned what had befallen Ambrosio, I made haste to overtake the Abbatte, which I was happy enough to effect at the time he stood most in need of my assistance."

"Well, I admire the rapidity of your movements," resumed the major, adding, in jest, "only, I fear, you will not find the world large enough for your perambulations, and, that, like Alexander, you will be reduced to shed tears, that there is no other which you can overrun."

"Never fear, brother," answered Mr. Faring, in the same jocose strain; "the world is round, you know. One may go over it without danger of seeing the end."

While the two Marylanders were thus exchanging jokes that appear rather vapid to our poor judgment, the captain was communicating to his grand-uncle a brief account of his adventures, and had not yet finished the recital, when they arrived at major Linton's cabin.

The travellers' mules and equipage had been left in

the *plazuela de los arrieros*, under the care of trusty
servants, and it being now too late to look for a house,
it was settled that the old clergyman should take possession of his nephew's apartment, in Sonora street;
while Mr. Faring would return to the plazuela, where
the servants had been ordered to erect the travelling
tent. Our hero, therefore, after taking leave of the
Linton family, and seeing his good uncle snugly bestowed in his bed, and in a fair way of enjoying a comfortable night's rest, accompanied his father to his tent,
and spent the night with him.

They were no sooner alone, than Mr. Faring opened
a confidential conversation with the young man. "Well,
my dear Ambrosio," said he, "in my absence, I find you
have been making up a match for yourself. Though
Sophia is all I could wish, and the very person upon
whom I had cast my eyes, and though this singular coincidence appears an interposition of Providence; yet,
was it dutifully done on your part to take so important
a step without my counsel or permission?—Youth is
headlong, blindly impelled by passion, and needs the
experience of age. Now, suppose you had made a
choice which I had reason to disapprove, and to which
it were my duty to refuse my consent, what an estrangement would it not produce between us?"

"Father, father, blame me not," answered the young
man. "It was not passion, I followed, but judgment.
My love for Sophia grew in proportion with my esteem
and admiration for her virtues. I was perfectly convinced you could not but approve of such a choice.
She will prove equal to what you have so often told me
my mother was, and, I hope, God will grant us a greater share of happiness than fell to your lot. But, after
all, can *you* complain?—Had you acted yourself according to the rule which you wish I had followed,
should *I* be here now."

"Come, come," interrupted his father; "you become
naughty. But let *that* rest, and let us speak of our ul-
terior projects. I do not wish to deprive the old count
and the good Abbatte, of your company. With them
you must remain as long as they live, yet, in the course

of nature, they cannot last long; and my earnest wish has been, that, when these ties which connect you with this country are broken, you should settle in the United States. The marriage you are going to contract will greatly facilitate the execution of such a plan; for you do not imagine that Sophia would part from her father, or, that the latter would willingly spend the remainder of his life in Mechoacan."

"I confess, sir," answered the captain, "that, ten months ago, I would have felt great difficulty in conforming to your wishes; but, during my captivity, I have had more lights, on the advanced state of civilization in the north, and it will, *now*, cost me very little to give my promise. We must, however, keep it a strict secret from the Abbatte, as well as from the Count, for it would give them incredible pain."

"Well, thank you, my child," said Mr. Faring, affectionately. "Now, indeed, I hope my old age will be spent in peace and happiness. For your sake, and for the remembrance of your mother, I have abstained from a second marriage. You are my only son, and with you I was determined to end my days, but it would have been gall and wormwood to me to live and die in this country. My fortune is considerable, nearly as large as the one you are to inherit from your grandfather, and it is my wish that we should form but one family—the major, yourself and wife, and myself, together with a sister I have in Maryland, whose husband has left her in poverty."

"Your desires, sir," replied the son, "shall be my law, and all those who are dear to you shall be dear to me."

In those fine sentiments of mutual love and reciprocal condescension for each other's wishes, father and son fell asleep, and when they awoke, the next morning, the most urgent thing they had to do was to look for a house, to lodge in, during their stay in Matamoros.

As they were leaving the tent, the captain happened to cast his eyes upon some *arrieros* that had spent the night in the square, along with his father's men, and was not a little surprised to perceive Flambeau amongst them. He went towards him and kindly addressed him in French, saying, "*Eh bien, mon ami*, do you still bear rancour?—Had you not better return to me?—Harkee! my fate is now determined. Nearly all my family have, by an unexpected concurrence of circumstances, met in this place, and in a few days my union with Miss Linton will be consummated, when we will set out for Mechoacan. Had you not better be one of the party?—I have an old uncle, amongst the rest, who is a priest, and a man of science and literary taste; I will place you with him, rather as a companion than as a servant. The old man will be delighted ·to have a *scholar* to serve his mass, every morning, and to take care of his library; and he will never find fault with you, provided you listen with patience to his metaphysical disquisitions, when he is in a chatty humour. You will be plunged in books, up to your ears. You, that once, so much envied the librarian of Underscratch college, and thought him the happiest man in the world, have it, now, in your power to secure the same bliss for yourself."

Flambeau had repented having left the captain, for he had, during their long and dangerous journey through Texas, contracted a strong attachment for him. He relented, therefore, suffered himself to be coaxed into the family, and, having briefly terminated his commercial business, he was, the next day, introduced to the Abbate, who, upon a further acquaintance, was delighted with him, and treated him with the utmost condescension.

CHAPTER XXXVII.

We will not enter into the detail of all the trouble our travellers had to undergo, in order to procure a house suited to their purpose. The best part of the day was spent in inquiring and looking about; and it was only just before twilight, that their equipage and servants were enabled to leave the square, which, in Matamoros, serves destitute travellers as a caravanserai, to go to take possession of their new lodgings.

We will suppose them already installed in them, their apartments decently set in order, their kitchen in operation, each of their servants punctually discharging his allotted task, and the whole family in the full tide of house-keeping; for, though they intended to stay but one month, in Matamoros, to such *a stress* they were reduced, through a want of houses of entertainment, in that city, which is the second sea-port town of a republic boasting nine millions of inhabitants.

Once settled in their new habitation, they had very little else to do, than to wait for the arrival of the papers from Mechoacan, and the dispensation from the Bishop of Monterrey, necessary for the marriage of our hero, who, either on account of the qualities of his mind, personal beauty, or the circumstance of his being the only scion of a wealthy and noble house, was a perfect idol in the family. Old Abbate Letinez, who, as we have already observed, was a man of learning, much addicted to thinking, and very shrewd in his observations, found an agreeable employment in examining the curiosities of the sea-board, which he never had visited before. Without having travelled out of his own country, he was well acquainted with geography; and pronounced the locality, at the mouth of the Rio Bravo, the best for commerce on the Gulf of Mexico, next to that of New Orleans; but, at the same time, he thought that, if Texas could secure her independence, these natural advantages would be rendered useless, by the superior facilities which the immense extent of frontier, between that country and Mexico, would give for the smuggling trade. He wondered much to see that nothing was exported, except coarse wool, raw hides and silver, when that port alone might furnish the half of Europe with copper, which could be brought all the way by water from the mines; when lead, sulphur, vegetable gums for manufacturing purposes, cochineal, and many other articles, might form considerable items; but, his wonder ceased, when he was informed that there was a general conspiracy between the government and the inhabitants, to prevent the navigation of the river; and that so many obstacles were, by the multiplication of formalities, thrown in the way of exportations, that it was a much more difficult operation to ship off a dozen of hides, than to introduce a whole cargo of foreign goods. "Of a truth," thought he, "if my dear countrymen do not mend their notions of political economy, they run the risk of becoming the poorest and most miserable nation upon earth.—*Santo Dios!* it seems they have borrowed their ideas on finances from the empire of Morocco."

Many other curious remarks did the shrewd Abbatte make, which it might be accounted pedantic to relate in this place. Of course, we will skip over a period of about three weeks, and hasten to the happy marriage of our hero, which forms the *denouement* of our story.

Mr. Faring, who was careful to visit the post-office every time the post arrived from the West, was so happy, at last, as to receive two huge packets, at one and the same time. With these, he returned home in haste, his face radiant with joy; and, the Sanhedrim of the whole family being immediately convened, they began to examine whether any thing was wanting, which might retard the nuptials so ardently desired.

They had the satisfaction to meet with no disappointment. All the papers were full and complete, and not the least formality prescribed by the canon law, or the ordinances of the kings of Spain, had been neglected. There came, first, the certificate of baptism of Ambrosio de Letinez, extracted from the regis-

ters of the parish church of Phelipa, duly authenticated
by the ecclesiastical notary of the place, and, afterwards, endorsed and legalized by the Bishop of Durango:—fees, twenty dollars. There came, in the
second place, an attestation in due form, from the
parish priest of Pasquaro, diocese of Mechoacan, by
which it was made known to all men, that Ambrosio
de Letinez, captain of cavalry in the Mexican service,
was a *single* man, and at full liberty to contract marriage, no other impediment intervening, &c. &c. &c.—
This instrument of writing was also endorsed by the
Bishop of Mechoacan, and charged only sixteen dollars. The third piece was a dispensation from the last
prelate, whereby our hero, being his diocesan, and under his jurisdiction, was permitted to contract marriage, *in facie ecclesiæ*, with Sophia Linton, without
any publication of bans; the above said Bishop being
moved, to grant that favour, by good and canonical
reasons; and, on the back, this pious condescension
was rated at one hundred and twenty-five dollars, as
a *multa*, (fine,) to be spent in pious works, by the
Bishop aforesaid. This, with a letter from the old
count, whereby he gave his consent to the captain's
marriage, did well enough for Mechoacan.

Now, came the other packet. It was from the
Bishop of Monterrey, who mercifully dispensed our
hero from the publication of bans, likewise, seeing that
the marriage was to be solemnized in his diocese; and
exacted, for this kindness, the light sum of seventy-
five dollars. A second paper contained the dispensation of what is technically called *disparitas cultus*,
that is to say, the religion of the bride; but, as this
was a matter of consequence, and which the Bishop
granted but with great reluctance, the grantee was
ordered to pay five hundred dollars, by way of expiation; and, moreover, it was enjoined upon him to fast,
and recite the seven penitential psalms, on the first
Friday of every month.

With these papers in his possession, our hero was
not more than half way through his difficulties, for, the
same formalities should, in rigour, have been required

of the bride. But how could she prove that she was *not* a married woman? She was a stranger in the country, and before she could get authentic certificates of *Solteria*, (singleness) as the Spanish law terms it, the marriage would be delayed, at least a whole year! In this emergency, our hero remembered what his friend had told him of the pliability of principle of Padre Robinez, and caused him to be spoken to by his uncle, who easily prevailed upon him to receive the oath of Mr. Faring as a complete proof of her being at full liberty to contract marriage.

The difficulty being thus smoothed over, the day for the ceremony was appointed, and, on the happy morn, the whole *cortege* proceeded from the house of the bride, to the parish church, where father Robinez, in his most splendid vestments, awaited them. A number of officers waited upon the bridegroom, in order to do him honour, and during the marriage mass a fine band of music played. The priest being expeditious, the ceremony was soon over, and our hero led his bride, in triumph, to his own house, whither major Linton also immediately removed. At night, there was a splendid ball, which, according to an ancient promise, was opened by captain Alvarez dancing with the bride. To him, besides, were paid the principal honours of the *soiree*, the family thinking that they could never do enough to manifest their gratitude towards the noble hearted man, who had saved major Linton's life, and we wish we had the powers of a Homer to immortalise his name, as well as that of his wife, for they are no fictitious personages, and well deserve to be honoured by the whole human race for their humane heroism.

Now, dear reader, our task is concluded. Our hero is happy, and virtue has been rewarded. A few days after the marriage, the whole family left Matamoros, for Mechoacan; the captain, his bride and major Linton riding in one coach, and Mr. Faring, Abbatte Letinez and Flambeau in another. Their journey was prosperous, and when they arrived at Pasquaro, the old count was so overjoyed that he crossed himself five or

six times, and actually recited the canticle, "Nunc
dimittis servum tuum, Domine, secundum verbum
tuum, in pace," from beginning to end.

Mrs. Letinez, or the young countess, as some of the
people thereabouts call her, is getting accustomed to
the town, and greatly admires the scenery of the surrounding country, which she finds superior to any thing
she ever saw before. Abbatte Letinez is delighted
with Flambeau, who has now learned Spanish sufficiently well to discuss with him questions of metaphysics, which furnish both with subjects for interminable
conferences, and Mr. Faring, curbing for a while his
erratic disposition, has promised to stay in Pasquaro,
until he sees the birth of a grandchild, for which, according to all appearances, he shall not have long to wait.

NOTES.

Note 1, *page* 9.—The *Sierra Madre* is a continuation of the Andes of Peru, which, after entering the states of Mexico and Puebla, divide themselves into two large chains, the western one running due north, at the distance of about one hundred leagues from the Pacific Ocean; and the eastern chain following the sinuosities of the gulf of Mexico, at the same respective distance, until it is lost, in the state of Cohahuila, in the immense plains watered by the Rio Bravo. The highest peaks are found in the state of Puebla, at the junction of the two chains, and are the Ixtacihuatl, or *White Woman*, and the great volcano of Popocatepetl, which is 6083 "*varas Mexicanas*" above the level of the sea. The limits of vegetation are at 1852 *varas* above the city of Mexico, and 4541 above the level of the ocean; the Ribes odoratum, a species of blackberry, being the last plant found on the sides of the mountain.

Note 2, *page* 13.—Don Vasco de Quiroga civilized the Indians of his diocese, and instructed them, not only in the Christian religion, but in all the necessary arts; and, to this day, the Tarascos and other nations of Mechoachan call him *Tata* Don Vasco, and cherish his memory with deep veneration. His tomb is in the beautiful island of Tzintzonzan, in the middle of the lake of Pasquaro. It has been the lot of that Bishoprick to have several prelates who were men of genius. The present Bishop, Don Juan Gaetano Portugal, is the only man of superior talents in the Mexican church. He had reformed his clergy, and set them on a somewhat more respectable footing than they are elsewhere. His predecessor, of whom Humboldt makes very honourable mention, originated the plan for the general and final enfranchisement of the Indians, and it is upon the rules he laid down, that the governments of the various states have acted since the independence.

Note 3, *page* 14.—The Virgin of Guadelupe, which is a very coarse and ill-executed painting, on a rude fabric of *pita* thread, was found by a pious Indian, of the name of Juan Diego, on the spot where, in the reign of Montezuma, had stood the temple of the Goddess Tonantzin. At the same time, a supernatural being, supposed to be the Blessed Virgin, appeared to this individual, commanding him to go to the Archbishop of Mexico, and direct him, by her order, to build a church on that spot, in honour of the aforesaid image.

As Diego required some sign, to prove to the Archbishop the truth of his mission, the supernatural vision gave him a handkerchief full of fresh roses, which was a miraculous proof—it being then a season of the year when rose bushes are not in bloom.

The image was first placed in a hermitage, situated where now stand the houses of the sacristan and servants. It was, afterwards, translated to a chapel, which forms the vestry-room of the old church. In the month of November, 1622, a third church was dedicated, on the spot where had stood the first hermitage, and the present fabric was begun in 1695.

In 1750, it was erected into a collegiate, with a prelate who enjoys the title of Abbot, and a number of prebendaries. The capital for the dotation of the chapter was $533,882, left by Don Andrew Palencia. The Spanish government took the money, and bound itself to pay the interest to the chapter, at the rate of five per cent. out of the king's share of the tithes of the dioceses of Mexico and Puebla. The votive offerings, in wax candles alone, amount to something prodigious, and there is no sacrifice which the Indians and Creoles are not ready to make for this image, which is for them a type of their nationality, and with which they suppose the honour of their race intimately connected.

Father Don Servando de Mier, a learned Dominican, having ventured to deny the truth of the apparition, when preaching, on the festival day of the Virgin, was well nigh torn to pieces, before he could get down from the pulpit, and had to flee the country, loaded with the public execration.

The present church was dedicated on the tenth of June, 1709. The building alone, without the sanctuary and sacristy, cost $402,000, which were collected from voluntary offerings. The silver-gilt throne upon which the miraculous image is placed weighs 1628 pounds, and behind the painting is a plate of the same metal, of one hundred weight. The principal tabernacle cost $19,000.

Note 4, *page* 17.—Vino mescal is a kind of brandy, distilled from the fermented juice of the Agave Americana, large plantations of which exist in the states of Puebla and Mexico, some of them so important as to afford an income of seventy and eighty thousand dollars per annum. The singular plant which furnishes this liquor flowers but once, and dies immediately after; but if the stem which is to support the bunch of flowers be cut before it begins to mount, it gives out, during three months, a sweetish liquid, which, being fermented into a kind of small beer, constitutes, under the name of *pulque*, the general drink, in the southern provinces of Mexico, and this, being distilled, constitutes the vino mescal—thus called from the river *Mescala*, on the banks of which the manufacture of it was first attempted. The pulque is generally supposed to be a wholesome drink, but it has a very unpleasant smell.

NOTE 5, *page* 51.—*Mexican Jesuits.*—Charles III. held, in 1767, a secret, extraordinary counsel, composed of the Marquis of Roda, secretary of state; the count of Aranda, president of the counsel of Castill; the count of Florida Blanca, the count of Campomanes, the archbishops of Burgos and Saragossa, and the bishops of Tarrazona, Albarrazin and Orihuela, in which the expulsion of the Jesuits from all the dominions of Spain was unanimously resolved; but the secret was so religiously kept that those who were most interested never suspected it. On the night of the 24th of June, in the same year, under the viceroy, Marquis de Croix, the Mexican Jesuits received intimation of the decree of expulsion, and all the professed members of the institution were embarked for the Pope's dominions, where they were maintained on a small pension from the Spanish government. Their church in Mexico was given to the Philippini, and their extensive landed possessions were sold for the benefit of the crown. In the colonies, they had done much more good and less harm than in Europe. To them, the Indians of the northern states, and of California owe the degree of civilization they enjoy, and the country, at large, what little literature it possesses. Amongst the old Mexican Jesuits who have left a reputation, may be reckoned Alegre, Campoy, Clavigero and Abad. Though they have, since their re-establishment, penetrated into so many places, they have entirely overlooked Mexico; it were, however, the most easy thing for them to pass over thither, from Louisiana and Missouri, where they are very rife.

NOTE 6, *page* 61.—*The Mexican Inquisition.*—This dreadful tribunal existed in Mexico till 1815, and the last public *auto da fe*, was against Morelos, himself a priest, and the most talented of the insurgent generals. He had a natural genius for war, and was for a long time successful; but being at last routed and falling into the hands of the royalists, they thought it more favourable to their cause to punish him as a heretic than as a rebel. The following are authentic accounts of some of the feats of that holy tribunal in the land of *Anahuac.*

It was solemnly established on the 11th of November, 1571, and three years after, held its first *auto da fe*, in which sixty-three culprits appeared, five of whom were burned. From the last mentioned date, to 1602, it held publicly nine *autos* more. On the sixteenth of April, 1646, and the thirtieth of March, 1648, there were two others, in the first whereof appeared fifty penitents, and in the second, twenty-eight, almost all accused of Judaism. But on the eleventh of April, 1649, was held the most famous ever seen in Mexico. An immense scaffold was constructed in the public square *del Volador*, and the ceremony was graced with the presence of all the corporations and persons of rank in the city. The concourse of people, also, was immense, because the news of the *auto* having been spread abroad, long before hand, they had come from a great distance

342   NOTES.

to witness the spectacle. The sermon was preached by a bishop of
Cuba, on the text "Peace be with you!" In this *act of faith* were a
Lutheran, thirty-nine persons guilty of Judaism, and seventy-seven
statues representing culprits, who had either fled or died. Of the
Jews, twelve were burned, although they had recanted. The only
favour shown them, on that account, was to strangle them, before
throwing them into the flames. Amongst them, were six women.
An old Castillian, of the name of Thomas Trevino de Sobremonte, a
wealthy merchant, who could not be brought to recant, was burned
alive, in the plazuela of San Diego. The other culprits were condemned to the confiscation of their property, whipping and exile.
Ten years afterwards, that is to say, in November, 1659, there was
another *act* of *faith* celebrated in the great square. The Viceroy,
Duke of Albuquerque was present, with all the tribunals, corporations and persons of note in the city. This *auto* was graced by
twenty-nine culprits and a statue representing an absent. Two
were strangled and burned, four were burned alive, among whom was
an Irishman of the name of Lamport. The remainder were condemned to confiscation, whipping and exile.

Upon examining the records of this abominable tribunal, one does
not know what to wonder at most, its horrid cruelty, or extravagant
puerility. One Palao, who was parish priest of Vera Cruz, was denounced to the inquisition by his own bishop, Dr. Campillo, and declared guilty of blasphemy, for having said, in speaking of a statue of
the Holy Ghost, represented by a dove, but clumsily executed, "take
it down, take it down. It is not a dove but a turkey cock!" A
merchant of the name of Briz, well known in Mexico, as a good
Catholic, was summoned before the tribunal, for having sold some
calicoes, the pattern of which was adorned with flowers in the form
of a cross, and he was obliged to cut the goods to pieces. A distinguished physician, of the name of Santa Maria, was ordered to be
taken into custody for having advised giving a patient, who was just
recovering from a fainting fit, a cup of broth in preference to extreme
unction!!—And yet there are still some people, who regret the inquisition, and publish books in its favour,—not in the Pope's dominions, but in the United States.

NOTE 7, *page* 82.—The civil year was among the ancient Mexicans divided into eighteen months, of twenty days each, and five intercallary days, called *Nemonteni,* something like the *Sansculotides*
of the French revolutionary calendar. We give here the correspondence of that system, with the Gregorian.

1st day of the month Titit Itzcalli . . . . . 9 January
    "   Itzcalli Xochilhuitl . . 22 January
    "   Xilomanalitzli . . . . 18 February
    "   Tlacaxipehualitzli . . . 10 March
    "   Tozoztontli . . . . . 30 March

1st day of the month	Hueytozotli	19 April
"	Toxcatl	9 May
"	Etzalqualitzli	29 May
"	Tecuihuitontli	19 June
"	Hueytecuiltontli	8 July
"	Micailhuitontli	28 July
"	Heymixcaithuilt	17 August
"	Ochpaniztli	6 September
"	Pachth	26 September
"	Hueypactli	16 October
"	Quecholli	5 November
"	Panquetzaliztli	25 November
"	Atemoztli	15 December.

The period of fifty-two years was for the Mexicans, what a century is for us; but they never reckoned them by odd numbers. Evidently knowing that the solar revolution exceeded their civil year by six hours; after the termination of each cycle of fifty-two years, they added thirteen days, before beginning anew the first month of the following cycle. Every fifth day throughout the month was a market day. Independently of this calendar, they had another manner of reckoning time, which was purely lunar, and constituted their religious year. How the old Mexicans had come by such a method of regulating their civil year is a mystery that shall, probably, never be cleared up; but it was not certainly of their invention, and denotes a people far more advanced in civilization than they were.

NOTE 8, *page* 91.—On the table land of Mexico, the atmosphere is so dry, that it is indispensable to water the wheels of carriages, every day, otherwise they would shrink and fall to pieces. Mexican wheels are exceedingly clumsy, but very solid and better calculated to resist the atmosphere of the country than the more elegant ones imported from the United States.

NOTE 9, *page* 94.—Hidalgo, parish priest of Dolores, was the first who raised the standard of Mexican Independence, on the 16th of September, 1810. He owed a grudge to the Spanish government, by whose order an extensive vineyard he had planted near the town of which he was pastor, had been destroyed. It was, in great measure, to avenge that injury he entered the first conspiracy with Allende, Abasolo and others. Some of the latter were practical military men, but, as Hidalgo's popularity, on account of his ecclesiastical character, was of more importance, he was declared chief, and in a few weeks raised a body of more than seventy thousand men, badly armed, indeed, but so fanatically devoted to the cause they had espoused, that, in many instances, they ran up to the cannon's mouth, and, in their ignorance, crammed their hats into them, to stop the balls. At

their head. Hidalgo advanced as far as Mexico, which he would
have taken, had not his heart failed him, after which he was repeatedly defeated, and, at last, taken, whilst on his way to the
United States, degraded from the priesthood, and shot at Chihuahua.

Note 10, *page* 100.—*Mestena*, which the inhabitants of Texas
have anglicised into Mustang, is the wild horse, immense flocks
of which are found in the large haciendas in the northern states,
and in the plains of Texas.

Note 11, *page* 111.—St. Philip of Neri established a society
of priests, who are bound together by no vows, and can leave the
institute whenever they please. They lead a common life in
spirituals only; but, in temporals, every one possesses his *pecu-
lium*. Their principal avocations consist in instructing the ignorant, by preaching, catechising, and giving spiritual exercises.
When the Jesuits were suppressed, their churches and houses
were given to the Philippini, amongst which was the *Professa*,
one of the most sumptuous buildings in the city of Mexico.

Note 12, *page* 177.—The virgin *de Los Remedios* is, next to
that of Guadelupe, the Madona that enjoys the greatest reputation in Mexico, although she labours under the disadvantage of
being *Gachupina*, id est, imported from Spain. It is a small statue, which one of the soldiers of Cortes carried with him as a
safeguard. When that general was obliged to effect the disastrous retreat, distinguished in history under the name of *noche
triste*, during which so many of his soldiers were taken and offered in sacrifice to Vitzliputzly; the owner of this little Madona
succeeded in making his escape, and having fled up the mountain, dropped the image which was picked up by his pursuers
and treated with great honour. They constructed for it a little
shrine under a nopal, decked it with flowers and burned per-
fumes before it. The Spaniards, at their return, finding that the
virgin had been so honourably treated by their enemies, looked
upon it as a miracle, and thought it incumbent upon them not to
be behind hand. In process of time, a fine church was built for
that statue, on the very spot on which it had been found, some
miles distant from the city, whence she is, in times of drought,
inundations, and other public calamities, brought to the Cathedral of Mexico in procession. In desperate cases, and when application to the virgin of Los Remedios has proved fruitless, recourse is had to that of Guadelupe, when the Indians manifest
the most extraordinary exultation. As late as 1836, under the
Presidency of Corro, the Madona of Los Remedios was brought
down from her sanctuary, with an extraordinary display of mag-

nificence, all the authorities going to receive her, in order to obtain the cessation of a drought which afflicted the country.

NOTE 14, *page* 199.—Account of the affair of San Jacinto, as
given by Santa Anna, in his official communication to the Mexican government.

Early on the 19th of April, I sent captain Marc Darragan with
some dragoons, to a point on the Lynchburgh road, three
leagues distant from New Washington, in order that he should
watch, and communicate to me, as speedily as possible, the arrival of Houston; and, on the 20th, at eight o'clock in the
morning, he informed me that Houston had just got to Lynchburgh. It was, with the greatest joy, all the individuals belonging to the corps then under my immediate orders, heard those
news; and they continued the march already begun, in the best
spirit.

At my arrival, Houston was in possession of a wood on the
margin of Bayou Buffaloe, which, at that point, empties itself into
the San Jacinto creek. His situation rendered it indispensable for
him to fight; and my troops manifested so much enthusiasm, that
I immediately began the battle. Houston answered our firing,
but refused to come out of the cover of the wood. I wished to
draw him into a field of battle suited to my purpose, and, in consequence, withdrew, about a thousand yards distance, to an eminence affording a favourable position, with abundance of water
on my rear, a thick wood on my right, and a large plain on my
left. Upon my executing this movement, the enemy's fire increased, particularly that of his artillery, by which captain Fernando Urriza was wounded   About one hundred cavalry sallied
out of the wood, and boldly attacked my escort, which was
posted on the left, causing it to fall back for a few moments, and
wounding a dragoon. I commanded two companies of cazadores to attack them, and they succeeded in repelling them into
the wood. Some infantry had also sallied out, but, seeing their
cavalry in full retreat, they withdrew also   It was now five in the
evening, and our troops wanted rest and refreshment, which I
permitted them to take. Thus was the remainder of the day
spent. We lay on our arms all night, during which I occupied
myself in posting my forces to the best advantage, and procuring the construction of a parapet, to cover the position of our
cannon. I had posted three companies in the wood, on our
right,—the *permanent* battalion of Matamoros formed our body
of battle in the centre,—and, on our left, was placed the cannon, protected by the cavalry, and a column of select companies
(*de preferencia*,) under the orders of lieutenant-colonel Santiago Luelmo, which composed our reserve.

On the 21st, at nine in the morning, General Cos arrived with
four hundred men, belonging to the battalions of Aklama, Guer-

rero, Toluca and Guadalaxara, having left one hundred under the orders of colonel Mariano Garcia, with their leads, in a swampy place, near Harrisburgh; and these never joined me. I then saw my orders had been contravened: for I had asked five hundred select infantry; and they sent me raw recruits, who had joined the army at St. Louis Potosi and Saltillo. I was highly displeased with this act of disobedience, and considered the new reinforcement as trifling; whereas I had, before its arrival, entertained well-founded hopes of gaining some decisive advantage with the new succour, which was to give me the superiority of numbers.

I disposed myself, however, to take advantage of the favourable disposition which I perceived in our soldiers, on the arrival of General Cos; but the latter represented to me, that, having made a forced march, in order to reach my camp early, his troops had neither eaten nor slept during twenty-four hours; and that, whilst the loads were coming on, it was indispensable to grant some refreshment to the soldiers. I consented to it; but, in order to keep a watch over the enemy, and protect the loads which were on the road, I posted my escort in a favourable place, reinforcing it with thirty-two infantry, mounted on officers' horses. Hardly one hour had elapsed since that operation, when general Cos begged me, in the name of Don Miguel Aguirre, the commander of the escort, that I would permit his soldiers to water their horses, which had not drunk for twenty-four hours, and let the men take some refreshment. Being moved by the *pitiable tone in which this request was made*, I consented, commanding, at the same time, that Aguirre and his men should return to occupy their position, as soon as they should have satisfied their necessities; and his disobedience to this order concurred to favour the surprise which the enemy effected.

Feeling myself exceedingly fatigued, from having spent the whole morning on horseback, and the preceding night without sleep, I lay down under the shade of some trees, while the soldiers were preparing their meal. Calling general Castrillon, who acted as major-general, I recommended him to be watchful, and to give me notice of the least movement of the enemy, and also to inform me when the repast of the soldiers would be over, because it was urgent to act in a decisive manner.

I was in a deep sleep, when I was awakened by the firing and noise. I immediately perceived we were attacked, and had fallen into a frightful disorder.—The enemy had surprised our advanced posts. One of their wings had driven away the three select companies (*de preferencia*,) posted in the wood on our right, and, from among the trees, were now doing much execution with their rifles: the rest of the enemy's infantry attacked us in front, with two pieces of cannon; and their cavalry did the same on our left.

Although the mischief was already done, I thought I could repair it, and, with that view, sent the battalion of Aldama, to reinforce the line of battle formed by that of Matamoros, and organized a column of attack under the orders of Don Manuel Cespedes, composed of the permanent battalion of Guerrero, and the piquets of Toluca and Guadalaxara, which moved to the front with the company of lieutenant-colonel Luelmo, in order to check the advance of the enemy; but my efforts were vain. The line was abandoned by the two battalions that were covering it; and, notwithstanding the fire of our cannon, the two columns were thrown into disorder, colonel Cespedes being wounded, and captain Luelmo killed. General Castrillon, who ran to and fro, to re-establish order in our ranks, fell mortally wounded; and the new recruits threw every thing into confusion, breaking their ranks, and preventing the veterans from making use of their arms: whilst the enemy was rapidly advancing, with loud hurrahs; and, in a few minutes, obtained a victory which they could not, some hours before, even have dreamed of.

All hopes being lost, and every one flying as fast as he could, I found myself in the greatest danger, when a servant of my aid-de-camp, colonel Don Juan Bringas, offered me his master's horse, and, with the tenderest and most urging expressions, insisted upon my riding off the field. I looked for my escort, and two dragoons, who were hurriedly saddling their horses, told me that their officers and fellow-soldiers had all *made their escape*. I remembered that general Filisola was only seventeen leagues off, and I took my direction towards him, darting through the enemies. They pursued me, and, after a ride of one league and a half, overtook me, on the banks of a large creek, the bridge over which was burned. I alighted from my horse, and with much difficulty succeeded in concealing myself in a thicket of dwarf pines. Night coming on, I escaped them; and, the hope of reaching the army, gave me strength. I crossed the creek, with the water up to my breast, and continued my route on foot. I found, in a house which had been abandoned, some articles of clothing, which enabled me to change my apparel. At eleven o'clock, A. M., while I was crossing a large plain, my pursuers overtook me again, and seized on my person. Such is the history of my capture. On account of my change of apparel, they did not recognise me, and inquired whether I had seen Santa Anna? To this, I answered, that he had made his escape; and this answer saved me from assassination, as I have since been given to understand.

NOTE 15, *page* 248.—*Graduado*, in the military nomenclature of the Mexican republic, means one who enjoys the honour of a grade, without the emoluments or command annexed to it. Thus, an officer, who in point of command, is only a captain, may be *graduated* a lieutenant colonel, &c. &c. The republic has been liberal of those titles, till it has become an object of satire, for the wits of the capital, who have made upon it some beautiful epigrams.

Note 16, *page* 268.—*The mint of Mexico.*—The mint in the city of Mexico is an establishment that has at all times command-ed the attention of foreigners, and been celebrated throughout the world on account of the prodigious quantities of precious metals which have been coined in it.

Till fourteen years after the conquest, that is to say, till 1535, no other money was current in Mexico than what was struck in Spain ; but, as this was not sufficient for the necessities of the country, the inhabitants made use of pieces of silver, of a certain weight, and hence the word *peso*. This giving birth to many frauds, a royal decree was issued on the 11th of May, 1535, for the establishment of three mints in America, one in the city of Potosi, one at Santa Fe, in New Granada, and the other, in Mexico.

The original cost of the building of the latter was $1,004,493. Its principal front, facing the north, is one hundred and twenty *varas* in length, and that which faces the east, one hundred and seventy. It is solidly constructed and in good style. All the principal officers lodge in it, and the apartments of the super-intendent are sufficiently sumptuous for a prince. There are more than three hundred men employed, and anciently many of these offices were sold by government, or passed from father to son, and as high as $60,000 were sometimes paid for the office of treasurer. Some of the most lucrative posts about the mint were in possession of religious communities, as, for example, the Carmelite friars, who possessed, at once, the offices of first smel-ter and assayer!

Now a days, this establishment presents but a very faint image of what it has been. The stream of precious metal which once made it so remarkable, has been exhausted, and it has, of late years, served for little else than to coin copper. There are, now, several other mints in the country, such as in Zacatecas, Durango, &c. &c.